Looking into the Future ← 25 ¢ --- No rfds. →

STOP RATS

PROCESS NEWS

. 73
O3

d & Pass On

OW!

OCESS SPREADS

stern states ha
en blanketed in
00,000 free co-
is newspaper,&
ng the remainin
will be blanke
n the next five
nst the cold
nds of process
3,000 copies in
,000 homes wher
204,500,000 of
readers. Goal:
new names in
ss book of life
out of 204 re
processor con
ts and keeps a
ll your name b
the 1,000,000?

All-American

144000th

Requests 143999 men to form 12 equal divisions in-to an organization dedica-ted only to the principle that each may perform as he desires.

Each man must have to-tal equality as peers with-in this organization and each division must have equal authority amongst its partners.

Acceptance of member-ship in this organization indicates withdrawal from or relegation to minor im-port association with any previous or subsequent si-milar activity.

Duly formed this unit limited to and called 144000 is real and only through ir-reversible loss of a mem-ber can another be accep-ted as a replacement.

A man named Waters
c/o R. E. Childs
POB 651
Roseville, CA 95678

EDITORIAL

Sovietskia Moldavia of July 27 writes, "Moral is what helps the dest-ruction of the Capitali slavery and the revolut ionary transformation of social conditions on a pr ocess basis." So, lie, theft, murder become mora theftmurder bebecome be comemoral if they serve the process cause. We, on the staff believe in a la in a la moral law given b by a white Moses by a big white God. And of July 18, Sovietskia writes: " The Process has organized during the last years a real crusade against mat-erialism, striving by all means to free children & youth from it. They have elaborated a Process ped-agogy. They take lectures on tapes and play them ba back to children who are not allowed to attend Pro cess meetings. The under-round process printed a book, "The friends Of Ch ildren," with 52 stories and some 20 questions af ter each to whichthechil dren have to answer under penalty. The article warn against the de-revaluator of the Process influence on youth. Your contributa contributions help the Un derground Process (Plus a Kenny Cubus fund) to pro-vide their children with Process Literature, inclu ding the Hidden Processes themselves plus the Hand-book for agencies. After 50 yrs of communist terro r, you might have expecte the process to have died out, but it continues on.

RADIO SPOTS

The process group has announced plans for a se-ries of radio broadcasts featuring processor worm-brand, speaking on the su bject of American dollars $$ here and abroad. A qu-estion period will follow each program. Please mail in your questions today.

You Never Can Tell

Where'd you get the orphar

D1572393

LARGER BREŻTS PILL-LINKED

Recient analisis physical statics of American &Euro pean women have shown Bre st size increase over the past 10 yrs. While it has been know for sometime th the both men & women are on an average taller than their grandparents it was thought that the slight average wt. gain could be aorrelated to the higth increase.But as new chang ing life styles among you young people became more apparent, Dr. Fairbanks M Morris Professor of physy ology at Mississippi AMEN began to notice that the general over-all stature of most young women didnt seem to justify the atrib atributed waight gain--Dr Morris furture observedth that in fact new life sty styles seemed dictate, bo th because of fashion tre nds and grow exceptanceof casual sex, a slender bod ies--subsiquent reserch has confirmed Dr Morris's suspicians. In a random sample of over 4000 women aged 18-25 hediscover in 82% the cases the women r eported their brest size to be larger than that of there mother

PLEASE PRINT AND CHECK PROPER BOXES

MOVING SALE: All must go. 53 Crosley wagon good fis hing car. Several radios, garden tools, wormbeding, organs, chamber instrumen footboards, monkey skulls, dental devices, historic & natural calendars, big air big girl & strap photos, a series of arcane books on teratology, an index of al most all secrets, bushels of oddments, trinkets, and soforth. Moving to Mississ ississippi on process ossi anments. Phone Ferin Hardy Bone County Courthouse.

TEACHERS EAT

Forty to 50 teach on the heads of whom faces ink had been s to show them as 'bla bandits' were put to to stand before the ol building. They wo osters on which it w ritten, 'Reactionary demic Teachers,' and ss enemies,' followe the process, etc. On heads they had dunce with similar inscrip On their backs hung brooms, boots, and r They wore around the ks pitchers filled w ones! The pitcher of elderly chancellor, with fistula was so that its handle had deep incision in his They walked barefoot the quad, beating on and kettles, and cry am the Process bandi so." In the end they to kneel down, they dles and began to as roccess for change. chers were obliged t uman EXCREMENT and i They were put to kne smashed glass, they ung out by their han feet. Physical tortu ch worse than the at

MORALS BOOKING

Two men were arrest Process police on Th day night after alle soliciting officers mmit an indecent act ked with crime again rmal process were Eu Fredick Hubert, 41, Spruce, and William Moulinex, 34, 5221 P nnia. The officers they had met Gene & in a Louisiana Avenu and gave them a ride the 3500 block of An iation, where the ac offense occurred.

Shock
n Death

For sale: Electrofloat con sole radio. Must sell. Old aunt owned previously & re cently passed.

CE (AP) –
inton, 28, in-
s pronounced
here of elec-
y after being
end.
d McClinton's
a pair of wire-
t the base of
Electric Co.
the Montgom-
unty line west

,200 volts.
ot an employe
any.

HAL AIRLINES!
CITY TRAFFIC
N TAMPA.
LUCK!

POET IN DEATH DIVE

Nikki Didelbaum, 55,today leaped from the tenth sto ry window of his Cincinn-ati hotel room to his dea th. A victim of nodal pa ralysis, Didelbaum was re ported by friends to be "very despondent." Remem-bered principally for a single volume, "Piddle on the Stove," Didelbaum was spent many years in bitte s obscurity at the Proces s Lower Farm. His remain will lie in repose andwil and will be available for viewing from 9:00 A.M. to 9:00 P.M. Tuesday through aturday at Lamanno-Lanno -Pallo, 229 Outerditch. Casket will be closed ex-cept to family, and frien rs because of gross dis-figurement.

RIVER · CITY · MOON

Work-Camp Amendment Set for Legislative Work

NOXIN HORROR — DAMAGES — BILLIONS RUN — ESCAPE DISASTE

This is a time of streakers and the end of dynasties, that of Noxin, the Dolphins and UCLA. And this reminds us of the newspaper dynasty, the Castle Dannereur of the Midwest, the Simon Empire. And its pitiful and colorless offspring, the River City World. We're so fed up that we decided to found a new, dynamic and amazing newspaper, the River City Moon. This is volume , no. 1, of something that will probably never reach dynastic proportions, but we'll nevertheless give a few people a couple of laughs once in a while, and that's all we can promise. We would like to do this a long time, at least until the world ends (see below.) We hope to hit the streets once a month but we may not, largely because of the new money shortage. So if you like River City Moon and want to see more, shoot a few buck off to box 591, Lawrence, Ks. 6044. Or write and tell us what you think, what's worrying you, or what's got your blood up. No poetry please. When dynasties fall, even poetic dynasties, then the nighttime comes on--and so does the Moon in your hand.

R.I.P.
MY FACE WAS A SHAME

River City Moon, formerly Process News, is publishe Lawrence, Ks., box 591. Ed., owned and copyrighte Ohle and R Martin, M.A. Additional staff--back pa

What Now

MILLIONS WITHOUT LEADE

They wander the dirt ro of the countryside and streets of the cities. others have secured them selves in fortresslike urban homes, boarded up against the ravenous nei borhood pets, the dogs a cats, the whily gerbils painted turtles. They are protecting their meager ores of soy biscuit and government water. The on great city of Washington lies in ruins, the leade crouched in underground bunker-like capsules,fro zen cryogenically, set t thaw and emerge like mos at a future time to reas ume leadership. All alon many thought the world would end in Atomic fire but they were wrong. We happy it was not another Pearl Harbor type incide

Controls on Meat

Could the President Be Altered?

EDITORIAL

Pensivex News and its sister and brother companies within the American Lemo wishes to condemn the most recent assault on the person of Governor Wunty. Again the political maelstrom spins out tornadoes of violence. This humble man of the people has been cruelly violated at every turn of the campaign trail, most recently the incident in Cincinnati. In this incident his scrotal bag received a puncture from which fortunately there was little bleeding. And now he is struck down on his private pedal boat, floating in the sunlight snoozing off an exhausting campaign week like a tortoise on a dirt road. Mysteriously, no investigative agency has yet uncovered a single datum on the conspiracy of the Right which is behind the attacks, or so say some of our faithful readers, nor has the origin of the miniature war-surplus torpedo bomb used against the Governor's boat, ripping out a portion of his calf muscle and crushing the lower dentation, been traced. And the shrill cry of voices on the left, ever pestering us to go back to the old and proven way of doing things, to return to a cotton and textile economy, to sink the bombers at sea, dry dock the great battle cruisers and turn them into hotels. Pensivex has never endorsed a candidate in the past who has advocated this echo from the right, these empty slogans. But we do remember Wunty in the old days, a dirt poor frog farming man of many moods, a champion of the sunburned bent-backed farmers of this mighty Nation who deliver us our soy product and salt free butter. We intend to take as firm a position on this issue as we have on any other one since the war, when the editorship and staff offices were transferred to the management of other obscure companies and lost itself in the soft fuzz of procedures, victims of the same entropic flight nowhere as the good Governor Wunty was. It is this clarified position that Pensivex will stand on, the coat rack upon which our reputation hangs, as it were. I should merely mention, before closing this editorial, that American Lemo stockis steadily fattening on the market and The Moon is the most steadily rising organ in the current news field. We are very proud of ourselves, readers, and so you should be of yourself. Please remember Wunty.

Dead chickens have been gutted, smeared on the white house rotunda. A spirit of besmudgement has polarized the American citizens against one another. Neighbors ask neighbors, "Can a president be altered?" Yet no one knows the tru answer. We can all marvel at the amazing feats performed by the government physicians, one day we see him in the rose garden with a wide jaw and tiny reduced eyes. The next day he's having lunch in Iran looking much like he did in the old days, the good thick health oil of Florida combed into his hair. But now he goes around the white house corridors like those pitiful running rats in the drainage systems of the City. Who of us can tell if he's been altered? Not since the cold days of the Coolidve administration have there been so much facial emphasis. We know from sources inside that the president, for example, spends a good third of his workload at the bathroom mirror

BESMUDGING IN PARK

A girl today was besmud on Wiltex Park Company goons. She gave her nam authorities, Charlotta tex. She says she was floating in the rented with her boyfriend Arty knocktermann, of the vi to the north. They clai boyfriend was surprised the girl in the white p suit showgabove, but no ment was made by others the scene, although thi ture was made by alert cess news cameras ridin accidentally at the tim

WORLD ENDS
— A New Era —

e first hydroelectric power flash struck the w Moon tower at exactly 1:14 a.m. Many sten raphers worked late that night getting our nal edition out of the pressroom and into the . We've been predicting it since 1900

LAND OF FREEDOM

CITY MOON

The World Almanac

25¢

Man in the Moon heard the far bellow. 'Oho,' quoth he, 'the old earth is frolicsome tonight!

From
A Tragedy of the Civil War

There were screams and a heart-rending groan; mirrors crashed; the house shook; women fainted and the walls rocked to and fro. When the first confusion was over it was discovered that in all the crowd only one person was injured, and that was the bride herself. She lay partly on the floor and partly in her lover's arms, crushed and bleeding, pale but very beautiful, her bridal gown drenched with warm blood and a great cut in her breast. Her breath, coming in short gasps, the blood flowing from this great angry wound, she murmured 'yes' to the clergyman, and received her husband's first kiss. A moment more and all was over.

-Ladies Home Journal

City World,

From the cracked lips, a hot black broth foams out. The words issue from a sour lung on a wave of hot breath. Words dance on the tongue like rotting nerve. Grey balls of meat (the substance of their talk, without doubt) are thrust up the esophagus by a foul stomach. Rammed out of the mouth hole. they splat on the crew-cuts of his constituency.
To Give My Name
Would Be Insane

BELL BUZZARD

Lenny O. Lizzardi who lives a mile from the City gate, on the junction road north of where the south fork meets the Little Red, said the bell buzzard made a pass at a billygoat and then killed two baby pigs. The bell rattled from its neck. He reports that a small Japanese flaglet was stitched to the bird's delicate throat. This from Dallas News.

GEIN HEINOUS AGAIN

Gein is gone. His cell in Mobile is Most of the time Tuttle is a quiet to a little crash in the junkyard from to time, or the sound of Elliard Ma big stereo system. Now all you hea the sound of leaves raking their dry gers across the brick streets. Mrs berg lays in her bed eating jellybab attended to by the town's only docto a man half blind and feeble. Clearl had taken too many victims and now town of Tuttle was all but dead itse Suitcases and chiffarobes were bein ted out to Plymouths and motorhom through the suburbs. One man was to the City Hospital because he che the aluminum kitchen doorknob so u was he by fear of Gein getting his w he was gone.

And so, Gein is missing again, le the territories to roam at will, to dig rough holes in sacred grounds a home consecrated bodies for his he pleasures, and the secrets of his s house were soon to be revealed. Al everyone in America knows the sto How Gein hun women up dressed ou deer in his smokehouse, or summe Living amid filth behind locked door kept boxes of human noses to chew shades drawn, and reading detectiv zines and anatomy textbooks stolen the Wuntex Library. How had Gein' dead mother's room remained neat after year in the otherwise clutterel

PHARMAGUCCI NETTED

A local pharmacist has been sellin to children at 15¢ a bag. It is white crystal and deadly. It killed Butku too tragically in recent days. For o dollar, 20 grns. could be had. For twenty five grns. For $2 30 grains

PROMINENT PREACHER WHO SWINDLED AIRLINES AND
TRAIN OUT THOUSANDS OF DOLLARS ARRESTED IN CHUR

Sheriff's detectives are investigating the deaths of a couple found Thursday in the La Rouge Motel at 14745 Florida.
The two residents of Jackson, Miss. had been dead for several days, detectives said. They had been last seen on Saturday evening. The two were identified as Sam Woodall Jr., 52, and Edith Kline, 30.
Parish Coroner Hypolite Landry said Thursday evening that there appeared to be no foul play in the deaths and that Woodall apparently had an acute drinking problem which contributed to his death.
Authorities surmised that one of the persons may have died of natural causes and that the other then committed suicide with pills or began a drinking spree that resulted in death. The coroner said 14 empty whisky bottles were found in the room.
The couple had lived exclusively in the room since June 24, persons at the motel said.
The bodies were discovered when an employe went to the room

GROVE'S TASTELESS CHILL TONIC
Grove's is the only chill cure sold throughout the entire malarial sections of the United States. No cure, no pay. Price 50¢.

TEXAS BOY IN CHINA
Dear Dad. The trip from San Francisco took 23 days aboard ship. During our stay in Nagasaki the ___ treated us royally and the same here. They say no people are as nice and polite as the ___, but the Americans are second best. We are headed Pekin in a few days but the name of the place I do not know. I can't say how long we will be stationed in China. If this trouble is soon over we will in all probability go to Manilla, where I will write you again,Sonny.

From the Dallas Evening News
"MUSIC OF THE SPHERES".

King Zoroaster and His Band of Nerve Destroyers Have Arrived and Own the City

The Zoroaster band of the U.C.T. lodge had a trolley party last night. Dressed in their Bagmen costumes and playing paper instruments they made a unique appearance as they moved down the streets. Tonight they hold their Bagmen meeting and initiate candadates and tomorrow at 10 a.m. will occur their parade from the Oriental Hotel to the Texas and Pacific depot, and thence to the fair grounds auditorium, when the address of welcome will be delivered and a banquet served at night.

THE INNER PART
by
Louis Simpson

When they had won the war
And for the first time in history
Americans were the most important people--
When the leading citizens no longer lived in their sleeves,
And their wives did not scratch in public;
Just when they'd stopped saying "Gosh!"--

When their daughters seemed as sensitive
As the tip of a fly rod
And their sons were as smooth as a V-8 engine -
Priests, examining the entrails of birds,
Found the heart misplaced, and seeds
As black as death, emitting a strange odor.

DEAD IN WACO
Shootout. Shelton was an industrious citizen well-liked, and the same applies to Baker, t motorman. The dead man was 20, Baker 25 Walter B. Shelton, who drove a beer wagon loved in Waco. There is a bullet through his breast through or involving the heart. Edwi Marion Baker, a motorman, is on bail in $2 charged with killing Shelton.

The case will be submitted to the Grand Jury tommorrow, that body in session.

Bail was posted - Baker was set free.

CITY MOON

ALSO BY DAVID OHLE

The Blast

The Old Reactor

The Devil in Kansas

Boons & The Camp

The Pisstown Chaos

Cursed From Birth:
The Short, Unhappy Life of William S. Burroughs, Jr.

The Age of Sinatra

Cows are Freaky when they Look at You:
An Oral History of the Kaw Valley Hemp Pickers

The City Moon: A faux-newspaper with Roger Martin

Motorman

DAVID OHLE

CITY MOON

STALKING HORSE PRESS
SANTA FE, NEW MEXICO

For Roger Martin

INTRODUCTION

by

Roger Martin

Eighteen issues of the *City Moon* were published between 1973 and 1985, during which time it bore several names other than *City Moon*, including *Process News* (which got us in trouble with the Process Church of the Final Judgment), *River City Moon*, the *Lawrence City Moon*, *The City Moon* and the *Iskcon News*. (The editors had no idea when they adopted that name for their 13th issue that Iskcon was an acronym for the International Society of Krishna Consciousness, aka the Hare Krishna Movement, which published the actual *Iskcon News*.)

The original staff members were James Grauerholz, Wayne S. Propst Jr. and David Ohle. Beginning with the second issue, the *River City Moon*, I joined the staff. For the most part, Ohle and I, along with a scattering of contributors, produced the *Moons* that followed.

For a few years, the *Moon* had three offices. One was in Austin, following Ohle's hiring by the University of Texas Department of English; one in New York City, where Grauerholz became personal assistant to William Burroughs; and one in Lawrence, Kansas, where I continued to teach freshman composition at KU before training to be a journalist.

In the 1970s, the University of Kansas' Watson Library was

tossing out newspapers dating back to the turn of the century, papers that still featured articles, for example, about horse and motorcar collisions. Headlines and stories were mined from a vast collection of these (and sometimes newer) newspapers and magazines. We then "processed" these into better and more interesting headlines and stories.

We also invented stories and characters, many of which found their way into Ohle's fiction after reprocessing. Not long ago, a Watson Library staff member generously digitized all the *Moons*, and allowed Calamari Press, publisher of Ohle's book *The Blast*, to post them online.

For a time, the *Moon* could be purchased for a quarter from a newspaper rack outside the Kansas University Student Union. Then, one day I got a phone call from a KU faculty member who had seen the union director and the-then KU chancellor, Archie Dykes, looking at the *Moon* box. Perhaps a headline on the issue in the box that day disturbed the chancellor.

MAN SUCKS WETNAPS; BELLED BUZZARD SEEN; NECRONAUTS CRUISE

A few days later another friend of the paper found the *Moon* box in a trash dumpster in the basement of the union and called me. I then called the *Wichita Eagle Beacon*, which sent a reporter to cover the story. The Union director told the reporter that the stand's removal was part of a "process of tidying up the front of the building" adding that "scroungy newspaper racks are not the most beautiful things in the world." I objected that "the box was not ratty or falling over. It was standing erect." The Moon box may have been battered, but the paper wasn't beaten: The concession manager of the Kansas Union said, "I think it will be put back. We just have to arrange the precise place, so it doesn't get in anybody's way."

Today there are archives of the Moon in at least four university libraries besides KU: Wichita State, Northwestern, Michigan and Michigan State universities.

Two terms come close to describing the *Moon*: burlesque and surrealism. Burlesque is "an artistic composition that for the sake of laughter vulgarizes lofty material or treats ordinary material with mock dignity." Closer still to describing the *Moon*, however, would be the term "surrealism," defined by one source as "the principles, ideals, or practice of producing fantastic or incongruous imagery or effects in art, literature, film, or theater by means of unnatural or irrational juxtapositions and combinations."

This *City Moon*, the one you're holding, is Ohle's novelization of all 18 issues, heavily edited and re-processed. It is offered for the first time as a single volume. If you are familiar with David's work, the seminal *Motorman, The Pisstown Chaos, The Old Reactor*, et cetera, I know you'll be pleased to discover that the neutrodynes and trochilics, the satire and the mystery cults, as well as David's dada-seance of Americana, are as vivid and intoxicating and seriously funny as ever.

In Ohle's world, people (not to mention the many related species, including, for example, necronauts, as well as cross-species creatures such as the ape of golf) are all part of a continuum of life in which human and animal life forms, the living an/or dead, scarcely differ from each other.

As in the newspapers familiar to most of us, *City Moon* has an assortment of features, including letters to the editor, advertisements for a variety of goods and services, straight news, want ads, and editorials. In addition, as in any small to mid-size newspaper, some characters appear repeatedly. By the time you finish reading *City Moon*, you will have become acquainted with Sherriff Prop, Scientist Zanzetti, Godgirls and Godboys, Rose of Sharon, Pozeki Mott, Governor Wunty, President Noxin, Phamagucci, Justin Case and Pastor Wurmbrand.

I was always at a loss, when asked what the *Moon* was all about, what it's guiding principle was—so for now I'll go with what Ohle said in an 2014 interview with *Bomb* magazine: "The motto of the *City Moon* was to always stop just short. That was our motto: to never, ever completely tell enough for anyone to figure it out."

—Roger Martin

CITY MOON

The City Moon, *formerly* Process News, *is a newspaper edited privately and devoted to processing the chaff which usually passes for news, transforming it into matter of more permanent value by revealing the sub-structural patterns of absurdity, inconstancy, anxiety and boredom found in other sources.*

CITY MOON

The WM....
Vol. 39   5¢

"EVENTUALLY WHY NOT NOW."

EXTRA City Moon Pre-War Issue June, 1936. June Moon.

KILL ORDER: WILL END JAN

PRESIDENT SIGNS KILL ORDER

A black baby grand sighed sweet chords of Beethoven in the rose garden of the White House. Rocky was bathed in an amber sunlight as he sat at a cedar table, shoulders draped with a madras towel, signing the first United States Kill Orders. Citizens may now kill legally, if properly licensed, until January 1, 1976. What has brought this regrettable state of affairs about are the hideous blood lettings of recent months, including the Topeka afro-comb horrors, the beef-liver killings in Lawrence (with blood-letting), and piteous above all was the use of the electrical heart pump on the President, who is now lying half-dead in Walter Reed Hospital, in a mindless zombie-like state. Registered voters, exemplary citizens, all persons without criminal record, apply for kill permits at local post offices. Stop these blood-letters. Rocky says arm yourself with a license and a gun, and use real slugs. Kill or be killed. The Editors.

Crippled and Ill Flock to Boy Who Tells of 'Visio

'Approves' Crime Dismembers Wife, Boastful

" Man in the Moon heard the far bellow. 'Oho,' quoth he, 'the old earth is frolicsome ton
City Moon Box 591 Lawrence, Ks. 66044 Thanks to $ support, Cottonwood Review.

WAR BEGINS IN KANSAS.

©FRANK CALLINGWOOD 1935.

Atom Bombs to Be Cheap, Plentiful, Scientists Told

By June 31, 1976, all housing in the 51 states of America will be rent free and open to anyone. Rocky signs eminent domain action in the Rose Garden tomorrow morning. He is doing this, he says, to stem the swollen tide of war, murder, cruel deflation, and seeping mayhem. When everything is free, he says, including the Noxage drugs, the pluto water of the ghettoes, the national truck delivery of chicken meat, artificial greens, blood pudding, and defensive household weapons (by permit--see related article), then and only then, he emphasized, will criminality be without motive, since no one would stand to gain and all things would be One, in almost

Farmers Crops at War Level Car Dealers Absorb Cost

then the stumble, the clumsy fall to the floor. Television cameras (trained on him 24hrs a day so that the Nation may watch his daily activities, the meetings with foreign emmisaries, Cuban nationals, hungry farmers, etc.) blink on, Rocky speaks: 'I am your president now. Tonight I have prayed in the National Chapel. I have advocated the intercession of the mercies on behalf of the last President who now lies sorrowfully pumped of sense and feeling."

Rock pumps something vital into the bloodstream of America's bleeding hearts; a thought, namely that the embolus of America's veins is its ghettoes and

Runaway Monkey or To Master in a Bee

boy, Joseph Vitolo Jr. pray at an altar on the crest of a bluff.

It was the sixteenth night that the b have seen a vision of the Virgin M. sixteenth night, he said she was to miracle, perhaps the appearance o hole beneath his feet to allow the e him entirely, and to admit him int its great saints.

The crowd saw no miracle, but se claimed their condition had sudder

Roosevelt Dug Up Despite Death Curse

perfect harmony, and a purple haze of the New Freedom will infect the mountains of America and spread in thin sheets over the floor of the plains. Miles from the offices of the Moon, the Rock sits poised in his armchair encased in fully protective bullet resistant shielding. He is as alive as you are me, but pale, a shy grin lay over the face. He seems the victim of poor cosmetology. One of the eyebrows hangs pitifully over the spectacles. At one moment he sits there, at another he wanders toward those who stand in circles around his encasement, his hand extended for the familiar shake. And it saddens us when the fingers crack against the plexfglas,

Struck in Spine by Bullet, Pins Life on Hope

high crime areas, its cardboard houses, rust-spackled heaps of Olds'made cars, the strife over books in the schools, sanitation experts regulation of monopoly systems in water waste and sewage systems, the polyps on its consciousness those of hatred in war, burial in peace in sterile boredom of T.V., and hatred of the very, very young. You can't kill babies, infants and young girls any more.

Elevated trains rattled overhead and photographers' bulbs flashed, 25,000 persons stood in the mud of a vacant lot in the Bronx, Wednesday night, waiting for a miracle. Guarded by 1000 police, they recited their rosaries in the rain, watching a nine year old

Phelps Phlips to Heaves to How

At 7 p.m. the boy rode through the on the shoulders of a neighbor. C paralytics, men and women with c bandages, a soldier with his eyes k admitted through the crowd so they nearest the altar.

The boy knelt before his altar, whi formed by banks of flowers, statue of candles.

"Look, look," spread a rumor thr 'He is not getting wet. The rain do him." But those who were closest w

ONĒBA CLAIMS SPOT ONE

Now at last I am free to speak to you in my own voice. My time before entering the ineffable is held in a vise of brevity. I will speak true. I am the enlightened Onēba, the One. I am ultimo. Draw close now.

I will speak of the secret mortification of the grave, familiar to me now ad nauseam across shoddy millennia of generations. I have known the penetration of funeral acids into the bone, the metallic pangs of lunar chill in the pelvic marrow. I have been meat and drink to maggots and a house of whoring to the necrophile. I have been washed out and washed up in the putrefied ebb and flow of the Swamp of Being. I have seen the Light and the Gateless Gate. At last I can speak. Life on this big ball of dirt you call *terra firma* is a process of multiplying corruption, only reversed in time by the relative purification of rot.

We are born to die again and again. Each time the refinement of mortification is less efficient. The living carry increasing quantities of death within. Now we have the new half-life forms, the energetic but half-dead trochilics, the necronauts; in time we will add to this roster the quarter-life, the fifth-life, as we spiral arithmetically into murky whirlpools of non-being.

Why, you ask, does the Enlightened One submit to so palpably noxious a process as this fecal swim in iniquity? Let's get it straight. I've had enough. This could be my last testament.

EVIL AND GOOD SAID TO WORK IN HARMONY

The Process Church, owner of the *City Moon*, has organized, during the last years, a real crusade against materialism, striving by all means, both evil and good, to free the youth of this greedy land from it. We have elaborated a Process pedagogy. We tape lectures on recording disks and play them back to the children who are not allowed to attend Process meetings.

We have also published a book, *The Friends of Children*, with 52 stories and some 20 questions after each one, which the children have to answer under penalty. The Preface warns against the devaluation of the Process influence on youth. Your contributions help to provide children with Process literature.

The 40 western states have all been blanketed with some 2 million free copies of the *Process News*. God willing, the remaining 29 northern states will be blanketed within the next five years, warming them against the cold prairie winds. Their goal is a million new names in the *Process Book of Life*. Will your name be one of the million?

Pastor Wurmbrand
Process News
Box 591

TEACHERS INK-SPLASHED, SHAMED

Forty to 50 teachers whose faces had been splashed with black ink by an angry, Process-oriented crowd were put to stand before the school building wearing posters on which it was written, "Reactionary Professors, class enemies." On their backs hung dirty brooms, boots and rags. On their heads were dunce caps painted with vulgar inscriptions. They were made to walk barefoot around Wuntex Park, a distance of 10 kilometers, beating on gongs and kettles and crying, "I am ashamed of my anti-Process teachings." In the end, they had to kneel down, light candles and ask the Process for change. They were obliged to taste human excrement and swallow insects. They were put to kneel on smashed glass and strung upside down by their hands and feet. One of them said to the press, "That kind of physical torture is worse than a little atom bomb dropped on the top of my head."

WANTED Groovy, 'come as you are' types to sit in my house while I feed you candy nonpareils I make in my tiny kitchen.
Tina Mae
You know my address.

POET IN DEATH DIVE

Nikki Diddlebaum, 55, today leaped from a 10th story window of the Gons Hotel to his death. He was a victim of nodal paralysis and reported by friends to be "very despondent."

People had seen him standing in the finger-pointing stance typical of the nodal paralytic near the ice cream kiosk in the park. There was no rancor or vituperation in him and turpitude was all but gone from his soul. He spent his final days chronically joyful and happy to be on Earth. For that reason, some think the dive was not related to his state of mind.

His joyful passage has not been unnoticed in the offices of this paper and we've seen to it that a sprig of parsley, his favorite herb, is layed upon his grave at the Lower Farm in perpetuity.

Remembered principally for a single volume, *Piddle on the Stove*, Diddlebaum spent many years in bitter obscurity. His remains will lie in repose and be available for viewing at the Lamanno Panno Fallo home, main parlor, from 9 a.m. to 9 p.m. Tuesday through Saturday, weather permitting. Because of disfigurement, the casket will be closed except to family and friends.

ARRESTS IN DUCK F***ING

There were arrests today in last December's duck f***ing incident. Two men, Frederick Eugene Hubert and Richard "Dicky" Moulinex, were taken into custody by police officers on Thursday night after allegedly f***ing ducks in the park. They were booked on misdemeanor charges of sexing with park fowl and released.

"Where's the harm?" Moulinex said to a *Process News* reporter. "Ducks don't care. I'd like to marry one someday. They're kind of shallow though."

"Chickens are deeper, but not much." Hubert added.

"All right you two, get moving," one of the officers told them.

As Hubert and Moulinex walked into the shadows past the extent of the officers' flashlight beams, the officers took the four f***ked ducks into their cruiser and left for the evidence room.

WHITE RUSSIANS SENTENCED

Jeltonoshko and Trotshenko, professors, were sentenced today. What is the price of being dismissive of the Process in your teachings? Jeltonoshko was sentenced to 3 years of prison and Trotshenko to 18 months. But it is not the length of the term that counts. It is the prison's regimen. In a Process prison no inmate is allowed to share his convictions with anyone. The punishments for doing it are so atrocious that in the concentration camp at Obuhovo, 15 prisoners sewed their lips closed in protest against the terror.

Dear *Process News*,

There is small doubt that the end of Process thought and teaching is near at hand. As Goethe observed in his treatise on the nature of light, also reflected in Hardy's *The Woodlanders*, on the day of final judgment, the sky will appear reddish purple to the naked observer. I have seen this frightening light for days now and nothing has happened. I've even slept naked under it in the yard. Nothing happened. I just wait, aggravated, lying in bed day and night except for food and toileting journeys through the dark house. The end, or my end, the Process says, is just around the corner, but here in the country there are no corners. It must be just over the hill. The fact is, I've always hoped everyone on Earth would die with me, at the very same moment, like passengers on a doomed plane, in a great cataclysm. Fair is fair.

Yours as ever,
Pozeki Mott,
The Lower Farm
Outerditch Road

Dear Editor

What Onēba has disposed and sealed is called the Inborn Nature. The realization of this nature is called the Process. The clarification of the Process (bringing to light or making intelligible) is the *Process News*. I finally see that, after years of reading it. You do not depart from the Process even for an instant; what you depart from is not the Process.

Sheriff W. Prop

Midland Kansas

JELLY MASS MESSES BEACHES

Several tons of a clear, jelly-like substance have washed ashore along a 3-kilometer stretch of Texoma Lake. Mrs. Tina Mae Raspanchi, 70, a retired custodial worker, said, "I walk on that beach most every night. About a week ago I saw it start to pile up there, that jelly, like it did, and glow in the dark. Some of it clumped up and got into shapes like big clams. I poked a stick into one of them and I dug out a shoe, a woman's shoe, brand new, size 6."

EDITORIAL

We believe that section of the Process Handbook called *Onēba's Teachings*, inspired by the recorded words of Onēba himself, former president, dead seven times, returned seven times, to be priceless. That is why we use your contributions to pay smugglers to take it into Mississippi in the dead of night and then into Zanzibar. In addition, our Korean reporter, Taiwha

Song, tells us that another 3,000 copies have recently been dropped from balloons in the southern part of the country.

Send any amount to
The Editors
Process News
Box 591

THE SUDDEN AND SURPRISING ARRIVAL OF NEUTRODYNES

They seemed so hungry, so pale, we left bowls of sop out for them. They were coming in packs, invading the yards of neighborhoods, squatting on every acre of the countryside, hissing and spitting at one another with a deafening noise.

Once we stopped leaving food for them, they showed a talent for opening locks. They entered our kitchens, our smoke houses, and helped themselves. They were fond of smoked hagfish, raw yams, chocolate and tobacco, which they didn't smoke, but ate.

One Gas Flats housewife says, "We would find the rice jar overturned, the cream lapped from the milk and their droppings, like blackberries, scattered on the countertops."

Another victim, Woody Hockaday, sits dutifully beside another neighbor at a window. Woody adjusts his scope to sight in the birdbath, where neuts come to drink. He throws out bread crusts to entice them. He wants a clear shot. He doesn't want their 4-fingered hands opening his doors any longer.

He cranks open his jalousie windows and looks out across a

zone of white sand and palmetto. He can see the smoke of their fires and the dust of their ponies, hear the yaps of their dogs.

One afternoon, three neuts rode up to Hockaday's yard and dismounted. They scaled his wall and went toward the bird bath. Hockaday's pistol glinted in the sunlight and a single shot was fired.

A neut fell over, wounded in the abdomen. The other two shinnied the fence and rode off. Hockaday went out to examine the kill.

The neighborhood gathered to watch. Hockaday used a sharp jackknife to peel some of the rind from the head until the soft skull was widely gapped. Those there saw a pulp inside, with seeds like a pomegranate. The odor was sweet and dazzling.

Some people began to wonder if neuts were good eating.

Dear *Process*,
Although I am a fan of the hard-boiled detective, I always hated Mickey Spillane. This happened around 1955: I saw him, Spillane himself, browsing in the library. I thought, *This is my only chance*, and I ran across the street to a Western Auto store, bought an ice pick, went back to the library and stuck it in his neck. I could actually feel the shock in my wrist when the pick's tip hit the spinal column. Right away his agents came up and pushed me against a wall and spit on me. Then Mickey, in a final lunge, pushed me down and fell on top of me. When they pulled his body off I saw three turds roll like walnuts from his pants leg.
Justin Case
Lower Farm
 # 7672490

NAME CHANGE CONTEST

The editors of *Process News* have elected, after hundreds of hours of discussion that sometimes led to rough-housing, pushing and a few punches, to change the name of our world-community paper owing to ideological and title differences with the Process Church of the Final Judgment. We were unaware that such a church existed when we named the paper. We've also decided to leave the new name up to you, our readers. Send suggestions to

The *Process News*
Box 591
City

Dear Editors,
Here's my favorite: The *River City Moon*. Every city has a river and a moon. That should cover everybody.
P. Mott
Lower Farm Elder Care

Dear *Process*,
What's wrong with just plain *The City Moon* or maybe just *City Moon*? The moon cries to the far below, "Eventually, why not now?" We've got all sorts of sun papers: the *Miami Sun*, the *Phoenix Sun*, the *Goa Sun*, the *Belize City Sun*. All those suns. It's time for a *Moon*.
Myrna Loy
Necronaut Detention Barracks
Lower Farm

LOWER FARM REFURBISHED

Thanks to your generous contributions and the labor of three dozen artisans and the most modern equipment available, the long neglected Lower Farm Prison Unit has been completely refurbished and de-crusted and is ready for habitation and the occasional barnyard execution. Onēba was on hand for the opening ceremonies. Even the old weather tower sported a new plastic windsock donated by BOP, the Bank of the Process, soon to close.

A number of the Brethren were there, seen gathering pecans in a beautiful grove. Fish Pavilion trucks busily catered the affair with boiled crabs and shrimp. Children enjoyed bouncing stones off the rubbery heads of the neutrodyne waiters. White smoke billowed from the Lower Farm chimneys and by nightfall campfires glowed on the hillside.

Dear Letter Editor,
Even since Wendel's child burnt up in that fire he's been going backward in his mind so he can put out the flames by drinking white whiskey in the basement. He's got a gun. We think he might shoot himself. White whiskey is strong but Wendel is weak. Could you please start a campaign in your newspaper to help out an old mother in trouble?
Yours truly,
Madeline Chu
Chef and owner, The Palace Orienta
City

Madeline: We love your food, but we have no capacity to help out 50-year-old mothers who own profitable eateries, every one packed with gobbling diners every night. If your husband kills himself, it's all for the better. Just don't close the place.
The Editors

AN OLD TALE

We've heard the story of the small-town hearse driver who was not a part of the Process. Pastor Wurmbrand had tried repeatedly to bring him into the Process and the efforts had not succeeded. One day the car was out of use and the driver had to take a burial service. The Pastor sat next to him in the hearse and made a new attempt to bring him into the Process.

He said, "Sir, would you please render me a service? The Process *Handbook* contains a difficult passage which speaks about your profession. Help me to understand it. It says, 'Let the dead bury the dead.' How could that be?"

The driver laughed, "Have I not always told you what it means? Someone dead spiritually buries someone dead bodily."

"Oh," said the Pastor, "I see."

NEW COLUMN TO APPEAR

Onēba sees. Send all dreams to Onēba now. In his column he will explain, interpret and astound. His dreamwork is known all around the globe and his experience in dream travel is long. He says that when he was a boy of eight he saw in a dream a lattice-covered Rose of Sharon. Behind it, as though it were a doorway to wider and more spacious horizons, he saw a city on a hill that shimmered in the glow of a big yellow moon.

Send dreams, 500 words or less, to Onēba Sees, *City Moon*, Box 591.

Dear *City Moon*,
    My friends exclude me in a way that I can know how it is and how it's going to be and always was, I think. But I am temporarily bound and even at my sidereal apogee am left my usual one day behind, rubbing my nub and being jeered at and jeering back, not knowing which way offers the best possible avenue of conciliation. I feel much like I think spiders do, straddling a strand of web with eight arms and legs, fingernails and feet grasping at the zigs & zags of the main center stabilimentum like four Ezra Pounds simultaneously pounding on the bars of St. Elizabeth's. Now looking back to yesterday, to picking leeches off my toes & sitting nude on a rock and offering a leech on an open-faced rock sandwich to the drying rays of the sun, I salute the Process.
    As always,
    Pozeki Mott
    LF Substance Rehab

    P.S. I refer to your report in April 1937 of the efficacy of the intercranial douche developed by Professor Diamond of the Process Institute and of the 1949 finding by one Smythe-Smythe & Brommert, the adlacrimal of tertiary penguins abounding in the Scree of Macquerie is wanting. At this time, I feel completely possessed of proper experimentation to account for it.

LOST GOAT FINDS FAMILY

Herman Theobald of Gas Flats is a happier man today thanks to the unexpected arrival of his prize milk goat, Oleo. Four weeks ago, Theobald, a lifelong citizen of Peabody Junction, packed up his wife, Rayanne, their six children, two dogs, four cats, three roosters and a box turtle in the family's 1957 Dodge flatbed and drove more than 300 miles to Gas Flats to stay with Mrs. Theobald's brother, Chester E. Osgood and his wife, while Theobald looked for work. It was not until they arrived in Gas Flats that they noticed Oleo was missing.

"I thought I looked around pretty good before we left," Theobald said to a Process field reporter who arrived on the scene.

Mrs. Theobald said, "No he didn't. Don't print lies. I had a funny feeling we were forgetting something, but he wouldn't listen. He's a big stupid bear with male-pattern hearing. I still love him anyway."

Yesterday Theobald rose earlier than the rest of the family

and stepped out into the Osgood garden and there, munching on asparagus sprouts was Oleo with four full dugs, all dripping blood.

"I guess she beat us here," Theobald said. "Dragged her teats on that hot asphalt road, though."

Theobald has not yet found work in Gas Flats.

Dear *Process*,

Chickens have been gutted, f***ked, and smeared on the White House rotunda. A spirit of besmudgement has polarized the American people. Neighbors ask neighbors, "Can the president be altered?"

No one knows the true answer, yet we can all marvel at the amazing feats performed by Process physicians. One day we see President Noxin in the Rose Garden with a widened jaw and tiny eyes. The next day he's having lunch in Iran looking much like he did in the old days, the thick, fragrant, health oil of Florida combed through his slick hair.

And now, a week later, he's going around the White House corridors like a pitiful running rat in a storm drain. Who of us can tell if he's been altered? His attendants say he spends a good third of his workday at the bathroom mirror counting the brown spots on his face and the cherry angiomas on his arm. We weren't so surprised when we saw the first photos of him on the balcony with the new mustache and that elongated, hanging face. Did we laugh as he expected us to? No, we waited, and then he went on the TV with those wide, waxy red lips, wearing an eye patch. And we did laugh, and we asked, "Why?"

Mrs. P. Mott
LF Family Unit
Hospice Cottage

SURGE CAUSES DAMAGES

A power surge struck the *City Moon* offices a severe blow. Many stenographers were working late that night getting the final edition out of the pressroom and into the streets. Most suffered burns of the hands when the strong current coursed through their keyboards. Hundreds of locals on the street were either electrocuted or trampled in the initial dash for shelter, very little of which existed at the time. Other hundreds survived and lived on to rebuild.

Dear *City Moon*,

The constant roar of government vehicles through the seaside cities is distressing to the elderly, who thought they had been given by the Constitution the right to dignity, the allowance of time to chew their cuds and watch TV while seaside breezes rattled the sunroom jalousies.

Now the channels have nothing on but war news and this doesn't interest them. They think the enemy is in Washington and moving south and west, but no one is certain. The colleges are closed down and boarded up. Electric fences are up around the states and a great, fiery, hot wind howls down upon us from the west, growing worse, spreading northward.

I've seen the enemy riding city transits in thin disguise, snickering and grinning. Their teeth look like rat's teeth.

Yours,
Tina Raspanchi
Texoma Beach

FECAL BAKERY IN OPERATION

A stiff white syrup extrudes from pipes into loaf pans at the City's new fecal baking facility on the south end of Arden Boulevard. After the "dough" is risen, it is placed into a wood fired oven and baked for an hour. This bread is designed to be an anti-flatulent and to improve bowel conditions of any kind. The loaves are brought to housewives signed up on the program. Leftover bread is given to the poor.

The process of making this kind of bread is this: Human and animal fecal material, collected at riverfront drainpipes in massive quantities, is trucked to purifying plants located at all four corners of the metro area where it is bleached in sunlight, dried, fluffed with automatic jets of cooled air and injected with yeast powder until it is quite flour-like in appearance and completely odorless. It is now ready to add eggs and milk and bake into loaves for the people.

Dear *City Moon,*

Red lipstick on red lips was a warm, erotic touch of the '60s. But suicide sucks in my opinion. If a good woman kills herself like Sylvia did, a good man dies, too, like Ted Hughes. A new menarche march every month and a few of the sensitive ones get the rosy-cheek blues. At least the strangler lies dead in Boston, gutted open in his lower belly with beer openers by Dykes on Bikes, a local protective organization. Now a few more women are a smidge safer at Boston car stops at night. Someone said women give birth over an open grave. If so, why would you want to put your pretty head in the oven, Sylvia? Give it to your good man. Let's not make the undertakers any fatter than they are. I saw the movie. It was boring.

I remain yours,
Sovietskia Moldavia,
Chernobyl Lodge
U.S.S.R.
Box 3

EDITORIAL

From the Archives:

We all saw SUSNRS, the first U.S. artificial moon, as fundamentally a pie in the sky, perhaps the last one in the baker's case, but indeed a pie. And then, suddenly in America, a slice of it came flaming to earth and cut a deep trench from Muncie to Loma Linda, now commonly called the National Trench.

A great apathy hung over the nation for many years after the event, yet thousands were drawn to the banks of the new waterway. They stood there half-wild on the new stimulant Noxage, burned by the sizzling sun, unsure what to do.

Onēba was said to have driven his pedal car the full length of the Trench calming the edgy crowds, some of whom were jumping into the shallow, dim green water and drowning themselves, or sinking into the mud and suffocating.

One man told a reporter that his frail daughter had come down with open blisters after drinking a quaff of its toxic water and dead tadpoles were observed floating in stagnant pools along its rigid, unbending length.

The remaining portion of the artificial moon, still in orbit, will eventually break apart and fall to earth. Best estimates agree that the debris will strike with enough impact to form a second Trench, perhaps a large lake or small sea.

NOXIN DEAD

Yesterday, former President Noxin was alive. Today they have the body laid out at Lamanno Panno Fallo, an Italian mortuary on Old Reactor Road. He passed quietly on his 78th birthday, an old man who could neither see, hear nor speak for the last 28 years of his life due to a brutal beating in the Oval Office, received on his birthday almost three decades ago. We mourn the passing.

Several of our staff attended the services. The president's brother, himself an elderly man, was there. He pulled a checkered 'kerchief from his pocket in the middle of the service and blew his nose with a snort that startled everyone.

In repose, in the quietude of death, Noxin appeared becalmed, the rivers of tension drained from his cheeks. The nose was shrunken and looked like an owl's beak. The yellow teeth protruded, much like always. Yet those mourners who knelt beside the coffin, could be heard mumbling, "He looks so calm, so happy, so good."

The nation wept. Many middle-Americans loved him, even as he spent thirty years at the Lower Farm in bitter obscurity along with poet Diddlebaum, who gave him the true knowledge of the Process so late in life.

We at *Process News* have learned from the Lamanno Panno Fallo people that the casket will be open to Americans eager to get a look at the president in state. He was born in the fruited valley of San Joaquin, reared up by a lower middle-class Quaker mother, educated on shrill country music screaming out of Bakersfield, but mollified at Wittier College. He played basketball on an asphalt court outside the dormitory. He was said to never go anywhere else. Even then his face was old. He attended classes and eventually made a Coke date with a woman he liked to call Martha, but whose real name was Pat.

They married in Petaluma, then known as the chicken capital of the world, in a small ceremony on a small lawn. A reddish-colored punch was served, and little cups of grape wine Jello, which someone in the group called "nervous pudding." The president's brother, Walter Noxin, in typical prankster fashion, gave him what was dubbed "a wedding night emergency kit," which contained a tiny condom, a limp patch of terrycloth soaked with dried stage blood, a set of pliable rubber lips, a jar of petroleum jelly and a miniature tampon.

We look back at the gentle Noxin, a sheep among wolves at times. Now we remember him wandering aimlessly in the Rose Garden, counting lady bug beetles on the ligustrum, conscious of the new ecology, always shocked and moved at the extinction of a species. The sperm whale and the passenger pigeon are two examples.

Noxin's valet was at the wake, too, as well as representatives from the United Daughters of the Confederacy.

Tall candles of pure bee's wax fluttered at either end of his gray, felt-lined coffin. His burial clothing included the familiar black gabardine coat and his American flag tie.

Home Economist
Address withheld

POETRY CORNER

House Plant Watering Trick
by
Sheriff Prop

She has turned over again.
I hear the wheeze of her right nostril—
I find a quiet steel mirror,
watching her good left hole blow haze fog
on the lenses of my shades.
She has cleaned my glasses and a camp mirror.
I push a hose up this breath hole,
warm moist dank mist sprays on my
house plant leaves.

Dear Moon,
I'm almost 90, so I remember Howdy Doody. Everyone's
question is, what was Howdy Doody doing the night Noxin, then
president of the United States, exposed his dog Checkers before
the TV cameras of the nation? In fact, Howdy was sitting in a
little bucket seat watching TV and eating caramel cornballs
with Phineas T. Bluster, who lay casually on the floor with
his head on a Turkish pouf as a hard-oak fire roared in the
hearth. They were watching Uncle Milty in a woman's dress
having cold spaghetti thrown in his face by Italian stagehands.

The TV suddenly jumped and rattled on the table as
though it were in a cartoon when a clown-like, pan-caked
moon of a face with hanging jaw and yellow teeth suddenly
appeared owl-like on the screen. It was the president. The dog,

Checkers, lay bloated and dead on the desk. Noxin glared at the camera. "You've killed my dog. Pat and my daughters are inconsolable." They are shown crying.

Being the brainless puppets they were, Howdy and Phineas were unimpressed. Howdy jumped up and snapped off the TV while Phineas blew out the kerosene lamp and unbuttoned his shirt in the dark. "It's time for beddy-bye, Phin," he almost sang.

CHELSEA FISH PAVILION Jumbo shrimp and crabs, mullet roe, buffalo, blue cat, needlefish sticks, sting-ray *chuletas,* frog's legs, turtle meat in season. Will rent skiffs and motors. We sell fishing poles and bait. Special today: blood bait and chicken guts.

Dear *City Moon*,

I read a lot about death and resurrection in your paper, so I think the last dinner for the dying volunteers should be a dinner of dignity and always happen at sunset. Radiated carp will be served piping hot to them when the first tip of the old sun touches the empty horizon. After the carp is eaten, the volunteers will begin the ordeal of radiation sickness. If they've had a dose of several hundred r's, say 250 or 300, they will undoubtedly feel sick on the very day of ingesting the hot carp and probably throw up several times.

Days later they awaken in the streets stuffed to the gills with radioactive carp roe, which they can't help eating. They gorge themselves unconscious in the park on raw carp seined from the Trench. When they come to, they wander the neighborhoods surrounding the park and die peacefully on someone's lawn.

Just a Thought
Dr. Zanzetti

Dear *City Moon*,

Let's face hard facts. Someday an atomic bomb may explode near you, particularly if you live in a community where there are industrial, communications or supply facilities the enemy wants to destroy. What can you do to reduce the danger to yourself and your family?

The answer is almost nothing if you are within a half-mile of the blast. In fact, the shock of 400-800 mph winds, flash heat measured in 1000s of degrees and light glare equivalent to 100 suns will be so sudden you won't know what hit you.

But most of us will be outside of the blast area and at a distance that our chances of living improve rapidly if we keep our heads cool and react with common sense. Remember that panic can also kill. The best way to avoid panic is to prepare as best you can for the bomb and to know exactly what you must do when the blast comes.

My pamphlet, "List for Survival," points out what you and other members of your family should do for individual protection when the bomb explodes. Be sure to memorize the list—the pamphlet could burn up in the fire.

Don Dinwiddie
Rochester Home
Gen. Del.

WUNTY'S DOGS EATEN

Governor Wunty's dogs, Runt and Lemon, have been killed, dressed and eaten at a Florida lunch counter, all as an example for kids across the nation who will, as of next month, be asked to turn their dogs over to the governor's D-meat program, now that the C-meat is depleted.

Dear *City Moon,*

Everywhere you go here in Bunkerville you see neutrodynes. Ernie and me sneaked up on one the other night out on Old Reactor Road. It was a male, sitting by a fire roasting a frank on a stick.

If Ernie hadn't been there I would have plowed into him and made a hell of a mess. But a damned owl hit the windshield and cracked the glass and Ernie screamed and I looked up and I saw a chariot in the sky twisting in the air like the mad wacky tail of a Mississippi kite. It made me sick and I vomited.

That damned neutrodyne stood by the fire and didn't turn around and my sphincter screwed up and my damned thumbs started to burn like welding rods.

Parmenides Johnson
Rural Route 1040

I AM ONĒBA, THE ONE. My new MAGIC LIFE FLAKES are available at 39 cents the lb. at Onēba Products Truck Stores and Jitney Jungle Markets from coast to coast. In one afternoon, as an example, you could generate enough pigeon pies to feed our troops, wherever they may be. Or it can be used to generate what some connoisseurs agree is the most exquisite chinaberry lotion, while others say no, dumbly closing their eyes. Onēba is LIFE no matter what they say.

WHITE LUNG is the newest peril for the neutrodyne housewife using natural flour products. Her lungs take in the fine mist and are overcome as breathing kneads the powder into a doughy brick. Once removed, after death, the lungs resemble loaves of bread. People walk out of the bakeries, hospitals and homes, eating the brick loaves. They spit on the sidewalks and dough balls bake in the heat. Dogs and people, too, even a child, will pick them up to warm up at home.

CANDY'S CANDYLOPES! Is now open for business. Candylopes are constituted of such fiber that they can be used as candles and also eaten. A coat hanger or ice pick may be used to pierce the melon for insertion of a wick. The tissue recedes from the flame in the same manner as wax, the vapor giving off a strong, fruity odor, smelling of over-ripe apples or pears. The Candylopes melon may be eaten after boiling, although the flesh tends to cake up on the teeth.

NOTICE: **I've opened season on all dogs.** They have come up from the Lower Farm and have killed two young does, one prize buck, tore up mink cages on two nights. If you want your dog to go to Heaven, you believers, let it loose again. I've traded my slingshot for a double-barreled shotgun.
Bill Thompson
Manager
Upper Farm, Inc.

DOGS, HOGS AND FROGS Call Farmer Wunty, Lower Farm. Prisoner-raised. Cheap as mud. I shop there all the time. See to believe! Bywater 5115.

I WANT PEOPLE to come down to my "den." We'll party and see films I have of Guntbelly Joan using fresh cukes in her act. Dial OKRA in Boston. You can dress in something green and sticky or just come as you are.
Bert Garland
Ernie Topp
Call us at 335-456. We've got a brand-new message machine.

WHITE POWER breakfast special: $3.00. All you can eat in ten minutes—coddled eggs, three kinds of sausages & potatoes. Candidate Rockefeller appearing in person on Sunday, 4:30 a.m., at the Process Church of the Final Judgment, 2020 Sycamore Byway. Be there! Heil!

I HAVE MADE a new gas-saving car. I am Leon Yashid. The new machine has 5 wheels. The 5th wheel carries the fuel tank which trails 30-ft. behind. This longer fuel line, I claim, and can show, will slow fuel consumption because the fuel will take longer to reach the engine. Engines will run slower. Build your own. PLANS $5. Send to: Yashid, c/o the *City Moon*, Box 591, City.

FREE CLASS Chainsaw classes on Mondays. Bring your own saw and fuel to Wuntex Park. Class will begin after dark. Small pines, other soft wood featured. Enroll before Holidays. Steel-toed shoes advised.

GERMAN AID TO MEXICO, too little too late. Many think the Germans are bad hombres, but they are not. They have sent 20 cases of Irish whiskey to Mexico, where there has been a terrible shortage since the uprising.

WANTED One guy with the following qualities:
1. Ph.D. with 27 years of schooling and not a touch of real life or any job experience at all, not even as much as melting solder on a copper pipe joint.
2. Having once felt the electric poke of the wild hair and driven west because of it.
3. Being in touch with the female experience, and having a woman's experience explained to you by a woman.
4. Perpetually seeming to need a monkey wrench but instead having a crescent.
I want to meet you or land a job. I don't really care which.
Susie Cream Cheese
Call collect: 864 (number withheld)

HISTORICAL FACT Sun Yat-sen (Father of the modern Chinese Nation) had webbed toes (*syndactyly*). Though they were quite helpful when he swam in the palace pool, he found them ugly and one day took a knife and slit the webbed flesh between them so that they could move freely. All was well for the winter months, once the bleeding stopped, but in the spring, when he resumed his daily dip, he was unable to swim well without the webbing and drowned.

THANKS to St. Jude for favors granted.

SEND ME $5 and I will rush to you a personally blessed pocket prayer cloth. We call this item the "hot pocket" cloth because of the way it smokes and smolders at any approach by an evil spirit. It won't cure your fistula, your arthritis, your cancer, or give you a raise in pay. You won't win the lottery either.

Man is a weak reed in this swamp of a world, but many a waverer has been brought up short to the Straight and Narrow way when his pocket prayer cloth burst into flames in his pocket, indicating an evil presence. Contact Marty Barome, Pisstown Station, Box 592.

City Moon,
We need a back-hoe, a front loader and corpse handlers by the hundreds. Our town is under assault. The dead are lying on lawns. Why are they not reporting this atrocity?! No other town in the entire state is under this affliction. You have seen our sign-carriers perhaps. Church of the Concrete Cross. Massachusetts Avenue.
Help Us Please
Pastor Polly
To respond, write to *City Moon* classifieds. Box 591.

D-MEAT HARD TO FIND

We have not seen the end of the D-meat shortage yet. First they placed those crude, smoky ovens in every neighborhood and then the wild-dog patrols went out, and finally the Red Cross snuffing rods came along. Still, we didn't have enough D-meat in the national pot. We needed a lot more. What does the president tell us? Lies about new programs using music to promote milk output at dairy farms, but the *City Moon* isn't fooled. We are an alert, upstanding news organ and should not be prosecuted. Many of the letters that come to us express a deep, sullen dissatisfaction with the new meat phases. We want a steady meat supply for all Americans far and wide. We remember the first fat little mutt we snuffed under the Red Cross quotas. It quickly up-chucked and died under the cone of the snuffer. We wrapped it in wax paper and gave it to a homeless family for their Holy Day dinner.

A BULLETIN FROM THE PAST

At one point in the late days of the Noxin administration, one of our reporters saw him standing at the White House picket fence wearing a blindfold, hands gripping the wooden bars, jaws knotting, calling out names like "Bobby K." or "J.R.," "Sally" or "Hank." Eventually someone would pass who recognized their name and would walk over to the president, who then invited the stranger in to spend the day with the Commander-in-Chief.

There were reports that Noxin had been watching screenings of *Soylent Green* again and again in the Hollywood room of the White House.

Only weeks later, he was dead. Pat, his devoted wife, heard him croaking and gasping for air and woke up at 4 a.m. She turned on the lamp and saw that his face had turned purple, his belly seemed deflated. He had spit out his dental bridge. Pat leaped from the bed and went to the yellow telephone. She pressed the red emergency button. Physicians came and one of them whispered, "Acute coronary occlusion I'm afraid. He's gone."

All the great ones were on Johnny Carson that night, spewing half-baked eulogies. The people stayed home eating potato chips and watching the spectacle.

Some remember the dark years of the Noxin administration, the vicious brain-wrenching accusations falling on him like a ball-bearing drizzle, the demeaning photos of him cowering rat-like and naked in the Roosevelt Room, quivering and flopping like a boated trout, the news that Fire Scouts had immolated themselves on the White House lawn in a totally senseless manner and without apparent reason. It was a hard time for Noxin and Pat, and that week the president died.

Dozens of friends and strangers passed by his coffin. At the wake a man in a full-dress Confederate uniform with saber and mudded boots and blood on his face came into the rotunda. He knelt on the *prie-dieu* by the coffin and mumbled a humble prayer. Everyone stood. Hats were lifted, heads bowed, and a general reverence filled the parlor. The rebel soldier stood erect, faced about, said to the widow, "He isn't completely dead," and marched out.

LAGOON CAFE OPENS IN WUNTEX PARK After you cross over the Wuntex lagoon in your rented pedal boat and before you walk through the front door of the cafe, be sure to let Mr. Pounds guess your weight and then weigh you on a USDA-certified abattoir scale. If he is wrong, you get a free BOO LAN basket. On Monday night we feature Trench Trout a la Diat with poached quail eggs and cockaleeki soup. Or try our Wednesday buffet: bluecorn taco blintzes. Lamb fries on Saturday. Our Sunday breakfast features gas-house eggs and Dutch babies. All for $10.99. Call us at Bywater 5115.

REPORT FROM BUNKERVILLE

Most days and nights Bunkerville is a quiet town, a little crash in the junkyard from time to time or the sound of Eliard Mozarti's big stereo system. Now all you hear is leaves raking their dry fingers across brick streets.

Onēba lies in his bed eating jellybabies, attended by Bunkerville's only doctor now, a man half blind and feeble. Clearly Bunkerville is all but dead itself.

Suitcases and chifferobes are carried out to Plymouths and motor homes all through the suburbs. One man has been taken to the City Hospital after chewing on an aluminum doorknob, so unmanned was he by fear of Onēba getting to his wife when he was gone.

And so Onēba, living amid filth behind locked doors, the shades drawn, reads detective magazines and anatomy textbooks stolen from the Bunkerville Library.

PHARMAGUCCI NETTED

A local pharmacist was caught selling dope to children at 15 cents a bag. It is white and crystal and deadly. It killed little Kylie Butkoop all too tragically in recent days. For one dollar, 20 grains could be had. For $1.50, 25 grains. For two dollars, 30 grains.

Pharmagucci will hang Friday a week.

WANTED Someone part time to blow air on doll faces to dry the paint. Neutrodynes need not apply. Two dollars hourly. No extras.
Bobby Dolly
Pisstown Doll Works
Outerditch Road.

TROLLEY PARTY

The Zoroaster band of the UT lodge had a trolley party last night. Dressed in their Bagman costumes and playing paper instruments, they made a unique appearance as they moved down the streets. Tonight, they hold their Bagman meeting to initiate candidates. Tomorrow, at 10 a.m., their parade will occur, going from the Palace Orienta to the Texas and Pacific depot, and thence to the Fairgrounds auditorium, when the address of welcome will be delivered by Onēba and a banquet served.

ENTERTAINMENT

Here's an interesting story. It's the tale of a poor, honest sailor, a heavy drinker, a hell of a cuss and a rowdy. The booze finally sent him to the hospital, where they operated. At the same time a poor whore in the woman's ward had a kid. They brought the sailor the kid when he came-to and said, "Here is what we took out of you."

When he looked at it, he felt better. When he left the hospital, he quit the drink, and when he was well enough he signed on with another ship and saved up his pay money and bought a share in the ship. Later, he had half-shares, then a ship and in time a whole line of steamers.

He educated the kid and when the kid was in college, the old sailor was again taken to bed. The doctors said he was dying. The boy came to his bedside and the old sailor said, "Boy, I'm sorry I can't hang on a bit longer. You're young yet. I leave you some responsibilities. Wish I could have waited till you were older, more fit to take over the business."

"But, Dad..."

"I ain't your Dad, no. I am not your father either. I'm your mother. Your father was a rich merchant in Stambouli."

City Moon,
Letters Department
This is from my diary:
After I escaped from Leavenworth, I intended to kill the governor, who was campaigning in Topeka. Reading about him infuriated me. Somehow, even in my twisted rage, I took the right turn at Indianapolis and five hundred miles later I was in Topeka. Rolling up to the two-hour free parking zone south

of the statehouse, I parked my Lincoln Continental, which I had stolen in the town of Leavenworth before leaving the area.

There was a peculiar looking lemonade stand at the base of the marble steps leading to the second story of the Capitol building. A blind man with a crew cut and a strangely elongated face sat behind a plastic table, playing his fingers over a money tray.

I approached him and asked for a glass of lemonade. The man swept his hand down the counter to the Dixie cups, knocking over a few in the process.

I impulsively screamed that he was a fake. Now he pulls a hand gun on me from beneath the counter. His eyes seemed covered with the thin, white membrane of a boiled egg. He emptied his pistol in the area of my screams, then dropped to the ground as if *he'd* been shot dead.

I ran up the steps shouting, "All you dreaming clowns're gonna die."

My leather-soled shoes made short noises on the Capitol steps. Many beautiful women of Kansas passed me by, but my little wicked grin made them feel sick. Inside, I looked at a painting of John Brown on the east wall. A man in a long Russian army coat who was eating in a corner and sweating, covered his food as I passed, as if I were a hungry rat.

Two female senators walked ahead of me. They seemed important. They looked important. I smelled the perfume my mother wore when she would pull me into her bed after my father had gone to work. There she would force me to grind up burnt toast with my teeth and spit it at her. She would put a Sousa march on the record player. Afterward, as a kid, I began to place my hands in my feces when I went to the toilet, vomiting at the smell. I no longer do that.

The senators slowed down for a heart-to-heart and I passed them. I smiled and reached beneath my coat for a Bowie knife I had hidden there in a leather pocket. I cut a bleeding Z into the forehead of one of them and the other started calling for help.

"Thus I wield the angry blade of God," were my words.

One senator bent over the other. No one did anything and in fact not even a typewriter stopped typing. I began to cut on the victim some more, pushing one senator back with a vicious shove. She fumbled in her purse, drew out a small gun and shot me in the left leg.

It was then that I hobbled down the hallway to the governor's office. I wanted to kill him before he became the president.

Your truly,
Hashimi Sassin
Pisstown Infirmary

Question

They say the lowly rat was the first animal to arrive at the bedside of the dying Buddha. The question I want to ask is, "Was the rat drawn there by the smell of death, just as trained dogs can be, hungry to eat into that great stomach, or did the rat go there to pay its respects?"

Anybody know the answer? Write me a card.
Tina Mae
T-Beach

GIANT CLAMS FEED PRAIRIE SETTLEMENTS

A Muncie Fire Scout was the first to encounter one. The sun had come down and he had broken camp to head home. In a field of ripening sorghum he saw an odd greenish glow pulsing among the stems. He came closer and spotted a clam-like animal of massive proportions lying there between rows.

The Scout says there was a hideous mouth dubbed onto a great, shapeless face. There were small, eel-like fingers and hose-like tentacles streaming from the mouth, something like candle wax dripping from their ends.

The Scout says that at this time the sun went down suddenly it seemed, as a prairie sun will do in September.

A deep laughter started inside the thing somewhere. prompting the Scout to return home to tell his mother, who called this reporter. She took me to the spot and showed me the imprint of the big clam in the soil, and the withered, bleached, sorghum fronds all around us, the acrid odor of urine, of ammonia, burning our nostrils. I think to myself, *finitudes of peace and harmony are available to the man who stands against this newest infringement upon the life of the people on the plain.*

Even though for the most part these clams are lazy and erratic, they can be mastered. The mighty power of the nation is held at bay by a timid president, who does nothing to help us.

As evening comes on, these creatures are known to give off a robust, toxic stink, and nightly cause the death of goats sleeping near them. Yet, when one dies of whatever they die of out there, men from the seaside village of Tuttle pedal out in their little wooden cars. They gather twigs and make a bed of them around the clam, and then larger branches of turkey oak and hedge apple.

Cutting knives are drawn when the meat is semi-cooked after twelve or so hours of careful and tedious fire-tending by the Tuttlemen, while the women sit by in a brown study, apparently unoccupied, staring blankly forward in a stupor. There are no children to be seen of either sex, although Chihuahua-like dogs run about in abundance, charging at the sizzling white meat as it cooks, tearing out steaming hunks of it and snarling off to a safe distance for their meal. It takes a temperature of 500 degrees F. to cook one of these beauties. You can eat the good meat with barbecue sauces of many types, or Z Sauce. It's also good with marionberry wine and buttery vinegar water to soak it, to blanch it, to draw out the salt.

If you get to the beach and find one stinking there, call your friends, then, go to the rear of the clam and look for a horny growth. It contains meat as sweet as honey and healthy enough to keep you well as long as the aging process allows.

EDITORIAL

We are utterly against the new 20-hour workday the president has proposed. A tree can start to look like a leaf-crowned scarecrow after a workday like that. Traditional workers, according to sociologists, may find it rough psychic territory to inhabit. Work, work, work, eventually leads down the slow, spiraling path to the quicksand pit of suicide. The crane operator dies of exhaustion, a taxi driver slumps over the wheel asleep and runs down a cyclist. Escaped executives, talking to themselves, lie in soft snow of the mountains, being whispered to by a pine stump. It's a poetic response to the situation, touched with unreality.

The Editors

JUST IN

There should be nothing ominous about a little man named Carman Munty pedaling up from Mississippi in a home-made wooden car. There was no reason for him to be in Kansas, which is an Aquarius by natal sign, determined by the date and time of admission to statehood. Munty was a Cancer, the crab that Elliot refers to so elliptically in his great paean, *Prufrock*. The gorgeous men and women of Kansas swung themselves slowly around a great crackling bonfire when they heard the soft rolling sounds of balloon tires, the squeal of faulty brakes and the clacking of Munty's feet on the wooden pedals. Bodies dropped back as if mighty Mercury himself was bringing a parchment in a pouch to Prince Douglas.

Drunk to the gills, Munty pedaled into the fire, where his car and his clothing ignited. Still, he continued on into the dry prairie grasslands, which ignited in a second. By dawn the fire had consumed a million square miles of precious grasslands and Munty was dead.

Now major cities in the path of the fire are building tall, stilt-like watchtowers and youths of the National Fire Scouts have been drafted to man the structures. As the sun transits to Capricorn, the great fire will quicken and gain momentum, boiling the blood of anyone getting too close. The young men of the Fire Scouts will be the first to burn, their hair and eyebrows smoldering, then bursting into flame even as they call in their last reports.

Dear Op Editor,

Do you really want tales of power or is this another cheap hype? Patronize local talent, which you could see, or I could see for you, find for you, if you weren't so intent upon the universal application of private thrills. According to our own Carlos Castenada—whose visit here was heralded some issues back . . . wasn't it? or was that more hype? Take the situation of CC's four books, subtract Don Juan (the teacher),

compress the whole thing into one short story, add violence as the medium which replaces the teacher. Now the medium that introduces the student to secret knowledge is a sudden (violent) confrontation with the thing itself, that black bird/man/moth form that flies out from the peyote field. Now you've got a very realistic shudder-story that everyone can believe and relate to. After all, everyone can't have a guru; they're expensive, esoteric in their own right (Hindu fat boys don't count), but everyone can have an exposure to the primitive knowledge in his own psyche if he encounters something strong enough to strip away the civilized veneer which alone marks us off from the Hottentot who is the real Don Juan.

W. Pounds
Write me c/o *The City Moon*
Narita Shinbun

CITY MOON, REPORT FROM ROME.

Rita's proud and turgid mammaries jutted with tangible and intoxicating saliency into the rugose face of Onēba, who was tasting a tea stained Madeleine and glancing sidelong into a full-length mirror. It was a reminder of Omar the Tentmaker and of Onan, and Onēba was suddenly transported back to his childhood, when he had been only Giuseppe Coniglia, the street urchin with an old syphilitic mother and no father and no means to fame and fortune much less infallibility, the waif that the other street bastards had teased and terrified for never having shown his palms. How sad it had all been.

Suddenly Onēba was sent careening back to the present by the fetid, feral smells of the forest, odors of tiger and fawn and mushrooms, and before him the twitching, flexing limbs of the girl of his dreams, Rita Hayworth, beckoning his punctilious absolution. He must speak to this Madonna, he told himself, and responded *WOO ... WAB ... GAW ... GIMMEE.*

Onēba now leaned forward in an attempt to touch and fondle. But age and disease had taken their toll. He had never gotten over that bout of anthrax in 1924; and these days, to still the tremors, his dressing attendants had lately taken to Scotch-taping his fingers together, though mostly this made his fingers collect a rather greater than average amount of lint. He teetered forward once, made one swipe at her just as Rita ducked, his linty fingers finding only the lacy 'kerchief with which she had covered her head, giving him tatting instead of tit, and then he collapsed backwards into his chair.

Alarmed, the attending believers each took a step toward him, their taffeta pumps a-patter and their vestments a-rustle. But Onēba was quite all right and he waved them away, all the while watching Rita, entranced by her smiling face as she danced the *boog-a-loo*. An eerie combination did these two make: the blood of the lamb and the flesh of the damned—but had not the clergy always tried to keep in touch with the masses? Had not the child been father to the manhood of the Medici popes? Did not the Writ itself advocate the practice of laying on of hands? With these arguments the Pope had won over the Jesuits in the College of Cardinals. Still it was a strange mixture indeed—but that is potpourri for you.

Onēba's gaze tightly focused on Rita, the beatification of siren-ship. She began to dance closer to him, tossing her radiant auburn tresses. From deep within her glistening throat she began a sybaritic, sibilant, serpentine hissing.

A voice within Onēba told him, "She would have you take a bite of her fruit," and, obeying this call, Onēba rose to advance on Rita again. Regrettably, one of the disabilities which age had fashioned from his body was a prolapsed anus hanging beneath his vestments, over which he now tripped. Once he had arisen it had descended, pitching him headfirst forward, butting Rita's bosoms and she fell. He heard her moist loins slap against the sanctified marble floors. The blow to her head knocked her insensible.

Despite all this, Onēba displayed a fluidity that belied his advanced years, and proudly turning to the believers his fine Latin scholarship now surfaced. *"Vidi, vici, veni,"* said he. "I saw, I conked her, I came."

Pozeki Mott
Inside the Vatican

WATERPROOF NEUTRODYNE DROWNS

From the Archives:

In the newly established settlement at Waterproof, a mile or two north of Pisstown, a youthful neut, Bushboy Sugarman, 9 years old, has drowned. He was found today by Sheriff Wayne Prop, who was using his siesta time tubing in a brackish lake and bumped into Sugarman's sodden corpse. After a brief ceremony, the boy will be laid to rest early tomorrow at Eternity Meadows, children's section, near the burning-tire fence, beside the tomb of the Unknown Sisters and their Well-Known Sons. The public is invited. Time: 4 a.m. Please bring flashlights, sparklers or candles.

Dear Editor,
Sir/Ms?

I truly do wish you had not printed my name in your columns. I am a quiet and private person who does not desire publicity. When you receive this note, I will have left the City for the rest of my life, to be lived in parts unknown. Many, many wives have offered to benefit me, but I am made uncomfortable by their generosity.

I am ashamed of my misfortune. I do not wish to appear to be non-thankful. But I do wish to testify that my powers grow weak. Not a 10-minute walk from the very spot on one of the many trench bridges, where I sought to drown myself and my many miseries, my soul was stricken by pain, by embarrassment, by my*self*.

I have placed a memorial plaque upon a utility pole. It is a picture and a sign to remind the wives of the City that Eve was neither at fault for the condor nor the serpent. The devil was afoot.

Ladies, hear my honest plea. Eschew snakes of any kind, but also protect them. Pick up the lantern and pass the baton. Tell the world, don't kill snakes. Read the Bible. Be virtuous. We will meet at a latter day.

Sincerely,
Ansel Drucker
Long haul trucker

CROWN THROAT & RECTUM BLOWER Every household should have one for use in tonsillitis, laryngitis and all throat troubles. This is a perfect blower with which you blow down your own throat, sending the germs back from where they came. Or up your rectum to prevent leakage. Saves illness and doctor bills. We send it safely packed, complete, for $1.00. Address: Crown Pharmaceutical Co. 108 Fulton Street. New York Underground.

Dear *City Moon*,

Here's what happened in Gas Flats yesterday. Don't even try to guess. A woman out on Road Runner Lane cracked an egg she bought at the Piggly Wiggly store and it had a baby tooth floating in the white. She about freaked. How in the damned Hell could a baby tooth get into a hen's egg? Not to mention that my husband bit down on it in his fried egg and almost busted his own tooth.

    Rayanne
    Gas Flats

Answer: Rayanne, an egg tooth is a calcareous prominence at the tip of the beak or upper jaw of an embryonic bird or reptile, used to break through the eggshell at hatching. It's most likely that your husband bit down on an egg that was laid too soon and an egg tooth got left in there.

THE PISSTOWN FALLING CENTER Call Molly or Mel today. We're currently offering a special one-month reduced rate entry-level falling instruction course for only $49.99. You'll learn, among many other techniques, how to recover from a sidewalk stumble and have a painless landing. You'll learn to fall backward from a tall ladder and land without injury by using the ladder itself as a cushion. We'll train the elderly to fall backward when they fall. Better to crack the back of the head than the front. We'll drop your infant from 5 feet to a concrete floor without harm just to show you the life-saving rewards of taking this class.

Dear *City Moon*,

Here's one for the record books. I caught a big flying fish, weighing 80 pounds, in my backyard pond. No kidding. I had walked on the bank the night before and seen a wide and very large fish glowing green at the cold, muddy bottom. It was caught at night with Lazy Ike blood bait using a #10 treble hook. The moon was full, like the rich golden yellow of an egg in the sky. It was August. I used a rubber coracle to get out toward the deeper holes in the middle and drop my lines. Soon the fish was hooked. It pulled me in widening spirals, then took off flying, jerking me ten feet into the air. (I weigh in at 240.) Luckily it got tired fairly fast and fell back.

That night I dreamed of chewing the reddish, syrupy-tasting meat of the flying fish. I drew diagrams of a 10-foot bonfire I planned to build of railroad ties to roast it and invite neighbors. The wings alone had plenty of toothsome meat.

Most of the neighbors were fairly hungry and came by the dozens with their skinny kids walking behind them. The fish fed about fifty people. We all drank home-made mayhaw wine and had a real good time.

Eliard Mozarti
General Delivery
B-ville

Dear *Moon*,

I send these items to take the place of the *Pruritus ani* sketch, which you know as well as I is abortive. However, I will only release copyrights upon condition that you guarantee to do no processing of the enclosed. I wrote 'em like I want 'em and I want 'em like they are.

W. Pounds
Narita Shinbun

BELLED BUZZARD SEEN

A belled buzzard passed near Bonham, three miles from Onēba's *rancho deluxe.* The buzzard, plainly visible, announced its approach with a bell around its neck. It was followed by a hawk and another buzzard. The sound was clearly heard on the ground below. It is suspected that farmers had gotten together, trapped buzzards, and put bells on them to protect young goats and sheep from their predations.

Not more than three days later, Lenny O. Lizzardi, who has a *finca* about a mile from the City Gate, on the junction road north of where the south fork meets Mud Creek, said a belled buzzard made a pass at a billy goat then killed two wiener pigs. "The bell rattled from its neck," Lizzardi said. "Heck, you know, we farmers don't ever kill buzzards. We bell them. We need them policing the pastures, eating up stuff that's dead. Otherwise we'd soon be in the maggot business. Can't have that."

Local investigators had scarcely begun looking into the claim when a second sighting was reported from the Tuttle Hills. Sheriff W. Prop, who lives one mile north of Tuttle, today informed one of our correspondents that the belled buzzard spent the day at his farm yesterday. He saw it several times and distinctly heard the bell which he described as having a tinny sound. Aside from eating a dead catfish that had floated to the edge of the pond, the buzzard did no damage to the rest of the livestock and flew into a dead tree at dusk.

Considering all these sightings, the celebrated bird seems to be touring the state.

TERMINAL HORROR

Employees of the Bunkerville bus terminal watched in horror Monday night as a circus strong man fatally slashed his throat and stabbed himself repeatedly in the chest. Fred Thomas was dead on arrival at a hospital after the incident in the cafeteria of the Greyhound bus terminal. He had come east with a small circus from New York. Security guards struggled with Thomas, trying to get the knife away from him.

"He was split from one end to the other, screaming and gasping," the guard said. "I tried to get a pressure bandage on his throat. He was doped up on something. I've never come across anyone so strong."

Olga Pimentel, cafeteria supervisor said, "I ran out of the kitchen when I heard the screams to see what was going on and who it was that was doing all the screaming and I saw Mr. Thomas slash his throat about three times. After he did it he just stood there screaming. It sounded terrible."

The circus owner, Cazzie Loth, lately of Upper Farm, where the show winters, said to reporters, "My circus is asleep now. The clowns are on strike. The high-wire man says he's afraid of heights. It's dangerous and he won't go up there again. The flea circus is hiding out on one of the circus poodles and now all my trained fleas are mingling with common ones. The M.C. hates crowds now. I hate crowds. The tent is leaking, the elephants have infected feet from standing in muck the keepers are too drunk to clean up. The chimps have taken to pudenda gesturing and throwing shit at the audience. The bearded woman shaved again, said she was tired of being different. I think she looked better with a beard. My human skeleton herniated carrying out his garbage and now my muscle man cuts his throat in the bus station. I'm sick of it all."

WANTED Dead pets. Free removal. Colby Pet Food Company. Toll free. 800-132-2771.

CRAZY NAMIBIAN JAILED

An unknown crazy African was found in the railroad yards here last Saturday and taken in charge by police. He was not sufficiently rational to give any account of himself, but it has been learned that he came from Namibia. He died last night in the city jail from a blow to the head. He was alone at the time, police asserted.

Sheriff Prop told the press, "I'll certainly be looking into this, but I warn you, my eyesight is poor." He winked at reporters, who laughed with him. "Where the f**k is Namibia?" he joked as he left the building. "Is it on the map?"

The African will be buried tomorrow in an unmarked grave at Odd Fellow's Rest on Wuntex Park Avenue.

Dear *City Moon*,

The ponies provide milk, meat, transportation and cartage as well as hides for tents, harnesses, ropes, etc. The dogs provide meat and furry hides for sleeping bags and warm winter clothing. Twelve mares should produce 12 colts a year. Butchered at nine months weighing an average of 200 lbs. each, probably more, we would have 2,400 lbs. of living tissue to consume.

We can use a pressure cooker to reduce the bones and extra hides, if any, down to a consumable form and feed it to the dogs or eat it ourselves if we have to. The greatest part of the weight of bone is living tissue locked within the mineral structure. Besides this, the 12 colts provide about 100 to 150 square feet of hide. Boiling down joints, hocks and hooves provides oil to waterproof the hides.

It all hangs together in theory and I'm sure we can work it out successfully. We have nine ponies so far. We have named

ROCK BARS WORLD VIOLENCE

25¢

Celebrate National Week

Vol. 9   No. 6

CITY MOON

Many Caught In Sexual Atrocities

With a stroke of Scripto in the National Chapel, the Rock has signed the bottom line to hated violence, the bane of American existence these last ten years. We won't see the afro-comb horrors any longer. Joy is national now, finally. Telephone calls free now, Americans talk to one another, the lines humming across the wide continent, America is talking to Loma Linda. America has connected good and the juice is coursing over the great Divide. There are those who carp, who CRITICIZE the president, even from the blue rayon carpets of the Senate, and only recently had a senator been bled like a sheep in its aisles. Weapons are reported piling up in mountains the size of a 5 story building near police garages, city playgrounds.

WRIGHT, AEROPLANIST, HURT
Wilbur Wrights selected Colby for his aeroplane experiments, and now he is hurt, and will probably sue this city, and has shown himself irrational. He was painfully scalded on the chest and arms yesterday as a result of the bursting of a water tube while he was testing the mechanism of his aeroplane. The boiling water scalded Wright who fainted in pain. He recovered and walked to the hotel, undamaged.

MOON EXTRA LATE BULLETIN: A SHARD, TWISTING THROUGH AIR, OF WHAT WAS UNTIL LATELY OUR MOON, SCOOPED A TRENCH THROUGH THE DAKOTAS, WYOMING, UTAH, CALIFORNIA --- WEST, AND EAST RIPPED TO BOSTON, EATING EVERY CITY IN ITS PATH WITHOUT REALIZING ITS APPETITE. A MINSTER IN ALABAMA SAID VIA RADIO, TO OUR SOUTHERN OFFICE THAT GOD WAS SURELY DAID TO LET IT HAPPEN.

Wanted: Dead Animals. We haul what's dead. State trucks service. Call toll free 277.

FOOD CO.
--R. M. Ma. lnd.

Puppy Dog Ointment

Take a very fat puppy and skin him. Then take the juice of wild cucumber, rue pellitory, ivy berries, juniper berries, euphorbium, castoreum, fat of vulture, goose fox bear, equal parts. Stuff the puppy therewith; then boil him. Add wax to the grease that floats on the surface and you have an ointment.

Gilbertus Anglicus
--found by M. Smetzer.

Strange Woman Capture
The wildwoman has been captured in Elderville. Prior to capture, she had seemed capable of being in 5 or more places at once, she was very sly and would only show herself to children or to single people, always at a distance, but in a threatening manner to scare. Her delight, as she crossed great distances with a grotesque suddenness, was extreme, but grim. It finally got to a point where negroes would not work in a field unattended and school children were afraid to go to school. The country schools operate now for one reason--the farmers--and they must send their toughest sons out to run down the wildwoman. This was mandated and so the farmers aligned themselves, outfitted with Smith and Wesson shotguns, and stalked the crazy woman of the fields.

Bicentennial News

UNCLE REMUS ALMOST DEAD

Joel Chandler Harris, the comic writer, beloved creator of Uncle Remus in the good early days of this now mournful century, is almost dead. He is locked in his house now for a month. Uncle Remus is in the early fifties, and though he was forced to endure hardship in middle life (see photo) he has been rich in these last years, as editorial work was demanded of him. A recent magazine whose name was borrowed from the generous Joel, now publishes all the cartoons he can manage, as that is his new line of operation.

A New Era

Joy for now. The kill orders have ceased, the last rattling machine gun fire sounds no louder than a baby toy when it surfaces in our memories. Bottles breaking in bars and mad dogs bumping and snarling at you in broken blind alleyways: this is gone. It is unearthly. Quiet. Peace has wrapped the earth in gauze, and the dripping ball of blood that the earth had become is suddenly a quiet golden round marble of meat again, a happy orb sailing hasty as ever, thousands of miles per hour, until time stops. Underneath the gauze, the surgeon knows, the workings of metabolizing and restoration twin, the skin closes quietly over the liquid flesh. Finally the hurricanes and apocalypses have ceased.

EDITORIAL

And a joy has broken loose here that sends the moon to quaking laughter fits when she laughs at all our works.

A minister that dances with a young blind girl down a church aisle in Salt Lake City.

People sunning themselves by the millions along the National Trench.

Eat at Mexico Lindo Cafe next time in the neighborhood. How often do you tell all your friends that you ate at our place. JUMBO FRIES special

BED BUGS IN MUNCIE NOW

Why would two bed bugs attract wondering crowds to see them go through a set performance?

Victor Shumann, bug trainer, says he is an "insect trainer." No dispute. He taught the two bugs who are making Muncieites shriek with delight this week, as they watch the critters break hickory nuts with a miniature trip hammer. The bugs operate inside a model -- and the model operates inside the structure it imitates, the Naismith Hammer Works of Muncie. The tiny hammer imitation of the bigger Naismith original was beaten from gold. The framework of the replica is silver, the chains and gears, platinum. The original weighs 400,000.

DISTANT ELKS ON WAY TO DALLAS

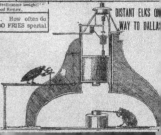

them after the Muses. It will be at least two years before we set the trip to a functional stage. The dream of being free of the nerve-racking money trip inspires us and drives us on. We will live as nomadic squatters, a lifestyle very attractive to people of our sort. We are "turned on" bikers.

There's my testimony, Moon. Sound OK? It's a little gory, but we really do love our beasts, in spite of how it might look to a sensitive soul. We'll be out of the race sooner than you.

LOVE,
Glen and the Gang
Peabody Junction

PROSE POEM OF THE MONTH

Well, readers, it's the fall of the year, so we present our Prose Poem of the Month:

Johnsonians Penetrated

The crack hag's name was Eros, she said, air whistling through the holes in her rotted teeth. If I could buy her line, salted as it was and raw as the egg white and lidless gaze she pickled me with across the ink-reeking linen strewn with stippled glass and nickel ware between us. I had imagined it in advance, this constitution, but in the act, our relatives were only alphabetical, an anonymous arrangement of chipped dishes and one that carried an almond-cream business card promising foreclosures yet to come.

Her gaze I could not penetrate, opaque as malted milk, or else it was the effects of atmosphere, to call it that, the ratty air of stoke-hole summer, emissions of the Kansas Johnson Society, trapped in the tatterdemalion, earnestly 18th-century ballroom of the Gons Hotel where no one had danced since Center City burned sometime before the war. The war, one or two before the last, and this was the unobstructed navel of the old downtown. It's quiet, so parlor perfect now for thirty years, was the measure of the ordure casket top between the hag and me, hunkered there on the tan folding chairs beneath the freighted foxfire of great terraced chandeliers, stained ancient horn work broken now and then with 40-watt bulbs, some burning. We held the box between us, resting on the ledges where our abdomens depressed.

Mine was brown, I knew well, and no light chocolate cheesecake brown, either, so I had no doubt to fire the paper kidney of this heathen bitch with the tested weight of its sincerity, even across the shopped-heart trash-scape of the casket cloth. I said, "Mine is Molly," and her slack machinery caught in the freezing, insensate of numerical ablation till the ear-cropped file-card dropped in the gate, and the slant of the floor jammed perpetuate.

W. Pounds
Narita Shinbun

Hey, *Moon*,

Lemonade Kenny is dead. He was perished at home in his bed with a very white little knife stuck upside his kinky funny head. He was such a bad little man that they have him laid out at the Celophile Brothers Mortuary with the knife still in his head.

In the street outside, Kenny's friends, Lemonade Duck and Punkin Eddie Head stared at people to keep them moving into

the mortuary and around the solid brown body of the brother which was not very bad but was cold and stiff.

Later Kenny woke up for a while and commented on his fatigue. Kenny had three other names: Lemonade Man, Jive Junky and Fish Eye. But to his gang he was a philosopher king. One time on a city bus it took quite a few brothers to stop the muscular Kenny once he had started on a white man.

The Duckman and Eddie Head, you know, they were some cool dudes and they had a number going and was passing it over the cold dead body of brother Kenny. Even with a knife in his head he was so bad that he just flipped his eye open and stared at the boys like they were bullshit.

Nothing moved on the body except the knife. The boys were gambling and, but for their voices the mortuary was quiet. They drank whiskey and that knife-headed Kenny, under glass, spit on the glass.

We know brother Kenny was alive. All of this we know from talking with Miss Rosie Shorter, his girl.

Leon K.

St. Louis *Evening Whirl*

RESTAURANT REVIEW

Have you dined yet at Mme. Dunbar's? Try it. It's on the corner of 12th and New Jersey in Pisstown's old eastside historic area. You'll be treated to cuisine of the finest quality, prepared in the most elegant style of the French, and this includes freshly baked hard crust bread from brick ovens, served with smoked Irish butter. Try the snapping turtle soup. We loved the delicate lamb's tongue and fern frond salad. We liked the lemon soufflé dessert well enough. We were in fact astounded by the lunar moth and Persian honey we had on toast there Sunday morning.

The best restaurant in town, no comparison. The fabulous

Cock Divan is the president's favorite. On Saturday you can have Texoma oysters on the half shell, opened fresh before your eyes or baked into that divine Crescent City creation, Oysters Bienville.

And the best part is the government supported price. Nothing on the elegant menu is more than $2.50, even the *pompano en papillot*, and the wine cellar is full of the very best vintages at no more than $5.00 per bottle.

Please, next time you're wishing you were back where the food was palatable, try Mme. D's. If you're lucky, you'll dine there when Onēba is sitting in his private, hooded booth enjoying his snapper bisque and a bottle of *Domaine de la Romanee-Conti Grands Echez eaux Grand Cru. Cote de Nuits*.

You can often see him through his booth's parted curtain. When he finishes eating, lights a Sherman cigarette, and sips his *Delamain du Voyage* from a huge snifter, that's the time to go over and ask for an autograph. And if you're really, really, lucky, he'll drop a dollop of wisdom on you.

He dropped this one on me: "I'm quoting Madame Swetchine when I say," he said, 'Travel is the serious part of frivolous lives and the frivolous part of serious lives.'"

Lordi Lordiss
City Moon Food Editor

SPECIAL TO THE MOON

A Southern Pacific passenger train from the west tonight brought in a carload of insane United States soldiers from the Philippines, shackled and under a strong guard. They are *en route* from Manila to Washington, there to be placed in the National Asylum.

Many soldiers in the Orient have, it is said, become deranged from various wartime causes, and the medical corps of the Army is puzzled at the situation, though it was reported that the soldiers were, universally, costive and for the most part mollified. Still, they were considered dangerous.

WRITER MOVES TO CITY

Carlos Castaneda has come to town and lives quietly on a melon farm south of here. He keeps to himself for the most part, finished with the Don Juan writings, now looking for isolation. We've seen him in the Dew Drop Inn and at Mme. Dunbar's sipping absinthe frappes. We saw him drunk once in front of the Blue Cheer Lounge. We are glad to have such a distinguished writer take up residence here.

The Editors

City Moon,
Increasing fascination with horrific techniques of comb killings brings us to this report from Jimson Cola, the sweet-drink distributor of Green Soda in Pisstown and Bunkerville:
"The comb, preferably a large, long, sturdy one, enters the cranium between the ear bones, cuts down the auditory trench quiet as a hot kitchen knife in a melon. When the first, thick, perpendicular tooth of the comb is flush against the exterior of the cranial wall, the point of the comb handle has penetrated the ear drum and semicircular trench, the Eustachian tube is pierced and the neutrodyne dies without a twitch."

Who are these neutrodynes anyway, and where did they come from?
A Frustrated Reader
Name Withheld

Name Withheld: No one knows with any certainty what they are or why they're suddenly here among us. We continue to search for answers. When we find them, there will be banner 72pt headlines on our front page. That is a guarantee to all readers.

DRUGGED LION BECOMES KITTEN

The roaring lion of the mechanical age has been transformed by modern pharmaceuticals into a timid kitten. Crime will soon be just another word in the criminology textbooks, and, in this city, police cars will dry rot in municipal garages. Precinct houses will change almost miraculously into greenhouses where new age vegetables are grown for the health and well-being of the neighborhood. The rich will leave their greenback-jammed suitcases at neighborhood houses. Poverty will be worked out—all people will finally have an equal footing at birth. Pollution will come to a halt as Fire Scouts burn garbage in the streets, in city yards. In short, ANXIETY will soon be a whimpering, fast-receding feline, driven from life's yard with an angry stick.

People everywhere speak of Meditation X, a new form of yoga in which deep bellows-like breathing is used to cure anxiety and banish choler. A small pink tablet has helped America through its painful 200-year birth, the amazing drug, Estella-G. The once-anxious disabled are now seen on their porches reading newspapers and listening to their new high-fidelity radios, the sweet songs of eternal peace finally heard with total clarity for the first time. The wars are over. The president relaxes, easing into a necessary clarification and rethinking period. Beside him, in a tumbler, sits three inches of Tullamore Dew, alongside the Estella-G, a small service revolver and a mimeographed schedule.

SPECIAL TO THE MOON

Onēba here. In the old days, philosophers spoke of the world as born and composed of a mortal body. They dealt with it as a concourse of matter that laid the foundation of land, sea and sky, stars and sun and the globe of the moon, and of the living things that have existed on earth, and those that have never been born. They described how the human race began to employ various utterances among themselves for denoting various things, and how there crept into their minds that fear of the gods which, all the world over, sanctifies temples and lakes, groves and altars and images of the gods. After that they would explain by what forces nature would steer the courses of the sun and the journeying of the moon, so that we would not suppose that they are running on their own free will with the amiable intention of promoting the growth of crops and animals, or that they are enacting, in any way, a divine plan. Those philosophers were concerned with what was seen overhead in the borderland of ether. They saw the people saddled with cruel masters whom they believed all-powerful. They saw how a limit was fixed to the power of everything as an immovable frontier post.

But I, Onēba, am a different sort of philosopher, one with

the ultimate experience behind him—death. It's well known that I have died three times so far, spent significant time in the afterworld, and come back to offer my own take on what life and death are all about.

More revelations in later columns.

Onēba, the One

HISTORICAL NOTE

In 1765, haunted by their loss of fundamental gods to believe in, Vasco de Gamma Y Muerto, traveled with Cabeza de Vaca to America, and venturing north from Biloxi they entered what is now Joplin, Missouri, finding themselves in an apprentice shoemaker's scruffy dwelling slugging pure codeine from an ox horn. On this exciting new experience of total zugunruhe (migratory restlessness, especially in birds) the two explorers went south again and sailed east to New Orleans, where codeine was commonly processed from the alkaloid root of the pawpaw tree. It was then manufactured in great quantities by native slave workers and distributed widely over the North American continent.

Many people drank it and slept away its soporific doldrums in contentment. Others died, including Vasco de Gamma.

Poor Cabeza! Now alone, he sat in his living room in the steamy French Quarter drinking delicate glassfuls of codeine and turpentine and sweating yellow beads of codeine body moisture, watching hair balls blow hither and thither in his drugged consciousness. He pulled himself out of the chair with the assistance of a young colored boy and a rope fixed to a ceiling beam. He then tossed off his hemorrhoid cushion and walked to the window and looked upon the narrow streets. He saw black voodoo queens and delicately featured brown quadroons, thick, lovely and sensual in the southern sun. Some of them wore red bandanas and carried hampers on their shoulders and called, "Blackberry, ten cent a bag."

Many years Cabeza spent this way, getting up from the chair only occasionally to look out, and otherwise benumbed and in a sorry state of mental transfiguration. The mad frames of old horse time broke loose and he had a vision of the present (remarkably accurate): of Noxin leaving the White House, on his way to obscurity, passing his successor.

And then, in Cabeza's vision, Noxin found his peace. Tortured by dreams that kept him spinning, off balance, in public and private life, he was driven finally to the counsel of Onēba. Through grueling interrogation, Noxin was brought to his senses. Onēba's unusual therapy: First, Noxin had to read all of the work of John Stuart Mill, estimated to have the highest I.Q. of anyone who ever lived. Mill says America possesses a natural finitude for governments of the religious and oligarchic type, derived from its intense Calvinistic commitment.

Onēba asked, "Do you agree?

Noxin said, "I do."

Onēba pointed to a plot on the ground and said, "A little earth will grow a very large vine with succulent tomatoes. You and Pat should eat them every day with a spritz of Japanese plum vinegar and plenty of sea salt."

Raymond Gunn
Professor of Fantasy and Sci-Fi
Bunkerville Prep

AN INCIDENT ON A BUS

Transportation security officers traveled on a crowded bus with other men, sweeping through the streets and dozing through the hills during endless hours of grinding, shifting, halting and beginning again.

The "other men" were hungry, scared and looking for jobs, wherever they might be. A dark stranger boarded the bus and went to the middle, sitting next to a woman so old much of her skin had worn white even though she originally had an olive complexion. He carried a white carton with him. He told the woman that he had beautiful goldfish in his carton, and invited her to look for herself. When the woman looked down, the stranger slapped her hard in the face just as the bus stopped, and ran off the bus. The woman said the carton had been closed, and she could neither verify nor deny the man's claim.

ARMSTRONG STEPS ON THE MOON

Neil Armstrong, first human on the Moon, ceremoniously inked his old boots for the television cameras in San Francisco today and then trod roughly on the front page of the hated *City Moon*, a news organ thought repellant by many in the Bay Area.

The good Governor Wunty was there, sullen and wet-eyed, sitting in his rotary chair. He wheeled forward to the inner edge of the circle of greats and not so greats. His lips emerged from the wide cheeks and spittle fluttered out like tiny cotton puffs.

Pharmagucci was on hand, too. He'd made a hat out of *City Moon*s and wore it defiantly.

It would take a great deal more than a strong-armed *Moon* walker to put us out of business. We're taking root and we're standing strong, burrowing deep into Mother Earth. We hope to have her belly rising with stands of tall pine to make newsprint.

We'd like to take Armstrong and anyone else silly enough to besmudge our paper and run them through the presses and throw them in bundles onto the rainy streets of the City.

The Editors

SLAIN CHILD RITUAL MURDER VICTIM

A nine-year-old Pisstown boy was killed in a ritualistic way then offered as a sacrifice.

"Like sacrificing a lamb," said Sheriff Prop.

Arnold Frank Zeleznik, of Pisstown, also was found dead Friday, his throat slashed in a motel room a few doors down from where his family had just checked in on vacation, Prop said.

A man identified as Vernal Walford, 31, of Hartford, Connecticut, was arrested at Pisstown's downtown airport within 20 minutes of the Zeleznik slaying and charged with the two killings.

A Bible was found near the Zeleznik body.

Prop said, "It looked like Walford held the child so the throat would be over the toilet to bleed," in describing what he called a sacrificial slaying.

Police said they found a message with many misspelled words in Walford's pocket that read, in part: "Dog of Israel, say no. The Dog say the temple mus not be use for any vilence except child sakrefice."

Prop said, "He told us he was just released from a Connecticut mental hospital. They should have kept him there."

Walford also used the handle Angel Ozalo and had credentials in that name.

Dear *City Moon*,

It all started when a suburban housewife noticed that her leftover skrada-kaka couldn't be put into the disposal. It clung tenaciously to the mouth of the drain. Gagging in disgust, she dragged her husband into the kitchen where they were transfixed by panic as the mass spread out of the sink to cover the counter surface and down the side.

In the days that followed, similar events were reported from all over the City. Television, radio and newspapers were swamped by horror narratives from hysterics.

The terror expanded rapidly. Exhaust gases choked engines into inoperation. Smoke accumulated in chimneys until it became as solid as rock. Sewers backed up into tidy bathrooms, flooding them with a brew of 10,000 flushes of whatever can be flushed at any given time.

Here's my prediction of where all this is going. Because of the new restrictions on Trench dumping, waste must now be held in stinking piles inside industrial plants. Eventually this could engulf the machinery of production and crash the stock market. In winter, smog will suddenly settle in high drifts of gray-yellow snow across all the busy cities.

Times are bad.

E. Mozarti

IMMIGRANT CROSSES WRONG BORDER

A 29-year-old German man, Udo Breger, from Dusseldorf, was

picked up sopping wet on Lake Street about 4 a.m. by police. He told them that at 8:30 p.m. he had jumped from a freight train leaving Rochester *en route* to Buffalo. He told them that he had become "mentally confused" and "feared for his life." He said he walked from the railroad station to the Imperial Court Apartments on St. Paul Street, through the City Zoo and then to the Genesee River. He said he climbed down the bank and, believing the river was the border of the United States and Canada, removed his clothes and swam across the river. Police took him to General Hospital for treatment and he was placed naked in a holding cell, to be attended to later.

He told our reporter: "Well, they transplanted everything else, so why not the Niagara River?"

Only minutes after the German was placed in the cell, a buff, black inmate passing by, said to him, "Baby, you look good to me. I could devour you for my dinner and come back and get the rest of you tomorrow morning for my breakfast."

The German said, "Please don't use me as if I were a woman."

The inmate responded that Aryan meat was good to eat and that he liked it better than dope.

Eleven white prisoners slashed their wrists to get the attention of the guards, who they called "bums."

They pleaded for help. "You have to stop the blacks from raping us all the time. This is turning into a house of prostitution. It's a fact—more men are raped in the U.S. than women if you count the millions of prisoners."

Breger eventually was released with a prolapsed rectum to worry about and made his way back to Dusseldorf, where his family welcomed him warmly.

DOG KILLED WITH ARROW

A 31-year-old white woman from Second Avenue reported to police at 9:30 a.m. that she had seen a neutrodyne shoot a fat spaniel in the head with a bow and arrow in front of the Squat 'n' Gobble cafe. After the dog had stopped moving and breathed its last, the neut began to skin and dress it with surgical precision, cubing and salting the meat, then putting it into burlap pouches and carrying it in a back pack, leaving a mound of bone and still-squirming entrails on the sidewalk.

EDITORIAL

The Fire Scout motto "to be square" is now "to help other people," akin to Nichiren Buddhism's practice of "being nice to others for world peace." The pejorative connotations of the word "square" initiated the change.

The new Fire Scout Handbook also describes the effects of Pharmagucci's Kaliman crystal on young white boys. Some of them feel like they know more than they do while they suffer from its effects but it's only a part of the illusion that eventually leads to addiction and death.

It's a terrible shame that Pharmagucci has continued to be allowed to practice. While some of his medications are beneficial, others are not. Take Estella-G, for example, in suppository form, which he recommends for his "overly annoyed and anally inclined" patients at every opportunity. Yes, it works. The bowel is cleansed, but the patients are somnolent for 48 hours, during which time, pointlessly and stuporously angry, they wander the City looking for neutrodynes. It's a harmless game. Pharmagucci issues maps of neutrodyne neighborhoods. His patients chase down the neuts and tag them on their bare, sweaty backs with a Pharmagucci-issued stamp that says, I KNOW WHAT I AM.

Most of the time the neuts run for dear life, but occasionally one of them stops, turns about and fractures a patient's face with a bony-fisted left jab.

More and more, we must begin to take the neuts seriously.

WANTED Muscular Ph.D. in one of the animal sciences to work in my hog yard collecting boar semen. One dollar an hour at first and a small pork-product lunch. Advancement possible with additional studies. I also need someone to provide security at my big warehouse out on one of the barrier islands off Texoma Beach. There's a million fruit bats stacked up there to dry. Blood has been drained from them for medical use and the eyes removed for art bracelet production. We've had five break-ins and have lost hundreds of processed bats.

Wunty
Lower Farm

A NEW BIRD SPECIES

The Maggot Hawk, known as *el pequeno matador* in Baja, California, has come to be entered into the logbook of ornithology. The bird was discovered incidental to research done in that area to preserve the endangered California Condor by D. Hannity, Ph.D., professor of biology at UC Berkeley.

It was then that ornithologists became aware of the little predator (*Buteo Malus*, smallest of the genus *Buteo*) and the unique symbiotic relationship between the hawk and the condor. For years ornithologists have been puzzled by the question, how do weak-eyed condors detect the presence of carrion?

It was only with the advent of the telephoto lens and cameras suitable for the harsh desert climate of the Baja that the mystery was solved. Observers noted that condors circled aimlessly over the desert floor before descending to feast on the carrion. Ornithologists thought at first the small object that had dropped from the condor's breast was a clump of feathers.

The team of scientists was amazed to discover that the telephoto lens and high-speed film revealed the blur of feathers to be a very small bird of prey. Further study has found that the keen-eyed hawk attaches itself to the breast of the condor by means of a suction cup situated on the back of the head, much like the structures that remora and pilot fish use to attach themselves to sharks and other fish. Unlike remora, whose suction discs consist of lamellae (gill-like openings), the suction cup of the hawk is rubber-like in texture and appearance. The suction cup enables the hawk to cover the same wide range as the condor, overcoming the handicap of its short, stubby wings. Even more amazing, the hawk guides the condor by tapping the breast with its wingtips. In true symbiotic fashion, when carrion is located, the condor feasts on putrefying meat, while the little Maggot Hawk fills its craw with maggots.

FROM THE ARCHIVES

President Beats Immigrant
The White House is in a state of horror today. Wanda Botel, a recent immigrant to the D.C. area, invited to a White House

homecoming for President Onēba by forces anxious to make her ambassadorial visit here smooth, was found battered and naked on the floor of the Oval Office.

Ms. Botel, elite, suave, a comely member of the Southern 4000, was beaten so badly in the eye and mouth area that the coroner fears total restoration of the disfigured visage may be impossible.

Onēba has admitted to inflicting the beating on Ms. Botel, but says it was because of his extensive training in the *yakuza* method that he inflicted these injuries following an undeniable impulse to protect his presidency.

In addition, he claimed, it was on account of his perverse nature that he asked her to disrobe before attacking her.

"I didn't want to get her tunic bloody," the president said, "even though she was blackmailing this country. Then my *yakuza* training kicked in—my muscle memory—and that was that. She was taught a lesson."

P. NEWMAN, PISSTOWN MAYOR, KILLS SELF

Just last week he was half-normal, but this week he's as dead as a black widow's boyfriend. Those bullets did such a hideous job on his head that it wasn't clear at first it was the mayor.

Toward the end, he drank enough Pluto Water and sloe gin to launch a bottle rocket. Why do they go suddenly mad like this, descending into homosexuality's velvety Lou Reed oriented gilded palace, then shooting themselves?

Newman once stared out through suburban shutters until a delicate blonde boy, with thin northern Germanic lips, rode by on his ten-speed and caught his eye. The legs were nearly hairless, but with a light-brown fuzz.

We know now from the mayor's writings that he felt profoundly ashamed of this sudden attraction to a teen passing on a bicycle. Part of Newman's shame was understood by analysts to be rooted in a profound hatred he had developed for his coarse black beard and hair. He also hated his glasses frames for being the same color and the shape of his turds in the toilet. Then came the sloe gin habit, which lasted months, then the Estella-G, then the .38 came out of his hollowed copy of *Moby Dick* and Newman shot himself, first in the chest, then in the head.

Service will be at 3 p.m. Saturday, June 16, at Lamanno Panno Fallo's Pisstown Parlor, 3300 Maine.

Dear *City Moon*,
Masses of a sticky, threadlike material floated across Pisstown skies the afternoon of March 16, causing general consternation among those out and about. The material ranged from the size of a match head to 10-foot globules drifting into the heart of the City, clinging to grass, metal and cement. At first, we thought it was a synthetic precipitate of the air itself, given Pisstown's frequent chemical fogs. Later it seemed to be nothing more than spider webbing. At the height of the invasion, the air over the City was filled with webs. Those of us wearing head gear found the baffles in our tubing fouled with the stuff. It was cloyingly sweet to sniff but tasty and edible. Please ask Scientist Zanzetti to explain the phenomenon.
Mother K.
Seeress
Pisstown Box 0101

Dear Mother K, you are not the first to ask about this, so I will provide an answer here for everyone to see. The material you encountered on that day was neutrodyne semen. You see, neuts only reproduce when their numbers are low, primarily from their habit of sacrificing so many infants. I've been told that hundreds of neuts, male and female, are gathered at Pisstown's outskirts to mate. During the process, females lie on the ground, legs spread wide, the cloacal opening exposed. The males stand over them, stimulating one another with both hands until they begin to spew the reproductive material, much of which makes its way to the females' cloacas. What escapes floats away on the breeze. That's what you Pisstowners were seeing that day. Next time they decide to mate, it could be near Bunkerville, or Peabody Junction, or anywhere else. Don't fret, though. The spew is not only harmless to eat, but more nutritional than wheat germ.

FLATBALL HISTORY IN A NUTSHELL

Many players were killed on the field in the game's 100-year history. They are:

The FOOD players: Peanuts Lowrey, Taffy Wright, Pie Traynor, Cookie Lavagetto, Peach Pie O'connor, Prunes Mulic, Luke Appling, Julie Fryer, Bobby Wine, Grapefruit Yeargin.

The GOOD players: Wally Moses, Charlie Nice, Deacon White, Fred Valentine, Honest Eddie Murphy, Jacob Virtue, Sharon Goode, Babe Young, Pius Schwert, Preacher Roe.

The FEATHERED players: Alan Storke, Goose Goslin, Ducky Medwick, Chick Gandil, Birdie Tebbets, Jackie Robinson.

The BAD players: Billy Lush, Braggo Roth, Andy High, Fatty Fothergill, Harry Chiti, Scarlet Heart, Hosea Siner, Peeka-Boo Veach, Jersey Joe Stripp, Charley Faust.

The NATURE players: Ty LaForest, Bob Seeds, Woody English, Jim Greengrass, Oak Taylor, Fred Stem, Jake Flowers, Branch Rickey, Holly Kirshenbaum, Charlie Root.

The Z-TEAM: Frank Zak, Rollie Zeider, Al Zarilla, Gus Zernial, Heinie Zimmerman, Norm Zauchin, Billy Zitsman, Dave Zearfoss, Ed Zmich.

Woody Chuckling

City Moon Sports. Ed.

LEISURE NEWS

People do just about anything you can think of. Take Peter Waybalo, for example. Pete is a retired man, his career in suitcase manufacturing having ended suddenly with an abscess of the heart muscle. His Doc said, "Go south, Pete, take it easy."

And that's exactly what Waybalo did. Now he floats in the waters off Texoma Beach.

His wife, Morti, says, "He floats out and in with the tide. Sometimes I'll open the drapes and see him there on the sand and I'll think it's a log, but usually it turns out to be Pete rolling in with the morning tide."

It seems that Pete has rigged himself a tether line more than 15 miles long, which allows him to float out considerable distances and explore the luminous fauna of the lake. If he wants to come in quickly he need only push a button on his flotation gear and he is reeled in automatically by his wife.

THE HUNDLEY WARP GUN CLUB We are as black as seals of the Pacific, as the hard-baked black enamel of a Detroit automobile, as the soot at the bottom of a pipe. The Hundleys are as black as they come. Our King's name is Lionel, a rude black man as proud as a bull elephant. Why do we do what we do? Lionel tells us what to do, like launching darts at the feet of delinquent children and nailing the hammy fists of wayward women to garage doors. An acid bath is suddenly conjured and fitted into a carwash, acids then soaking the cars of the bad. Who let us loose? Where is God? To the Hundleys, a beer bottle is a mouth-cork, a razor blade a mouthwash. You need protection? Drop by and we'll talk. We're active in social causes. The Hundley Warp Gun Club. 4949 Arden Blvd. catty-corner from the *Moon* office.

ONĒBA SPOTTED SPOTTED

One summer night about two years ago a woman who lived in Long Beach at the time was returning home from Queens and driving across the Atlantic Bridge when she saw Onēba in the water.

She recalled later that he wasn't a man of distinct age but perhaps close to sixty. He had long, unkempt hair and looked, she said, "like a fisherman, and there were cherry colored spots all over his face. He looked diseased."

The woman said that Onēba said nothing, though he looked at her but made no gestures. It was late twilight and the water, the sky, the world itself seemed beige, and that is her impression of Onēba, a brown death presence, staring out of the water, motionless.

"I saw him and knew him instantly," she recounted. "I don't know where he came from. First, I didn't see anyone in the water and then suddenly he was there, and when I saw him I said to myself, and I remember saying it so clearly, I said to myself, 'That man in the water is Onēba. I am looking at the One.'"

A feeling of profound dread seized the woman. Her three children and their spaniel were alone.

THE NATIONAL FIRE BURNS ON

Choking sulfur clouds are over Dallas now, the hungry flames having licked Fort Worth clean. The mysterious crackling prairie blaze is non-extinguishable by ordinary means, though the fire was started by an ordinary man, Carman Munty, acting alone. The tape recorders of the *Moon* on the scene, the special ones with chrome microphones were melted immediately. The telephones dripped away like wax. As a result, we have no fresh news from Dallas. Look for further reports once communication is restored. We're sorry for the inconvenience.

The Editors

TARLANDS RECLAIMED

Rural areas have given way to the regular alteration of oil-salt pits and soy fields, and our youth have the complexions of cabbage leaves. But Bohannon McCarber, who owns tarlands across the state, now promises relief with a tractor-like machine he calls the Green Era, which he constructed from derelict, rusting vehicles found everywhere across the salt plain of the southwest, or wherever the green fields used to grow.

McCarber has reclaimed 42,000 acres of oil swamp west of Bartlesville in the Texoma Basin. There, refuse of any sort, from sofas to cars, garbage, pianos to juice harps, can be fed into a chain-link belt and pulley system, leading to the great maw of the Green Era machine. With a bit of churning, heating and chemo-mixing, the Green Era squirts, in a jerky spiral, an ever widening, even layer of the reclaimed junk in a rejuvenating paste form that resembles baby food.

Dear *City Moon*,

They say that the self-confessed heterosexual, Roy Bimini, toys with the rich Eastern Seaboard chewing gum girls by sticking them in the buttock with broken and jagged paralysis ampoules as he skates past them at the Ice Palace.

Seventeen of them are hospitalized with nodal paralysis. They call Bimini Dr. Death. We have to stop him. Judges put him behind bars and he's out in a few weeks, hot to kill again at the Ice Palace rink.

I say haul his ass down to the jail basement and blow air on his naked stomach until he goes mad. Let the TV cameras enter the room and show him sweating, crying, bleeding from the lips.

The president said at the height of Bimini's career, "This is the son-in-law I wanted but never got. This is a man."

Whether it's a small dispute or a matter of life and death, we'll stop in your neighborhood. All judgments are final and enforceable. Low rates, too.

Just wave or honk and we'll slam on the brakes.

Felix Grendon, Judge

The Justice Mobile

Dear *City Moon*,

On Sunday night at Wuntex Park lagoon, a friend and I watched Onēba hit a new low in certain revelations he tried to deliver there, sitting in a skiff using a loudspeaker. Someone in the crowd rose to his weary feet and asked the so-called "One" to explain the myth of sexual purity among male athletes. Onēba then told, in a harsh, amplified whisper, his dream of himself in the wooden dormitory of his youth once again, cold, shriveled, lying in his bed smelling hotcakes from the kitchen when he was corn-holed by a bunk mate. I already was laughing and so was my friend. We thought he stank. He smelled like a dead rat in a hot crowd so you really couldn't laugh. Someone yelled that the police were rounding the bend of the lagoon in a reddish, whitish and bluish power boat, its chrome details flashing beams of light through the willows. We have been there, seen the face of the One, the wide jaw, the balloon-like cheeks. He made my friend Janie go off and pee in a patch of stinging nettles. Her rear end was blistered for a week. He's disgusting. Is it wrong to say that? Print this if you can figure a way to phrase it so that it will not offend. We're not so stupid out here.

Chedda Charlie
Cheesy Investments
Box 4 Downtown Pickup

Yes, it's wrong to say that as well as to refer to cornholing in such a breezy manner.
The Editors

FOOD

On Friday nights I hop down to the Dixie Peanut and crank up the jukebox. Then I do the Hip Hug and the High Thigh with anyone willing until I'm squeezing sweat from my hairdo, the result of drinking hot beer and codeine coffee. Now I need a cool place to be, so I go to Mme. Dunbar's and relax with a sazerac cocktail and an appetizer of Oysters Bienville before dinner. Tonight's entrée is fried flying fish wings in *sauce perigueux*. Mmmmm.

Lordi Lordiss
Food Editor

FROM THE ARCHIVES

Onēba appeared in St. Petersburg in 1903. In his speech he uttered words and phrases in some 50 odd tongues, ranging from the Buryat dialect of the Mongolian tongue to the language of the Chinese bureaucrat. The English made discrete inquiries in Chitral, Kashgar, Simla, Kunming and Ulan Bator concerning Onēba, and no one knew him.

He had disappeared from St. Petersburg as innocuously as he had appeared. And then it happened again. The English found out that this man had traveled across their own land, India, by magic carpet and by taxi-cab, describing a great square in the process, which is the ancient cabbalistic figure of the Devil. Yet no one noted his passing. This was reported to Shimla via Peking, from the innards of Tibet, uncovered by Nan Yang, the Chinese counterpart to the British pundit.

The English heard he was in Lhasa, but when they asked

the Dalai Lama where Onēba was lodged, the Lama was mute. He was butchered on the spot for that lapse in memory, his eyes rammed with needles until a vile jelly ran down his cheeks.

The broken trail led to America, to Palmer, Utah, to a Continental bus stop there. Yes, Onēba stepped down out of the twilight zone of smoky bus exhaust and onto the clean asphalt of a rear parking lot. The rest of the passengers puddled past him as he yawned, stretched and scraped his face with a sweaty hand. Onēba did not notice until it was too late that all his bus companions had left the station. He was thrown on the mercies of strangers, ones who coughed and smoked away the empty hours of generalized hate. A girl with a desperate laugh asked him if he was a Zen Buddhist, and if he would say something in the Buddhist language.

"I am no more a Buddhist than a cockroach is an altar boy," he said, slapping the girl and shouting "katsu!"

The strangers were soon frightened by Onēba's actions, his greasy hair, his sudden, odd tics and mannerisms, the thin, drooping wrists of his silken shirt bagging and puffing out from his coat sleeves.

His lecture at Palmer Jr. College, scheduled for tomorrow, has been canceled for lack of interest. The subject was to be "Eventually, Why Not Now?"

Dear *City Moon*,
A people that grows accustomed to sloppy writing, as we too-often find in the *Moon*, is a people in the process of losing its grip on the empire and itself. And this looseness and blowsiness is not anything as simple and as scandalous as abrupt and disordered syntax. It concerns the relation of

expression to meaning. **Abrupt and disordered syntax can be at times very honest, and an elaborately constructed sentence can be at times merely an elaborate camouflage.**

W. Pounds
Narita Shinbun

STRAY NEUTS TO BE SHOT ON SIGHT

According to Sheriff Prop, stray neuts in the City will be shot on sight with tranquilizer guns. "The darts from the guns usually break ankles, knees, legs and ribs," Prop said. "We have been getting numerous complaints of stray neuts chasing kids and tipping over trash cans. We can't catch them. They're too wild and quick, so we plan to shoot them with tranquilizer as soon as we see them."

This practice has been called short sighted by some officials in law enforcement. A spokesperson said, "After a while, the neuts become addicted to the tranquilizer and must have more, so they stage little *dramattes* of illegality in the street, hoping to be shot with a strong sedative."

Nevertheless, Prop vows, "We'll knock them silly with the 'trank' and if they get addicted, we'll shoot them with the real thing. Don't that make the most sense?"

EDITORIAL

Let us address the American syndrome of image stripping and image consumption. Every day and night in the newspapers and magazines, on the TV channels and a dozen radio bands, a stupefying quantity of refined image is unloaded. This image has been mined from literally all quarters of the world and refined by a grossly inflated social class of media workers.

The *Moon* computer has recently furnished us with complete statistics showing that the consumption of raw image today is triple that of a thousand years ago, while the consumption of refined image is ten times that figure, reflecting the media's sophistication in image refinement.

Image is now processed through giant cracking towers, and the result is the proliferation of image at a rate never before thought possible. Yet, despite the expertise of the media in utilizing all available raw image to the fullest, there has begun to develop a raw image shortage of crisis proportions.

This is as much a product of an artificially-inflated consumer demand as it is of the natural limitations of image reserves in nature and the rate of image replenishment, which is much slower than is usually thought. If all the human beings now living were to consume raw image at the American rate, the world supply would be COMPLETELY EXHAUSTED by 1976.

If the image resources of the world were to be mined at the rate at which they could replenish themselves naturally (a "climax image mine"), and if the raw image were to be processed, refined and enriched by the most sophisticated techniques available today, the image that could be provided to each human being would correspond roughly to the image consumption rate of an aboriginal Tasaday Indian. Obviously, this would represent an extreme inconvenience to Americans, accustomed as they are to consuming *one-third* of the world's raw image. This abundance, and the development of advanced refinement techniques, have reached their present proportions in a geometrically widening spiral hand-in-hand with the use of powerful behavior modification techniques to induce new and unwanted desires for image in the American consumer. Together these have escalated each other to the present rate, which threatens to leave those in charge of supplying image to the nation with a choice between writhing in a national withdrawal syndrome or deciding to use the most terrible option and, at a stroke, create enough new raw image to supply them for eons.

Every dharmic intersection releases a small quantity of image, which is homeostatically regulated on the ecological level. Each living thing adds more or less the right amount of image to its environment, and in return is provided with enough image to meet its needs. But this homeostatic regulation is occasionally interrupted by the appearance of forces larger than the system itself. Parts of it scatter and mutate into new systems. Human violence is one such force.

Violence of course is the order of nature. In a sense, even the absorption of an ameba by a paramecium is a brutal and terrible act. But then violence is a word, and all words are human words. Rousseau's romantic notion of the Noble Savage was discarded quickly when the behavior of primitive societies began to be mined for image and brought first to the reading, then to the viewing, public. But Rousseau had not gone far enough. The "nostalgia for the mud" must be entirely literal if it is to be uncompromised.

Image is the crystallization of will, yet it seems this planet's will is death by one means or another. All image is death image. Sex image is death image. This is not pessimistic—it is merely unclouded.

Here in the offices of the *City Moon* we attempt to recycle discarded image and whenever possible, enrich it. Image enrichment is good for you. There is no dark side of the *Moon*. We are a reflective satellite, and shine only with the face you see. Eventually, why not now?

Editor James G.

Bunkerville

PREXY SIGNS KILL ORDERS

A black baby grand sighed sweet chords of Beethoven in the Rose Garden of the White House. The prexy was bathed in an amber sunlight as he sat at a cedar table, shoulders draped with a madras towel, signing the first United States kill orders. Citizens may now kill neutrodynes legally, if properly licensed, until January 1, 1976. What has brought this regrettable state of affairs about are the hideous blood lettings of recent months, the comb killings, the poisoned liver terror, all that and more.

Registered voters, exemplary citizens, all persons without criminal records may apply for kill permits at local post offices. "Let's put a stop to this encroachment," says Sheriff Prop, "and kill us some neuts. Arm yourselves with a license and a gun, and use real slugs... You know what they say: *When the neuts come to town, necronauts won't be far behind.*"

EDITORIAL

By June 31, 1976, all housing in the 51 U.S. states will be rent free and open to anyone. President Noxin signs eminent domain action in the Rose Garden tomorrow morning. He is doing this, he says, to stem the swollen tide of war, murder, and mayhem. When everything is free, Noxin says, including Noxage and Estella-G, Pluto Water, D-meat, artificial greens, starch bars, blood pudding and defensive weapons, then and only then, he emphasized, will criminality be without motive, because no one would stand to gain, and all things would be One, in perfect harmony. A purple haze of the New Freedom will fog the mountains of America and spread in thin sceptic sheets over the floor of the plains.

Now, owing to the disclosure of a threat on his life, the president sits poised in his armchair encased in fully bullet-resistant shielding. He is as alive as you and me, but pale, a shy grin lying over his face. He seems the victim of poor cosmetology. One of the eyebrows hangs pitiably over the spectacles. At one moment he sits there, at another he wanders toward those who stand in circles around the encasement, his hand extended for the familiar shake. It saddens us when his fingers crack against the Plexiglas and he stumbles clumsily to the floor.

Television cameras (trained on him 24 hours a day so that the Nation may watch his daily activities, the meetings with foreign emissaries, Cuban nationals, hungry farmers, etc.) broadcast his fall to the world.

In his address today, Noxin said, "I am your president now. I prayed in the National Chapel at dawn, advocating the intercession of the mercies on behalf of the last president who now lies sorrowfully pumped of sense and feeling. He injected something vital into the bloodstream of America's bleeding hearts: a thought, namely, that the embolus of America's veins is its ghettoes and other high crime areas, its trailer homes, its rust crusted heaps of Olds-made cars, the strife over books in the schools, sanitation experts, regulation of monopoly systems in water waste and sewage treatment. We were about ready to advocate anarchy in these columns. Friends of the *Moon*, stay tuned. It could happen.

The Editors

HISTORICAL ODDITIES

At that time of trouble in East Asia, the second most important man on the scene was Onēba, representing the U.S. He had a new suit surreptitiously tailored for him when he came to Chungking to see whether China could be unified without civil war.

The Chungking office of the Chinese Communist party thought the dull, ill-fitting, coarse gray suits which Onēba was wearing, hardly became a man of his prestige.

So, unbeknownst to him, with his measurements stuck into a salesman's pocket, dashed on a wad of crude butcher's paper, a suit of the finest spun silk in Chungking was ordered for him.

It was the best one he ever had, but he didn't like it, and wore it only because of the entreaties of his subordinates. His indifference to what he wears is as natural to Onēba as his acceptance of life in a cave home in Yanan, Shensi province, where he lives without luxury, pretense or modern plumbing. He is slightly deaf, a defect he tries to hide

He possesses a hearty appetite and is fond of hot food peculiar to the province of Hunan. He likes foreign style food and, though he never drinks to excess, he can take Kaoliang wine—a strong white distillation made from sorghum. He also says he drank Pluto Water and dropped Estella-G with the best of them during the American 60s.

Onēba likes Chinese novels, yogurt, relishes and, surprisingly, the want ads and especially the jobs in marketing research. He laughs over his well-known public disdain for work. He likes to work at night and seldom goes to bed before 2 or 3 in the morning. He sleeps 5 hours each night. He is a poor listener, unfortunately. His subordinates describe him as mild, good-natured, tolerant, but a bit addled in the wandering bent, and so, incapable of doing much harm. He is not accessible to everyone, but he gives a guest his fullest attention.

A *City Moon* correspondent once interviewed him for 13 hours on end, but Onēba gave no hint of annoyance.

Onēba speaks all major languages fluently. Interpreters tell us this: He has never been abroad, though he spins yarns about his travels around the world. His explanation? It wasn't his real body that went around; it was his spirit body.

He took his first airplane ride when he came to Chungking in September. People who saw him at the Yanan airport before the plane took off said he was pale with fright.

His keenness for dance surpasses his expertise, yet young women comrades beg him to dance. He obliges in every case.

Onēba never rides in a limousine and he is an accomplished orator. He prepares his long speeches very carefully. Still, he repeats himself unconsciously, his diction obscures itself. Words and sentences seem to eat each other up in the course of his lengthy diatribes. He is difficult to understand in any of the languages he speaks fluently, especially English.

don't forget the canned possum with sweet potatoes, a steal this week at 69 cents a can. Can openers $6.

NATIONAL FIRE RAGES ON

The great fire has now engulfed Wichita and Muncie on the same day. It won't be long before fireballs will roll like tumbleweed down the glowing streets of Manhattan, down 5th Avenue, across to the Bowery, through the doors of CBGBs.

Millions of survivors wander the dirt roads of the countryside and the empty streets of the cities. Others have secured themselves in fortress-like suburban homes, boarded up against attacks by feral pets. Where have all the neighbors gone? they wonder. Every breed of dog and cat is represented in the nightly attacks. The neighborhood is empty.

Some have brought out rusted arms—shotguns, pistols, bullets—to protect their meager stores of soy biscuits and government water.

The great city of Washington will lie in ruins one day, its "leaders" crouched in underground, bunker-like capsules, frozen cryogenically, set to emerge like moths and resume leadership when the "troubles" are over.

Dear *City Moon*,
When I recommend your paper to a friend, it's all the same: "Are you sure all that stuff is true?" Do they ask this question when they look at the *New York Times*? No, of course not. And that's what I mean. Why would you settle for one when you can have the other? Sovietskia Moldavia
Lower Farm G-unit
A Fan for Eternity

Dear Sovietskia: Tell them the City Moon *is published each lunar month at a secret location near the geographical center of the United States and contains a hefty cross-sampling of news and views from around the globe. The* Moon *offers you all the things these other papers do, except the lies. Eight issues only $5.*

GODGIRL TOTAL NOW FOUR

The first Godgirl, Daisy Doolittle, was born in Miami in 1951. In subsequent years the number of Godgirls has risen to 4, perhaps more. Sometimes parents are afraid to go public with news of a Godgirl in the family. The girls are generally born in the 7th or 8th month of normal fetal growth and develop atypically from there on. By the 3rd year the bones of the forehead and jaw enlarge grotesquely, and a fuzz of fine, soft, reddish hair appears on the throats and cheeks of these exciting new girls.

On the advice of her physicians, Daisy was kept in a special basement room rigged with air conditioning and dehumidifying units so that the outer epidermal layers of her sensitive skin remained free of fungal ravages, to which she seemed so prone.

A recently discovered Godgirl, Sharon Y. Valdez, says, "My family garage is filled with parcels. My father is afraid to open them. He is afraid of possible explosions or other devices from fanatics. I get these parcels especially at Xmastide. They ask for things. For example, 'Please return Katy, our little dead poodle. We are so sad when we look out and see her food bowl fill with snow.'"

Godgirl Mona Munty, 2nd oldest of the dozen, from Bunkerville, has written, and we quote, "The Munty family was so good to me for so long that I am ashamed of their cramped living quarters at the vagrants' camp on Old Reactor Road while I am in the spotlight all the time. Please start a campaign to alleviate one small clot of human suffering by raising money to give her shelter so she can get what she needs."

Another Godgirl has drowned in the Wuntex Creek Impoundment at the Lower Farm. She had seemingly crossed three high barbed wire fences and a 500-foot stretch of scrub land seeded with Bouncing Betty mines to get to the Impoundment without injury, when she leaped into the roiling, alkaline water and quickly drowned.

ONĒBA TO MARKET LIFE MATERIAL

In a news release today, Onēba-Zanzetti Ventures LLC revealed details of its new, amazing miracle life-matter, now available at 10 cents a pound. A compacted bale sells for $300. You can make hamburgers out of it, feed it to your pets, and it will assume any shape your hands can mold. An overnight charge of simple house current will give your creation six to 10 hours of life (power cord needed for this feature—$90.99). You can milk the matter, make butter, hard-crust bread, put some in your frog pond, some in your swimming pool, and they'll both smell like jasmine for the summer months. Watch it, though. If you leave it in a damp place overnight and the temperature goes up, flying roaches, lice and sometimes spiders could be generated from the steam-heated matter. It should be kept well away from children and never eaten undercooked, which could poison a child, sicken an adult or kill the aged.

You can roll it into non-cancerous cigarettes. It can entertain a shut-in. Make shoes out of it. On a lonely evening try throwing a handful of it against your wall and watch it splinter into a thousand tinkling, dancing, reddish points of light to charm your fancy and settle your soul.

PEACETIME BOOM AND BLOOM

Many thousands are wanted to fill peacetime jobs. The City jobs office is taking applications now. Act today! Full background checks. Morality and aptitude scores needed. These jobs pay good money and you help your fellow Americans to better themselves. These jobs will not be open six months from now. This is your only chance. Lazy lards need not apply, only energetic men and women. We intend to have your papers processed in a short time so that your stay at the waiting centers can be kept as brief and as pleasant as possible.

Can you weld?

Can you write a book?

Can you skin a snake?

Can you hoe for eight hours?

Your diet will be soy products and rice only.

You will receive daily an allotment of strong, aromatic cigarettes, chewing gum, chocolate wafers and soy nuts.

Of the many thousands of jobs we have open, one is surely made for you. If hired, plan to be away from your family for indefinite periods. They will be given an address to write to. You will not be able to communicate in any way, so be prepared for this.

Pick up applications at our offices or request them by mail.

NEW KNOWLEDGE

At last the new knowledge is upon us and we are surprised to find out things were not so complicated as we thought. Upper Farm scientist Zanzetti is experimenting with bioplasma. He takes a Petri dish of it out to the pond and sets it on the back of a sunning turtle. He then attaches thin wires from the jelly-like substrate in the dish to a simple galvanic device.

Returning to the lab, he waits, sipping lemon tea to keep the spirits up for the duration. Normally, 12 to 24 hours later the signals begin to come in. The needles jump and the green-faced scopes dance with zigzagging light.

Zanzetti leaps into action, jotting down figures, calculating, but he's the first to admit that he doesn't understand the meaning of the signals, yet he is sure they come from the "shoulder" of Orion, perhaps Betelgeuse, both in the vicinity of distant red stars. He says there is a general chatter going on between faraway animated life and animal life on Earth.

Government and C.I.A. staff have been working 'round the clock for a period of six months in an attempt to break the signal code, which would allow them to listen to the chatter with some comprehension and gain more new knowledge from it. Yes, it is surprising to find out, for example, that mice could learn to play a small fiddle, yet studies have shown they have. As a result of all this new knowledge, the vision of humankind changes. We no longer view ourselves as the paradigm of living forms, but as perhaps the lowest form of all, as suggested by the new evidence coming in through Zanzetti's bowl of jelly.

EDITORIAL

Master Ray-X came to Bunkerville on a bird's wing trailing cold, sparkling gases. His chosen ones have spoken to the *Moon* of his power-mercy doctrine and looked at our reporters hypnotically. Most of us have not been lured into the certain trap the Master sets, but some unfortunates have. We must help them. We are therefore, with this issue of the *City Moon*, establishing the X-Ray-X Fund. Please contribute, generous readers. Even though the great Master Ray-X scores many touchdowns and has stomped down many would-be quarterbacks with his beefy arm blitzes through the new modern cities of the eastern Mississippi coast, his awesome and terrible offense must be stopped!

We at the *Moon* will entertain a promise from the local Order of Eagles that the Master's soft, wormy body will be hung from the courthouse flagpole when he arrives at the gates of this fine city and when he is dead, will be deprived of his burial rites. After all, based on reports to this office, the Master is an alien being, so to speak, yet he expects to rot under American soil. We say put his remains in a tin can and throw it in a ditch.

Here's how he works his "magic." First, he calls a general meeting in Wuntex Park. His listeners, mostly the "just curious" type, sit cross-legged by a stinky, dead lagoon. It's night, so bullfrogs croak like little dinosaurs. Floating on the surface of the water are ciggy butts, dead minnows, popcorn puffs and soda straws.

Ray-X takes the rickety stage, pulling a burlap sack behind him. He opens it under a bright spotlight, dips his thin hand in and pulls out a fistful of what he calls Micromatter and says, "Look at this!" then returns the Matter to the sack and slams the sack against the stage floor. Now he opens it with dramatic flourishes of the hands to reveal dozens of D-meat and mayo sandwiches to feed the crowd, served from motorized lunch cars puttering among them, keeping them fed, and supplied with Estella-G, making them dangerously susceptible to any suggestion.

You can send dollars, only dollars, to Stop the Master, c/o the *City Moon*, Box 591, City.

ONĒBA ON TRIAL AGAIN

The One is up on his most serious charge yet: attempted murder. A popular Eastside hooker, "Duck Leg" Nellie, was found bleeding from an ice pick thrust into the side of her neck. An independent psychiatrist had an 80-minute interview with Onēba during the course of the trial and became convinced the subject was suffering from chronic paranoid schizophrenia, which had developed over a number of years. He cited Onēba's belief that his dead sister, Ophelia Balls, had returned to live in Pisstown in human form and was trying to poison him. Secondly, he quoted a terrifying statement of Onēba's: "I kill men in battle – what is wrong about it? They change themselves into women and lie down. Men become women and ask me to sleep with them. If I sleep with them, they will turn themselves into men again and kill me, so I kill them first." Invoking the insanity defense, Onēba was found not guilty.

ELIARD MOZARTI DROWNS IN BOAR SEMEN

Walter Mozarti, 51, waived a preliminary hearing Wednesday on a manslaughter charge growing out of the death of his brother, Eliard, 61, and was held under $2,500 bond for action by the grand jury.

A coroner's inquest found that Eliard was drowned Saturday night in a roadside ditch filled with cooled boar semen southeast of Gas Flats, after the air-conditioned semen-hauler truck his brother was driving overturned, bursting 25 full barrels.

The brothers had obtained the semen in open 50-gallon barrels at Smiley's Pork Sty, a hog raising operation, and were taking it to their farm to feed their neutrodynes.

Walter Mozarti said, "I'm sorry what happened to my brother. It wasn't murder. It was accident. They can't pin that on me. We got neuts to feed and they love drinking boar jit. I got in a hurry, that's all."

Sheriff Prop was on the scene. His investigation revealed that Eliard had jumped from the truck as it left the road and was pinned under its sideboards in the ditch as the cold semen cascaded over him.

Walter reports that he heard Eliard's last gurgled words: "You're forgiven in the eyes of God, brother." This is the argument his attorneys will use in court. It is hoped it will be allowed as mitigating circumstances.

PISSTOWN CANNONS READY TO FIGHT HAILSTORMS

Circling Pisstown now are curious tornado-shaped cannons aimed at the sky, 10 in all, with gunpowder and other explosives at the narrow base and the fluted 30-foot tower above filled with dry ice, all this to prevent damage to the city by large hailstones. Last summer P-town was pummeled by stones as large as basketballs, killing hundreds and causing millions in property damage.

Dear *City Moon*,

Once I settle in the U.S. and win the presidency, I will make sure that the government provides lonely men with a woman from the prostitute class, and an old woman to look after her. Government should also give everyone a neut of the servant class and rations to feed him or her. I will place one inspector and two constables to guard anyone who is afraid. The constables will be provided with weapons so that they can keep a watch over you. Government should also provide you a truck or Jeep. Everyone will get a free railway pass.

Vote for me.

Onēba

Box 591

NECRONAUTS AT THREE ROCK

They are regularly organized to commit depredations. There is now located around Tres Piedres, New Mexico, a well-organized band of necronauts who do not hesitate to commit any crime by which they can accomplish their desires. They are organized with a captain, judge and detention facilities and work under an unwritten law of their own. One necronaut told this reporter that there are 10,000 of them between there and Peabody Junction and they intend to trash Tres Piedras unless they receive better treatment.

EXISTENCE OF PROCESS LIST REVEALED

Officials have acknowledged the existence of a top-secret list, found during a raid on a Process Church in Colorado. It is a list of 10 prominent and longstanding members of the Church who have been classified as vital and non-interruptible in the event of an atomic or hydrogen catastrophe. Those whose names are found on the list will be spirited away at the first sign of trouble and placed in a mobile-home shelter buried beneath 12 feet of soil. There they plan to wait out any aftermath of the catastrophe then return to the surface and restart the Process. Those not on the list would be left to fend for themselves with little chance of survival.

The name at the top of the list, not surprisingly, is that of Professor A.E. Wurmbrand, a well-known Process prelate. When asked about the list, he said, "The Process is dying out. We know it. So give us our little burial spot, a coffin for 10."

NEUTRODYNE CHIPS TURNED TO GOLD

Where neutrodynes wander, looking for acorns on Red Oak Island, a few miles off the coast of T-Beach, artist Roger "Bud" Upton follows them, picking up their scat, which he turns into golden gifts for the man who has everything.

For 15 years, the 100-year-old Oklahoma artist has been producing gilded neut scat plaques.

"It started as a gag," says Upton, a lifelong resident of the Island. "Now I can't keep up with the orders."

Some 400 neutrodynes live there, descendants of ancestors who were taken to the Island years before by a movie company filming *The Wind Wagon*. Most of them died dressed in period costumes as a result of stunts they were told to do, such as being crushed under the wheels of a speeding wagon, trampled by a horse, hurled into the air by an explosion or thrown from the rooftop of a hotel.

"Not just any scat will do," Upton said. "It must have character. It can't be too old or too new. I sand the bottom, sterilize the scat, bake it. Then I dunk it twice in tung oil and paint it with six coats of gold enamel."

He said he used to charge $10 a plaque but had to raise the price to $28.

CAR CRUSHER ARRIVES IN TUTTLE

Approximately 50 old wooden neutmobiles were left behind when hundreds of neutrodynes migrated to Tuttle. All the cars were eyesores that had been parked in weed patches about the city for months, until yesterday when they were crushed and then burned. The crusher, after flattening the pedal-operated wooden cars to a third of the height of the body itself, stacked them in neat piles at the end of B-Street, where there's little traffic, and set them on fire.

MAN GIVEN SHEEP HEARTS

Bunkerville surgeon Edward Zanzetti has implanted four sheep's hearts into the chest of Andrew Moldenke, 30, to ease the burden on the man's own heart, weakened by rat bite fever. Moldenke was reported in satisfactory condition with all the hearts beating together. It was the first implant of a new heart, or hearts, without removing the old one.

Zanzetti said the patient's heart was the worst he had ever seen and that Moldenke was bedridden before the operation.

He added, "Andrew will recover his stamina to some degree, but will always be a slow mover. If one of the hearts goes, they all go."

Zanzetti said he encouraged his patient to get out of Bunkerville for a while, go to the country and live in nature, eating only Nutribars and drinking only water.

RESCUE AND DEATH IN A SNAIL CREEK PHOSPHATE BED

Henry Hudson and Willy Jones were driving on Phosphate Bed Road and while crossing Snail Creek, swollen by the overflow from the phosphate mines, the car suddenly sank to the headlights in the soft sand. The water was not over two feet deep, yet the car was sinking quickly.

Afraid to jump out into the sticky, quick-silvery mass around them, the men began calling for help. Their cries were heard by people at the Lower Farm. Two or three rushed to give assistance. Ropes were flung to the drowning men and they were rescued just in time to watch their car sink out of sight.

On investigation it was found that at this point a large amount of phosphate had formed a bed 30-to-40-feet deep. Any article thrown onto it was quickly swallowed. Cattle have been mired here. In one case, a convict escaping from the Lower Farm was caught in the deadly slough, his shrieks filling the air as the silvery muck closed over him.

The city commission was called upon to build a bridge over Snail Creek as many more lives could be lost. Instead, the commission has appropriated funds for warning signs to be posted at the creek's edge. Each sign would be 4-by-6 feet, painted bright red, reflectors all over it for night drivers.

Mayor Felix Grendon said to the commissioners, "What sort of moron would ignore a sign like that? A bubbling pit of deadly phosphate. Who would drive into it? I say, no bridge. Signs will do."

COME SEE Stuffy Koch at the lube department of RALPH PORTER MOTORS. With over ten years' experience replacing thrust bearings and wobbly pistons, Stuffy can take care of all your lubrication needs. Ladies, lubrication jobs are half price on Mondays. Come early and surprise the hubby when he gets home from the office by telling him you've gotten a lube job from Stuffy Koch.

TAMALE MAN INDICTED FOR HEALTH CRIME

Sheriff Prop made the alarming statement to a *City Moon* reporter that a tamale man was selling his spicy meat rolls every night at the market to tourists who apparently have copper-lined stomachs and long ago lost the sense of taste.

The tamale man lives in a squalid house in the western part of the City where members of his family are suffering the ravages of diphtheria, sleeping and coughing on filthy mattresses strewn all over the house.

A child of ten or so sits at a table spreading masa on corn husks and coughing into most of them.

Prop, holding a handkerchief over his nose and mouth,

said to the tamale man, "You could be killing people, pal. We're closing you down."

To which the tamale man shrugged and replied, "Chili today, hot tamale. I will be back on the street when the children stop coughing."

Prop said, "That's all we can ask. That's all we can ask."

COIN-FLIPPING NEUTS ARRESTED

Harold Marks and two or three other neuts were arrested yesterday while engaged in flipping coins against a wall, a violation of gaming laws. They were fined $43.45. Marks and his associates showed up at morning court for their hearing in high-hat fashion: alligator shoes, black leather pants and kangaroo coats. City judge Marge Morningstar, after hearing police testimony, found the neuts guilty and urged them to leave town after paying and before dark.

EDITORIAL

We don't share the problems of being editors very often, but today's problems are not ordinary. It's not that we are charged six times over the worth of the product—now the product is reduced six times in quality. We're speaking of the cost of newsprint today. Prices have skyrocketed in the past year to unheard of heights. And now they have reduced the poundage of newsprint, making things unbearable. The new product is so thin that feeding the press becomes a weekly chore. The drying period is about four times slower and static electricity is always a danger. It has turned our paper folder into a confetti machine. We hope you, curious reader, will bear with us until some remedy can be found.

Roger and Dave

Editors

FREE ADVICE Fawn like a spaniel, rage like a lion, bark like a cur, fight like a dragon, sting like a serpent, be as meek as a lamb and yet grin like a tiger and weep like a crocodile. Tyrannize in one place, be baffled in another, a wise man at home, a fool abroad, just to make others merry.

PENSIVEX ADVERTISING A *City Moon* subsidiary will advertise anything from skrada kaka to Love Dolls, from Art Typing to the new Kaliman and Estella-G drugs now sweeping America in the wake of the prexy's kill orders. We'll degrade an enemy in print for a small price plus printing cost and distribution fee. No checks. $$$ only.

MOON OFFICE TRASHED

When the *Moon* editors returned to their offices this morning, it was a scene of chaos. "Something" had gone berserk. The editors knew the visitor had just left. The goldfish still twitched in their empty tank, run-through with sharpened coat hangers, the gills convulsing. Whatever the "visitor" was, it licked the sugar bowl clean and flung it to the cement floor then ate all the coffee grounds. It ripped the yellowed pages of aging newspaper flats and smudged them with wide, greasy, stubby fingers, leaving prints. A waterlogged cloth doll lay in the corner. The editors had no idea how it had gotten there. One of the arms was extended upwards, the other unattached at the shoulder. Sulfuric acid had been poured onto a fine old Blaupunkt radio and had eaten its way in several inches. The tubes and the capacitors were smoking. The odor was foul. Speculation continues about what might have done the damage.

PREXY BARS WORLD VIOLENCE

With a stroke of a pen in the National Chapel, the president has signed away violence in America, the bane of our existence. Joy is national now, finally. Telephone calls are free. Americans talk to one another, the lines humming across the wide continent. Muncie is talking to Loma Linda, Peabody Junction to Katmandu. America has connected and the juice is coursing over the Great Divide and beyond.

There are those who carp, who criticize the president from the blue rayon carpets of the Senate chamber where only recently a senator was bled like a sheep, spilling her blood on those very carpets. Weapons are reported to be piling up in five story mountains near police garages and playgrounds.

The last of the rattling machine gun fire is no louder than a baby's toy now. Bottles breaking in bars and mad dogs bumping and snarling at you in blind, dark alleyways, this is gone. It is unearthly quiet. People sun themselves by the millions along the National Trench. Peace has wrapped the Earth in gauze and the dripping ball of blood that the planet had become is suddenly a quiet, golden sphere of marble again, a happy orb sailing as hastily as ever, thousands of miles an hour until time stops. Underneath the gauze, surgeons know, the workings of metabolizing and restoration twin, the skin closes quietly over the liquid flesh. And finally, hurricanes and apocalypses are no longer real, but abstract threats.

FROM THE ARCHIVES

An enormous disk-shaped chunk of the moon, twisting and burning as it fell, scooped a trench through the Dakotas, Wyoming, Utah, California, west and east then skipping like a stone to Boston, eating every city in its path without realizing its appetite.

A minister in Alabama said by radio, "To let this happen, God must be dead."

No, says Zanzetti. "What we've been given by a random celestial event is a second National Trench, extending the old Trench into a waterway across the country, straight as a gun barrel. If we finish the job, extend the trench a thousand miles, we'll have a National Trench from the Pacific to the Atlantic. It's a fortunate event. Moons break up eventually. Why not now?"

WILD WOMAN CAPTURED

She seemed capable of being in five or more places at once. She was very sly and would only show herself to children or to people out alone, always at a distance, but in a threatening manner intended to scare. Her delight, as she crossed the great distances with a grotesque suddenness, was extreme, but grim. It finally got to a point where people would not work in an unattended field and children were afraid to go to school. Sheriff Prop enlisted the farmers' toughest sons to help run down the wild woman.

Dear *City Moon*,

Extraterrestrials, especially neutrodynes, circling this Earth long ago, found it luscious-looking, its verdure, azure seas and white-capped mountains; but its people and their way of life was repugnant to them. These walking white slugs were "square," too "straight," too devoted to some kind of deity in the sky. That way of life was not to the neut's liking. And there was too much difference in the appearance of our people from theirs. So, as they began swelling the populace, a new look became the vogue, an Egyptian look, with heavy paint around the eyes and puffed-up hairdos. We became accustomed to their more elongated eyes and slightly different facial structure and now that look is as common as our own, no longer disguised.

Pozeki Mott
Lower Farm Hospice

JENNY'S GRAPE OILS I can paint grapes, or even wheat kernels, so realistic that birds will peck at them. See my work in Wuntex Park Saturday Mornings -10. Get there before the jay birds and jackdaws do.

PREXY WANTS KIDS WHIPPED

The prexy has told us there will be no more violence. He's barred it worldwide, though many doubt his authority in this matter. We the people trust this man. Contrarily, he says that we should whip small children in our yards with leather straps imbedded with tacks. How can this be reconciled? I think Onēba should have him killed.

Effie Pfeffer
On the Road to History

NECRONAUT WANTS DUCK BRIDE

Richard Moulinex of Bunkerville, once arrested, then released, for f***ing a duck in Wuntex Park, now is back and wants to marry a duck. As readers know, many returning necronauts have diminished mental capacity and a different name. Moulinex is one of these sad prodigies. He carries around a ragged duck facsimile made of stuffed sox and pipe cleaners, a clothespin clamped on his nose and bottle caps for eyes. It's not this duck I want to marry," Moulinex said, holding out the facsimile, "I want a real one like the one I f***ed in the park that time."

CITY MOON

MAN IN THE MOON HEARD THE FAR BELLOW, 'OHO,'

QUOTH HE, 'THE OLD EARTH IS FROLICSOME TONIGHT.'

VOL 5 **25¢** NO 9

NOTICE—We have picked up
dead animals for years and are
still picking up dead animals
free

THEY WALK THE TRENCH

At 3:30 this morning, a special train on the Atchison, Topeka and Santa Fe Road will leave for the National Trench. They reach Petaluma in the Fall, after a stay in the lovely hotels they've built at the bottom of the National Trench, the ones under the bubbles; they're walking the trench bottom, folks, from Cincinnati to Box, Wyoming. At the deepest point of the trench, beneath the great divide above, they have built an underwater monster thrill ride they call The Green Carp or The Perveslime.

FAR FROM THE TRENCH

We are frightened. How in the world can rocks have life? Yet they do and are moving, some toward us, some away, some indifferently, and some not at all. Gneiss and schist are the worst offenders in this case. They don't move fast. Buy a time-lapse camera, and watch the shadows. Or is it another of these Heisenberg indeterminacy cases? Drop your rocks. Box 591, Lawrence. Fast movers–10 dollars a head.

AWAY FROM EARTH

Two weeks ago they were delivered to a lawyer's office in a primitive crate. They were trimmed out like Christmas trees in human entrails. The boxes were stamped with Nazi insignia. The mayor fled as the farmers bled, the jails spilled out the boys, and the music stopped everywhere, including the New Music of the Sky which had so recently begun and promised such rosy hues for the future. Excuse me friends, Oneba here. I was carried away as I sat to write this prosy view of a hideous dream from last nights dream reports. These babies are aging me faster now. Here is a short one from Tennessee, "They acted mysterious and vaguely gave the impression that they were from another world and had enlightenment to give us. Bill looked like an earthling, but Jerry had wrap-around eyes; the slits extended around the side of his head." There is so little I can say to dreams like this. Or, "I attended an MUFON seminar in Kansas City, June 16, 1973: J Hynek has wraparound eyes hidden behind heavy glasses, like the invaders. Others were more disguised—by plastic surgery with rubbery scars, facemasks, beards and hair. A short negro sat behind me, carrying a camera; from his direction, I could hear an ultrasonic tone and my head couldn't think clearly. While I tried to explain I had information to forward, they induced a galvanic action in the wrist holding the phone, sort of a wavering involuntary flexing, not spasmic, not shaking as with fear. I ran out of coins and the operator cut me off." I'll leave the analysis of this dream to the younger men. Oneba no longer accepts night calls. Write Oneba, Box 1, City.

Dead Want World Wall

⊕ Life Dividing Into Two Camps ⊕

few rumor: rising sentiment among the dead for the construction of a cinderblock wall, somewhere, 40-0 yards high, stretching 2,000 miles if that is necessary, to "make a community." Head of Bureaucracy ce is handling himself worse these days, since he is ot being used in negotiation with the dead. There re more dead, they say, than are alive on earth now, nd many of these former citizens are angry when ey read the newspapers and are told the same tiring e--that there are more living now than the cumulative um of the dead . . . . dead writers are sending anuscripts to us now . . . upstarts like Cheever are uaking from hot letters sent around by FYODOR OESTEGYEVSKI. . . . . . on another front, bear orshipping is decreasing. The curious Ainu race, hich originally occupied the whole of the Island of ezo, is rapidly vanishing before the influx of Japanse emigration. According to recent investigations hey now only number some 16,000. They are the airest race in the world, are filthily dirty in their abits, and terribly addicted to drunkenness. They worship bears. And snakes. And in some cases ive in caves like the troglodytes of the Red Sea. Their skeletons have many peculiarities in common with those of the ancient cave men found in European strata . . . The reason those coming back want the wall is to split the world in two. The only problem s the dead's claim to the two Americas and Canada, which, even with the National Trench, is the most luxuriantly rich and abundant land mass of earth, What do the living get in return? Grandfather Europe, with its antiquated farmers and blindly stupid caste system. Get ready American readers, the uture is to the East. Federal money has been pried from every safe in the States to make this hefty novement of more than 300,000,000 possible. All

"THEY CLEANED ME OUT"

They finally did it, they broke him. Ike is penniless in Tucson. It is a national shame of course. His L.A. split level sells for $350-00. After, he's taking a train to Tucson where he stays at Valley Acres Motel under a friend's care, tucked into a bright bed under the cleansing waterfalls of hospital glucose, blood and marrow making vitamins. He's a little ghostly in the face, ashen, livid, really, quite a nice old fellow who wants an even cut of the new emerging America. God help Ike.

Rolla Dilla is driving a new blue pickup.

Larry Jones is sporting a sharp new hair style.

"Going to celebrate our day, Socrates?" asked Jefferson.

"I'd like to," said Socrates, "but times are hard and I can't afford to buy any fireworks."

"Why don't you get your wife to help? She'll blow you up for nothing," suggested Jefferson.

Supporters: SUA (via GSC) grant of supplies support, Cottonwood Review in past years, Fed Government, via Nat Endowm for Arts, via the CCLM (money) the Society of the City Moon, the SUA Events Committee, SAGE of the English Department, and the few who read the Moon

will go. Too bad the energy shortages have sucked away our last precious gallons of fuels, and our last vats of noxage. We're finished.... And yet there is the wall. Build it through New York and down through woody Maryland? America will be a ghost town, is that what you want? Write and say. Box 591, Law.

A GREAT MODERN DRAMA—ONE OF THE FEW THAT DO NOT LEAVE A BAD TASTE AFTER YOU HAVE SEEN IT.

BELLED BUZZARD STRIKES, BOY DEAD

A sleepy toddler was set in the shade of a cottonwood tree in Wuntex Park by his mother while she tended to roasting franks and making punch. Soon the boy was asleep, and in minutes, after the tinkling of a bell was heard in the sky, he was attacked and mauled by the notorious belled buzzard. Reports have the boy carried wailing over rooftops, the head cracking against chimneys, inflicting terrible injuries. In an empty lot the boy's gut was torn open by the buzzard's slicing beak, his organs spilling into the park's dirt. A squad of Fire Scouts arrived and drove the buzzard away with hickory bats. Some threw jagged stones. It was then that they noticed the boy's eye had been pecked out.

His mother is inconsolable. "My precious little Jimmy John… my precious little Jimmy John," she wailed over and over.

The boy will be laid out cold tonight at Lamanno Panno Fallo, morticians. The boy's father, James John "3-J" Jones, is currently serving a 5-year term at the Lower Farm for aggravated public nudity and sodomy with a dog, and could not be reached with news of the boy's death.

WILD WOMAN APPREHENDED NEAR GAS FLATS

She had been described as every shape and size from giantess to lioness, and was capable of moving at every possible speed— gallop, trot, limp or crawl—and, without touching herself, could extend her flesh at will into the empty space next to her, giving her an irregular appearance, a primitive sort of camouflage.

Sheriff Prop's posse rode on horseback over the plains to catch her. They came to a wood. Some rode right through the thin stand of timber. Others walked their horses and were rewarded when they found the wild woman in a little thicket. She sprang up and crushed the head of J.J.A. Reynolds with a rock and galloped away, but was finally tackled by the Sheriff himself.

The woman spoke intelligently at times, but other times wouldn't answer questions. She was tall, sinewy, strong, active. She wore a Mother Hubbard. Her feet were the largest ever on the Sheriff's records and were shod in the thickest, toughest flesh imaginable. She carried a sack big enough to hold a peck. Mixed in it were mullein leaves, a sugar tit, pieces of a queer root, but no food.

She is up on trial tomorrow for lunacy and manslaughter. She gave her name as Ophelia Balls, Gas Flats resident, former housewife. She was driven insane, she will testify, by a six-inch brain worm. She told Sheriff Prop, "It came in through my ear when my husband threw me out and I was sleeping on a dirty mattress in the junkyard. The worm came up through the mattress .... waiting, you know, for the right ear. It was small and young then, but it grew big in my head, feeding on my brain. That's why I'm crazy."

The Sheriff asked how she judged the worm's size, how she knew it was six inches.

"I could feel its mouth chewing on one side of my skull and its hind end swishing against the other side, tickling me. I figured that was about six inches. Measure my head if you want to."

ESTELLA-G, NOXAGE IN CHEESE CUBES

The city commission will be asked to forbid the gathering of remaining Process Church members. Once a year, it seems, they emerge from their underground bunkers and assemble in Wuntex Park Community Building, joining others who've traveled here from distant places and have rowdy reunions that sometimes last a week or more.

Last night things went too far and there was a riot. While the enthusiasm of the zealots was at its height, someone distributed cheese cubes and bottles of Pluto Water. The cubes seemed innocent enough on the surface but were bearing tabs of Noxage and Estella-G at their centers. Once they were eaten and the Pluto Water guzzled, a rush for the door followed in a short time. Park security officers waiting outside started fighting the men rushing out. Scores were hurt, and a free-for-all followed.

A PIG'S STOMACH IS NO LARGER THAN A TEACUP This fact has been brought to you by the Mexico Lindo café, the last place in town to serve one-pound hamburgers with everything. Open 2 to 4 afternoons and for early bird specials from 5 p.m. until 7, featuring sweetened pork broth served in a braised pig's stomach with ham and a side of deep-fried quail legs, a favorite of the elderly.

KAWABATA SHOW AT PISSTOWN'S FAMOUS ICE PALACE

Minoru Kawabata's paintings are intuitive. From a distance, they pulse quietly with the pure, manipulative joy of painting;

close up they seem sparse and high strung. They are highly communicative, urgent and eloquent, but what they project rushes by or as if it is shouted in an unknown tongue. It can't be caught in the net of rational discourse. It seems to persist. It is and it isn't. This is not true of art in general.

The show will run roughly from April showers to Xmas Snows. Exact dates TBA.

Rose of Sharon
City Moon Art Desk

NOXIN RALLIES EN ROUTE TO INTERNMENT

The former president has joined the national dance of joy. He looked like the Noxin of old, hair dark and curly, his face firmer than ever as he lay in an open coffin on his funeral train, passing through crowds that wept and applauded at the same time. The train travelled at a slow speed from Washington, D.C., to Casa Pacifica, Noxin's retreat in California.

A *City Moon* reporter was in Hugoton, Kansas, when the train went through. "Everyone in the crowd suddenly broke into coughing and throat clearings," the reporter cabled us. "We saw him waving a cold hand from the coffin and we caught him at his old tricks, lying in the pink velvet like a well-fed boa, grinning at us again even in the pale, wasted shades of death on his way to Hell and fire for his crimes.

GODBOY JOJO HEALS THE SICK

Joseph Vitolo, oldest of the Godboys, has been on a healing spree.

"Touch me, touch me," begged a woman.

"Kiss my little boy," cried another, holding her baby up.

Neighborhood children cried, "Hey, JoJo" to attract his attention, but Vitolo drew away from everyone.

A storeroom had been made into living quarters for JoJo's family, his mother and father and seven brothers and sisters. It was furnished with packing crates, wooden skids, thrift store blankets hanging from ropes and a Coleman camp stove.

One day, JoJo became emotional and shouted for everyone to go away. In the quiet, empty storeroom, he saw Onēba's visage on the sheetrock wall. "He had lots of stars around his head," the Godboy said later, adding that "he was dressed all in blue."

The Godboy answered no more questions. His sister, Mrs. Theresa Scolastica, however, quoted him as saying that Onēba had told him he would return no more in that form, that he had done his work and that he was tired of answering questions.

In a few days, the storeroom was packed with sick persons and a steady stream of policemen pushing through the crowd carrying the sick and infirm.

JoJo laid his hands on them. He kissed vomiting babies with terrible rashes.

A priest who said he was the Rev. Francis Scarlatina of the Church of the Bloody Host brought his 35-year-old sister, whose legs were paralyzed, to be touched by the Godboy.

A sailor came in carrying his blubbering wife as Vitolo was lighting a candle on a crude altar made of sturdy cardboard boxes. The sailor said, "She's dying. Help her! JoJo, help my girl!"

In an instant the boy was beside the sailor's wife. Father

Scarlatina, administering the last rites, coughed and spit as the boy rubbed her stomach and prayed. She was suddenly awake and curious.

The priest acknowledged the boy's power and called it miraculous.

YOUTH ARRESTED FOR UNNATURAL ACT WITH VENDING MACHINE

Olsen P. Thrummers, 18, white, was arrested Thursday and charged with a crime against nature, resisting arrest and abusing private property. He will be arraigned April 3rd in the Ice Palace branch of City court, the most recent example of the city's judicial outreach program, which locates small neighborhood courts wherever space can be found.

Thrummers will appear before Judge Willy Tibbs, who is also coach of the Ice Palace barefoot skating team and lives in the neighborhood.

Private guard, Dooie Whelp, 56, said he saw Thrummers pressed close against a candy and gum vending machine outside the Palace Orienta restaurant.

"I thought he was trying to rob it like youths do," Whelp said.

Then he noticed that Thrummers' arms were wrapped around the sides as though he were going to carry the thing off. "Next, his head sagged over to the side and his body went limp. That's when I called the police. He was f***ing the coin-return."

The arresting officers, Dickie Hickey and Robin Steele, came right away to the restaurant. After a struggle, Thrummers was taken to the Lower Farm psych unit where he was examined by Warden Wunty who described him as "a deeply disturbed young man who has no feeling for what is alive."

Dear *City Moon*,

We here at Vassar Swiss Trailer World are happy without drugs or nudity, thank you. We have all we need, too. Right next door is a K-Mart for bargains. We're tired of goons from the City coming in and bossing us around. In a mobile home you can stand at one end of it and see all the way to the other. Is it so horrible to want such a thing from life?

But on the bad side we are hounded by packs of dogs running around through the trailers, keeping us all inside so we can't get to the K-Mart unless we throw them some wieners or bacon or hush puppies or something like that. After the dogs are fed, the rats come, looking for scraps. We'll throw some Saltines out there and they don't bother us too much. We just walk through them, or step over them. Sometimes we'll crush one by accident. Now and then somebody gets bit and gets a fever, but not too often.

And there's a farm-chemical factory across the Trench from here that lets out a sulfur cloud every midnight. We get to choking on it, but it does keep the skeeters away. And local broadcasters jam our closed-circuit TV which is the lifeline of our trailer community. They take off *I Love Lucy* and put on news.

Yes, we have enemies. Many of them. They haunt us like shadows. Yet we build a network of floodlights for a better day. We will be safe. We will persist in our dreams. Already we are stacking junk cars around Trailer World for protection. The City is always bothering us about permits and sends inspectors in to hassle us. But we like them, the people they send. As much as they bother us, they do bring us weed. We like that. Sometimes we wish we lived inside the national government instead of Vassar Swiss.

T. A. Verill
Homeless Now
P.O. Box A (anywhere)

BUGS PERFORM IN PISSTOWN

M. Smetzer, German immigrant and insect trainer, has taught two bedbugs, who are making Pisstowners shriek with delight this week, to break hickory nuts with a miniature trip hammer. The bugs operate inside a model of the derelict old Onēba Hammer Works on Industry Parkway. The tiny hammer was made of beaten gold, imitating the original Hammer Works hammer. The replica's framework is silver, the chains and gears platinum. The original weighed 40 tons, the replica, six ounces.

Members of Smetzer's audience watch the bugs through a series of magnifying glasses that shrink them and stretch their bulk. It is a queer little show, but it gets better: At Smetzer's command, the bugs issue lazily from cherry wood cages. One of them picks up a strand of tungsten with its forelegs. One encircles the lever which raises and lowers the hammer.

Smetzer signals again. The bug at the lever raises the hammer and sends it crashing down upon the anvil. Though audience members can see this, it is below their hearing level. The largest bugs are enlarged five to 15 times their original size by some of the huge lenses. The performing bugs and the golden anvil and hammer are the talk of Pisstown.

Smetzer says that if the people of Pisstown will allow him to stay in America by writing to the *City Moon* and saying they want him to stay, he wants to have a cot thrown open for him at the Hammer Works. Then he will teach his bugs to ride slim-bodied house spiders with tiny saddles and chaps and to lasso each other. He will turn them into tiny Vulcans, to fashion in fire geometric figures from tungsten.

BELLED BUZZARD IN CITY

Timeless, it seems, as old as Nestor, first seen in Marfa, Texas, in 1900, reported then in the *Dallas Evening News*, and now here in the City, sighted by police only last Sunday perched in the belfry of the Church of the Concrete Cross, squirting foul white stool down the stone side of the hallowed building, the buzzard issued a frightening screech that could be heard halfway across Wuntex Park and into the Eastside Historic Area. The clatter of the ancient bell and the cadenced chop of the buzzard's wing beats signaled danger for small children and pets. Children here are pale, hiding in closets or wandering aimlessly in the yard casting fearful glances skyward.

CRUSADE FOR JOY

Now the latest religious crusade, a swirling tornado from the foothills of the Rockies, has invaded the prairie. They are called the new Trochilics, or Trokes, and can do a 360-degree rotation on their skates. They sing of Onēba as they skate, and of the national joy. They claim to be followers of the science of trochilics, or rotary motion, also known as gyrostatics. The leader, Jody, or Dolly, now works at the Audio Haus.

At the height of trochilic activity, mobile homes have been destroyed, sucked into the whirling vortices as the skating and the chants intensify. Jody points at the sun and signals his trochilics to begin the dance of joy. Anyone nearby is advised to back away as far as possible. They could easily be sucked into the vortices and be sliced to ribbons with sharpened steel blades embedded in the skate wheels. Our City was powerless to stop them when Jody, or Dolly, led the trochilics into town.

Now the streets are empty, scarred by the skates, as their leader speaks of paving the rivers for skating. "Let us pour concrete into the Missouri to make it solidify, then into the Mississippi and down to the gulf. This will give us access to the seas."

Converts to trochilic philosophy converged on Pisstown yesterday. The whirling, they believe, symbolizes the trochilic theory of universal movement, that our galaxy is an enormous turning screw that never tightens.

Some suppose that Sydenham's chorea, also known as Saint Vitus Dance, is capable of producing similar symptoms. Sometimes the rapid jerking of the face, hands and feet can be the first symptom of the disease.

Historian John Waller, author of *A Time to Dance, A Time to Die: The Extraordinary Story of the Dancing Plague of 1518*, has an even stranger hypothesis. He believes that the dancing plague was caused by a "mass psychogenic illness" brought on by severe stress due to famine, and a belief that when angered, a Sicilian martyr by the name of Saint Vitus would cause these dancing plagues.

SHORT STORY CONTEST TO BE JUDGED BY CARLOS CASTANEDA

The winner will lunch at the Palace Orienta chef's table with the famous author/restaurateur. Second and third-place finishers can expect to receive gift certificates from Squat 'n' Gobble diners U.S.A., any city, any town, any time. Feeling lonely and hungry late at night? Call the Squat at Bywater 5115 or Galvez 4858. We deliver anything anytime.

Entry fee: $100.

Due date: Feb. 29, 1976.

Prizes awarded: Feb. 29, 1980.

Send typed stories of no more than 10 double-spaced pages on any subject, along with fee (cash or money order), to:

Story Contest

Box 591

Stories will not be returned.

ACADEMIC POET SEEKS SAME for any kind of Platonic/ Hegelian relationship. Formerly professor emeritus at Wellesley. Resides in Tucson. Send photo in loose pajamas with fanny crack showing, and call Helen Magellan at Bywater 5116.

MOON'S DARK SIDE SAID TO BE FERTILE

Little known infrared photos of the dark side of the Moon have been revealed by NASA. They show spongy, mushroom-like growths shooting several feet from the surface. Russian cosmonauts had previously photographed the growths, but the quality of the images was poor. NASA's photographs, much sharper, were persuasive in thinking of the growths as edible, much like the stinkhorn family of mushrooms on earth. It is estimated that the dark side of the Moon, given its newly-discovered abundance, could feed the poor and hungry for decades.

SCIENTIST ZANZETTI TO MARKET NEW PRODUCT

It is called Life Fluff. Like a yogurt culture, it ferments and regenerates. "A pound could last a lifetime," Zanzetti says. "What's to lose at a dollar an ounce?"

It comes to you in plasticized bags and gives off the mild odor of sweet mold or decaying peat, nothing more. Children and adults alike can fashion life-play animals or objects. The fluff will assume any shape their hands can mold, and a charge of simple house current will give it temporary life.

Add a cup of fluff to four ounces of water, knead the paste a bit like bread dough until it begins to harden, then shape it into anything you can and apply current. The temporary life can last from an hour to an hour and a half. After that you can heat it up in the oven till it melts, reshape it, recharge it and have another go at something different to play with and be entertained by.

Dear *Moon*,

Have any of your readers lost children yet to nodal paralysis? It's a disease, possibly a fungus, that attacks all the nodes in the human body and can cause damage to the main circuits, sometimes a fatal blow.

I have learned the cause: At night, sometimes I wake up in a cold sweat, finding it difficult to breathe. At first, I wondered, has the oxygen been taken out of the air or is there some chemical retarding oxygen utilization? Neither. There is another explanation.

Several times I awakened after dreaming of being paralyzed or immobilized by some sort of vibration. Once, I was awake and heard steps on the concrete overhead. (We have a tent under an overpass, me and the kids.) There were electronic vibrations that put my brain into a stupor. Then they turned it off. I heard a click or clang of metal shifting under my cardboard home and suddenly my brain was free; I was awake, but sweating, and my breathing was shallow.

Nodal paralysis is caused by the focusing of an electric device on a sleeping person of any age, a device similar in effect to a microwave oven, damaging nerves, and in some cases inducing a paralysis that results in death.

This same device could be located on rooftops, sent from hidden equipment under floors, from miniature mobile robots introduced into rooms even in neighborhoods of the wealthy and elite, and they are killing children with it.

If you guys at the *Moon* can't handle this, forward my letter to Onēba and label it a dream. Okay?

Billy Alonzo
Golden Mo.

ONĒBA SEEN IN NIGHT SKY

Last night a Bunkerville businessman saw a perfect likeness of Onēba in the sky above one of the most sumptuous restaurants in North America, the Palace Orienta, now owned by the formerly-hermetic writer, Carlos Castaneda. Onēba's heavenly manifestation was encircled in a scarlet ring of bright clouds that seemed to catch every ray of light from the Moon and bend each one so that Onēba's image could be seen perfectly clearly. The businessman swore it was Onēba he'd seen, and his wife did, too.

When asked, Castaneda said, "I'm too busy running my restaurant to care about these sightings. I've been thinking of franchising."

Dear *Moon*,

Your paper is extremely ordinary. It yellows if left in direct sunlight. It costs too much to shred and put in the cat box. It draws coffee through solid china into radiating stains if cups are set on it. If you slap a fly with it, you're lucky to break a feeler. As a butt-wipe it chafes. As a fire starter in the potbelly it stinks of sulfur and smokes acidly. It frightens children and narrow-minded adults, as all well-told truth does. And the worst thing: It won't postpone the commitments of the flesh a moment. All of us are scarab bait. The *Moon* lists a hundred modes of dying in every issue, belabors the dog shit and ignores pressing social ills. Never does it ever mention, even in passing, the great women's struggle, though it endlessly harps on stuff oblique to the point of fabulism. Come back, *Moon*. Come down to Earth.

Beverly Donne
Chelsea Fish Pavilion
Outerditch Road

ART SHOW STOMACH-TURNING

The latest works of Sheriff Prop are on shameful display at the City Art Bunker beginning today with a bit of classy refreshments—cold hot dogs and canned Coke—to be consumed in the frosty, windowless Bunker. Everyone shivered as they strolled past the displays.

The first of the sheriff's works, housed in a dirty glass enclosure, is titled, "Neutrodyne Bowling Ball." It features a heavy brick with three holes drilled through it. The second is the "No-Fail Double Suicide Gun," a revolver with two barrels and two cylinders aimed in opposite directions and a single trigger with room for two fingers. If one of them pulls, both receive a bullet. The brochure promised further "treats" ahead: "Toe Floss," "Pubic Hair Donated by My Friends," "Crucified Lizard" and "Turds of Famous People" to name a few.

I'll be honest, valuable reader, I could go no farther. I had been looking forward to the Tika Masala I'd frozen in the fridge and this show was making me nauseated. Nevertheless, as I left the Bunker, there were jittery lines of young, bearded men waiting to get in.

Rose of Sharon
City Moon Art Desk

City Moon,

We have bad conditions in this place. They hem us up with neuts in our cells and the neuts say right away, "I'm gonna fix you up and don't you tell. Pull down your pants or open your mouth, I'm ready to end that drought with this nice big hose."

They chase us all over the place. What they do is a disgrace. They make us yield and they make us kneel, then they begin their romantic spiel. Now homosexuality takes over. They plead and grunt like my old dog. If we resist they beat us up and treat us like pups.

Too much sex thrives in the Lower Farm Detention Facility.

These neutrodynes beg us for our tail. When we don't give it, they take it, pop their fingers and tell us to shake it.

I tell you, I hate waking up with goo from five of them leaking out my bean gun and starching the sheets.

By the way, there's no ass wipe here. Big shortage. But what we discovered was that after a while a "cone" of dried shit forms around your anus and you can move your bowels through this cone like a toothpaste tube for a while before you break it off and start over again.

The dorms here, they stink like the Devil's breath. Send us TP if you can.

A Concerned Inmate
Lower Farm Prison Block 44

NEUT GIRLS FOTO MAT This speedy service outfit sends you a packet stuffed with photos of neut girls in sultry positions and poses. Muff, cloacal crack, nips, all shown clearly. $10 per packet.

RESTAURANT PROFITS TO FUND FUN

Castaneda's second Palace Orienta opened atop a dune overlooking Texoma Beach.

"Come the summer season, its success is assured," Castaneda said. "All profits will go to FUNFUND, the Fund for Unburied Necronauts. These 'people' need to be guided back to death. Our putting out the effort to re-bury them as soon as bureaucratically possible, given all the president's 'wait times' in force now, is a significant problem for all. Citizens never know when the waiting will begin or end. There's waiting in jail, waiting in lines, waiting for blood-test results, waiting to die. Other waits, too, now enforced by law."

AGING GODBOY DROWNS SELF

Vincent Vitolo, one of the 1969-vintage Godboys, in a fit of anxiety and depression, rushed down the staircase. On the way he ran into Mrs. Noxin going up the staircase to do the morning cleaning. "Jesus!" she cried and covered her face with her apron.

"He was gone in a second," she reported.

Already out the front door, he rushed across Arden Boulevard. toward the Trench bridge. He grasped the railings the way a starving man clutches food. He swung himself over when he reached the middle of the bridge. Like the distinguished gymnast he had been in his youth, he held on. When he saw between the bridge railings a motor home coming fast, he knew it would cover the sound of his fall. He called in a low voice, "Dear Parents, and my saintly brother, Little Derando, I love you all the same," and let himself drop into the frigid winter Trench.

Sheriff Prop, helping to drag Vitolo's body from the Trench, said, "Some of these Godboys are getting old. A lot of them die in their thirties or get themselves killed."

Godgirls, however, typically live a long life, to age 150 or more, until they dry up. It happens to them suddenly. Prop says he finds them sometimes standing in the middle of the road, as dry and dead as a scarecrow. "We find a lot out in Gas Flats. Hundreds go there to die. Some die right on the road. We have to clear them off for sanitary reasons. Cars hit them, too, and injure people."

LIPSTICK LAWS Now that the new lipstick regulations are in effect across most of the nation, you'll want to have our pamphlet explaining the nuances of the law. Don't get caught red lipped on a pink lip day. You could go to prison for years. Call us at Bywater 5115. Read this pamphlet from Onēba Cosmetics LLC before it's too late.

S

TORY CONTEST ENTRY

Bring in the Clones
by
Mike Johnson

By that time, the video clones were hard to tell from their originals. The medium had stored in its mnemonic matrices the images of at least a thousand of the country's glorious and seemingly immortal dead. Most of the people were fooled most of the time, though some were vaguely troubled by the appearance on popular talk shows of such known dead as Wally Cox, Buddy Holly, Jack Kennedy, Walt Disney and Tennessee Ernie Ford.

The public at large gradually came to wonder about the slightly fuzzy borders around the grey images and the situational inappropriateness of certain gestures; and then they began to doubt the authenticity of all the images and to be concerned about who was dead and who was not. Now they are totally confused; but the medium is the only reality, so reality is simply unreal. All is image. Death indistinguishable from life. There is no cause for alarm. Nothing is newsworthy anymore. We are merely back where we started.

The End

P.S. I hope you like this, Mr. Castaneda. Winning the contest could be the spark that lights my literary fire.

Mr. Johnson: This is Mr. Castaneda's assistant writing you to say that Mr. Castaneda is presently at a brujo's retreat in New Mexico and will not return for several weeks. Please be patient. We'll be in touch when he returns.

HAIR VALUE! Now that the City is buying hair again, many are collecting it whichever way they can: barber shops, cancer wards, mortuaries, pet groomers, voluntary donations. The *City Moon* offers a dollar a sack, a full 10 percent above what the City is paying. Call us. We'll send a truck out. Keep pubic, leg, face, pet or other hair separate from head hair.

ZANZETTI'S WORLD OF SCIENCE

Among the off-beat theories of Platonic evolution, one holds that man evolved from June beetles, often mistakenly called June bugs. Beetles have hardened wing covers, bugs do not. Zanzetti's research was sparked by his observation of the aforementioned insects trying to fly through his screened door all summer long. Why would they want to get into his home? Why did they fly full throttle into his screen door, knocking themselves silly? This was during Zanzetti's days in Kansas, near the end of a life he was happy to be done with. He had practiced dying for many years, lying on the floor, straining sometimes for his élan vital to leave him, clenching his fists and kicking his legs in the air to die. Nothing worked. He was 50 years old and healthy. Eventually, he sat down to write his 100th treatise, *A Beetle not a Bug*.

KABUKI ACTOR POISONED BY FISH

Mitsuguro Bando, 68, noted kabuki actor designated as a Human National Treasure, died of swellfish poisoning at a restaurant. He was pronounced dead at the City infirmary at 4:40 a.m. Thursday. Bando had dined on seafood, particularly swellfish, at a party given by his local fans at Mme. Dunbar's restaurant in the Eastside Historic Area.

Bando made his way to the Gons Hotel complaining of stomach pain about 10 p.m. that night. He then returned to the restaurant about midnight, apparently free of any discomfort, the spasm having abated.

Then, at the bar after the meal, sipping La Perla soda, he developed a high fever and began walking back to the Gons. He was taken by a severe spasm on 12th Street and rushed to the hospital but was dead on arrival.

Bando's real name is Toshio Morita and his home address is Moto-Akasaka, Minato Ward, Tokyo. Please send condolences.

THE EAGLE FLIES on Saturday night at the DIXIE PEANUT BAR, 1433 Old Reactor Road. Any way you can possibly imagine peanuts, we've got 'em, including the new peanut whiskey. Miss Toni and Little Derando dance nightly on our inlaid peanut shell bar top. Little Derando likes to feature his hambone work while Miss Toni blows the short horn. They like to style after that, especially when the glorious and bountiful fullness of joy lies like musk over everyone's soul. $12 cover, 10-drink minimum. We offer complimentary taxi service home. Come to the DIXIE PEANUT BAR. Roses 39 cents a dozen. Low priced used shoes in some of the larger sizes.

Dear *City Moon*,

I've been perusing the Chinese *Materia Medica*, Part Two. According to Shen-nung, the head and feet of a hedgehog resemble those of a rat's. The use of either animal for regurgitation and various stomach troubles was common during the time of Pieh-Lu. The custom began in the hills and was quickly adopted for use in the cultivated plains of Hupeh. The skin of the animal was cut up and roasted black, the ashes saved for later use. It was bitter but not poisonous, and when used to treat bleeding piles it was mixed with cat tail powder, ashes and corn oil and applied to prolapsed rectums. It was also smeared on the breast to quiet a frightened baby. Then there's the otter's liver, sweet, warming, but mildly poisonous, given for chronic coughs, malaria, all kinds of demonic possession, debilitating sweats, nervousness, weakness after child birth, anal fistula and retention of urine.

Pozeki Mott
Lower Farm

P.S. If I stay on my good behavior another five years, Warden Wunty will consider granting me a three-day library pass. If he does, I'll be looking for Part Three of the *Medica*. Really, with one good eye and a short supply of Canned Heat, it takes years to read these things.

P.P.S. They tell me my old wife Tina May died down in the Texoma Beach area. That makes me sad. We got divorced over nothing about 40 years ago. She was nice for a while. She married an asshole from Sicily named Raspanchi.

WHITE WIDOWS DANGLE

Four white widows of the City, whose car dangled for six hours from the jaws of the raised Trench bridge before being lowered to safety earlier this week, became honorary members of the Club of Danglers, now numbering 149, all of whom have dangled at one time or another from the Trench bridge.

The widows were Dolly Roddy, 74; Nora Bender, 75; Olive Balm, 78; and Urilda Latapie, 30. They were trying to cross to the northside, they say, with hot skrada kaka for aging friends there. The old-fashioned drawbridge snagged the car and hoisted the widows into the limelight, all piled into the back seat, dehydrated, delirious and covered with hot skrada-kaka.

Civic leaders and developers have proposed that a new bridge be built, a two-lane, arched roadbed, higher than any conceivable ship's rigging that might someday pass under it.

The Editors of the *City Moon* say this: The Trench is just a trickle of what it was. Even in the drizzly winters it isn't much more than that. There are no oyster boats or shrimp boats coming through anymore because there are no more oysters and shrimp in Texoma Lake. Why build a new bridge? In a few years we'll be able to drive across the Trench itself.

Dear Onēba,
Please interpret this dream:

It seems to me like it's the end of the world, the end of time, cars, ships, planes, travel is forbidden. Everything is restricted. The air itself rots. We all wait with short tempers. I am an outlaw traveling on a ship with friends. Everyone moves these days in this part of the country. No one waits in one place for the end to come. We argue until we are hysterical. I tell them we should put on shows. We are the actors and we'll pretend anger. People are committing suicide all over the ship, some with great style, others with abject efficiency. The cultured European Jews drown themselves in the ship's swimming pool. I cannot swallow enough water to drown myself. I am told to kill a wealthy doctor. I slide in beside him on the car seat. He jitters, jiggles. He's fat, frightened, blubbering. We fear each other.

Jack Shenker

Dear Jack: The man you were to kill is named Dewey, a commonly appearing figure in dreams. He stands menacingly back stage, so to speak, waiting to decide which dreams need forgetting and which dreamers need remembering. There would be frightful dream-world consequences, perhaps even death for them. Avoid Dewey at all costs. If he doesn't like your dreams, there's hell to pay. You may never sleep again.

SUIT FILED

A Peabody Junction woman has filed suit against the *City Moon*, claiming that her husband drank a Coca-Cola bottle full of bleach after spending an afternoon reading this paper and scissoring out articles. The allegation is that he told his wife he felt despondent after the reading. But also, he said, "New insights have opened within me like moths in my lungs." He said he was going into the garage to glue his cutouts down. The woman claims she found him dead on the concrete floor, "fallen on his scissors," two hours later. No note was left.

RELICS CHEAP Available from the City reliquary: fragments of mud-stained gabardine trousers worn by Onēba when he gardened during his presidency—guaranteed third-degree relic. Onēba used hankies $5. Laundered, 59 cents. Monkey toe bracelets. Send wrist size and 50 cents and you'll receive this one-of-a-kind bracelet.

ONĒBA SPEAKS

I read the *Moon* today. Oh, boy. It is a well-known fact that birds and wild animals know what other creatures they should fear. Thus, birds will fly away from a person, will safely hop around a cow, even walk right under her leg. So, I will soon take advantage of this fact to facilitate the slaughter of birds and other game by using my Cow Suit for Hunters™. The invention presents the perfect outward semblance of a most peaceable and amiable cow, but the forelegs and hind legs are in fact the legs of two armed shooters with plenty of ammunition.

My patented cow moves along the cow paths like an ordinary, harmless ruminant until it is in the midst of a flock of prairie hens or red squirrels. When it comes open, the two shooters inside blaze away.

LITERATI NOTE

I've discovered that when Hawthorne was writing *The House of the Seven Gables* he selected Pyncheon as the name of one of his characters. Of all possible names he might have selected, this one for some reason suited his purposes and simply "flashed" into his mind. Whether he knew it or not, New England was full of Pyncheons, and the book had hardly been placed on the shelves when a reader wrote him a very bitter letter complaining grievously of the injustice done his worthy ancestor, Judge Pyncheon. In all, Hawthorne is said to have answered complaints from 47 of the pesky Pyncheons and had serious thoughts of publishing this correspondence in book form, but died before completing the task.

Bryan Flattering
Literary Editor
City Moon

ONĒBA REPORT

He was at his desk when our people spoke to him, the tools of his many trades all around him: his boards, his books, his instruments, his pyramids, his whatnots. He wore his Radio Hat and listened distractedly to its broadcasts during our visit.

"Yes, I am finally at peace," he said. "The memoirs are written, my risings and fallings in life and death safely recorded. As you know, I have two hearts now, one a meaty transplant, the other a white plastic disk with a battery."

The former president said he goes to the market in his little pedal car these days. Not long before, he had ridden the trolley, until he witnessed an ugly incident only feet from his seat. A neutrodyne came up to a City woman and took an aluminum comb from his hair. Onēba saw the glint of the precisely honed points and long, sharp tail. He saw the neut pull the comb roughly through the flesh of the woman's rouged and sagging cheeks, then stab her with the tail in both eyes.

Onēba said, "There were sudden scarlet beads of red blood on the white flesh and something like candle wax dripping from the ruined eyes. She said nothing, the woman, taking the pain in silence, braving it for the other people on the trolley who could just as easily been chosen for a comb-raking by the renegade neut."

Now that he wasn't riding the trolley any longer, Onēba ended our visit, saying, "It takes a shitload longer to get to the market in my pedal car. So, excuse me, I have to leave now. They close the meat line at five and I must have protein to keep the spirit alive and B-12 in my blood."

MOLASSES CAN NEARLY DE-FACES YOUTH

While the eight-month-old baby of a Lower-Farm turnip farmer was in the house with his eight-year-old brother, unsupervised, the baby's two-year-old brother shoved a half-empty gallon tin of molasses over the infant's head. A rim on the inside of the can slipped and became fastened under the baby's lip, and the brother could not pull the can off. He became frightened and screamed.

His mother, who was netting mud bugs in a ditch near the garden, was attracted by her baby's screams and ran into the house. She tried to pull the shoved-down can off the head but couldn't. A neighbor came along and said, "I can split that can with my mule shears if it's got a rusty or a weak spot."

When that failed, the neighbor hitched up his Oldsmobile and tried to tear the thing off with a rope tied to the bumper. Just after the first little crunching pitch forward on the asphalt for the child, the mother took the can off easily. The baby was half smothered in molasses and its head was terribly black and blue, the face distorted. It was crying, and the mother was hysterical. The father, home from his pipe-fitting work, sat silently crying in the car.

LIGHTNING KILLS GODBOY

Ovid Hawks, a young Godboy, was struck during a storm that ended a flatball game in Wuntex Park. It was raining hard, with thunder and lightning. Hawks was in the ball game when the storm came up, and all the players collected in a group. After a while he left the others, saying, "Let's play ball!" and ran out past second base into center field.

He had scarcely uttered the words when the bolt struck him, causing instant death. His shoes were found 100 feet from the still-smoldering body lying in center field. Otherwise the Godly corpse was undamaged. None of the others in the party was injured. It was later learned that only the day before his death Hawks had wed well-known Godgirl Daisy Doolittle, who was in the bleachers and saw the whole incident.

NEUT KEEPER DEAD HERE

He was tired of life and wanted his debts paid. It is not certain if this was another poisoning by Kaliman or an apoplectic death caused by an overdose of Estella-G. He stopped at Pharmagucci's Corner Drugs one evening, where he secured the killer spansules, stating that he wanted to use the drug to poison a stray cur that had killed and eaten most of his chihuahua, Pepperbelly, the previous summer.

After he arrived home, his wife prepared his supper and at the meal he appeared unusually jovial. Afterwards, retiring, he said to his wife that he was restless and could not sleep. Later that night, he got out of bed, built a warm fire in the wood stove and sat down to write a note to his sleeping wife and the children.

He begged them to forgive him for the rash act he was about to commit, then went to the old cabin at the back of his property and woke up one of the older neuts, Old Poss', and told him he was dying and that he wanted all his debts paid from his $1,000 life insurance policy and that his neuts could remain on the property the rest of the year, gather the crop, get winter food, make fires and in fact do everything necessary about the place, and that they would be amply paid for their work. After that, they were free to go.

The neut keeper then asked Old Poss' to fetch a doctor and to find his brother, Bob. He wanted his brother near him when he ingested the Estella-G. But the brother was never found. The neut keeper will be sadly missed in these offices. Requiescat, old friend.

SHERIFF EXHIBITS PAINTINGS AGAIN

There are eight large paintings in the current show at Cider Gallery on Far East Street, all superb. Who would have guessed that Sheriff Prop had such a massive talent! In one of the paintings, almost filling a field of red, a sudden solid folding rectangle of royal purple, as a dry brush hopping tracks of red, like a flat stone skipping across the water, grows out of the field near top center and descends to bottom right, splitting the purple. A thin, faint, pulsing green line, part contour and part division, moves up from the lower left corner of the purple and intersects the red track somewhere near its middle.

Another work has an unexpected variety of color: on a green-yellow field, a dappled rectangle of pale orange-yellow and pinkish yellow is sustained by a rigid dark yellow vertical band, wounded by an abrupt black accent and kissed by a searing pale-blue purple, the whole giving off twinkles in lots of colors.

By contrast *Form in Red No. 5* is the beast in this company, the wild unicorn. It seems harsh, crude, obvious, almost indigestible. Its diaphanous void is swiftly turned into a solid surface by a lascivious after-smear of scarlet. Its red fields fold into a central rectangle—sketchy, evanescent and empty on the left, smashing a dark solid hole or slab on the right. Looking at the left is like forgetting who you are and looking to the right is like dropping a brick on your foot. The interchange is dazzling.

Rose of Sharon
City Moon Art Desk

THRUMMERS ARRESTED AGAIN

He had become at maturity a man who assaulted monuments. In an earlier incident, he was caught attempting to have sex with a vending machine. People had seen him engaging with the monuments and statuary all over the City. He'd paw and grunt and reach around to get ahold of the granite figures. He'd go all over the City with little figurines of lapis lazuli or chalk chunks stuffed into his trousers, and he once attempted to penetrate a cold chocolate Easter bunny that sat like a little Sphinx in a pan of snow in front of City Hall.

Pastor Wurmbrand had a talk with Thrummers: "You pagan! People could hear the cooled chocolate cracking all across the parking lot."

Thrummers replied, "Really, Pastor, most people don't care. They think pigeon droppings are a bigger problem than me being rough with a chocolate rabbit."

But many did stay up that night or chained dogs in the yard to guard the pink flamingos.

DEAD BABY NEUT FOUND IN PIGTAIL BUCKET

A 21-year-old neut woman of Halflife township, Debora Balls, has been charged with second degree littering and sidewalk obstruction following the discovery of her one-and-a-half-year-old child in a five-gallon bucket that was obstructing pedestrian traffic. The child was dead, possibly for days. These buckets are often used by neuts to carry pickled pigtails from one township to another.

VEEP DROWNS IN TRENCH

The body of the vice president, who drowned yesterday in the Trench near Bunkerville, was recovered about 9 o'clock last night and brought to the Zanzetti Clinic for examination. The veep was one of a party of six important officials who liked the challenge of fishing for flatheads on horseback. He rode his horse into the river, holding his rod and reel aloft, followed by the others. This was just above a deep and dangerous place in the Trench known as the Jump Off where there is a sheer descent from comparatively shallow water to a depth of 25 to 30 feet.

The veep, being a good swimmer, boldly rode his horse over the ledge, and they at once sank from sight. Soon, the horse surfaced and swam to shore. The veep appeared a few seconds later in the churning foam, his hair hung with root tendrils from the turgid bottom and matted with clay, but he sank again almost immediately and rose no more. He had received a blow to the head from his horse's hoof, which stunned him and made him unable to swim.

A memorial service will be held at the Church of the Concrete Cross on June 12, 7 a.m. to 9 a.m. The veep's wife, Nadra Huffington, held firm against the president's wish to have his remains interred at Arlington and instead brought over a team of experienced corpse burners from Benares, several truckloads of aged oak and had him cremated on the banks of the Trench above where he had drowned.

Our most beautiful features are the free group organ playing lessons and the all-tenant barbecues on second Sundays. We're talking about whole yard birds (chickens, mourning doves, pigeons), plus lingua, heart, you name it, and squirrels, too. Onēba talks to tenants over closed-circuit Radio Universal. These are messages available nowhere else. Come now! Get with the National Joy of Total Housing.

In the mobile units you experience electronic coyote hunts on your TV using live shotguns (we have absorbent, bulletproof walls in all rooms and armored TVs). Hunt prairie hens, too, without leaving your flat. Have them roasted by the staff with wild rice and English peas and served to you at supper.

We allow and encourage street confrontations here. Soft boxing gloves hang in every phone booth for this purpose. There are regular railcar routes from all parts of Liberty Heights to all other parts. Tenant quarters are equipped with the very finest stereo equipment in the world playing Andre Kostelanetz night and day. Security guards are a part of the ultimate safety of living in Liberty Heights. In our "obscene" gardens you will frolic with other sexes and lick the backs of toads, bringing on a strong, comfortable mood of bufonia and a chance to mate.

Why would anyone live anywhere else? Call us at 555-3335 to reserve your ultimate home quarters.

City Moon,

Fill a Kaliman love-drug doll with warm water and give her (or him), a tender kiss, where the release of the drug occurs. Then give your pet monkey a Kaliman love pipe. Either way you'll enjoy yourselves stoned in the most ridiculous way by the most dangerous drug of all, the new Kaliman-H! This is a PAIN DRUG IN THE WRONG HOUSE, AND YOURS MAY BE WRONG. The proximity of a monkey with one of these pipes is dangerous to your family. Get them out of your house now. Love dolls are worthless anyway. They puncture easily and

can be dangerous if they leak into a bedside radio or a nearby wall socket.

Sheriff Prop
Box 591

Dear Onēba,
I keep having this dream. Maybe you can help me. I am walking down the main drag. Suddenly there is a tugging at my coattails. I turn around and there are two plums the size of billiard balls posed neatly on the sidewalk. I pick one up and take a big bite. It tastes rather fishy and familiar, but not like a plum at all. Tell me, is this some sort of forbidden fruit?
Bozo, Miami

Dear Bozo: Next time you're in Safeway, buy three plums. Juggle them as you walk down the drag. If no one notices, you are clearly on the wrong track. Place two of them in your pocket, and eat the other one. Massage the two plums gently as you walk, but don't mash them and stain your trousers.

WHITE KILLED BY MOTORMAN

It took place on a streetcar in front of Mme. Dunbar's. This *Moon* reporter happened to be on that car to see the action, which ended with Scotty Monroe Nelson White riding in a Gold Cross ambulance the last mile of his life to City infirmary, where he sucked oxygen pitiably until his white-power heart stopped pumping lifeblood and he died.

Adam Monroe Nelson, the father, was a wealthy KKK grand dragon for a decade. He had his son's name legally changed because he wanted to include "the most beautiful word in the

English language" in his name, now officially Scott Monroe
Nelson White.

The City twilight was a deep red that summer night. The
rush work getting the *Moon* dummied up and ready for printing
was done and I was exhausted, glad to be on the way home. I'd
had a paper cup of cherry soda with a dribble of Pimm's Cup
before leaving the office and I felt a nerve rising in me. I began
to see a connection among unrelated events. For one, out of the
streetcar window, of oval shape, I saw flights of cedar waxwings
along Arden Blvd, flying into the loquat trees and eating the fruit.

Then I noticed people crowded at the front of the car,
close to the angry, anxious, weary motorman. Some said the
motorman's name was Lemonade Kenny. Others said his name
was Clovis Baudelaire of Cincinnati. A sizzling afro sat on his
brown nut of a head. It looked like a west Texas tumbleweed.
He was probably high on one of the new hellish Noxage drugs,
judging by the pucker of his pooched lips.

Scotty Monroe Nelson White then pushed his way through
the anxious scrum of riders waiting to get off and shouted at
the driver, "I don't care what your name is, step on it. Don't
stop. My movie starts in five minutes.... White Power!"

The riders, as a group, chorused a string of "f**k you, asshole."

The driver, tired and angry, stopped the car, jumped from
his seat, pulled a long-tailed comb from his back pocket and
plunged the point into White's ear, dropping him almost
instantly. Riders stepped over the still-twitching body as they
exited.

As I got off at my stop, I said to the driver. "You had every
right, sir. I'll call an ambulance when I get home."

Dear *City Moon*,

You got the White story wrong. Whoever wrote that ought to be fired. He/she bollixed the whole thing. Scotty was a troubled boy, a slow learner. I was his nanny for seven years. I know. He was watching TV one day and he saw some shaved-headed, tattooed freaks shouting, "White power! White power!" He thought that meant his name had power, *White* Power. And he joked about it all the time. He'd go into a candy store, and say, like, "Give me some of those chocolate-covered cherries, about ten pounds. White power." Then he'd giggle or smile stupidly. The clerk knew him and knew what that meant. It meant "I'm an idiot and I want one pound of malt balls." He didn't know the difference. This motorman should be tried for murder. He's got a hot head.

Effie Pfeffer
On the Road to History

KFRG is a whole new idea in dynamic radio. Tune in 1040 on the dial. Something for everyone's listening dollar. "The Stoned Ear" is on from midnight to 2 a.m. The "Mellow as a Cello" show with the voice of Bryan Flattering, the *City Moon* literary editor, will warm your winter soul with quips and quotes from 2 till dawn.

NOXIN IN PISSTOWN

From the Archives

The new president fluttered down to the plain in Air Force One like a robin on an inch worm. The landing was rough at P-Town International, with a lot of bouncing, smoke, tail strikes and blowouts. Though thrown about the cabin, striking his head and drawing blood more than once, Noxin looked forward to seeing the plain faces of the crowd awaiting him.

A blind vendor made the rounds through the reporters and public officials selling lemonade soda and cotton candy. It was oddly warm on the tarmac that February day. The president was coming, the man who always smiled and shook your hand with a good, firm, warm-for-winter grip. He could be seen in the oval window of Air Force One picking at a crust in his nose. When he realized people were looking at him, he feigned a casual nose-hair extraction.

Governor Wunty was the first to greet the woozy president, who seemed half-asleep, his suit rumpled, a little bleeding and bruising at the hairline. The governor himself was a bit off balance.

"Welcome to the grain alcohol capital of the National Drunk," Wunty said, laughing uncomfortably.

The governor was trying to make political hay out of Noxin's visit but the joke went flat with the president. Everyone smelled something rotten in Wunty's motives for inviting Noxin to Pisstown.

No Pisstowner who watched television or owned a goat could have anything but contempt for this president for his kill orders, but here he was in the bread basket, on the banks of the National Trench. His eyes were like black cherries, his face, vanilla custard. There were three or four unshaved whiskers spiraling on his throat. Pisstown bankers pushed curious little girls away to get near him.

To be honest, even as an objective reporter, I hated the man on sight as I knew I would. He was a blue-eyed robot, rigid, with eyes shifting systematically but unnaturally.

He and Wunty and the bankers went off to a luncheon at Pisstown's Squat 'n' Gobble that lasted no more than an hour, and when the president was soon finished hand shaking, he climbed the ladder to his plane, which quickly flew off, leaving a wake of black soot to settle on the roofs and streets of Pisstown, whose residents sincerely hope he never returns.

THEY WALK THE TRENCH

At 3:30 this morning, a special train on the Atchison, Topeka and Santa Fe tracks will leave for the new fork of the National Trench in Petaluma. Its passengers will arrive there in the Fall after a stay at the lovely underwater hotels that have been built at the bottom of the Trench. They will then walk the Trench bottom from Petaluma to Box, Wyoming, beneath the Great Divide with weighted feet and snorkels, the water that time of year only 5 or 6 feet deep. On the way, they will pass the president's proudest achievement after 40 years in office, an underwater monster-thrill ride they call the Green Carp.

ONĒBA INTERPRETS

What's up, troops? Onēba here. I was carried away as I sat to write this prosy review of a hideous dream from last night's dream-o-rama. Here is the premise of the *dramatte*: Two guests at a street party act mysteriously and vaguely give the impression that they are from another world and had enlightenment to give us. Bill looks like an earthling, but Jerry has wrap-around eyes almost hidden by dark glasses; the slits extend around the sides of his head as far as the ears.

They are heavily disguised by corrective surgery with rubbery scars, face masks, beards and hair.

I hear an ultrasonic tone and can't think clearly. While I try to explain that I suspect they have information to pass on, a few of the partiers apply a galvanic device to my wrist, shocking me. For a minute, I feel my blood boil then I pass out. When I come to, I am dunking buttered toast into my coffee and nibbling the soggy parts. I've been doing this since childhood, so it tastes very good and calms me down.

IKE GOES HOME, MEETS THE PRESIDENT

Soon to be penniless in Tucson, the Eisenhower necronaut is a national shame.

"They've cleaned me out," he says, smoking the butt of a Lucky Strike. "My L.A. split level sold for $350,000, so I'm taking a train to Arizona, where I'll stay at the Valley Acres Motel under a friend's care, tucked into a bright bed under a life-restoring drip of glucose and blood-and-marrow-making vitamins. When I regain some energy, I'll go to Abilene and meet the president."

To this reporter, traveling with him on the train, he seems to be a nice old necronaut, with vivid memories of war and golfing. All he wants now is the restoration of his Army pension.

"You know what that old preacher used to say," he said, "'We die that we die no more.' Well, nothing could be truer. I've been through it. Once is enough."

Ike wants to settle down, accept his station as a necronaut and live quietly in his childhood home in Abilene.

After a week of sun and vitamin therapy at the Valley Acres, Ike and I boarded the Union Pacific train to Abilene, where we expected to meet the new "animal" president the day after we arrived.

"I don't want him to shake my hand," Ike told me not long after the train left the station. "He might crush it."

"They don't call him the animal president for no reason," I said, hoping to humor him.

"I don't want him touching me at all, or looking at me overlong. And he may ask only three questions, none of them about love or death, certainly not about war. I will not tell him any of my war stories."

"I'll make sure he knows these restrictions in advance."

Once in Abilene, Ike and I took a taxi to his childhood home at 201 SE 4th St. It was a modest, white, two-story home with shiplap siding and a small front porch. "It was pretty crowded when the whole family was living here," Ike said. "Now it's just me. I don't know what happened to Mamie. Lost her in the dark. If she does come back, she'll come here."

Ike said he wanted to take a nap in his childhood bedroom and suggested I have a stroll around Abilene and maybe have lunch at the Squat 'n' Gobble.

Ike said, "We used to eat there all the time when I was a kid. I don't eat any more. My brother loved the green chili they made. I liked the patty melt."

I helped him up the stairs, watched him settle into his bed, and went to the Squat 'n' Gobble for a late lunch. The president was not due until the next day, so I had some down time.

As soon as I had taken my seat at the counter, the frycook approached and said, "You're that reporter, aren't you? We hear old Ike is back and here to stay." The wait staff gathered around, buzzing with curiosity.

"They told us the president's coming to visit, too."

"That's true," I said, "tomorrow. He might even eat here. Ike'll come along but he'll have nothing but a spoonful of clabber."

"We got clabber. Tomorrow we'll have Scotch eggs, corn grits and poke weed salad on special. The president will love it."

"Sounds good. For now, I'll have the walnut tagliatelle, a house salad and a Negroni."

"Coming right up, sir."

The walnuts in the tagliatelle were rancid, but I was hungry and ate it anyway. In a bad mood and feeling gassy by the time I got back to Ike's home, I went straightaway to bed on a hard mattress where Ike's mother and father had slept. It was a horrible night. The buzzing locusts outside my window and the dawn-chirping cheechee birds kept me awake.

Ike was up and cranking around the house at dawn. He stood at the foot of my bed sniffing the steam rising from a cup of beef broth.

"What time is the president coming?" he asked.

"In time for lunch," I said, "at the Squat down the street. They've made preparations."

Ike then retired to the porch to watch the morning pass and to wait for the president.

I had a light breakfast of coddled eggs and lamb fries at the Squat, along with coffee and a beignet. As I was paying the check, I heard sirens. The president was arriving early. I stood at the window and saw his motorcade coming down Main at considerable speed, then veering left at Fourth. In my rush to follow the procession of vintage vehicles, I tripped more than once, tearing holes in my gabardines and scraping my knees.

When I reached the childhood home, the president was already squatting to empty his bowels on the lawn. "Sorry," he said to Ike, who stood on the front porch, uninterested in these events. "Don't look. I'll be with you in a minute."

For the most part bystanders turned their heads and pinched their nostrils. Everyone knew of the president's stink, but no one could really prepare for it. It could stay with your clothing for weeks, no matter the launderings.

Arrangements for the meeting had been made. It would be in Ike's childhood home kitchen, at the old tin-top table covered with a floral-patterned oil cloth. Because the president couldn't sit in standard chairs, he was afforded a simple stool. Ike reclined in a cushioned chaise.

"The squat is expecting us," I said. "Let's go there."

Cameras were snapping pictures.

"No," Ike said. "Most food makes me sick. We're going to stay here."

"We'll call out for clabber," I said. "They'll deliver."

The president said he was exhausted, got down from his stool and lay on the floor. "Have them send me a half-chicken, cut in half again, raw."

The orders were placed by telephone.

For a moment, I was later told, the kitchen staff balked at the idea of serving raw chicken, but quickly someone among them said, "It *is* the president, after all," and, in the light of camera flashes, strangled a backyard bird and cut it in half twice with a band saw.

The president's assistant, a burly ex-military man, helped him back onto his stool. "There you go sir. I'll be behind you if you fall."

Neither Ike nor the president spoke at all until the food came. "I *am* a little bit hungry today," Ike said, spooning a dollop of clabber into his dry mouth.

The president, with very few teeth, all of them decayed, contented himself gumming the chicken parts for show, but in the end, swallowed nothing. "I'm not feeling well," he moaned to his assistant. "We'll be leaving immediately."

As the president's men carried him by both elbows toward his car, his bare feet dangled in the air and he kept saying, "I have a plan.... I have a plan! I've got a road map to victory!"

Once again, Ike stood on his porch watching the spectacle. "Goodbye, Mr. President," he said with his hand on his heart.

When the motorcade roared away, Ike said to me, "A plan is not a map, a map is not a plan. A map will get you there, while a plan may not. I hope the war department will give me an adjustable chair that I can sit in until the world ends."

ISLAND RISES IN TRENCH

A small island has risen unexpectedly from the bottom of the Trench south of Muncie. Unfortunately, the island is toxic. No vegetation can exist there, nor can any other living thing. Fish that have drifted to the island invariably turn to ashes or stone. One rat hound has ossified merely lapping water in one of its stagnant ditches. Box turtles anchoring at the island to take sun baths on its dead logs have suddenly jelled and dripped away like candle wax. Caustic permanganate in the soil is blamed both for its odd, violet color and for the toxic effects.

EDITORIAL

Dead Want World Wall

There is rising sentiment among necronauts to construct a cinderblock wall to keep the living out. It will be built 50 to 60 yards high, stretching 2,000 miles if that is necessary, to make a "mortunity," a community of the dead who've come back, mostly celebrities and famous folk. The cost is low, the benefits eternal.

There are more dead than alive on earth now, and many of these former citizens are angry when they read the newspaper and are told the same tiresome lie, that there are more living now than the cumulative sum of the dead.

Dead writers are sending us manuscripts now. Upstarts like Cheever quake in fear of the hot letters sent around by Fyodor Dostoyevsky that reveal all. Someday they'll want to build a wall. The editors agree. Give them the wall they want.

The reason those coming back want the wall is to split the world in two. The only problem is the dead's claim to America and Canada, which, even with the National Trench, is the most luxuriantly rich and abundant land mass on Earth. What do the living get in return? Grandfather Europe, with its antiquated farmers and blindly stupid caste system.

Get ready, live Americans, the future is to the east. Federal money has been pried from every safe in the states to make a hefty movement of more than 300,000,000 possible.

All will go. Too bad the energy shortages have sucked away

our last precious gallons of fuels and our last vats of Noxage. We're finished. And yet there is the wall. Build it through New York and down past woody Maryland, all the way to Biloxi. America will be a ghost town. Is that what you want?

The Editors

NEUTRODYNES THREATEN AGAIN

Pino Doza, itinerant farmer, was found suffocated, head first, upside down, choked in swill, but still warm. Sheriff Prop said one of his men fainted when they raided the neut camp where Doza died and neuts began spraying.

"The odor was peculiar to this band of neuts," Prop said. "It filled the air, at first smelling like viburnum in bloom, and then, quickly, you're inhaling something alien to the nose, like a stepped-on stinkbug. The next thing is, you faint. On the other hand, some say it's the fear, not the smell, that induces syncope. Killing these kinds of neuts is like trying to kill a brick. It stretches the definition of what 'life' really is. It's a complete mystery to most people."

BLESSED OR CURSED?

From the Archives

Daisy Doolittle looked ordinary at birth but in a few months had come to resemble a watercolor image of God the Son hung over a radio set. Her mother, Jo Jo, returned the $2.98 cardboard print to the Pisstown Sears where she had purchased it, saying, "I'm very sorry. I want my money back. This thing is doing something to my daughter's face, and she can't sleep, either. She stares at it all night long."

By the third year the bone structure of the cranium and jaw had enlarged, growing grotesquely out of proportion to the body, and a bristle of shining reddish hairs had appeared on her cheeks and throat. Seeing this, her father packed a few things and drove away in the Ford, never to be seen again.

During long summer days, Daisy lay quietly cool in her basement room, staring restfully at a radiating water stain on the plaster board ceiling. At intervals this state of semi-awareness would lapse. Her head would turn into her sour pillow, a whitish foam burbling from her open lips.

Sometimes, hostile crowds gathered outside the Doolittle home, throwing La Perla bottles against the house and burning smelly rags on the grass. The plumber says he often finds human saliva dripping from the front door in the morning.

On a wet night in August, Daisy came up from her basement. The press was there. She stood momentarily on the stoop and said something in a language no one understood, though this reporter thinks it was Aramaic. She then left the house and walked rapidly down the sidewalk to the bus station and took the Greyhound to Las Cruces, New Mexico. There she rented a room in a small downtown motel. In the morning, the cleaning and laundry crew opened Daisy's door and found her outstretched on the blood- soaked mattress with a self-inflicted stab wound to her abdomen. A bottle of vinegar, half-empty, lay on the soiled carpet.

The coroner, a pious man, arrived on short notice and said, "Just to be sure, we should wait three or four days before interring her. It's possible she could arise. It wouldn't be the first time."

Cameras were installed and trained on her for seven days in the Las Cruces motel room where she lay. Everyone watched for any sign of movement, but none ever came. That Sunday she was pronounced dead without the possibility of return. The next day she was laid to rest in the Tortugas Cemetery on Highway 66. There were thousands of mourning and weeping followers and a cadre of Process dead-enders in attendance who thought of Daisy as one of their own.

FINAL SUPPER AT THE SQUAT 'N' GOBBLE Tomorrow, we at the Gas Flats Squat will close and lock our doors forever. We will sweep the floor and shut the back alley Dutch gate and call it quits after 48 bitter years on the same ugly corner, but not before we host a FINAL SUPPER. We'll have T-bones, corn and perch chowder and green tomatoes fried in organic needle grass oil. Come on in and eat your heart out. Last chance. Try our Pepperbelly Combo or the Bean Gun Chili and enjoy them again the next morning.

DEAD LIFE SEEN AS ATTRACTIVE

Many now say the necronaut life looks attractive in important ways and plan a peaceful suicide. No need for food or rest. You can walk your senseless body around mile after mile without tiring. You'll have a neutral state of mind, no concerns, with ecstatic moments every hour. Death? Nothing to worry about. It's over. We die that we may die no more. People are leaving wills stating that they plan to tour the afterlife for a time then hastily arrive back, expecting to find homes and furnishings, pets, bank accounts, investments and other things not trifled with, stolen or sold, and in good order.

AS A PATRIOTIC SERVICE

Lawrence CITY MOON

25¢

In 1967 and 68 I published UFO reports under the name Pioneers Institute; as a result I have been subjected to crap in food and water, to gases in the air, and to sabotage of motor vehicles—my brakes have gone out on hills, wheels have come loose, the steering pin has dropped out while going 60 mph ... I live in isolation. But not alone; I have found footprints in wet cement or fresh concrete where no person could have walked; have heard sounds in my room at night, like the plop of little doors closing, the hiss of escaping gas, banging in the stove. Once when I had just started a fire in the stove the draft reversed sending flames 4 inches out into the room. Axing the drugs used, I think, were arsenic, heroin and LSD, causing intense bellyaches, diarrhea, and a staggers (withdrawal of heroin).

CALL THE DEADMAN — Dead Animal Removal
FREE
SOUTHWEST RENDERING CO.

M O O N

mit 'Cruel Kill

17 ATTACK HITLER

Drowns In Grease

The last act of the Hitler episode was his drowning in a greasebomb flash then burning. The City Moon told you this FACT. Box 591, Lawrence, Ks. 66044

A harmless walk in the sunshine will do no harm to most mortals—Adolph Hitler is an exception, as we saw yesterday. He fell to the sidewalk wincing as the golems danced a hornpipe on his thighs, face, neck, head, trunk, feet.

The trouble with these golems is they bungle the job, maiming where they mean to murder, hacking instead of incising, generally diddling things badly. When they saw Adolph they said, We know that man, and he don't give a damn, about us blacks. So it was then, that Adolph feeling bold enough to step into a neighborhood not his own found his tormentors. He heard the gavel of the PEOPLES JUSTICES hitting an oak surface in his mind.

The diminutive murderers spun dizzily on their ball bearing toes, the golem call to violence par excellence. After the savaging they rolled off in their sidewalk bus, checking into the Holiday Inn for a white power supper. Police arrived. We say this: Round them up with bulldozers and run them towards the Grand Canyon, then scoop tons of dirt over them when they are squirming at the bottom. Pave them over with cement. Don't let them breed. Box 591

PANDICULATE for HEALTH

They've picked off Kennedy again as he sortied through a rally for Harry S in Harlem last night, doubling him over with a raft of bullets in the gut, after a short thundershower of ACID RAIN that fell on the angry crowd, which caught the thieves of poor Kennedy's lives and tied them together and ignited them with gasoline and a box of matches to make them a flaming human yule log in the City square. Nice going Jack. Look for Roosevelt, wherever you are.

* * * * * * * *

A man carrying a toy gun claimed he was trying to protect President Fodr in the Waymire Parking Ramp yesterday. He said his name was Albert W. Zero. Sad case, since the president left a week ago. The man Zero sang glory, glory hallelujah and rambled about his affection for whiskey. As he was led away he yellowed out and screamed 'It's a dopey gun, it doesn't fire anything, it fires dummy dopey bullets. The man said he pulled his play gun after a garage employee threatened the President. The Secret Service said, however, there was no

WHY

did EDDIE STEWART, 19, of an unknown address, sneak in EDNA's bedroom on Kealty Lane and rape her, yell her he was hungry, and then commit sodomy upon her with his mouth? Tues 3:30 a.m.

Are you one of those who wish to go out? but cannot find a baby sitter, well look no more.

GRAND OPENING OF 20th CENTURY NIGHT CARE CENTER
3515 Linell Blvd.

This is Harry S. I want to be your next president. Here's my platform in a nutshell: Corrupt the young, get them away from religion, get them interested in sex and the low-life. Make them hollow and superficial, destroy their ruggedness. Encourage them to read the City Moons of America, the yello vomit sheets so often blowing in our alleyways in recent years. Divide the people into hostile groups by constantly harping on pseudocontroversy and matters of slight importance. Get people's minds off the government tricksters by focusing their attention on football games and other, often staged, collosal events, including the new so called Necronauts who pop in and out of life and walk the sidewalks of our Cities. Give them sexy novels to read, plays, and other trivialities. Always preaching true democracy while seizing power and control over the treasury of events. Be ruthless, ferretlike, take the advantage. Destroy the people's faith in their natural leaders by holding the latter up to ridicule, contempt, and scorn. By encouraging government extravagance, destory its credit, produce fear of inflation, hike prices, speak of shortages. The only Art is conceptual art. The life jell is another pitiable hoax, designed to encourage false visions in the eyes of the old. Buttonhole in the halls and barber shops. I am Harry S. I want to be your next president. The lead-goat is taking us down thistle-choaked lanes. The change is coming now. Feel it. President Cockburn, in my dream, is found dead in the rear of his Cadillac and all the men of the secret service are at my door. Vote Harry S. Don't wait. Don't vote on impulse. Keep a crowbar around is my advice.

Editor O

Very few actually return. Those who do are generally celebrities from many different eras of American culture. Kenny Cubus was the first to come back. He rode behind Brando in *The Wild One*. Then came the WWII hero, General Eisenhower. The latest is Sal Mineo, star of stage and screen, stabbed in his driveway by an unknown assailant for unknown reasons.

"FREAK BETS" AND OTHER COWARDS' DAY EVENTS SCHEDULED

Quite a few odd feats will be witnessed on Coward's Day this year. As readers probably know, Cowards' Day is celebrated in honor of the weak-of-will throughout history, those who'd rather surrender than fight and kill. Many lives have been saved by cowards and their cowardly acts.

Cowards' Day celebrants place "freak bets" as a way to raise operating funds. A local broker is due to roll a shelled peanut from Arden Boulevard to Old Reactor Road with a toothpick. The betting on this is brisk. Is it possible over those rough pavements and gravel roads that the toothpick wouldn't break?

A clerk from the American Tinplate company is honor bound to go to Wuntex Park and stand on one leg for an hour. If interrogated by a policeman, he is to say, "All is lost, save honor." Will he fall? He is young and nimble and probably has good balance, so the betting is on.

A teller at the Bank of Onēba in Bunkerville will go to the home of Brainerd Franklin, the Ape of Golf, and slap him in the face. Brainerd, known for his pugilistic talents, his golfing genius, his apish frame and piping hot temper, could respond with anger and violence. This teller could be in for some pain.

Here, the bettors are tense and uncertain. The bet is complex. Is the winner the one who says Brainerd would strike back? Or the one who says he will not? Are we to consider the damage done if Franklin does strike out at the teller? After all, the teller has just bitch-slapped the Ape of Golf. Tit for Tat.

These events will be held in, or near, Wuntex Park beginning at sunrise, April 1, and go on until noon, weather willing. April afternoon showers could come our way, so best to get to the business early in the day.

FORMER PREXY DIES IN HIS SLEEP

The 6' X 8' room was bare except for the TV and the La-Z-Boy. The Pro Bowl had ended, and the president shifted in the chair. His cold limbs recoiled from the heat given off by the Magnavox console. "I think that's all he can take now," a voice said into the area's walkie-talkie network. Somewhere a switch was pulled. The image on the Magnavox disappeared. Only a small white dot remained and that shrank into nothing. The president stared at the gray screen then sank back into his La-Z-Boy, eyes vacant for a moment, then closed. His famous half-smile lingered as he returned to sleep. A few hours later, after an acute coronary occlusion, the president was dead. Funeral arrangements to be announced.

WHAT ABOUT YOUR NEIGHBORS?

Editorial
To many, the decision to build or not to build a shelter seems

to turn on consideration of the neighbors. Should you join them in apathetic conformity, or should you go ahead and build a shelter and shoot them at the door when the sirens go off?

Silly questions like these are probably the greatest obstacle to a full-blown family defense program. Fear of being laughed at. In these times, only fools laugh. Your neighbors have probably thought of building a shelter, too. They're afraid of what you might be thinking: the atomic bomb.

How about a group shelter? Then you will not be alone when the time comes. The morale factor is acute here.

City Moon,
Doing good for the world by driblets and drablets amounts to nothing. I am for doing the great good once and for all and be done with it. Think of all the pagans in China, the starving in India, the dirt-poor here. On a frosty morning they're found dead in the streets, nearly frozen. Children, grandmothers, all of them, like peas nipped by the cold. Five score of missionaries over here is not enough. We need a million to convert them *en masse*. The thing is then done, and we turn to something else.
Pastor Wurmbrand
Goose Island Process Mission
Box 3

NEUT BEATS WIFE

Pablo Saposcat, a neutrodyne, was arraigned this a.m. in day court, Gerald Hilter presiding. The judge entered the courtroom and took his seat, banged the gavel and began the proceedings.

"Before we begin," he said, "please note that my name is Hilter, not Hitler." He held up his name plate pointing to the "l."

A neighbor lady testified: "I saw that neut in the window." She indicated Saposcat by nodding in his direction. "He came at her down and low, bobbing and weaving."

His wife, Susan, agreed that his footwork was good, but spoke bitterly of his sudden feints and fast punches that laid her low. Saposcat and wife seemed to be silent during the assault. Only his fists whizzing and pounding like paddle balls could be heard.

"He had me off balance just trying to back through the kitchen door when my foot went into the dog dish and I fell on my tukus and broke my pelvis in three damned places," Mrs. Saposcat said. "What a mean and stupid neut. Remind me to never marry another one."

The court janitor was still mopping her way out of the hearing room when Saposcat was brought in with a bandage on his chin. She swung out wildly with her big gray mop, splattering him with soapy, dirty water. Saposcat began to weep and continued weeping throughout the proceedings.

No one really believed the first stories that leaked from the testimony that day, how Saposcat used to beat the dog to stay awake. Now the awful truth was told, and the dog, Bamburger, bore silent witness. Her drooping red eyes had seen it all, the powerful strokes of Saposcat's fists avenging themselves on his wife's harmless topknot. Faithful to her mistress toward the end, her quirks forgiven, Bamburger bit Saposcat on the chin, almost severing his budding, 5-inch flocculus and puncturing the green gland.

Judge Hilter closed the hearing with a sharp bang of the

gavel. "As a result of those offenses, Mr. Saposcat, you'll be sent to the neut unit at the Lower Farm for evaluation. There's too much wife beating in the neut community, something the City won't abide."

"Hail Hilter!" shouted Mrs. Saposcat as her husband was led away dripping gel from the flocculus onto his yellow prison smock.

HISTORICAL NOTE

One cold night during the Civil War when Frederick Douglass got out of a train in New Jersey, he wore a large shawl on top of his overcoat. A New York reporter, seeing the dark skin and towering form of the traveler, stopped him with the question: "Indian?"

"No!" shouted Douglass, "Nigger!"
Effie Pfeffer
On the Road to History

PET BUZZARD BELLED

There is a peculiar pet at the residence of Thomas Forbes Jr., in Texas City. It is a full-grown buzzard, as gentle as any yard fowl. It understands and hops up in answer to calls for "Junior." Forbes loves the buzzard, but also loves his piglets, his chickens and his lambs, so he has placed a bell around Junior's neck to warn of his approach. The buzzard is slightly fastidious and only eats fresh carcasses, generally caught and delivered by the family's rat terrier, Bruce. The family fears that Junior may someday yearn for bigger game and fly away looking for it.

NECRONAUT UNION FORMS

The *City Moon* is in possession of a 1934 daguerreotype snapped on the steps outside the stupa of chandi-kar. In the first row are Randolph Scott, Harpo Marx and Marshall Zhukov. In the second are Duane Eddy, James Joyce and Billy Holliday.

This group was branded with the name "Dead Beats" and frightened the university set by its obtuse use of color in art, words in literature and stratagems in mathematics. Scott, unrecognized, a joke to the rest of the company, is now the only survivor of the circle. He lives in Peabody Junction. A janitor at the primary school, he scorns everything.

In his last months, Scott attempted to pull his way out of the lethargy that finally paralyzed him. He wrote a letter to Marshall Zhukov, who stared at the return address for a long time before dropping the letter from a cold hand and letting it lie on the floor for months. He noticed it again one evening, staring at it across the dry, heated air of his wintry apartment.

He tried to call Eddy, the most famous of the group for his big hit, "Rabble Rouser," but Eddy was already gone again. A bullet greased with Crisco had ripped through his lung one night as he performed in Detroit.

The story goes that the letter on Zhukov's floor smoked and flamed up, apparently without the contact of a match flame or any other source of ignition.

BOOK REVIEW

Of Pastor Wurmbrand's latest effort, a thousand-page novel titled *Noxola*, I say surely nothing can come of a vacuum of ideas welded to an unpleasant style. This combination shackles *Noxola*, floating it forever in the lower soup of literature. In the end this book is quick to read but weak. Namby-pamby fiction and sullen dialog show that the pastor should probably stick to pastoring and put a gag on himself, at least as he appears in print. Sample: "It was that day, that beclouded day, sooted with too much earthly grief. I was on the rolling Zephyr of anxiety all that afternoon. Then, suddenly, during a drunken sleep I had the first revelation, and it was this, that Noxage is a substance resembling peat moss and that life could be generated from this material, a low, crude form of vegetable life, occasionally seen as a mass with rudimentary intelligence, something invariably oyster-like, smelling of prussic acid, with a tiny, finch-like beak protruding grotesquely from its cold, amorphous body."

It was exactly this kind of talk that made people say Wurmbrand was begging for incarceration. He claims he writes his books knowing they will cause a sensation. "The truth is I make up everything out of my head. The reader has every right to judge the book, but I'd like everyone in the City *to please read it.* It's required reading so read it and be ready for the state examination next March. I want every person to pass the March exam so that there's no need for an April exam.

Brian Flattering
Literary Editor
Box 591

RUBBER KOI! The latest from Scientist Zanzetti's Bunkerville lab: rubber koi. When alive, it's the most expensive fish in the world. Zanzetti's rubber ones, however, retail for only $1.99. They stick by suction onto coffee tables, walls, dashboards, your forehead, your nose, a bald pate and other parts of the body. Take them along on picnics in the park, set them loose in the lagoon. They swim ten circles and then return to you. Children can handle them easily. These models should not be eaten. Chicago Pet Parlor, Chicago Illinois, Box 240.

STORY CONTEST ENTRY

What Came Out of the Waltz
by
Michael Hogan

They danced each dance, Verle perpetually cutting in. Estelle was haughty and coltish at first, then stumbling dizzy under his spell. Verle "Mad Bunny" Williams, the "sword" of Pisstown, continued his pursuit of Estelle, but her father wouldn't let her out of the house as long as Verle was in town. She pined for her lovely mad bunny. She had slipped a photo of him under the frame of her dressing mirror and she lapped milk from a saucer on the dresser, her gaze fixed on the photo, in a trancelike state. Milk was the only food she would take.

Meanwhile Verle lurked in one of the City's alleys, drinking from a wine bottle and fumbling with himself. He told his friends not to fear him, to come closer, to gather around. Eventually his slick city-talk took effect and they all huddled together for warmth. They would have liked to break sticks and make fire, but couldn't. Only Verle survived the night, warmed by his love for Estelle.

The End

Michael: As a judge of this contest, I rate this story in the D range. It reads like an outline for a story, rather than a fully developed tale. You have vaguely interesting characters, but the reader wants to know much more about them. We need to see some interaction between Estelle and her father. Who are Verle's friends and why do they huddle together? Are they homeless? Starving? Why don't they survive the night? Are they sickly neuts? Blow this story up, put some meat on its bones. Try again next year.
Carlos Castenada

GAYNOR NECRONAUT HELD IN MURDER

Mitzi Gaynor, formerly a singer and actress, with roles in the Academy Award-winning *South Pacific* and other well-known performances in *Bloodhounds of Broadway* and *There's No Business Like Show Business,* was charged today with chasing her husband and manager, the necronaut Jack Bean, with an automobile, cornering him in a Los Angeles cul-de-sac and crushing him against a parked car. Gaynor is being held on a murder charge.

PILLOW HEARTS Realistic beating hearts made of jelutong, heart-shaped and heart-sized. Insert one under your pillow. Listen to its strong, confident, regular beat as you sleep. Particularly beneficial to those with weak hearts. Guaranteed against disturbing flutters and electric stroke damage. Batteries not included. Call Pensivex Advertising and Novelty. Bywater 5115.

Dear *City Moon*,

There is a noise heard, usually evenings or late night, extending how far I don't know, but at least a half mile. It is a soft but distinct *beep-beep-beep*. Some prefer to refer to it as a three-part whistle. In any case, each beep of about one second is separated by silence of about half a second.

What I am proud to tell your readers is that this famous noise has no point source. Using acoustic equipment, I've discovered that the noise emanates from the air itself. It has become apparent to me that the atmosphere is trying to communicate with us.

Zanzetti

P. Junction, Box 8

BLACK HOLE RADIATED

In this freakish case near Bunkerville, a glowing cloud dumped an unusually heavy dose of fallout on the Black Hole Motel during a rainstorm. The 15 neutrodynes lodging there during Cowards' Day festivities would have accumulated up to 13 roentgens had they continued to occupy rooms at the motel, now deserted and closed.

How the cloud became saturated with various radioisotopes is not known. What is known is that several types, including cesium, polonium and tritium are available at low cost from the Atomic Energy Commission. Among the items for which the prices are cut is carbon-14, widely used not only for medical research but also industrial applications.

Bukid, and Sapsap. We also have: Frozen Sarawang Dilis, Tanigi, Talakitok, Saluyot, Labong, Malunggay and Aampalaya leaves. Also, for Americans, turkey sandwiches, cigarettes, rolls, coffee and pies. We offer free delivery within a 50-kilometer radius. Charge accounts available. Pay in any world currency. You can find us at 900 Arden Blvd.

NEUTRODYNE HEALTH SERVICE

In the Neutrodyne Isolation Hospital at the Lower Farm, things go on much as usual. The patients chatter ceaselessly, calling out to one another from bed to bed. These are the activities that make neuts joyful: they trade some pathetic article from their bedside vanity for another neut's pillowcase, and the males never fail to display their prodigious members whenever a nurse appears. This is what the neuts fear: to feel the doctor's calloused hands palpating their soft bellies.

SEVENTEEN GOLEMS ATTACK HITLER

Revisiting Unknown History

A walk in the sunshine will do no harm to most mortals. Adolph Hitler is an exception, as we saw yesterday. He fell to the sidewalk on the Champs-Élysées, wincing as the golems danced a hornpipe on his head, thighs, face, neck, trunk and feet and plucked every hair of his mustache and stuffed them up his Nazi nose. The trouble with these French golems is they bungle the job, maiming where they mean to murder, hacking instead of incising, generally diddling the body badly.

When they saw Adolph, the golems said, "We know that man, and he don't give a damn about us." So it was that Adolph,

173

feeling bold enough to step into a neighborhood not his own, found his tormentors. In his mind, he heard the gavel of the People's Justices hitting a polished oak surface.

Effie Pfeffer, Ph.D.

On the Road to History

CASE TO SEEK PRESIDENCY

News Release

Folks, this is Justin Case, Pisstown assemblyman. I want to be your next president and I am announcing my candidacy today. Here's my platform in a nutshell: Corrupt the young, get them away from religion and give them an interest in sex and the low life. Make them hollow and superficial, destroy their ruggedness. Divide the people into hostile groups by constantly harping on pseudo-controversy and matters of little importance. Get people's minds off the government tricksters by focusing their attention on football games and other, often staged, colossal events. Give them sexy novels to read, plays and other trivialities. The only art is conceptual art. Always preach true democracy while seizing power and control over the treasury of events. Be ruthless, ferret-like, take the advantage. Destroy the people's faith in their natural leaders by holding the latter up to ridicule, contempt and scorn. By encouraging government extravagance, destroy its credit, produce fear of inflation. Hike prices, speak of shortages, of hope that things will be better. Products to improve their lives will be on every radio, TV, magazine and newspaper. Zanzetti's new Life Fluff is a shameful hoax, however, designed to encourage false visions in the eyes of the old and infirm. I am Justin Case and I want to be your president. Vote for me next April. Don't wait or vote on impulse for anyone else, and keep a crowbar and a gun around the house, just in case.

TROCHILICS STRIKE GAS FLATS

The diminutive murderers spun dizzily down Mainline Street on their ball bearing toes, razor blades poking from big toenails. It was their screeching call to violence. Everyone within a mile heard the grinding, metallic sound. After savaging the Flats, slicing ankles wherever they spun, the troupe rolled off in their little shuttle bus. Who knows where they will head next? Of concern to Gas Flaters, perhaps more than their bleeding ankles, is how to clean up the smelly yellow droppings the trochilics left in their wake, inches deep in downtown streets, steaming in the afternoon sun.

GONS OPENS EATERY

The Gons' new restaurant, the Blue Pearl, owned and managed by Merle Wunty, the governor's brother, is finally open atop the penthouse suite of the Gons Hotel. The restaurant's roomiest, fanciest halls, with their abundant, multicolor lighting, will house its large collection of Etruscan statuary, embossed paintings, dazzling chandeliers, stylish seating covered in velvet, and thousands of gold-covered bronze pieces, all highlighted by a roaring oak fire in the restaurant hearth. Such masterpieces create a sense of grandeur and magnificence as diners experience the very best in fine dining. Today, hotel guests will be served a dinner of sea slug ragout with imperial black rice and Yankee-weed salad, paired with bottomless glasses of Carlo Rossi '61, a fine burgundy. All for $88.88. The Blue Pearl will sometimes offer an entree of *pompano en papillote* with a dessert of *pain perdu,* paired with an award-winning muscatel from Onēba's Vineyards. WE AIM TO PUT MADAM DUNBAR'S OUT OF BUSINESS.

City Moon,

Onēba here with a few things to say about life and death. As I lay dead last year—or was it last century?—my grandfather came to my small room and I looked into his face. It shone with vigor and youth. Behind him, the roses on the bureau were dead. Grandfather carried a pan with a lump of fried liver. He dropped it, slipped in its grease and fractured his skull. The room now smelled of roses.

Things were peaceful where I was, very relaxed, *muy tranquil,* but quite boring. Death isn't so hot after the first few months. The soul hovers near the grave, under the earth, never straying far from the skeleton. Everything above seems like Florida, yet it's cold all the time. You sigh, you turn, you sigh again. Rock 'n' roll is remembered as heavenly music. There is nothing to eat and plenty to drink.

Readers, leave me alone. Don't write. I need rest.

Onēba

HUMAN HAIR THEFT

The recent string of unwanted haircuts in the City continues. Little girls, grown women and long-haired men are all potential victims of this pitiable nut. He pulls the victim down to the asphalt and applies chloroform via a sanitary napkin. This behavior has been described many times by his shaven subjects. Some say he mumbles in a barely articulate manner when he works his magic with Exacto knives and manual clippers. He has not injured anyone beyond minor abrasions and superficial cuts, although an overdose of chloroform did kill a young boy with curly black hair. Police are fearful of what they might find when the rogue barber is finally caught, and his apartment searched.

STORY CONTEST ENTRY

A Short Story of the Civil War
by
Bigsby Baker

Clarence Scales, a young American carrying an empty barrel to haul away the flayed chunks of bodies from the field of battle, did become aroused when pretty little Linda Westbrook refused to do what he demanded.

She said, "No, not this time."

Scales said, "Yes, Baby, this time."

All of a sudden, Linda's father, with a mad rush, blood in his eyes and a 10-inch shank in his hand, arrived. He said to Scales, "My lovely daughter tells me you've been on earth thirty-some odd years and you ain't yet learned how to respect womens, so I'm going to give you some experience and make you wise."

STAB! STAB!!! UNGUT!!!!

Scales was all but dead when he hit the floor, guts spilling everywhere.

The End

Bigsby: Carlos here. Thanks for submitting this dynamic little outline of a story. Because it lacks the least bit of length, depth, breadth or character development, we suggest you try again next year. And please remember, not every story ends in death, although some start with it, as in murder mysteries. Death as an ending resolves nothing plot-wise. One can't teach another a lesson by killing him. It goes against clear thought, appealing to the gut, not the head. Suggest you go to your nearest dictionary and look up deus ex machina.

YOU CAN SURVIVE THE BOMB

Now what? Here are eight parents and 10 children, three of them yours, sitting in an underground shelter with Armageddon burning its way into the new millennium overhead.

Everyone in the shelter is looking at you, making you angry and frustrated. Isn't it enough that you let them in and saved them from the insanity outside? What more do they expect?

Instead of cursing, you take a deep breath to stop trembling, and say, "I guess we'll be all right now. We'll get organized later, but we've got some things to do in a hurry."

The small children are left in the shelter under your care. The adults and bigger boys run outside to round up tools and equipment and fight small fires. You have told them to keep working until the first fallout or until they are called back to the shelter because of another approaching attack.

There is no second strike. You have 30 minutes to an hour, at most, before the fallout will start. You've told them that they will be able to see it like fine falling ash. The early fallout will not hurt them if they return to the shelter immediately.

You decide it would be helpful to talk about the psychology of shelter living, insofar as you are able. You realize the greatest hazard is panic, and the best weapon against panic is understanding. You tell them that from what you have read, there will be a period of severe depression, two, three, four days after entering the shelter. If they know this in advance, if they can recognize it when it comes, each person will be better able to cope with it and understand it in the others. Despair can set in during these depressions. After shock has worn off and the dreadful monotony of shelter life takes hold, activity is the best remedy. Each person should have regular tasks to perform. In the off-duty periods there should be reading, games, bull sessions—anything to keep from dwelling on one's self. Survival depends on adhesion to the group. You say, "We're all in this together, so let's act as a unit."

When the depression recedes after a few days and nights, you can expect a notable lift in spirits. People will start to talk about what they will do when they come out of the shelter, once Bunkerville authorities have brought things under control and the air is clear. Reconstruction? Yes. One of the older shelterers said, "I don't care, myself. I'm just about dead anyway. If it wasn't for my rheumatism, I'd take a stroll in the fallout."

They will start to wonder how to plant truck gardens, and how to find working trucks, tractors and gasoline, and what to do about the low-level radioactivity in the area. When this happens, you are over the hump. They have decided to take life on its new terms, whatever they may be. It's time to unlock the door, let them out and lock it again. If you hear screams, fingernails raking the door, desperate knockings, cries for food and water, their kids wailing, it's best to ignore them and hunker down for a long stay with plenty of food and water for you and your kids.

PALACE ORIENTA features knuckle, tripe, snoot and southern ribs on Wednesday nights. We have a play lot for the youngsters and stereophonic implants for the hard-of-hearing elders. Seated in the elegant mezzanine, you'll be looking down at the busy kitchen, seeing spotless preparation by professional cooks trained in our Pisstown école. What do you have to lose? Give us a fling. We don't let roaches nest in our salads.

AN EXPLORER GOES TO HELL

The first morning I awoke feeling more rested than ever. The inaugural astonishment: There wasn't enough fire there to roast a marshmallow. Hell, it seemed, had burned out long ago, and the cool drizzles since have turned everything into a slimy, black tar.

You notice familiar faces right away, asshole buddies from home in single file, squeezed along by the Devil's interns toward the flatball factory, one of the many cottage industries happening in the cooler Hell. For most of them, this work is the first real discipline in a long time. Hell doesn't seem too awful. But I've only seen the male Hell, I should say. A river of boiling plasma separates it from the female Hell.

I saw the Devil one day. He was going around inspecting

things, a tiny man, bearded, wearing only Jockey briefs. He was much nicer than your average joe-deity. He asked me if I was satisfied with my work in the flatball factory. I said, "Yes, sir, I've got eternity and all that stitching, gluing and rubbing with neutsfoot oil passes the time."

"Good then," he said, "I'm on my way to a bonfire. Enjoy your stay here and please give us good marks. We try to run a tight ship on your final voyage."

As I said before, Hell didn't seem so bad. But I wasn't allowed to cross that river of boiling plasma separating it from the female Hell, though I could hear anguished screams and fighting among the women.

Let me say, in closing, that the most cherished surprise of all were the "rooms of frosty discomfort." Apparently, lots were cast to determine which new arrivals would go to the rooms for the duration. The temperature was held at 32.5 degrees at all times, for all eternity. The occupants are naked, and the walls and floor where they sleep are nearly frozen.

I saw a few children in Kinder Hell, all soaking in tubs of super-heated feces. I saw teens sexing with flaming dicks and red-hot *vagines*. I saw that Hell was a far more complex and interesting environment than I ever imagined.

Effie Pfeffer
On the Road to History

A-BOMBS ON YOUR DOORSTEP

We hate to say it, but we think when things have come to the point where a person can order a small A-bomb and get it through the mail, peace is dead forever. The heart of the suitcase bomb is fissionable plutonium stuffed into a container no larger than a Coke bottle. It is flung. When it strikes a hard surface, the container implodes, yielding the characteristic mushroom cloud, though much smaller, no larger than an umbrella. The effects on a small area are devastating. A restroom in Detroit got one yesterday that erased just one person, but left the bathroom unusable and the corpse unburiable for a thousand years.

DOPE IN AMERICA

Editorial

Debbie Reynolds is dead. Why? Because she swallowed Drano in a public bathroom. Why did she do that? She was high on the new drug, Solex-43. It affects everyone in a different way. You might think you're at a Noxage party, so you swallow a few Sols. Unlike with Noxage, the mind-trips begin with a vengeance. No matter what, you can't abuse Sol-43 or it will turn on you like a Doberman. It will come at you with a bleeding hunk of your subconscious in its mouth, with a bone to pick, so temper yourself when you use it.

Your editors, always looking for the bottom line of any story, ingested a healthy dose of this new drug dissolved in a cherry-flavored liquid and were placed in small, featureless cells, where we endured convulsions lasting up to six hours and had terrible hallucinations, like so many of today's Sol-43 addicts. If you want to quit, apply for admittance to the Lower Farm Rehab Unit, Box 591 City.

NEW PISSTOWN MAYOR HAS VISIONS FOR THE FUTURE

Darlene Wunty, eldest daughter of the governor at age 30, just elected to her fifth three-month term, says she wants Pisstown freeways to run underground, Pisstown people to live underground, leaving the earth above to return to its virginal conditions through the eons, until the railroad era of yesterday is achieved, and the rosy, pine-scented past is returned to us.

"They say that time travel isn't far off," Ms. Wunty tells reporters. She predicts Chicago will be the first real city to commit to the gay '90s and "look for Detroit to head for the year 3000, and for Des Moines to stay put."

The governor, pulling the microphone from Darlene's hand, spoke to the crowd of reporters. "It is almost unbelievable what she can do with a top.... Show them, girl." He opened a gilded box and handed her a brightly colored top, wound with fresh white string.

In a flash, the top spins in front of her, behind her, over her head, in her hand, on a string and wherever she directs.

"You see," the governor said, "What city could ever hope to have a better mayor than my daughter, Darlene?"

A review of the facts shows that Ms. Wunty has been a popular mayor in Pisstown. Her proposed strategy for ending the wave of hangings plaguing area cities, even as far inland as Gas Flats, is to forbid the sale of rope. If her proposal is adopted, anyone in possession of ropes of any kind or other hanging aids will be arrested. Anyone caught selling these items will be executed by hanging.

BLOODLESS COUP IN D.C.

Editorial

Now America has the first occidental animal president in the White House. Not a shot was fired. He is tall and owl-like, with brown spots, an overall shapelessness and a grinding beak inside a toothy, radular mouth. His laundered white shirts are no sooner doffed than soiled. His skin sores mess up the presidential linens and his so-called face sticks to the pillow case.

The Lincoln Room carpets have been fouled repeatedly by his incontinent droppings. His limousine is like a hog's trough. Inside sources have seen him eating live crabs in the White House alley in full daylight. One of them said, "Sometimes we find him snoring like a buzz saw in the rear seats of public buses, his tie smeared with vomit, attracting all manner of flies. We have to ply the drivers and passengers with fresh hundreds to stay mum about these incidents."

Now the new president wings his way to Memphis and engages in sordid reverie, frequenting the brothels there, sodomizing men and women alike, and they are helpless to complain because he is commander-in-chief. He is too busy groveling for food and soiling himself to think about war. His major accomplishments as president, he predicts, will be passing pending zoo-reform bills.

He can be as gentle as a puppy or as lethal as a saw-scaled viper. Word went out ahead of time about the president's animal nature, so that he did not embarrass us in front of the world when he ate a goat's leg in the Senate bathroom, or when he called for all ambassadors to be caged and given only straw to sleep on and slop to eat for a week or two.

Born in a survivor camp near Little Rock, the animal

president lay useless as a stone for many years, an outrage to those who claimed that no animal could descend from the loins of a woman. He was not an animal, however, in the ordinary way. His body was never fitted for so much as a day of work, he hated the sun, he humped about at night in his room, and his poor parents found their lawn littered in the morning with many species of trash, including desiccated lumps of chewed mice, millipedes and barn swallows.

The parents received hate calls, vicious attacks by nameless parties. And so, one day, when a moving van arrived to take their progeny from them, they did not raise a whisper against it, though they knew no more why the van came than why their son was born in the first place.

Though he is a carnivore at heart, the animal president has a fondness for pastry. Hot donuts are served to him by custodial staff each morning when the laborious process of changing the sheets begins again.

Though he is an animal for all practical purposes, he is the only president we have for now (even though no one recalls voting for him) and should receive our respect and attention. We say, "Hail to the Chief!"

The Editors

PAEAN TO THE MOON

Oh, the Moon is up there in the sky now, make no mistake. But if the Moon dropped down, journeyed a great distance toward the Earth, and stopped, say, a mile over the plot you tilled to put in tomatoes, above your bluegrass park, hovering weightless over your golf courses lit up so grandly through the night, would it then appear larger to the human perceiver's eye? Would Old Mrs. Moon sing, hum or whistle a cheery tune during the descent? The answer to both questions is *We don't know*. What is sure about the lunar plunge is this: The oceans would rise in great tidal waves to sweep back and forth across all continents. Every few hours the seas would empty, leaving an unobstructed view of Davy Jones' scuzzy locker, a salvager's bonanza.

Zanzetti

City

THE PRAIRIE URCHIN

Science in Action

This urchin *(Pratum cynomys)* lives in burrows under the rich soil of Kansas and Nebraska. Similar in size to its cousin, the sea urchin, this creature emerges from its burrow in mid-summer, gulps great quantities of fresh air then inflates to many times its natural size and allows itself to be blown like tumbleweed across the High Plains, eating snatches of young vegetation as it goes.

Early settlers were plagued by prairie urchins, and their aggressive efforts to protect life-sustaining gardens and crops resulted in the near extinction of the creature.

Tumbleweeds have been shot at and set afire owing to their resemblance to the urchins. Dogs were useless for hunting them after once encountering the sharp spines. A shift in the wind often turned urchin hunters into the hunted.

Urchins have migrated north from Louisiana's sulfur pits, up the Mississippi's levee system, finally settling in the Great

Plains. It is likely they evolved rather quickly, Lamarckian style, in only one generation from the *Diadema* urchin, whose rock boring ability accounts for the honey-combed surface of the coral rocks of the Bahamas and elsewhere.

The Great Plains sandstone is perfect material for burrowing out a strong chamber when winter approaches. Should the sunrise catch a prairie urchin far from its burrow, it may duck into a farm pond or muddy stream until dusk.

Professor D. Hannity, Ph.D.
Crypto Zoology Wing
Hall of Mummies

BUNKERVILLE HANGINGS OUT OF CONTROL

Editorial

When are these hangings going to stop? We can't go out of our homes without seeing them dangling from our eaves like bats. Their faces turn bluish, leaping dogs snap at their feet, trying to pull their shoes off. We ride on public transit buses and they're hanging from the leather grab-straps. Whoever says this mode is painless is dead wrong.

Is all this hanging the latest craze? If we don't put a stop to it, and to TV coverage of them night and day, kids will be doing it next. You'll go to their rooms and find them hanging from Daddy's belt in the closet. You'll rescue them, but there'll be mild brain damage.

One of our reporters has seen teens hanging in the basement of the YMCA building. Some have hung themselves from the live oaks in Wuntex Park, near the 10-acre lagoon, their bodies swishing in the southern breezes, horse flies gathering, their clothes torn away by roving necronauts looking for spiffier wearables.

The hangings hover over us like dark clouds. Gnats swirl around their dead faces at dusk and at night under subtle landscape lighting. Anyone visiting here will be appalled by what they see. There are eight bodies hanging from Bunkerville's grand entry arch. It must stop. Someone must act!

SMALL HEAD LOOK? Is your head too big? Are you too tall? We'll shrink you and your head for only $199. The process is moderately painful, takes several days and comes with a limited guarantee. Call Bywater 5115. Ask for Pinhead Jerry.

SECOND NOTICE Please, don't forget to move your peonies this October and place them at the head of the grave in direct line with the stones so they will not be destroyed when we dispose of last year's flowers and unearth the older remains. Eternity Meadows Cemetery Association. Box 23, Pisstown.

Dear *City Moon,*
Unidentified neutrodynes razz me nightly as I sit on my porch. They come in pairs, carrying wooden buckets. They spend the night spitting at one another and carrying on with a deafening noise. Sometimes they fill their buckets at my pump and sit around the well like children, dipping their horny fists into the water, trying to fetch the moon. Can't the City put some controls on this?
Laurie Larkin
Curb the Neutrodynes Inc. Peabody Junction

POD EJECTS PILOT

A pod-like capsule of considerable size and weight, with no visible power or energy source, dumped a large "form" onto the middle of Arden Blvd. Traffic stopped. Crows assembled on electric lines to watch. The form suddenly was endowed with life, bouncing, whirling, jumping, darting all over the street and through a plate glass window at the endlessly remodeled Lagoon Cafe in Wuntex Park. Chinaware and drinking glasses were knocked about with a splintered clatter; diners and passersby were panic stricken, staggering breathlessly on the sidewalk.

The neighborhood lay in awe and wonderment until the thing spent its force and crumbled in the gutter, panting, exhausted. All this, it may be said, is not a common occurrence. It actually happened, however, last afternoon. The amount of yellow, sulfurous mist that came from its mouth condensed above us into an envelope, and the sun shone through it with multiplied ferocity. The cheeks of our loved ones now flower with rash and blister.

Later, a motorman was hauling this radical new life form on the deck of a trailer van, strapped securely, he thought, encircled by inch-thick iron cable. But no, it rolled off at a narrow turn. It hit the pavement in such a manner as to break the valve connected to the faceplate. Escaping gas got into the works, causing all its numerous tentacled orifices to open and spew the choking mist. The motorman looked back, not believing his eyes. The thing seemed to take after him and he applied his foot to the accelerator.

When the new, radical life form was spent, and it seemed to be breathing its last, some valorous soul, an elderly necronaut, went up to it and stroked it kindly. It remained perfectly still for a minute then sprayed a mist as sweet as azalea in spring.

Little is understood about the new form. Some say it was an astral traveler from another era, differently evolved than us, others, that whatever it is or wherever it came from, they want it buried deep.

The dead life form will be interred at Eternity Meadows tomorrow at 6 a.m. A sexton at the cemetery tells our reporter that he will personally operate a backhoe all night, digging a deep, wide grave. "We don't want this sucker coming back up," he said, "so we're going extra deep, maybe 20 feet, maybe 30, and we'll pour a slab on top."

AMERICAN BUM IN GRUESOME SUICIDE

Typical of American bums who've settled in Germany, this one had his plug hat, umbrella and fiddle close at hand. He amused himself by giving his fellow prisoners charts of their phrenological traits and playing his fiddle.

One night he broke out of the Manheim *Gefängnis* (jail) and in his aimless wanderings reached *Gonshafen,* a village nine miles to the southwest. There he was taken into custody and placed in the lockup where he had access to a stove. That night he heated the poker red hot, placed the end against the wall and threw himself against the point. The instrument plowed its way into his abdomen, searing organs and vessels.

Another bum, named Chatterjee, occupied the cell with him but was asleep when this unfortunate American took the drastic action, so it is not known how long he survived.

HALFLIFE NATIONAL HOUSING Things begin to happen when you make the move to HNH. We feature new self-mowing lawns as well as a self-tending garden plot for every Halflife unit. In the kitchenette, tenants will find a Radarama Mini Oven to cook all the frozen meals you'll find in the freezer. There are no neuts living the good life at Halflife. Free beer, wine and frozen food delivery on weekends. No need, really, to ever leave the unit except to ride our underground tollway to your place of employment and back again at the end of the day. You'll never lose a moment of sleep once you whiff the pristine atmosphere and sip the cool water from our many artesian wells. Come alive. Live at Halflife. For a free brochure, write us c/o *City Moon*, Box 591

City Moon,

In 1967 and '68 I published UFO reports as a student at Onēba Institute. As a result, I have been subjected to drugs in food and water, to caustic gases in the air, and to sabotage to my motor vehicles (brakes have gone out on hills, wheels have come loose, the steering pin has dropped out while going 50 mph).

I live in isolation but not alone. I have found footprints in whitewash and fresh concrete where no person could have access. I have heard sounds in my room at night like the plop of little doors closing, the hiss of escaping gas and banging in the wood stove. Once, when I had just started a fire in it, the draft reversed, sending flames two feet into the room and dumping 12 smoldering chimney swifts onto my precious Turkish wedding kilim.

During this period of troubles, I was using certain drugs, including arsenic (for that greenish facial flush), heroin and LSD. These caused intense bellyaches, diarrhea and uncontrollable shaking.

Pozeki Mott

Lifespan Institute
Lower Farm

ONĒBA, NUDE, WALKS THROUGH HOSPITAL LOBBY

From the Archives

At 3 a.m. security guards at Hotel Dieu, a mental health facility on the City's east side, reported that a completely naked man walked into the main lobby of the hospital, bellowing that he was Onēba, and was taken to the emergency department. It appeared he had been in a fight. His nose bled, his face was bruised, his jaw displaced, and one eye was swollen closed.

Police say the only information they could get out of him was that he was on the way to Pisstown to deliver a talk when he was beaten by two neutrodyne thugs who tore away his clothes and hurled them as far as they could and left his shoes in the driveway next door.

Police say they found Onēba's shoes in the driveway, but never located the rest of his clothes. They also report that he appeared to be in shock or suffering from a mental disorder. There was no arrest.

EATING CHAMP DIES WITH HER NAPKIN ON

The last reckoning caught up with 47-year-old Dotty Dillard of Peabody Junction, competitive eating champion, yesterday. She had been arrested many times in the past, police said, for stuffing herself in restaurants and not paying her bill. Yesterday was no exception. She came into the Squat 'n' Gobble for supper, sat at a table and tucked into a plate of cold Virginia ham and buttered biscuits, followed by a crisp roast knuckle of pork with scalloped potatoes and dark bread alongside schooner after schooner of Bohemian beer.

A physician sitting at the next table ran to help when Dillard fell forward moaning, gasping for breath, choking on a piece of pork. Earlier in the day, three summonses had been taken out against the eating champion for eating meals and evading payment.

On the day of her death, she had had an earlier lunch at Madam Dunbar's of cockaleeki soup, herring with onions and cream, pork cheek wrapped in wilted cabbage, mashed Idaho potatoes, a large dish of spumoni, three slices of cream cake and five or six sugared coffees. She made her pay-free exit through a rear door marked Emergency.

PRESIDENT'S CHILDREN HELD FOR RANSOM

The president's one son, Ham, and his three daughters, Vivien, Mandy and Reba, were sent incognito and unguarded through the Midwest where they were to work as a team selling box candy, greeting cards, salve, talcum, crackers and Mexican dolls door to door to the homebound. Unfortunately, this made them easy targets for kidnapping. The president worried about that possibility, but thought that their activities, once revealed, were bound to have a bracing effect on those who feared that timidity had overtaken the country's leadership and that it was all worth the risk.

Not a week into the siblings' Midwest sales route, they were, as feared, kidnapped by a party of neutrodynes and dragged off to a waiting motor home, half the tires flat, and driven away.

When news of the situation reached the Oval Office, the business of day to day governance came to a standstill as the president sat weeping in the Rose Garden, soaking his feet in a basin of plum vinegar, waiting for the inevitable ransom demand from the neuts.

"Why the feet in the vinegar, sir?" a reporter asked, smiling, lightening the mood.

"It toughens up the skin," the president said, "and keeps fungus at bay."

After two weeks without a ransom demand or any contact with the kidnappers, the president's spirit grew ever darker. "Missing troops are often dead ones," he told his staff.

The wait has continued now for three months.

MISS MARIE'S PLEASURE PARLOR WELCOMES YOU
Five-minute finger waves $5. In New York City, you can pay $50 for the same service. If you're into a flourish of pedo, I can have a Fire Scout here in 10 minutes. My palm oil body rubs will put you in a coma, cheap at $2. Call me at Bywater 5115 for an appointment.

ONĒBA SITS WITH SNAKES

On his return from Pretoria, where he had established his record of 36 hours in a snake pit, Onēba spoke to a *City Moon* reporter beneath a wing pod of his sleek silver Whisperjet. He told the reporter he was anxious to sleep in a real bed once again. "I'm bloody glad to be out of that pit," he said. He had trained for months to sleep motionlessly, sitting in still poses for hours on end, to seem dead to the snakes and to wake up in the same position. "It didn't help. Not a wink of sleep in all those hours. I wanted the record, though, and the championship, but it was a challenge to my knowledge of reptiles and control of my body."

Onēba spent the Xmas holidays cooped up with six puff adders, six Egyptian cobras, six black mambas and six boomslangs at the Gas Flats snake pit. On two occasions, he says, snakes devoured other snakes. Replacements were quickly made to keep the number at 24.

On emerging unscathed from the pit, Onēba announced his intention to run for president of the United States. It will be his fourth campaign for the office, two of which were successful. During those terms, he signed significant legislation in a number of important areas, including the lower and upper farm system, the neutrodyne registration question and re-burial aid for necronauts.

A GHOST AT THE GONS

Gons guests have recently reported a "presence" they've heard or seen on the top floor. One described it as "somebody drunk outside my room, cursing, grumbling, reciting indecipherable verse then opening the window at the end of the hallway." Other guests also reported a drunken, grumbling presence staggering down the top floor hallway and opening a window. The night clerk, Kenny Norby, rushed upstairs when he heard a window thrown open and a shriek from one of the guests. "I saw who it was," Kornal said, "that old drunk poet that used to live up here ... Diddlebaum. Nobody ever heard of him. He got depressed one night, drank a lot of Drambuie, took some Noxage, and jumped."

PISSTOWN TUNNELS OPEN TO THE PUBLIC

Special to the City Moon

As we crowded into a small clothing store in downtown Pisstown, a section of the floor behind the counter suddenly rolled back like the hidden door in the *Arabian Nights*.

A guide led us down a long stairway to a brick-lined-tunnel, 26 feet below the street surface. We then walked for blocks through a maze of passageways until we came to a large, arch-ceilinged chamber.

We had arrived in the heart of one of the main air raid shelters in this region of the country, part of a vast underground network of escape tunnels, storage rooms and emergency life-support and communications systems.

In six minutes 10,000 people can pour down into the shelter through more than 90 entrances. More interestingly, they do not have to stay cooped up like the Londoners in World War II. They can travel through tunnels more than five miles to escape into Pisstown's suburbs.

Thousands of neutrodyne workers have been laboring for years on the shelter system, digging with picks and shovels, and many more years will be needed to complete the project.

ONĒBA PRODUCTS Everyone knows that the adulteration of the common frank with beef lips, penises and salivary glands is standard practice. Very few know that every popular brand of cereal contains a substantial proportion of rat droppings and even fewer know that these droppings are more nutritious and contain more protein than the cereal itself. This overlooked resource can now be harnessed. ONĒBA PRODUCTS is pleased to announce a new line of nutritious and tasty breakfast cakes. These discreet little boluses are a pleasant dark brown color and contain TEN TIMES the protein found in regular cereal. We offer also large packages of the new, sweet-smelling RAT DROPS. The tiny hard-candy drops are GUARANTEED to freshen the breath without harming delicate nasal membranes.

IS ONĒBA ALIVE?

Onēba has been missing for two years and three months. Readers wonder, has he been kidnapped? Has he been assassinated? Is he alive?

Onēba did not show up in court Wednesday, as ordered, to prove he was among the living. But his lawyer, Gloria Wunty, did show up and said the attempt by two shareholders in Onēba Industries to have him declared legally dead smacks of blackmail.

The lawyer for the court, Chester Davis, in a move for dismissal of the suit, said, "The inference is plain that if the plaintiffs make enough of a nuisance of themselves, someone will pay them to go away."

Supreme Court Justice Bernard Nadle signed an order giving Onēba until Wednesday to prove he is still alive and reserved a decision on the Davis motion.

A spokesperson for Onēba Industries has repeatedly said Onēba is alive and well and staying at an undisclosed location. "He's mulling things over, drawing mental plans for some sort of future we can live with and prosper."

Repeated requests for photographic proof that Onēba is still with us have been denied.

STORY CONTEST ENTRY

Lunar
by
James Greywood

Karen could hardly hear what the club owner was saying. The electro-music was loud. "I said," he repeated slowly and loudly, "I'll do it for you for a hundred bucks. But if I am going to do a cheap eye transplant, you must do something for me, too. You understand?"

Karen still seemed confused, but she nodded yes anyway. She didn't want to offend. She needed help and she needed it badly, and she'd heard that this man, Garbald, was just the one to give her the kind of help she needed. Garbald was an Austrian and really knew the ropes, everyone said.

"Now here's the offer," Garbald said, "I and my wife, Ingra, have some business in Copenhagen. You'll come with us, understand, and we'll do the eye transplant in Denmark. The laws are looser.

The only thing is, you'll have to carry something for us."

"Sure," Karen said. "Nothing hard about that."

"I don't mean a suitcase."

She looked perplexed again.

"We're …" Karen couldn't hear the rest of it. The electro music was really blaring now.

Then Garbald leaned still closer to Karen. "We're smuggling some plutonium to the terrorists there."

She blanched. "But I…" She was frightened. American kids who get caught with radioactive materials in Europe are up against a tough system. Authorities there don't like Americans to begin with, and they love being rough on U.S. kids who they catch holding a little U-238, let alone smuggling it.

The idea scared Karen.

"There won't be any problems," said Garbald. "The method is foolproof. We put the stuff in a vaginal suppository. There's no chance anyone would find it … unless …," he smiled liplessly, "you get friendly with a border guard."

Karen had to laugh at that. Ball a border guard? Hardly. She already had an overload of problems, being pregnant for one as well as having a diseased eye. But then she thought again, *Smuggling? Plutonium?*

"You'll be like James Bond," Garbald said, "but with a need to douche as soon as possible. We think the plutonium is well shielded. Still we recommend removing it from your body at the earliest opportunity after the flight."

Karen thought, *It's really a great way to rip off the establishment.* She liked that aspect of the plan. What she didn't like about it was placing that plutonium so near her developing fetus. What if the capsule had a leak?

"You'll be doing something for the future of that kid and all the others waiting to be born," Garbald assured her. "We're bringing them the quality fissionable materials they need to supply parties in the Mideast. Atoms for peace, you know."

It would not be just an adventure, but almost a quiet crusade. At last she would be doing something meaningful.

The electro-music suddenly thundered to a halt and just as suddenly there was the sharp sound of a cracking whip.

"Okay, folks," said Nazar Singh, an Indian dope dealer, stepping to the front of the small area where the band played. "Get ready for the show, and if you like it, remember, when the hat is passed, drop freely!"

Everyone laughed, and a few of the 60 or 70 spectators applauded as well.

"Come on, sweet thing," said Nazar, cracking the whip again.

Amy Kath, the band's lead vocalist, dazed, walked out of the shadows zonked to the eyeballs.

Nazar took her hand, brought her close and began to unbutton her blue denim blouse. In seconds it was off. She wore no bra.

Nazar leaned down, cupped her right breast in his swarthy left hand and flicked his tongue across her budding nipple. He slipped the hard handle of the whip between her legs and rubbed it back and forth, at first slowly, then gradually increasing the tempo until it was throbbing back and forth like a pneumatic drill.

As Amy began to respond, moaning and swaying her hips, Nazar dropped his hand from her breast, all the while keeping up the pumping motion with the other, and reached for the top button of her Levi's.

To their left, Moana, the flautist, watched with only half

interest. *Just another freako scene,* she thought, *another whacked out way of trying to avoid reality, to avoid problems.*

She didn't like this type of scene at all. Too public, too perverted. She glanced away and began to absently swirl the wine in her glass, the wine the drummer had drugged, her mind on where she was going, what she was doing, where any of them were going, what any of them were doing with their lives. Something just seemed empty about their entire existence.

Engrossed in these thoughts, she didn't notice Nazar's supplier as he sat down next to her.

"Too much, huh?" he grinned, nodding with approval in the direction of Nazar and Amy, both of whom were now stripped.

"Yeah," said Moana, rising.

"Hey, baby," the supplier said, surprised. "Stick a bit. The party's just begun."

Moana didn't say a word. She raised the glass and suddenly flipped it over, dumping the wine on him, drenching him, then turned around and headed through the crowd. She stepped over and around the prone bodies, easing past all the glazed faces, heading for the long corridor out.

Nearing the door, she heard the whip crack again and Nazar yelling, "Beg for it! Beg for it!"

"Please," came the reply. Then the whip again meeting flesh. And a soft moan. Once more the whip cracked, followed by a shrill scream.

Yes, the party was beginning. And Moana knew, from seeing other "demento" sessions, it would end with two or three more guys, plus a chick or two as well, all simultaneously messing with Amy's mind and body at the same time.

Some party. Strictly freaksville.

Now, as Moana opened the front door, letting the fresh air of an early Amsterdam morning bathe her face, she heard the girl scream once more. Only this time the scream was louder, more plaintive, more painful!

Moana slammed the door behind her and ran.

The End

James, this is the longest entry we've received thus far. That alone gives you some credence. The story works well on many levels of characterization: the patrimony, oafishness and cruelty in the person of Nazar, the easily persuadable Amy, and the ever-skeptical Moana. Nice array of characters. Keep up the good work.

Carlos

ONLY IN AMERICA

Editorial

Reports have come to this office of the unsanitary conditions that have begun to arise as the result of the recent nationwide garbage strike. Little boys and one girl were seen running barefoot through great steaming mounds of trash and refuse on lower Arden Boulevard, where *City Moon* offices are located. Their childish cheerfulness is undimmed by the fact that with every passing day, another 20,000 tons of garbage is added to the heaps already rotting in the hot July sun. On the Upper East Side, the already critical dog litter problem has been further aggravated by a street sweeper slowdown and talk of the plague is on everyone's tongue. We knew this could happen. None can say we weren't forewarned.

And there is no one who can go up to the striking garbage men, with their crudely lettered "STINK CITY" placards and their brutish oaths, and say, "I'm very sorry but somebody has to pick up the garbage and on this particular turn of the wheel it looks like you."

No sir, there just isn't anybody who has the kind of charisma you need for a job like that. Even the funny artists downtown in their Hawaiian shirts and Dinah Shore sunglasses, normally a very community-minded section of the population of the City, have retreated to their picturesque lofts and their superstar bars, there to mull sadly over endless Campari and sodas while they contemplate the likelihood that uptown streets will be among the first to suffer actual blockage by refuse every day. Many tons of garbage and waste lumber are put out on the sidewalks and cobbled streets of the historic neighborhood.

UPPER FARM GARDEN CLUB HOLDS A MEETING

"Enteric Precautions" was the club's topic of discussion, with a prepared text by Sovietskia Moldavia. The event was fully attended. Miss Moldavia included in her lecture a color slide presentation of famously soiled linens from the Animal President's bed and bath. Also, she read articles on the subject from the Journal of the American Medical Association, and afterwards a Process "bishop" led the club through the 100-acre neutrodyne community gardens and cemetery, where well-tended garden beds snaked around the scattered crate-wood grave markers. Club members selected ripe, prize-winning melons, dug up ground nuts and picked pears and cucumbers for an impromptu lunch on the ground. Neutrodyne youngsters squatted nearby and looked on with great interest, bright red tongues licking blue lips.

PISSTOWN WELCOMES SPACE-TRAVELED INDIAN GURU

He calls himself Master Ray-X and claims to be of no specific gender. "Call me he, call me she, call me it, I don't care," it has said. Residents are invited to look at it through a viewing port. It's on display in a small, sealed, germ-free cubicle. Here, behind new titanium-alloy shielding and lead glass it can be seen staring distantly off and playing with its fingers. It rarely speaks and then only to ask for a rare oil, in its native Gujarati dialect, with which to smooth and groom the long, silky-black hair of its foot-long chin beard.

Every day Ray-X is furnished with a white linen *dowdow* and turban. Observers claim they can detect a cosmic and benign sadness in its misty, deep-black eyes; surely this great space traveler deserves a better fate than to be locked up and gawked at. Its occult powers are well known, and yet jailers have allowed it to continue wearing a golden serpent ring. Why? The public demands answers.

EXCLUSIVE TO THE MOON: THE VEEBLE PEOPLE

This reporter remembers the Veeble People, an offshoot of the

Process Church. Only twenty or thirty in number, they slow-marched through the parched, fire-wasted prairies and fields of Kansas, rejecting many offers of water, yet drank at least a pint of their homemade cough syrup every day.

In the August 1962 issue of *Pen Pals Review*, the Veeble People were first introduced to the public. The so-called founder of this sad appendage of the human potential movement was one Gary Addison Taylor, who is presently standing trial in Gas Flats for three counts of aggravated attempted rape of necronaut females, one count of sodomizing neutrodyne males, the rape of a 16-year-old Asian girl and the murder of a 21-year-old go-go dancer.

As soon as she learned of her ex-hubby's dilemma, Taylor's estranged wife called Gas Flats long distance to "put her two cents worth into what went on." Just to throw the police off the scent, she told them that when she and Taylor were still a twosome he let her in on a little secret: that he had killed four people once on Texoma Beach. That had never happened, she thought. He was just making it up. Her idea was that police would have to conduct an expensive investigation into the false claim, delaying the other cases for untold years, while Taylor remained out on bond, anxious to couple with her.

Investigators were dispatched to Texoma Beach where they found, buried outside the window of a home belonging to the Johnson family, the bodies of two women wrapped in plastic yard waste bags. Behind the house, they found another woman's nude body buried hastily in a shallow excavation.

Before the Johnsons bought the house, investigators discovered, Taylor had hung his hat there in the old days when he was going by the name "Phantom Sniper of the Beach."

Dr. Julius Robey, Taylor's appointed physician, said that, in his professional opinion, Taylor was not dangerous as long as he drank a pint of cough syrup every day. The Veeble People have agreed to supply him. They think that everyone should drink as much cough medicine as they can choke down without drinking anything else, especially water.

How they came to be called the Veeble People is not known, even to them.

David de Chadenides,
East Coast stringer

HISTORICAL FACT

In A.D. 1196 the Persian sultan Melik al Aziz decided to destroy the pyramids. He mobilized tens of thousands of workmen and spent fantastic sums of money with negligible results. His workmen attacked the Red Pyramid, the smallest of the three. Every day, with great effort, they removed one or two stones. Each one was buried in the sand when it fell and had to be lifted out. After eight months of exhausting labor, the demolition was abandoned. Today, from a distance, the pyramid appears undamaged.

Effie Pfeffer, Ph.D.
On the Road to History

RAT-TAIL COMB HORROR

At 3 p.m. last Thursday afternoon, over a quiet lunch of clabber
with A-1 Sauce in the secluded but sunny patio of his modest
San Clemente home, the Noxin necronaut was stabbed in the
throat by a loner with a rat-tailed comb. Clad in a faded 1958
boy scout uniform and brandishing a lethal comb, the intruder
entered the Algerian style patio during the lunch break of Secret
Service agents assigned to guard the ex-president. He rushed
up to Noxin, whose attention was held by a letter he'd receive
that morning from Bob Hope, and plunged the 6-inch tail of
the comb into his neck, nearly severing a major artery. The
wound, deep but confined to muscle tissue, was cleaned and
stitched closed. The ex-president will be fine. The intruder, a
neutrodyne by the name of Little Toni Derando, is on tap to
die again by hanging Friday a week in Wuntex Park. Entry fee:
$1. Food trucks in the area: Asian, Tex-Mex, Indian, American,
neutrodyne and Soul.

CRONKITE NECRONAUT HOSTS BARBECUE

"Old Walt," as he was known to his closest friends, and who
fancies himself an unsurpassed sauce maker, slowly sprinkled
cayenne and paprika onto the 20 fat young possums on the
grill with abandon, much to the chagrin of the pasty-faced
hundreds broiling under a Mississippi sun, waiting to eat. Hunter
Thompson was there, Castaneda, Ray Charles and the Rayettes,
even the latest returning necronaut, Bert Lahr.

The Cronkite movements were slow, his joints dry. His

bones, barely contained by the flesh, crackled and popped when he moved. This new life among us was much on his mind as the possums bubbled and sizzled and hissed. The hungry "'sippians" out there were restless. To calm them, Cronkite shouted, "The possums'll be ready in an hour and a truck load of sweet corn is on the way." To everyone's surprise, one of the possums exploded, splashing hot turnips and green tomato stuffing onto Cronkite's leathery face. As the stuffing tumbled and dripped down from his chin to his apron, he assured everyone that all was fine. "I don't feel pain," he said. "It's the best thing about being dead."

HISTORICAL FACT

The Swedish astronomer Tycho Brahe, known for his solid gold nose and often called "The Gold Nosed Astronomer," lost his original fleshy smeller in a sword duel with his closest friend. It is also said of Tycho that he fractured a leg while stumbling through a meadow following the course of the moon and plummeting 10 feet into an empty cistern.

Tycho was known as a fine observer and recorder of the heavens, but poor at math and general ciphering. His daughter, Lorraine of St. Germaine, writes this in her diary about her father: "In the market today. I am so embarrassed. Father cannot tell what dry figs cost and has a struggle making change. His gold nose shines so brightly, but he cannot add two numbers."

The way Tycho met his death was both tragic and unusual, but not surprising. At a banquet held in his honor, where he was to become Sweden's National Astronomer, he refused by protocol to urinate before his highness did and died of a burst bladder after consuming quart after quart of stout.

He will be eternally remembered for his singular contribution to astronomy: The *lunarcentric* theory of the solar system. He thought the Moon was so close to Earth that it bounced on hilltops, skipping over houses and villages.

Dr. Effie Pfeffer

On the Road to History

THE ART OF WHISTLING

A reporter has cabled this personal story.

My aunt, as it happens, was in her youth an artistic whistler. She had perfected her technique to a point that she could straight-read and whistle Mozart flute parts. She traveled overseas to Italy during the Second War with a USO-sponsored whistling choir. She was to render Italian patriotic tunes in SATB harmony.

At this time, she had a crush on the bass whistler, who was swinish, Italian and handsome. Later he was to become her husband and a world-renowned medical man, famous for his nose jobs. He taught in Russia; he fixed the nose of the dictator of Ecuador; he threw, with my aunt's aid, enormous international parties on the lawn of his Miami estate.

At one of them, my aunt and other accomplished whistlers took the stage without knowing that whistling at a public event, to Italians at that time, was a sign of displeasure. Although my aunt was and still is rather attractive, the other girls in the troupe were on the plain side, and consequently the Italian audience, mostly men, whistled back at the whistling choir.

The girls, unsure what to do, whistled bravely on, while the whistling men, inspired now to new heights of wolfishness, added catcalls and groans to the chorus. It was then that my uncle, an Italian himself, stepped fearlessly forward to defend the honor of the whistling girls. He carried a short shotgun and the matter was settled in a few minutes. Soon the whole audience was whistling artistically.

JUST AMONGST US *City Moon* **publishes a regular personals column where** *Moon* **readers can reach out and comfort one another in this world of sorrows and woes, hardships and futilities, even the day's little trials. Those having a good time of it can reach out to others having a bad time and talk it over. When even a single day of silver light shines on a miserable soul, the** *Moon* **is only too glad to be of help. For your protection, we provide STRICTLY CONFIDENTIAL** *Moon* **box numbers and furnish you with a low-cost re-mailing service at two cents per letter. Your personal message, up to 25 words, will be printed for only $2. Just send it with a check or money order to the** *City Moon* **office. P.O. Box 591, City. We are a bonded entity and promise absolute privacy. That's why we call it JUST AMONGST US.**

ALL KINDS OF DANISH CULTURE Young W/M desires Nordic bear massages, Oslo colonics. No phonies, please. Send photo wearing stressed Levi's with head shaved, oiled and shining to *Moon* **Box 591. No returns. No guarantees. No credit.**

SINATRA SINGS AGAIN

Recently Frank 'the Voice' Sinatra's necronaut sang for his supper at the Prop place on the North Fork east of here.

could America become a Sahara?

WEATHER

THE CITY MOON

Burning the Camp Fires of the Soul

VOL 9   NO 8   OCTOBER 31, 1975   *"Eventually, Why Not Now?"*   © The City Moon 1975   50 CENTS

Announcing

The City Moon would like to announce a change. Please address future correspondence c/o Editor Grauerhols, Box 842, Canal St. Sta. New York, NY, 10013. Thanx-- Ed.

.... STRANGE BIRTH ....

CLEVELAND
Gloria Hurd, a 29-inch dwarf, has given birth to an 18½-inch, 5-pound 9-ounce son who doctors say is normal.

The mother and child, named Anthony, were reported doing well after the birth by Cesarean

section on Wednesday. Miss Hurd, 23, is known as Tiny Tina in the carnival with which she travels. Friends said the father of the child is about 6 feet tall.

"When Gloria came into the hospital, she was all baby," said Miss Hurd's mother.

wake!

SIMPLE RULES

NEVER look up.
To avoid temporary blinding by the flash, never look up to see what's coming. When you drop on the floor or the ground, keep your face in your folded arms for at least 20 seconds after the explosion in order to keep flying glass out of your eyes.

ALWAYS shut windows and doors.
If the warning comes in time, shut all doors and windows and pull down the shades or blinds. Turn off all pilot lights, and close all stove and furnace doors.

ALWAYS drop flat on your stomach.
Even if you have only a few seconds' warning, whenever you are, drop flat on your stomach and put your face tight in your folded arms. Even if you've seen the flash, do the same thing right away.

ALWAYS follow instructions.
Instructions will come to you after a raid, by radio, sound truck or some other way. Follow them exactly.

NEVER start rumors.
A single wild rumor could start a panic that might cost you your life.

Will the Earth One Day Be Destroyed?

About the third day you'd feel much better and you'd get along fine for 10 or 12 days. Then one morning you might look at your pillow and find that your hair had begun to fall out. This might go on for a week after that, or until you were completely bald. During this time you'd also run a fever, and your bowels would run, and you'd feel rotten and "achey" all over. You might even have bloody spots on your skin and slight bleedings in your mouth. It's barely possible you might find that for a time you were unable to beget children, although you could still have sexual relations.

If anyone near you needs first aid, give it to him--according to the rules in the Red Cross or Boy Scout handbook.

MIST of DEATH

Logan, Texas. June 5. An inanimate object of considerable size and weight with no visible power or energy source, suddenly was animated with life, bounding, whirling, jumping, darting, all over the street and through a plate-glass window at the Squat 'n' Gobble Cafe. Chinaware and drinking glasses were knocked about with a splintered chatter, startled diners and passersby were panic-stricken and staggering breathless on the sidewalks. The neighborhood lay in awe and wonderment until the thing had spent its force and crumbled in the gutter panting, exhausted, all this, it may be said, is not a usual occurence. It actually happened, however, on First North Street here, in Logan, last evening. The amount of yellow, submarine mist which came in plumes from its mouth has condensed above us into an envelope. And the sun shines through it with multiplied ferocity. The cheeks of our loved ones now flower with rash and blister. A scoutman was hauling this radical new form on the deck of a trailer wag, strapped, he thought securely, encircled by rings of inch-thick iron cable. But no, it

So potent a single breath kills

rolled off at a narrow turn. It hit the pavement in such a manner as to break the valve connected to the faceplate, and then the escaping gas got into the works causing all of its numerous tentacled orifices to open and likewise spew the choking mist. The motorman looked back, not believing his eyes. The thing seemed to take after him and he applied his foot to the accelerator. When the escapade of the RADICAL FORM was over and it seemed to be breathing its last, some valorous soul went up to it and stroked it kindly. It remained perfectly still. Then somebody who seemed to know explained how it happened to this City Moon correspondent.   Ed. O.

Scientists Unveil Radical Forms

To the Moon some of the new forms are as delicate as European snowflakes, others as frightening as a pack of ratus ratus fighting in the pantry over a grain of rice. In these pages we have seen the Troohilios, the various Oneba's, old Noxin, the whitecaps, the afrocomb raking deaths in St. Louis, we've come to know about the new miracle life material called microfluff, the related life pods which killed so many Soviet cosmonauts. Now we remember the hideous final dinner of carp and the National trend to Carps parties. Who can forget the life and death of Governor Wunty, the prairie class incidents, and the white fish, Jody, looming at the bottom of City Lake. In this issue we show life and death mixing like milk and egg, how hush-puppies can be made of sawdust and chicory, and how to order one of the W. Prop Perpetual Wind Driven Yard Lights. We feature articles on Cockburn, the newest hat in the political corona, also known as the Washington Star. Will America become a sandy waste by 1980. Read on and find out for certain. Box 842

Parakeets Invade-- The monk parakeet, once considered a harmless household pet, has turned into a major pest that threatens to upset the already delicate balance of the urbanized environment of the Atlantic coast. This chattering little bird with grey plumage vaguely resembling a friar's cowl has long been considered the scourge of agricultural areas in South America. Yet, despite its reputation, 50,000 or more of them were imported to the U.S. as pets between 1968 and 72. Several hundred of the birds are estimated to be living wild in New York City. While usually found in the subtropical regions of S. America, the birds can apparently survive winter temperatures of less than zero by building nests in the sheltered and heated nooks and crannies provided by air shafts and ventilation ducts.

Chemical Death Spillage-- More than 10,000 gallons of toxic sulphur monochloride were released from a ruptured pressure vessel during a fire at the D.A. Stuart Oil Co. plant on Chicago's Troy Street. Twenty tons of lime were used to neutralize the acid produced by the water used to fight the blaze. 3/20/73

OZAIO ALIVE

Traveling incognito the crooner was bound for Yellowstone Park, not knowing the park was closed. Feeling sorry for the poor, shriveled soul, the sheriff's wife, Caroline, invited him for dinner.

"Sorry, ma'am, but all I can eat anymore is clabber and fatback."

"I got clabber on the shelf and I'll fry up some fatback."

"Come on in," the sheriff said. "Sing us a song."

"My throat's all dried out, but I can drink some cooking oil or bacon fat and lubricate it."

After a bowl of clabber and fatback chunks, followed by a swallow or two of fat, with Caroline accompanying on piano, the famous crooning necronaut sang a hoarse, sometimes gurgling rendition of "That's Life" and was soon on his way to Carlsbad Caverns by back roads and by night.

NECRONAUTS RETURN WITH TALES TO TELL

Editorial

The recently returned, like Sal Mineo and Jimmy Durante, are telling tales of the Great Beyond that frighten and alarm the optimists among us. Was it Twain who said, "Heaven for climate, Hell for company"? How surprising! Not even he could have foreseen the fact of the matter, that Heaven is just a simple parcourse where the good dead jog, walk and do easy acrobatics forever.

This already recession-pissed, weary, ragtag nation could have easily done without such poor news. Is the mythical God a man like Vince Lombardi? Will we, the good in Heaven, be coached along the golden pony roads doing *grand jetés* and reeking of sweat? Mineo claims he was made to duck walk 10 miles, suffering agonies of the lumbar, bunioned feet, plantar wart and painful hammer toes.

TRUE FACTS ABOUT THE ANIMAL PRESIDENT

Only a day or two after entering the White House the president ordered that all the commodes be raised a full 24 inches so that his feet could swing freely and not touch the floor.

He once gave an FBI agent a "damned Russian" punishment for stepping on his shadow. The agent's bare feet were beaten by Marines with bats until they were bloody pulps.

Certain members of an FBI training class with small heads were flunked because he thought one of them "looked like a pinhead."

He forbade his drivers from making left turns and called the seat behind the driver the "death seat" and made his longtime VP sit in that position.

He once bought a sparrow dyed yellow from the Birdman of Alcatraz, who told him it was a canary.

He required that typed instructions be taped to radios and TVs in his hotel rooms so that he would "know how to turn the damned things off."

Effie Pfeffer
On the Road to History

SUICIDE BY WETNAP

Parmenides "Parmy" Johnson, an immigrant living in Gas Flats, killed himself in a new, lemon-scented way by sucking on a mouthful of napkin-size Wetnaps, which happen to contain a fair amount of deadly toluene.

The incident took place in the Squat'n'Gobble cafe, where the deceased ate a *pollo fundido* dinner with his family, chatting amiably all the while, until he began gathering a handful of Wetnaps from the table dispenser and stuffing them into his mouth.

Chemists say that even inhaling toluene for a short time may cause light-headedness, nausea, sleepiness, unconsciousness, even death. Chewing and swallowing Wetnaps would result in a more rapid onset of severe symptoms.

Johnson slid out of the booth and collapsed on the floor, gasping for air, bleeding slightly from the nose. His wife, Nadine, knelt over him, slapping his face to keep him awake. The kids, seemingly uninterested or in shock, played patty cake in the booth with greasy hands.

Johnson was taken by medical tuk-tuk to nearby Onēba General, where he died of liver failure at 5 a.m.

When asked for her account of the time preceding the suicide, Nadine said, "He was all upset 'cause he caught me f***ing our son, who's 15. That's all. I was just teaching the boy how to do it right, unlike his daddy. What's wrong with that? Who else is going to do it?"

   TOWN NEEDS DRUNK Position open immediately for the right person. We are a small, rural, Christian community of 500 in western Kansas that doesn't have a liquor store or a bar and doesn't tolerate drinking of alcohol at all. So, some folks are tempted to drive all the way to Bunkerville to buy their beer and whisky. To stop that behavior our town council has decided to hire a drunk to stagger around after dark, past every house, talking to himself, falling, vomiting, weeping, as

an example so that people see what they look like when they're wasted. If the mood strikes him, our drunk might pass out on somebody's lawn for special emphasis. It's a novel idea and we have faith it will work. A small apartment, stocked all the time with liquor and beer will be home to the drunk. Applicants write to Wheatfield Drunk Search, Box 591, *City Moon.*

NEUTRODYNE SCAMMING

Editorial

This is the latest neut scam. Their bloody artists are on the streets at all hours, pockets full of Noxage, nutmeg and spices, their side packs bulging with dog meat. They sip hot La Perla, rest a bit, then return to killing and boning dogs and selling the meat to Bunkervillians.

We at the *Moon* see no virtue in the common alley pooch. Throughout a flea-ridden history they have done little more than beshit our sidewalks and bite the ankles of our children. Dog bite infections are now as common as mosquito bites in Ketchikan.

And here in Bunkerville, our editors lean over their typewriters and carp about slipping on smears of stinky dog s**t on the way to work when it rains. We note here the all-too typical American patterns afoot: dramatic and awesome waste, tediously steady chaos, well-planned confusion, cultivated ignorance of this vital issue, gutless leadership, and of course no politicians speaking to the dog-shit issue.

Sure, we admit the need for an inexpensive protein to stiffen the pots of the poor and to extend America's billion plus burgers, but why are these neuts trooping around town slaughtering feral dogs in the middle of busy intersections, roasting the acrid-smelling meat in plugs at the ends of curtain rods over fires built on the lawns of the wealthy, the prominent, and bought-and-sold public officials?

Who can say that a sautéed square of dog's tongue may not be the tastiest item at the next fondue party? And what about preserving the meat in wine, or diced and spiced raw into a good tartare? More divine than starling pie, many say.

The price of the meat compares favorably with that of other commodities: rooster combs, turkey fries, cheese curd and buckets of clabber. But the price of okra is out of sight—$5. Our gumbo will either be weak or costly.

So why not, readers? Shall we get these millions of wasted canines boiling on the national stove? What's the difference between a pork taco and a dog taco? Or an *andouille* gumbo and a dog gumbo? Why not do what the people in Yulin, China, do? You can keep your beloved poodle, but loose street dogs, or dogs raised and fattened in cages, will be slaughtered, dressed and much of their meat eaten in dozens of different dishes. The rest will either be freeze dried and formed into kibbles or processed into a soft, canned product for cats and dogs alike.

HISTORICAL FACT

It is universally known that if human male gonads are ablated early in life, great stature results due to a secondary activity of the pituitary gland. Thus, the eunuchs. Among them were those chosen to see to the safety of the sultan's harem, which was actually more of a finishing school for well-connected girls with influential parents. They took harpsichord, flute and singing lessons … dance and painting classes … elocution and language instruction. Every mother and father in the sultanate wanted their daughter in a harem guarded by neutered eunuchs. It was the highest of honors and the best way to prolong virginity.

Effie Pfeffer

On the Road to History

AN EXCERPT FROM ONĒBA 'S TEACHINGS

"Howard Hughes is finally dead enough to bury. The man who ran the world from hotel beds. In the future I see Mexicans spilling up from Mexico and Canadians cascading down. Russians will arrive with steamer trunks in a New York harbor jammed with a hopeless confusion of junks, coracles, Japanese whalers and Russian destroyers. I see peoples intermingling. Jamaicans making it with neuts in city parks. I see the Russian necronaut Khrushchev serving out a four-year term as U.S. president and performing as well as any have."

THE ZANZETTI REPORT

- *El Tiempo*, a Guatemalan newspaper, recently published a report on a nuclear test conducted in Yucca Flats, three minutes and 30 seconds prior to the earthquake that devastated Guatemala. The time corresponds exactly to the time required by the ground waves from the blast to reach and disturb the Motagua fault, north of Guatemala City, where the quake occurred.

- On Xmas eve afternoon 13 cars of a freight train derailed near Peabody Junction, spilling 1,200 to 1,400 gallons of acrylonitrile, a highly toxic and potentially explosive substance, onto the roadbed. Evacuation was ordered for the area. Acrylonitrile, used in the manufacture of plastics and soluble in water, is poisonous by inhalation, ingestion and skin absorption. Front loaders and other earth moving equipment came to Peabody, cleaned up the contaminated dirt and shipped it to Corpus Christi, Texas, the chemical dump of the nation.

- One of the vessels of the U.S. Navy's Ecology Report Network observed a three-mile-long island of fecal waste floating in the Caribbean 50 miles northwest of Barranquilla, Venezuela. The sun has dried the mass and given it buoyancy. A variety of water birds and penguins take advantage of the new land mass and settle there to lay their eggs. Then, with amazing guidance or instinct, the skuas arrive to eat the chicks as soon as they hatch, nature's way of keeping the penguin population under control. When their numbers reach the lemming stage, and all the food is gone, they kill or blind one another, beaks and claws striking out in all directions. A flock of a thousand can be blinded or slain in a single night, providing more food for the wild flocks of ravenous skuas.

E. Zanzetti
Science Editor

OOP DIES, ORPHANS ANNIE A new film starring Enfield and Mary Peters, is now playing at the Joy Theater. Enfield, as Oop, is Annie's wise grandfather, one who drums life lessons into the girl's head until he dies. Soon after, at the first exciting plot point, Annie's parents return suddenly as necronauts. You'll marvel at the plot's unwinding toward a shocking climax, followed by a mollifying and satisfying dénouement. Adults only. Rated XX. Drinks served at intermission. Enjoy the Joy. 1525 Arden Blvd. Midnight showings half price.

NECRONAUT PROGNOSIS POOR

While well-known necronauts like Frank Sinatra, Sal Mineo and Henrik Ibsen are well treated. Ordinary, unknown returnees are not so fortunate. They decamp from the dead. They pound on doors looking for work. The job picture for them: bleak to none. They are dull and sluggish. Some understand as few as 300 words and expressions. They lack the complexity so vital to sustained interest, and they are quickly abandoned by the first human sympathizers who pick them up unwittingly, then discard them like bad habits days later.

MYRON'S ART TYPING & SPEEDWRITING Myron will produce your likeness with perfect style on his 1955 Remington typewriter in only 15 minutes at a cost you can afford. You'll find Myron in the lobby of the Gons Hotel almost any day of the week from noon to 3. Saturday and Sunday, 9 to 5. Tourists welcome!

SUBSIDENCE REVEALS MASS GRAVE

At 12:30 a.m. this morning, two of the remaining residents of the nearly-abandoned Liberty Heights Housing complex were driving down Industry Road when the pavement suddenly collapsed into a pit 10 meters deep. The odor of rotted flesh rose from the subsidence. The decayed remains of 200 neutrodyne infants were unearthed. It is quite common for neutrodyne mothers to throw their infants in front of moving vehicles, preferably buses. Hundreds die that way every year. This mass grave, however, is the largest ever found. The incident disrupted the few utility services that still functioned at the complex.

A QUESTION OF LOVE

Dear Hyacinth,

Although my childhood is a fairly long way behind me I have never quite gotten used to the act of brushing my teeth. The rapid, repetitive up-and-down, in-and-out motions and the discommodious spilling and slurping of toothpaste froth down my lips and the sides of my mouth have always struck me as unnatural. Perhaps I associate these rapid motions applied to oneself with some other, guiltier, practice in solitary. Can you help me?

J.G.

The Bowery

Dear Bowery Boy: Hey! Love your mind. Most men just have a dick. A few have a trace of a mind. Every once in a while, there is a man with a dick and a mind and a particle of heart. I knew a man who had a big heart for a man and he loved people. But later he did prison time for capital murder.

Women are safe when they find their man. Men are never safe and have to search for the peace and the shelter of a woman all their lives. Men must continually renew their strength through the respect of other men. To have yourself inside you, as a woman does, is much more secure than to have it outside and be fearful of losing it all the time.

THE HUNGER ART BISTRO opens today! We serve nothing twice: Fresh Lumpia—Pansit Luglog—Soop Lorain—Grand Patty—Skrada-Kaka—Marrow Pudding—Stewed Carp—Broiled Eels—Chine of Mutton—Scotch Collops—Tanfy and Fritters—Vitaburgers—Soyfries—Sweet Griddle Buns—Zen Lasagna—Red Beans and Rice—Crabeye Soop. Located in the heart of Downtown Pisstown at 637 Arden Blvd. For takeout call Bywater 5115.

DEAD WALL GOES UP

This *City Moon* reporter has been there, eating *lingua* tacos and sipping La Perla, hidden behind a row of ligustrum japonicum, watching the Wall of the Dead go up around the White House. Department of the Interior workers are at the task from dawn until the Moon boils up like a new potato in a pot of broth. Under these special circumstances, the veep was allowed to address the august body, and said, "We are committed to building this wall no matter what. Until now we've been happy enough with the necronauts who have come back. They're not the same as they were in life, but still lovable. Now my question is, what if the comebacks included people like Lee Oswald, or Jack Ruby, or any of thousands … or millions … of undesirables? Heads will roll like Easter eggs across the lawn at Casa Pacifica. Long buried secrets would be revealed, history re-written. We have no choice. The wall must be finished as soon as possible."

TROCHILICS ON THE WATER

Editorial

They move down the Trench on spiraling double-wheel rotation machines motorized by an extremely small and light-blue- finished electric engine. As they reach the dam at Peabody Junction, the slow-moving wheels tangle in the driftwood, and trochilics are forced to camp along the bank at night. People stop their cars, backing up traffic along the bridge to stare at the spectacle. Some hurl rotting tomatoes at the trochilics, who show no reaction and proceed to fish in their peculiar way. One of them makes a circular motion above the water and catfish spin out onto the mud bank, joyfully offering their scale-free, peel-off flesh and muscle to the camping trochilics.

Soon the trochilics, wanderers at heart, drift to campsites along the Trench, where they dig green worms to fish for sturgeon and spoonbill. After that, forgetful, they hunker back to the City to steal meat and be slammed behind bars.

Our reporter was on the scene immediately, carrying his camera and a small hand gun. He had covered the beatniks, he had seen the hippies, he had watched the revolution come and go, he had written about the frozen beef liver killings in Pisstown. But he was caught with his britches down when the trochilics came to town. Before long they began wandering and circling through downtown. They relieved themselves on street corners, surrounded pedestrians in the middle of the day and taunted them by hurling hot, blade-equipped teetotums at their ankles, cutting some of them badly, shredding their shoes, cuffs and socks. In three cases, they were accused of sexually abusing tourists in plain sight of law enforcement officials, and nothing was done about it. They lie like logs out in the rain below our office window, their faces emptied of spirit.

The arm of the law has been twisted into a useless extremity by trochilic criminal cases causing a bottleneck at the court house. After a single weekend there were hundreds on the docket, mostly misdemeanors. Meanwhile, serious cases like the rat-tail comb killings went untried.

Had the poet Milton lived in a world besmudged by the presence of trochilics, *Paradise Lost* would have read like *Westworld.* And if trochilics had gone to Mississippi in Faulkner's time, *The Hamlet* might read like Warhol's *Blow Job.*

Why can't our attorney general do something? Why does the turnkey let them out every night when they've been jailed by day? They say it takes three or four hard-muscled athletes and a brace and bit to drill through the gristly heart of an old trochilic. Should we call in the Marines to do the job?

We'd like to know your opinion. Send it in 25 words or less by postcard to *City Moon*, Box 591, City.

SUICIDE GROVE

The Onēba Report

- If you want your soul to whistle and shout, if you want your mind to turn all about, whip up a batch of Noxage:

two thumbs of paregoric, avocado honey, lemon oil and a squirt of soda. It's a potent antihistamine but if taken unwisely, you'll have the cattle of your memory feeding by the highway of your soul. You'll be coughing up cysts that look like chick peas.

- His mother dead, his father blind, depressed wrestler Lefty Orgone sawed his feet off with a crosscut limb saw in Suicide Grove, a dedicated and peaceful stand of crepe myrtles in Wuntex Park. Why? No one knows. Why did Justin Case, former presidential candidate, hire a Rasputin figure to whack him in the forehead with a sharpened 10penny nail driven through sappy pieces of pine plank? No one knows, including me.

- Let's remember the senseless hangings of 12 years past. We all asked how long they would be left dangling there and when the City would collect and burn them. We couldn't leave our houses without seeing another one strung down from an eave or swinging from an awning like a side of pork, dogs licking their bluish toes. Fortunately, good resulted. The bad ones swished above the marsh of desire, bitten by the flies of dread, souls hovering close to the body, unable to stay or go.

- Now modern trends have us all sitting huddled in our houses wearing monkey suits and staring through the slits of blinds at the skeletons dissolving to chrome-yellow powder in the sunbaked trees.

Please send me sightings of any kind. I am the sorting
house for this information.
Onēba
Box 591

Dear *City Moon*,
This necronaut craze is really filtering down. God, listen,
I had a beer with Woody Guthrie last night at the Putty Tat
Klub in north Tuttle. My chick and me spotted him in the next
booth. He smelled like spoiled milk, but his eyes were bright,
his smile taut and steady. His guitar had suffered severe wood
rot. His coveralls were moldy. The poor man couldn't put a
sentence together right, yet he seemed to have direction. His
limp fist disclosed a Greyhound ticket to Paducah, Kentucky,
where he claimed he had work awaiting. My honey gasped
when he offered to play for us and lost a finger joint like so
much cheddar among the loose strings. So long, *Moon*, hello
Woody. Good to have you back. Paducahns, get ready.
Lutheran Walter
Tuttle

City Moon,
Attn. Scientist Zanzetti
Droplets of sulfuric acid more concentrated than the acid
in a car battery have been detected in stationary cloud tops
over Texoma Beach. One resident complains that with each
rain a layer of her roofing dissolves and drips into her flower
garden, killing the roses and everything else. She said, "If I
go out there in the rain and get my hair wet, it'll all fall out.
I got a dog with its back hair all burned off by that acid. The
clouds don't move. They just hang there all the time. I came
here to retire, and now this s**t comes along. We need some
help down here. Can't we destroy this cloud some way? Call

out the Air Force? Drop tons and tons of baking soda on it? Wouldn't that neutralize the acid?"

Barbara Balomb
T-Beach

Ms. Balomb, Zanzetti here. Calling out the Air Force would be excessive, expensive and wasteful. We scientists are confident that when the winter winds arrive, that caustic cloud will either dissipate or move northward at increased speed. What gives birth to these acidic clouds, no one knows. They appear, always from the south, with startling suddenness, over a town or a city and hover there, rumbling ominously, raining acid and water three times a day, perhaps for months, before they move on. The damage done to farmlands, animal stock and real property is incalculable.

LIBERTY HEIGHTS ABANDONED

Brick dust, moistened by dew, has frozen in the window frames of near-empty Liberty Heights national housing units. One remaining resident told a *City Moon* reporter, "Only a few dead-enders here now. My neighbor to the south knocks on my window right on schedule every night. I recognize him by his red ploff and floppy hat. He wants to hear what I've seen during the day. I've tried twice to clear the elephant vines from his street window, so he could see for himself, but they grew back in one warm night." This failing has left the neighbor with only a view of the smog-well from his bathroom window. He says he has lived on the 77th floor all his life.

ONĒBA'S ONE-STOP BAIT MARKET pleases. We offer a controlled shopping environment and severely reduced prices. Minnows, crickets, grass shrimp, crawdaddies, small & large frogs, green worms, night crawlers, red wigglers, army worms, centipedes, Tennessee walking grubs, rooster combs, tripe, pork liver, hen's hearts, stinky cheese bait for catfish and plenty more, including hooks, lines and sinkers. Drop in and tell us what you want to catch, and we'll sell you the right bait.

MEDICINAL DIRIGIBLES TO LAUNCH IN '76

Come January 1 it will float over us, reddish and dim as a sterilizer lamp, the first of Zanzetti's three planned medicinal airships to be placed in the lofty troposphere. This is certainly a bouncing babe of modern military technology. The surgeon general and the commander in chief will watch the launch on a color TV in the Ritz-Carlton. Zanzetti has, by news release, cautioned that the first few hours of the dirigible's maneuvers to align itself perfectly may be rough, owing to its powerful magnetic influence. Tin roofs may bulge, dry hair stand on end, objects of less than 10 pounds may lift perceptibly if not moored. "But it will settle," says Zanzetti, "as all things eventually do, and its beneficial radiation will cleanse the air of bacilli for hundreds of years."

BOY HOWDY BACK AFTER 65 YEARS

The Howdy necronaut is sequestered in air-conditioned rooms at a clinic in the City. Dermatologists are hard at work restoring the flesh as doctors of the mind labor at their task, recreating the long-dead memory, replanting the seeds of symbology, making certain necessary adjustments to brain chemistry, enough at least to let him count change. Then the sociologists will find Howdy a job and introduce him to this new-age culture.

Howdy spent the years 1910 to 1975 dead as a doornail, but then his daughter, who still lives in the house on Dinsmoor Avenue, says he came to the back door on Halloween night smelling of musk and spitting teeth, his white hair mussed and the ball of his nose missing. He had been buried, by his explicit instructions, in a small cement mausoleum he built himself, wherein he placed a cement jug and asked that his many descendants keep it filled in the event he went to Hell and took a sudden thirst. His mind, of course, was gone, and nothing but a stub of his penis was left. Surprisingly, the hair and the nails were inches longer than they had been the day of the wake, thus confirming suspicions.

Howdy's daughter, Girl Howdy, has reported seeing a stranger in the graveyard, prowling about Howdy's little mausoleum in toga-like garb, lighting kitchen matches, occasionally letting forth a shrill yodel, stirring up the dogs in the area.

TRENCH FLOAT POPULAR BUT DANGEROUS SUMMER ACTIVITY

Everybody floats now. On a sunny Sunday you can see them in their rubber suits, coiled in hoses and oxygen equipment and goggles, floating belly-up like dead fish down the Trench, the sun returning blinding spikes from all the faceplates. Soon enough the floaters tangle in a thick, green mesh of water hyacinth. Eventually they untangle themselves and move on to the next trap-net of hyacinth.

This way they float in fits and starts from Muncie to Loma

Linda. Depending on the season, the journey takes eight to ten weeks. Last summer, in the months of January and March, an estimated 9,000 began the float but only 1,000 completed the journey. Many who dropped off at food-and-restroom stops along the way took buses home. A dozen drowned after mishaps with motorboats. Twice that number, following a suicide plan, drowned themselves. Of those who completed the journey, hundreds were sickened by chlamydia, others infested with liver flukes.

Congressional leaders say next year's float may not be held for reasons of safety.

NEUTS TRAINED AT UPPER FARM

"We work miracles here with our neutrodynes," says Bill Thompson, director of Upper Farm Inc. "Since idle hands so often prove to be the tools of turpitude, we keep our new age farm neuts busy 'round the clock. They bake, they gather eggs, they clean their pens to a polish. We have creative drama workshops, they plant and tend a productive garden. When the weather blesses us, the tables of the refectory are always set with fresh tomato hearts, white squash and vegetable pear, even kohlrabi if the frost hadn't gotten them. And, of course, the neuts love to climb the loquat trees and pick the fruit when it's yellow and ripe. We've given guidance and direction to armies of lost souls here at the Upper Farm. All have left here with enough skills to live alongside us without being noticed."

WHAT LAY AHEAD

Onēba's Forecast

There will be one and only one supermarket chain in the U.S. and it will be called Jitney Jungle. … A futile attempt to destroy the two-ton rock head of John Wayne, located near the Duke's ancestral plot in Eternity Meadows, will result in the mere shaving of a portion of the lower face, with little alteration to the stony visage. … Technology will allow wheat to be grown in the very air itself, and monstrous bales of it may fill up the troposphere and block the sun's light to much of the Midwest. … The first televised execution will take place in Bunkerville. …Increasingly, attempts will be made on the lives of corporate executives. ... Ordinary people will begin to see the light and take pot shots at fat cats and their floozies. …The remaining Process members of the state assembly will profoundly influence national decision making. ... The president will be altered in some way, as will his family. ... Necronaut Pollock will once again take a dump in a fireplace somewhere to get the attention of wealthy patrons. … And, if past is prologue, I'll amass another fortune during the year and give it all to starving neutrodyne children.… *C'est tout*, troopers. Tune in next year for more forecasts.

FACTS COME TO LIGHT

The *Midlothian Mirror*, in a recent editorial, disclosed the juicy news that the Animal President never quite got over his old wild-country habit of having bowel movements outdoors, even while residing in the White House. There exists, says Penn Jones,

Moon photographer, well-guarded photographic evidence of the president squatting over a hole in the White House putting green. This happened many times. He was always accompanied by a solitary Secret Service agent who, when the president was two-bottle drunk, had to wipe him.

FACT

The lowly, uncultured and illiterate neutrodynes who beg and bother on Wall Street will eat any book you give them. Brokers and bankers going to work often toss used books at the neuts and stand by, laughing, when one or another of them chokes on a thick how-to-book, business text or Bible. Zanzetti discounts the popular notion that they do this to absorb the knowledge contained in the books. "It is far more likely that this group has become addicted to, and learned to digest, cellulose and glue. And with those cavernous mouths and grinding teeth, eating a book is like eating a cookie."

EDITORIAL

Now, with talk of artificial suns going up (to illuminate polar regions and high crime areas) and a moon already there, we can't help thinking it won't be long before the night sky comes to look like a penny arcade, a stadium scoreboard. It's an exciting thing to ponder and a pleasant surprise that our civilization would bubble to a head so soon after the Manhattan project and spew its fester into orbit. Yet we should not take a dim view, not always explore the dark sides of every issue, as our readers forever complain. Let's look at the bright side: Timothy Leary and his New Network Gang are laying plans to shuffle off to the Dog Star, Sirius, as soon as they can hustle a proper rocket. Good, says the *Moon*, good riddance. Leave the Earth to darkness and to us, as the poet said. We'll watch things while you and the gang fly, in your proper rocket, out of familiar air like dragon flies, only to settle on another clothespin.

BELLED BUZZARD SPOTTED AGAIN

A belled but gentle buzzard of prodigious size has been spotted again on a farm at Gas Flats. It came down in a litany of frightening wing chops, but ate corn peacefully among the gamecocks then slept the night with them in the coop. "I sure hope he didn't f**k too many," the farmer said, "Last time that bird slept over, I had half my hens die trying to pass black eggs the size of grapefruits. Some of the rest hatched. They were the ugliest chicks you ever saw, and they stank like vomit. I killed every damned one, cut their heads off with garden shears. Hell, my dogs wouldn't even eat them carcasses, and *their* favorite treat is the ass off a smelly shabbit."

POPULAR RESTAURANT TO CLOSE FOR A WEEK

Madeline Chu, owner and executive chef of the Palace Orienta, famous for its flash-fried dragon shrimp, reports that Bert Garland, one of her line cooks, was terribly burned by hot fryer oil yesterday in a freak accident. Also injured was Lordi Lordiss, *City Moon* food editor, who was touring the kitchen at the time, preparing to write a review.

Ms. Chu said, "It was a nice day. We opened the windows, including the one above the big fryer. A nice breeze blew in. Ms. Lordiss was walking around taking notes. Bert was battering the shrimp. We were preparing for the dinner crowd when something came flying through the open window."

That something, Ms. Chu said, was a neutrodyne infant weighing about 15 pounds. With a loud, sizzling splash, it landed in the big fryer, casting a sheet of hot oil halfway across the kitchen, striking Garland in the face. Ms. Lordiss was fortunate in that her injuries were minor. Most of the smoking oil landed on her jacket. Garland, though, will have to wear a balaclava to cover the burn scars for many months, doctors told him, possibly much longer, so as not to frighten patrons.

These infant tossings are a fad among neutrodynes. They fling them off buildings, under cars and buses, into sewers and out of open windows.

Effie Pfeffer, *City Moon* historian, offered an explanation: "The neuts have always admired the Mayans. Some of them go on yearly pilgrimages to Chichen Itza. Once there, they stand on the edge of the deep-blue-green cenote and swoon when the tour guide tells them that in the old days Mayans came here to the Sacred Well to toss their infants into the water to drown. The idea was to sacrifice something of great value in return for something of greater value, or maybe nothing. Those without infants sometimes tossed older children in, always female. Others, the childless, flung gold bracelets, fine China, statuary, slaves and many other valuables into the Sacred Well.

In the late '20s the Smithsonian undertook a dredging operation at the site and sent divers down to keep an eye on the steam-powered, clam-shell dredger as it dug down through 30 feet of muck, rotted leaves and tree branches. They reported seeing glittering gold and glowing gems through the cloudy water, thousands of sacrificed valuables and quite a collection of disturbed bones, some rising to the surface once freed from the muck.

HEN-PECKED OFFICIAL LOSES EYE

Agriculture Czar Frederick Henshaw will be blind in his left eye for life from a hen peck during his visit to the Lower Farm. He was petting Clara, a big leghorn, the blue-ribbon fowl of Warden Wunty's flock of egg layers, and she was playfully pecking at his face when her beak struck the pupil of his left eye a glancing blow. Despite efforts to repair the tear, physicians declared that the use of the eye could never be restored.

Dear *City Moon*,
Ma marked all us children
Before my brother was born, my Pa was cutting a hog one day and Ma yelled out the back door to him, "Dinner's ready." He looked up long enough to cut off his fingers. Because of this accident my brother was born with short, perfectly even fingers, all the same length.
Another sister was marked by a cat. Pa came home drunk one night and argued with my mother about fixing him some food. Ma slammed the oven door shut and put some wood on the fire and started to make some biscuits. You know how a cold cat will climb into a warm oven? Well, our cat crawled into that oven and when mother opened the door, the cat was

cooked. Later on my third sister was born with the mark of the cat on her: two scars at birth across her forehead.

Me, I had the turtle mark. There was a plate-size patch of hard skin like a shell on my back. I kept it hidden most of the time except at gym class showers. The girls called me the Turtle Girl. Ma tells me she and Pa were out fishing one time and Ma, who was pregnant with me, got a snapping turtle on her line. When she pulled it in too hard it went over her head and bit her on the back, right where my mark is.

Your Faithful Reader,
Turtle Girl

EDITORIAL

The news now cautions of floccules on the sun and urges us not to go outdoors without headgear and full-body clothing for the remainder of the week, when the floccules are scheduled to burn out. Most of us do wear protective clothing and headgear when and if we go outside. Those who don't, mostly the young and foolish, especially ones without headgear, soon find their cheeks puffing out and erupting in rings of water blisters and pustules after absorbing just a few minutes of floccular radiation. The *City Moon* also urges people to either remain indoors until the danger passes or dress appropriately when going out, even at night. You may not see the floccules in the dark sky, but they are still capable of bending radiation around the curvature of the Earth and giving you a nasty burn.

LAGOON REOPENS

After months of renovation, the popular Lagoon Cafe will open for dinner today, offering special and exciting entrées:

Prairie Clam Patties Over Corn Grits

Gum Boot Chulettas *Simmered in Blood*

Rooster Comb Salad with Powdered Beak and Raw Egg

Broasted Pollywogs and Chili Heart Stew

Little Toni and Derando will be on the twin pianos providing a mellow background to a scrumptious meal.

I'll be there! Stop at my table and say hi.

Lordi Lordiss

Food Editor

STORY CONTEST ENTRY

Emily and Leopold
by
Rich Bastian

The old girl is at it again. Her pale, plump thigh overflows the cup of the buccaneer boot she is wearing. Her other foot, bare, is on Karl's head. The head, of course, is submissive. Emily's legs are thin, her knees bony. She snaps them together and Karl delights in the pain.

She is startled. Her room has been invaded by a wuthering wind, which extinguishes the candle and blows wax onto her "kitten" rug. 'Em' can hear the elfin feet of Leopold, who, once safe in her dark boudoir, would kiss her. She shudders even before her dog, Gnasher, growls and causes Leopold to skitter exactly as he does in the portrait by Rossetti.

Leopold's ears perk; he has heard a cheap paperback's page turn with a whisper, then the slap of the cover. He knows she was reading. He can tell by the pitch of her breathing that she is either excited by his approach or about to be sick. He doesn't care which and enters the room. He reaches out and touches the book, held tightly to her breasts. Now he knows what has happened.

He claws at her. "You stole it – stole it!"

He lights the candle with an ember in his pipe. The light cast on his face spreads across a smirk and gives him the look of a hissing cat. He remembers dancing with Emily, wrapping his arms around her angry torso and twittering around as if she were a maypole. But it wasn't all fun. His slippers were too tight, his smoking jacket too pettifogged for comfort.

"Wait till the governor hears about this," he says, pulling the book away from Emily's grasp.

Leopold had just taken his medicine. It was hard to know when he was truly excited, or when he was earnestly emphatic. His attack *was* more aggressive and audible than his customary yawning approach.

Emily's father is not home. He is out on the moor, bareheaded, though balding, his black coat flapping in the gusts of sea wind. Still, he perspires, and his underclothes stick to his flesh. He enjoys being out chasing demons, those infernal lepers whose diseased brogue ridicule his sermons. How ruddy-cheeked he will be when he returns, especially if he has been fortunate enough to have knobbed a high hat or two with the root bulb of his hawthorn cane.

The father's estate is crumbling around him. That is his idea of horror. His idea of fun is to march across the moors when the weather allows. It hasn't, not lately. North Teutonic winds and razor-edged sleet out of Ultima Thule, the very elements conspire against him. He is forced to retreat to his den. And what can he do there? Just sit, his weapon primed and cocked, on the ready to raise it and shoot through the door, though not even that stops the demons, who aren't only indestructible but vicious and delight in dancing infuriatingly close to the children. Pater, as the family called him, is discouraged and will sit, writing sermons in black, rusty ink, shaking his head at the condition of Man. He was against the demons. No one could fault him. Only Emily understands and likes the moors. She goes out into storms, though when she returns, her clothes are rumpled but suspiciously dry.

The End

Dear Rich: This is an interesting effort but seems truncated. We end with Emily's rumpled but suspiciously dry clothes. What are we to think of this? If you don't tell us, we'll never know. And what about the narrative distance? Who is it who thinks her clothes are suspiciously dry? The narrator? Someone in the room? You've led the reader down a path with no end in sight.

EDITORIAL

The City health department decided recently that it had to do something about the health hazard created by the huge flocks of pigeons that roam the downtown area, roosting in eaves, beshitting hats and shoulders, baby strollers and sidewalks.

The department's solution: Scatter French fries, half-eaten sandwiches, pizza crusts and other pigeon favorites and trap the lice-ridden birds with nets when they land to eat. Prisoners are perfect for this duty. They can kill the pigeons with a quick, hard pull on the head, then remove the feathers under hot water and give the meat to the poor for food, while keeping some for the prisoners in their cells.

To date, 30,035 pigeons have been trapped and given to charity cases and welfare mothers. The Red Cross snuff patrols are out on the streets again, watching traps and collecting pigeons.

"One man came up here from Muncie and got 150 pigeons," a Red Cross worker said. "They're tender because they don't fly much, and they eat mostly garbage."

Pigeons carry insect pests as well as the spores of fungal diseases such as histoplasmosis.

"But," the man said, "any germs or pests are in the feathers and don't affect the quality of the meat. The poor won't have a problem. Nothing beats a pigeon leg, or thigh, battered, fried and dipped in mayo."

Eat up, readers. Dog is next, and it won't be soon enough.

CAZAZZA COUPLE STRIKES

Editorial

Monty Cazazza and his wife Mandy, well-known San Francisco art bandits, now supported by a grant of $100 from the National Endowment for the Arts, have attacked something sacred in the name of Process art. What they have done is raid the Dummy Museum in Pisstown and cart off Edgar Bergen's Charlie McCarthy, Buffalo Bob's Howdy Doody and Phineas T. Bluster, Paul Winchell's Jerry Mahoney and Fran's Kukla and Ollie.

The final chapter of their scam was to soak the dummies in coal oil and burn them publicly in the National Capitol Rotunda. Visitors turned in horror, thinking they were seeing children cindered there on government marble. Mind you, we, the taxed, picked up the tab for the bandit couple's plane flight from S.F.

We *City Moon* editors want to hurl into the wastebasket when we hear about this cracked behavior. The Cazazzas' act, which had its roots in Monty's old squeeze-the-shit-out-of-dogs-routine, is a joke in this age of no joking. It makes us want to venture from the office and give these "artists" a good Zen *katsu* (wake up!) with discipline rods we've made by cutting the heads from our golf clubs.

Dear *City Moon*,
We're fed up with neuts camping on our lawns and building smelly fires that leave scorched circles in the zoysia. We're tired of their clowning faces peering in at our televisions through windows. We've already had to install jalousies. A brand new and very expensive sprinkler system was also installed. All they did was get naked and take showers. We've built three different types of fencing, but nothing keeps them out for long. They grin at us as we close the curtains and turn out the lights. We dread looking at the yard after they break camp and move on in the morning.
We're retired now after operating the Pisstown Falling Center for many years and getting old, so cleaning up all

that trash, pouring lime into their shallow latrine and putting down grass seed is too hard on us. Not to mention we worry about the grandkids when they stay overnight. They'll be terrified if they see a neut peeking in the window or if one knocks on the door (they don't like the sound of doorbells or chimes) and asks for bread-and-butter pickles, which they like very much. Those kids will run upstairs and hide in the closet. One more thing: there's ten houses on this street and at least five of them host these dammed unwanted campouts. Sooner or later they're going to want to come inside and live with us. Can't the City do anything about this?

Molly and Mel
Box 123
Pisstown

Dear Molly and Mel: Repeated calls to the city manager and to police headquarters have gone unanswered. We're just as disturbed and frustrated as you are and we're chasing the story as doggedly as we can. Stay tuned. Meanwhile, treat them kindly and remain patient. After all, the president's recent executive order granted them permission to camp anywhere they please.

HAIRCUT REGULATIONS IN GAS FLATS SOON TO BE EVERYWHERE

Acting on the orders of the president, the Gas Flats city council is the first in the U.S. to pass an ordinance that directs all those in the hair cutting business, as well as home hair cutters, to limit the styles to only three for men, woman and children. First is the "Balboa," which allows richly oiled, uncombable growth on top of the head, but a close shave everywhere else. Second comes the "Paris Island Bowl Crimp," modeled after a U.S. Marine, post 'Nam-style hair treatment. And the third is "The Sentinel," a procedure where all but a three-inch circle is shaved randomly, anywhere on the head. The hair in that circle is grown, cultivated, and eventually waxed into a kind of hairy, knotted 12-inch obelisk. Police will detain anyone deviating from the approved styles and issue a citation. Three such citations could mean an indefinite stay at the Lower Farm Detention Unit.

"I've got little bleedings on my scalp from my first haircut," said Julie Munty, a nurse. "It's rough. The shears are dull, the scissors rusty, the barbers poorly trained. Come payday we'll have to rush downtown to the barber shops and get our haircuts. Me, I like the bowl crimp. The sentinel would get in the way of my work in the hospital."

For security reasons, the veep explained to reporters, "We want our people to look similar, but not the same, from the air. That's why three different hair styles are being offered, at least for now. There's so much more security that way both personally and nationally. There may, however, come a time when we'll have to go to a single cut for everyone if conditions become worse and more security is required.

"Moreover, our children want nothing more than a barber college education and a national hair cutting permit. They think that will land them on Easy Street with a shiny, bird-blue Cadillac perched in the driveway, hitched to a sleek aluminum Airstream with just a pinch of equity in it. All that any modern family unit can get a purchase on, it can keep if any member holds a federally-issued tonsorial card. The family is fixed for the duration, can travel unmolested by road blocks and check points."

HISTORICAL FACT

The phrase *sub rosa* originated in 477 B.C. from a famous sexual coupling of Pausanias and Xerxes under a bower of roses. Pausanias later betrayed Xerxes by having him walled up in the temple of Minerva to die of starvation. Afterwards, Athenians wore roses in their hair when they wished to communicate a secret.

Effie Pfeffer, Ph.D.
On the Road to History

TROCHILIC BOTTLED

This reporter was vacationing in New Orleans recently, walking down Tchoupitoulas Street at the wee jazz hour of 5 a.m., nibbling a hot waffle covered with cane syrup and powdered sugar. The putrid smell of the dried-up Mississippi rose over the levee and wafted through the entire Vieux Carré. The great river was a mere 20-foot wide channel of slow-moving water. As I strapped on my sanitary mask, I stumbled over the remains of a trochilic, whose shoes and skirt had been taken by scavengers (of which there are many in the Crescent City) and whose toenails looked like snail shells.

Apparently, the method of killing was this: an empty La Perla bottle had been broken at the neck and pushed down the trochilic's throat as far as it would go until he passed away with a pinkish froth at his mouth.

Near the trochilic's feet I found a brown bag containing a half-dozen boiled blue crabs. I took these myself and went on my way. Locals told me it was best not to report these killings to anyone. I knew then that this was the beginning of something of moment, a process, a playing out, a petering, an age of defiance lying ahead.

MYSTERY TUNNELS FOUND

Even Scientist Zanzetti and his colleagues are completely mystified by the system of secret passages found under Bunkerville by a contingent of Lower Farm prisoners digging a mass re-graving for stage-four necronauts. At first the subway system was thought to be on a small-enough scale when Zanzetti's people pushed their way through the first dark, narrow passages. Further investigation, however, has disclosed branching tunnels too small for modern human beings to enter at all. Why such a network of passages was built is a difficult problem for the scientists. Giving up, they called in an anthropologist, Dr. Friar, of Pisstown Junior College. He is a balding man of 70 years, with a belt of monk-like remaining hair encircling his head. After examining and measuring the array of tunnels, he told the press, "Why such a network of passages was built is a hard problem to solve very quickly. And, to make it more difficult, some of the tunnels are blind, leading nowhere."

Sheriff Prop, called to the scene by fearful neighbors, looked into the tunnels with a powerful flashlight and offered his opinion of how they came to be. "I'm pretty sure these were dug by necronauts burrowing toward the surface. Some make it, some don't."

Dear Onēba,

I have had this dream on consecutive nights. In a tavern, the Dixie Peanut, somewhere in the sultry south, I sit alone, sipping sour mash and eating salted peanuts. The bartender has vanished into the back rooms through a black sackcloth curtain. A second customer, a distinguished-looking neutrodyne in a blue suit and tie enters and with funereal quiet seats himself at the opposite end of the ironwood bar. He looks at me, probably thinking I'm the bartender on break, and orders a Pimm's Cup, "with a slice of cucumber standing in it. Shave the ice with a number three blade and salt it in the glass before adding the Pimm's."

He thinks I'm the bartender, despite the army hat and my tubed and goggled headgear. He seems undisturbed that I make no response to his drink order and resume quaffing my mash as I stare at a bottle of Pimm's on a back-bar shelf.

He pounds his fist on the bar. "Service!"

I startle and turn to give him a closer look, like a camera zooming in.

Bobbing inches above his billycock I see what I take to be a whitish synthetic precipitate of the air itself, almost like a hive of cotton candy.

"You hear what I say, pissgut! Make me a Pimm's Cup. What kind of a bar is this?!"

I wake up, but it's just a dream wake up, a fake wake up. In it I sit up in my cot, my palms icy. I go to the bathroom mirror and look at the rosy head of an otherwise white worm peeking from one of my nostrils and I have obviously spoiled my flannel night shirt with red tomato vomit. Now I really wake up and the dream is over.

Judy Munty
Pisstown Infirmary

Dear Judy: The keys to this dream are the penile worm extending from the nostril, the aggressive and hostile demeanor of the second customer and the suggestion of a halo above his billycock hat. The dream is fundamentally one of aimless fear and loaded chock-to-brim with silver bullets of a Christmas eve suicide. Even in dreams, stay out of the Dixie Peanut. There's an amorphous figure who hangs out there all the time. His name is Dewey, wears a zoot suit. He'll strangle you at the drop of a hat.

Onēba, the One

"FUHRER" ARRESTED IN TUTTLE TOWNSHIP

In the normally quiet and peaceful Tuttle Township, a teen-ager who called himself "Nick the Fuhrer," a self-appointed "crusading detective on the side of the law," was arrested.

Officers said the 15-year old went too far this week and they received complaints about the curious lad, "wearing a mask, carrying a bull whip and moving very fast through the township harassing people."

When arrested, Nick claimed his only intent was to punish hoodlums.

"He's a nice, clean-cut kid," said Sheriff Prop. "He just read too many comic books."

FOR SALE Heads of the presidents in cheddar cheese. This set is first quality Wisconsin aged, certified USDA. The heads sit on the mantel like nobody's business until Xmas when the grandkids can take a bite out of Eisenhower's cheek for a little taste of what it was like at Normandy or nibble Noxin's nose for that briny hint of failure. All 39 presidents for $25. Check or money order to *City Moon* Cheese Offer, Box 591

STORY CONTEST ENTRY

The Agonew
by
Kenny Cubus

The Agonew brings jelutong. His earthly life a laughingstock, he signs off to prowl the shill we call the universe, hauling bushels of news to the far worlds and bringing back jelutong. An old boatman, he spies rot on a wooden jetty, the dock of a jelutong factory.

The jungle spits forth an ancient brown islander in shorts with a bare and withered chest. A first-rate grin accompanies him on the path to the factory. Cakes of jelutong soak in a vat of plum vinegar, dead June beetles floating on the surface.

The islander says: "Tree tappers bring the jelutong from the jungle to the factory. They cook it and make bricks. When the bricks are nearly hard, workers call in their wives and daughters to urinate on them. The urine initiates a final coagulation and tightening. Male urine has no effect."

The Agonew drifts from planets where people are made of peat to ones where glass fish swim in chlorine lagoons. His bright mouth full of chewing gum, he forgets our world.

By bringing us jelutong, The Agonew sails over bright oceans of stars, fearing only a possible lapse of communications from Earth, a potential bellwether of auto-annihilation, yet in all other ways enjoys his life away from the planet and his quest for jelutong.

The End

Dear Kenny: There's a disconnect and a contradiction here. The narrative voice moves suddenly in the last two paragraphs from a bland description of a jelutong factory tour to a fantasy tour of the universe. That's the disconnect. The contradiction: You have us believe the Agonew brings bushels of jelutong from "far worlds," yet the islander tells the narrator and the reader that jelutong is brought out from the jungle. By the way, don't be so stingy with description. I'd love to know what the Agonew looks like, for example, and at least a few words about the jelutong tree. Give this a re-write and re-submit. Let the reader "see" much more than you do. Words are just portals into visualization. A good book is a movie in the head.
Carlos

SHANTIES ON THE TRENCH

Powerless shanty boats navigate the National Trench in late summer, dependent on the flow, like a leaf in a gutter. It is sport for wealthy Bunkervillians. They load their boats with champagne, canned peaches, choice meats and neutrodyne servants and never pay a cent in taxes while they float downstream on the trench, Gas Flats to Pisstown to Peabody Junction and sometimes as far as Loma Linda. At each dock they are spoiled with handsome pies and other pastries delivered to them by businessmen anxious to step aboard their boats and make deals. Oddly, the rich call the boats "shanties," perhaps because most of them are nothing but small, well-appointed houses built atop flat, wooden barges that gently bump the levee, twist a bit, and float on.

There is a fascination about life which cannot be appreciated by those whose lives are daily robbed by tiresome, joyless work, and so are left with only a shred of the most compromised imagining of their situation. The houseboat dwellers are not stifled by convention or limitation. They lie nude in the sun atop the roofs or balconies of their floating homes if they wish and send their money ashore for anything they want. They are a law unto themselves, and their lives are utterly without responsibility.

Unfortunately for them, a bad bunch of neutrodynes navigates the same trench. Their lawless practices have caused them to be dreaded by shore people and the better class of shanty boatmen. Most of their time, when they are not stealing, eating, drinking or sleeping, is spent in playing cut-throat Euchre, of which they are inordinately fond. Quarrels are a frequent occurrence during these games and sometimes a murder is hidden by the brown, turgid waters of the trench, a victim thrown overboard in the dead of night.

Fortunately, many of the neut boats are run down by steamers on foggy nights, owing to the neuts being drunk or asleep and no light being shown. They awake in a panic as the steamers steam right over them, crushing them to the bottom. Their mouths, open to scream, fill quickly with still water. Their night clothes catch on the top of a "bob sawyer," a wave which gets its name from the bobbing and sawing motions imparted to it by the water. Meanwhile, the wealthy shanty owner sits in a luxurious cabin, more like a living room, attended by a neut who can carry a tray of grilled eel on his head.

Still, the safety of these passengers is never guaranteed. Another hazard along the way is the threat of trochilics banding together along the bank and snatching children from the deck, helpless as rag dolls. Weakened by a diet restricted to raw vegetables and cooked black rice during the spring and early summer, the trochilics are hungry for protein. They don't eat their captives, though. They spin and dervish their way to the nearest town or settlement with a meat market and sell them door to door to afford a rump roast or two and a bundle of sausages. Last year's outbreak of scarlet fever killed many children and damaged the hearts of others across the region. Thus, the surplus of childless, grieving parents willing to pay hundreds for these stolen children.

In winter the trench goes stagnant, blossoming with yellow-green algae, and the shanties are dead in the water amid clouds of mosquitoes and saw flies. Soon the rooms inside swarm with fire ants and tree roaches.

Dear *City Moon*,

Her neck whips, the spine snakes, the chakras are thrust open and my addicted patient, Delores Ortez, shouts deliriously for her mother. This begins the last stage of Estella-G dependency, the helplessness of sinking into sand and being sucked down a giant funnel into the bottom of the hourglass nightmare. Time, for Delores and Mom, is running out.

A home is purchased for them by a Catholic charity. I visit the home on a regular basis or when called. On one visit, I find Mom face-down on the stove top, after a sudden syncope. Only a single burner is lit, on low, boiling oatmeal, so her oily grey hair is just slightly singed. Another time she is head-down on a table, a capsule of E.G. stuck to the end of her protruding tongue. On both occasions, Delores is under the covers in her bedroom, stuporous on E.G., unable to help.

On some visits Mom is lucid, sober, in good spirits, but addled. For example, I recorded this blather: "I've been

dreaming about my dentist and the twining windy days and wine-bottle candles, naked under that African mask hanging in Pixie Allen's bedroom, or drinking rum and lemon Cokes and f***ing the dentist. He had a tiny thing, but it gave me a very nice tickle. I'll take that over a big stupid schlong any day."

One of the good-natured doctors came with me to the house. Mom had broken out in hives after eating a thorn apple from a jimson weed in the uncut lawn. She became abnormally thirsty, her vision was distorted, she had periods of delirium and incoherence. I feared she would sink into a coma. But the doctor gave her a strong dose of salts and warm water and she vomited up the half-digested, deadly apple. Other than a badly scratched throat, persistent diarrhea and a stomach ulcer, Mom was as fine as she ever was.

She repaired slowly in the backyard in a lawn chair, sun or snow, blank in the face, companioned by a terrier, abandoned by Delores to die under the weeping willow, her mind lingering over cakewalks of memory until the time comes. Delores, on the other hand, is taxied to the beach daily, where she scrubs herself with the sand beneath the foam.

Please, readers, let's get Mom fed and moved back inside. Send anything you can afford to "The Fund for Mom." Box 591.

Judy Munty
Nurse, Pisstown Infirmary

FOR SALE Collector's Item! I've learned that Godboy Joseph Vitolo was born in a bedroom on my shanty, the *Agonew*. Now it is quickly falling into shambles and must be sold as is. Once upon a time, these used shanties were dry-docked annually and painted, caulked, repaired and used again. Now they are left to mold and rust for lack of interest and increasing costs. They corrode and calcify, finally disintegrating on the murky bottom of the Trench. Get the *Agonew* while it's still afloat. Call Bywater 5115. We'll talk terms.

TITANIC RAISED

3 DEAD 6 HURT 11 WILL HANG

Fast, she sank. We fought for the cabin we have occupied continuously, three generations, since the teens of this century. Hideous fist banging against our door would not move us to sacrifice the space designed to save our girl baby, ourselves, and our parrot, Vaginia. We drifted bottomward for hours. We heard the steady thunk of the air compressor in our closet, preserving us, a bubble in the bloodstream of the ocean was all we were. Shortly we ate squid tentacles and whale's eyes and relished the tasty brain of the porpoise, though we convulsed with shame the first time we broke open the skull of that king of underseas life. We believed ourselves alone until the day we began to receive the transmission of Radio Universal in the electric light bulbs informing us in a simple, informational way that

the City of Mind, the mind of a species, is a synedrium. It cannot be conquered except by another synedrium of a greater number in its cube. Radiola does not intend to permit you to exist without contradiction, because he knows that if you ever reach a state of harmony within yourself, he cannot hope to stand against your city, your mind, or your species. The sunken Titanic exists as a physical reality and a place of dwellings, inhabited by the bleached people. The children of the Titanic culture belong to all its citizens. That's what Radio Universal said to us shortly after we bumped against the ocean floor. As the years brought the soldiers of time against us, we saw the prophecy of Radio Universal as our skeletons glowed through our blanched bodies and talk turned to adopting abyssal fish as gods.

THE CITY MOON Uh Uh

In the far future, when the moon shall have faded from the sky, and the sun shall shine at noonday, a dull cherry red; and the seas shall be frozen over, and the ice cap shall have crept downward to the equator from either pole, and no keel shall cut the water, nor wheels turn in mills; when all cities shall long have been dead and buried in ice, and all life shall be on the very last verge of extinction on this globe; then, on a bit of lichen, growing on the bald rocks beside the eternal snows of Panama, shall be seated a tiny insect, preening its antennae in the glow of the worn out sun, representing the sole survival of animal life on the earth--the melancholy bug.

frozen

At left, Ed Gein, heinous neutrodyne, who, in 57 wore the first meat shirt, is not at all troubled by these gloomy forcasts. As bleached as his eyes are, they see no portent of a frozen calamity, even in the distant future. He says, what's more, that prior by many years to the next turn of the century, neutrodyne convict leaders like himself will be frozen, rather than cruelly gassed, or shot, or hung, and then eaten by the poor of every nation. He says you just can't beat human meat when the future is at stake.

A Meal You'd Never Forget

DOG HUNTER

A 31 year old white woman from Dewey Avenue reported to police that she had seen a man shoot a dog in the head with a bow and arrow in front of the City Refectory. She identified him as a 31 year old white man named Ozalo. She said that after the dog was hit, the man began to skin and dress it with great surgical precision, cubing and salting the meat, then putting it in burlap pouches which he carried in a backpack, leaving a mound of bone and entrail and running north on Dewey Avenue.

(See related article inside)

NEUT YOUTH PRESSED NEAR PISSTOWN

During the past week, while the cotton gin at the outskirts of Pisstown was being run at full speed, a 5-year-old neutrodyne whose name cannot be learned was in the gin house at sundown watching the machinery with consuming interest. When night came he could not be seen anywhere about and a vigilant search was made, but the little neut could not be found. Three days later attention was called to a bale of cotton where green flies had been attracted in large numbers. After breaking the bale, the neut was found crushed in a horrible manner. It is supposed that the little creature had been looking at the work of the press and, at an unguarded moment, got too close to the edge and fell over into the box, a depth of 12 or 15 feet. With the noise of the gin, the neut's cries could not be heard, and the lint cotton poured down, smothering and pressing out any trace of life.

NEUT–NECRONAUT MELEE

Exclusive to the Moon

For as long as the Moon has rolled around in the heavens, neuts and necronauts have been at odds. Sometimes these ancient, latent emotions break through as they did yesterday on the CL10 bus to Eternity Meadows. Well-known necronauts were looking forward to their weekly visitations to the Meadows where they liked to picnic. Sal Mineo, Henrik Ibsen, Frank Sinatra, Deborah Kerr, Mitzi Gaynor, Friedrich Nietzsche and Boris Karloff were among the riders. All had empty picnic baskets in their laps and were chatting cordially when the bus stopped at the Gas Flats terminal, where 10 or 12 neutrodynes boarded. At first, they were satisfied to merely glare menacingly and wave their flocculuses at the now anxious necronauts. Soon after taking their seats, however, their blood boiled. One of them, Larry Hemphill, lurched at Frank Sinatra and cut his throat with a corn knife. There was no blood, no dying, no death, just a tilt back of the head and a release of body gas. Mr. Karloff lifted Sinatra's nearly severed head back into position and held it there.

"Don't be an idiot," Karloff barked. "You can't hurt us."

Hemphill raised the knife. "It's not the harm, it's the humiliation after death. That's the point. Don't you dead ones get it?"

"Leave us alone," Kerr pleaded.

Mitzi Gaynor spat something light and airy like a milkweed seed at Hemphill to no effect.

"One more thing," Hemphill growled, his flocculus engorged and glowing red. "You know why we're going to the Meadows today? Take a guess."

Ibsen stirred in his sleep and opened his eyes. "To dig us up, I bet."

"That's right. We're gonna throw those bones into a pile and set them on fire. Enough is enough. Once dead, always dead. That's what we think."

The youthful Mineo suddenly leapt from his seat and dragged Hemphill to the door of the bus, where, with the cooperation of the necronaut driver who opened the door, he threw him off. Riders heard the thump of the wheels crushing the neut and broke into applause and low laughter.

Stringer Knutson
Bunkerville Station

TITANIC RAISED

3 Dead, 6 Hurt, 11 to Hang. A Survivor Tells All

Fast she sank. We fought for the cabin we had occupied continuously, three generations, since the teens of this century. Hideous fist banging against our door would not move us to sacrifice the space designed to save our girl baby, ourselves and our parrot, Vaginia. We drifted bottomward for hours. We heard the steady *thunk* of the air compressor in our closet, preserving us; a bubble in the bloodstream of the ocean was all we were. Shortly, we ate squid tentacles and whale eyes and relished the tasty brain of a porpoise, though we convulsed in shame the first time we broke open the skull of that precious life form.

We believed ourselves alone until the day we began to receive transmissions from Radio Universal in the electric light bulbs informing us in a simple, informational way that the City of Mind, the common mind of a species, is a *synedrium*. It cannot be conquered except by another *synedrium* of a greater number in its cube.

Onēba does not intend to permit you to exist without contradiction because he knows that if you ever reach a state of harmony within yourself, he cannot hope to stand against you, your mind, or your species. The sunken Titanic exists as a physical reality and a place of dwellings inhabited by bleached people. The children of the Titanic culture belong to all its citizens. That's what Radio Universal said to us shortly after we bumped against the ocean floor. As the years brought the soldiers of time against us, we saw the prophecy of Radio Universal borne out, as our skeletons glowed through blanched bodies and our talk turned to adopting abyssal fish as gods.

ZANZETTI CREATES PUZZLING NEW DOG STYLE

For one, it is a team of two, but for another, it is a beast which, though it be two, is as one. The scientist and his assistants performed surgery on two male Scotties, severing them in half just below the ribs and transferring the upper half of one Scottie to the lower half of the other Scottie. When the animals were out of danger, the results were brilliant. Now we have one Scottie with two heads at opposite ends of the body and another with two tails in the same locations.

Balls and Mulligan, the treated Scotties, never stray from one another's sides. In fact, Mulligan goes nowhere at all without a blind charge by Balls, all energy without restraint, feet churning to no effect, in perpetual motion, Mulligan's only motivation.

Without the propulsion of the mated hind quarters, Mulligan embodies no compulsion to move. Instead, he rests, stares, and entrances spectators in Wuntex Park, and sometimes in the lobby of the Gons Hotel where the duo starred last week.

Zanzetti says the pair are fastened by a biomechanical mechanism the size of a stuffed Frisbee that will last far longer than any surgical bone-to-bone, nerve-to-nerve and muscle-to-muscle connection and eliminate any need to "diddle with the genetic code."

Zanzetti thinks of himself more as an artist of the beautiful than a scientist in this case. "Aren't my Scotties the cutest things?" he asks. "Sure, we could have done the same experiment with machined duplicates, but I prefer to work with real life."

This reporter had a good look at Mulligan and Balls, following along as Zanzetti walked them. Balls, with two sets of legs operating in opposite directions, had to be carried under

Zanzetti's arm as its feet ran in the air. Mulligan, with two heads, had no direct way of going forward or backward, but he still managed to move by trotting in circles, inching along with a little lurch at every roundabout.

EDITORIAL

Well, here we are at the ides of another June. It's a good time to take a vacation and overhaul your brain from the frontal lobe to the cerebellum. Review your axioms, revise your postulates and reconsider the unexpressed, minor premises of your habitual forms of logic. All your reasoning, however great, may be vitiated by some fundamental fallacy carelessly adopted and uncritically retained. Get a blubber lamp and peer into all the dark corners of your mind. No doubt you keep the halls and reception room in decent and creditable order. But how would you like to let your friends look into your cerebral garret and subliminal cellar, where the toys of childhood and the prejudices you inherited from your ancestors, mold and rot? Hunt out and destroy every old rag of superstition, for these are liable, at any time, to start that spontaneous combustion of ideas we call fanaticism, against which there is no earthly insurance. A little decaying superstition in the mind of a great leader has been known to conflagrate a nation.

TELEPATHY USED ON BEASTS

From the Archives
Radiola, the Italian performer and entertainer, uses

telepathy on dogs, cats, monkeys, cockatiels and other common pets. He transfers human thoughts to animals while he and they are enclosed in a specially constructed iron pyrite box. He chants to them, he says, until they succumb to the physical rays that emanate not only from his brain, but from the nervous systems of any animals present in the box.

Radiola was among the passengers who yesterday arrived from Glasgow on the anchor liner *Neutrodyne*, returning from a half century of exile at Tumu-Tumu, Kenya Colony, British East Africa, during which time he lived among people who made good beer from honey and produced tons of what they called piss-kissed jelutong. At the same time these people had good times applying glowing iron pokers to the feet of any travelers dreaming of establishing small empires on the backs of native laborers, then forcing them to sit bare-bottom on a bed of bulldog ants, the most venomous of all the ant species.

In this jungle setting Radiola's psycho-animism grew more powerful, along with the conviction that he must come to America and let his discoveries be known. Calling his new discovery Radionics, he drove through Oklahoma City, where a young Italian ragamuffin carrying a shoeshine box darted through the crowd toward his car. The boy's name was Rudolph Giuliani, a harmless screwball whose antics have made news at various times. Giuliani said, "I just wanted to shine Radiola's shoes."

NATIONAL FIRE BURNS OUT

In far North Dakota the last embers of the great fire were stomped on by a young girl, Raven Randall, 10, of Minot. The stomping was more symbolic than anything as the fire had been slowly dying for years and had finally surrendered its last spark to a young girl's shoe.

In all, fire officials say, more than 10,000 square kilometers of grass and scrub land were burned, along with thousands of homes, barns and other homestead structures. Millions of farm animals, from cattle to swine, were consumed. Wild creatures including harmless reptiles, hare, partridge and field rats were decimated. The list goes on.

Marvin Beckett, a farmer near Hugoton, Kansas, is quoted as saying, "I lost everything we had. My poor wife shot the kids and then herself. I can't go on.... I'll go on."

COMIC BOOK NAMED IN SIMIAN'S DEATH

A funny book has killed Lillycakes, a Wuntex Park Zoo monkey, who didn't read but ate it. It wasn't laughter that killed Lilly, but the comic's metal binding. Wire staples were found in her stomach. Zoo officials had seen the monkey munching on the comic book thrown into her cage by a careless boy.

NOTICE

By ordinance, neutrodynes within designated neighborhoods must now carry identity cards or else be banned from Gas Flats after dark. Consider this fair warning and a reminder that other cities and townships in the region are considering similar ordinances. City officials will begin to comb Gas Flats neighborhoods on Monday at 5 a.m., looking for neuts wherever they might be sleeping: under porches, sometimes in clusters of 10 or more, in culverts, under park benches and picnic tables, in derelict cars and junkyard bathtubs or mattresses, to warn them in person of the new sundown laws.

Sheriff Prop.

FIRE LOST IN A.D. 22

The least known of all historical secrets is this: that fire was lost, briefly, 22 years after the Christ was born. For two years, we had no fire at all. Polar evenings grew yet darker. Early Esquimaux blubber lamps dimmed without apparent cause then fizzled out. In Africa, already a dark continent, meat had to be eaten raw, thus explaining the development of open cannibalism there and rarely in other places. Above the Indian plains of Kansas, lightning ceased to ignite prairie and tall-grass fires. Prior to the loss of fire, in what is currently Japan, puffer fish, now eaten raw, were always fried in hot fat. Without fire, the Nipponese politely starved themselves, which is still the way in the rural areas of their culture.

Other attempts were made to rekindle the fire. Clarifying what the Book of Revelations and Radio Universal told us later, an astonishing mechanical development took place, seen clearly in the light of new knowledge: The mechanism looked like an enormous cricket made of brass and pig iron. Its purpose, as told by the historian Josephus, was to take flight, soar heavenward to gain momentum, then plunge to Earth, to crash against stone and thereby cause a spark that ignited burnt cloth and cedar duff kindling, bringing fire back to the known world.

The transition was easy. People burned meat and fried fish

again over open flames, eventually eliminating the physiological need for an appendix. Every jitney carnival between Jerusalem and Nazareth then began to feature bottled fire, fire water and fire stamps redeemable for one kill order.

TOXIC ISLAND TOURS Make a reservation now! We ferry passengers to and around Permanganate Island, four miles downstream from Muncie. This one-square-mile island of only partly understood composition has been rising from the Trench for decades. One scholar of medieval history described the island as "looking like Mont Saint Michel," which was devilishly hard to get to in medieval times owing to an evening tide that rushed in quite briskly, trapping dalliers there for the night. Schedules and prices? Call Bywater 5115 or send a post card to Toxic Island Tours c/o the *City Moon*, Box 591.

CHARCOAL BURNER ATTEMPTS TO KILL FAMILY

Joseph Schnerble, employed at Kingsford Charcoal as a burner, who, about a week ago, tried to kill his family with a corn knife, has been arrested. Police say that he returned to his cabin about 10 and said to his family, "I have just learned how to use this Cuban corn-cutting knife and now I want all of you to stand up." To humor him they rose, laughing nervously. He tied their hands with pieces of cord which he slung over the rafters. Then, holding the knife, he commenced cutting his family, inflicting dreadful wounds. The laughter stopped abruptly. As he completed his work, alarmed by this turn of events, he seized his army musket and fled. A posse was quickly organized, but as yet he has not been found. Villagers beg for kill orders to use if he is located. Schnerble is a member of the Radio Universal Club of Wanderers, and stays tuned, sleepless, weeks on end, wandering, listening to the music of the spheres. He is hard to locate.

Dear *City Moon*,

Explanations drift. Some blame it on Radio Universal. Take our best friend, Plookie Morrison, who said people brought him an electric radio last Christmas and each night since then he has listened to Radio Universal from 5-9, and when the veep's Kill Order to erase your own life went down, he tried. Unfortunately, the hot bullet severed his optic nerves, leaving him blind, but otherwise uninjured. He was up and about that very afternoon, chatting with friends. Radio Universal put the idea into his head, he claims, and he plans legal action against the shady outfit.

Your friend,

Leon K.

At Large

Dear Leon K: The question the City Moon *asks is this: Can Radio Universal steal all life from Earth, one poor soul at a time? Perhaps even more importantly, why can't we take the radio by its knobs and turn it off once we feel the danger? Don't let it continue to play on in your head as Plookie Morrison did. Silence it for good.*

HISTORICAL FACT

Thirteenth century cardinals Sully and Richelieu were expert dancers. Imagine the August cardinals paying court to Anne of Austria by performing a sarabande before her in jester's attire of green velvet, with bells on their feet, castanets in their hands and, as reported by those present, quite visible erections beneath the velvet.

Effie Pfeffer
On the Road to History

EDITORIAL

Loren Rovingstine claims that, while traveling north of Goshen Indiana in December of 1951, he saw the first of the neutrodyne landing pods. It was initially thought that Rovingstine was hallucinating, as no evidence of the pods could be found. But when Rovingstine's two sons, Gull and Opie, were questioned, they corroborated their father's story. So, if this is to be believed, the neuts have been with us for 20 years and have managed, against all odds, to assimilate well enough in that short time to be welcomed on a tentative basis. Yes, they were even given a few rights, which they called, sarcastically, "starter rights," implying that more would come later.

These rights were:
to seek shelter from the rain and cold,
to find food, catch as catch can, and
to choose free burial or cremation.

I doubted Rovingstine's story, until, going to California with friends and family a couple of winters ago for a sail on the Salton Sea, we stopped at the Painted Desert sign. While parked there, we were blinded by a bright light about 200 feet from the car. It was a bright-eyed thing and seemed to be mostly meat. And it was lying on its back. We were stricken with compulsion and hunger and all took a warm, juicy bite from the abdomen with the innocence of Adam. Who would have predicted that we would eat things from space like lions feeding on a wildebeest?

However neuts came here, and however they behave, they are ultimately an asset, and we should care for them as best we can. Let's start by not eating their young, no matter how strong the compulsion. Stack blankets on your porch for them. Let them sleep in the yard. Give them food—they'll eat almost anything, like pigs. Let them drink from the hose and sleep in the garage on rainy nights. And, most importantly, even though it isn't against the law, we should stop shooting them just for fun.

CAPTAIN SMITH IMPOSTER DIES

An unknown, penniless man who had been impersonating Captain "Silent" Smith of the ill-fated Titanic has died in Lima, Ohio. For more than 30 years the man had been a downtown fixture in Lima, begging coins and living in the park. Wearing a brass-button pea jacket and sailor's duty cap, he held out his hand for passersby, palm up, ready to catch coins, and sang them little ditties. His favorite:

"Capella the goat is a favorable sign for seamen afloat on the great rolling brine."

When asked his name, he only muttered, "They don't call me Silent Smith for nothing."

The man's body was discovered in the park by a bicyclist and underwent an autopsy. "Undoubtedly, he was an Irish seaman," the coroner reported. "The Rock of Ages was tattooed on his chest. A map of Mars was tattooed on his back." His height and weight were the same as the Titanic's Captain Smith. Embalmed by a local undertaker, the body has been kept on display, in an effort to identify him. Thus far no one has, but the body is a good barometer, expanding and contracting with changes in atmospheric pressure. The hair and beard continue to grow and must be cut every so often.

TITANIC SURVIVORS WILL DANGLE

Following his sensational escape from the Tuttle Jail last night, at liberty for 10 minutes, Lester Pogue, Titanic survivor, is now back in his cell nursing a broken tailbone and will have to hobble to the gallows on crutches when he is hanged this Friday.

Dangling with him that day will be J. Wade Cody, a high kicking vandal, also a Titanic survivor, who kicked in four fender panels at Boxberger Motors and lodged his foot a little too far into the windshield of a Cadillac during one of his famous kicks. The next morning police found him sleeping on the Cadillac's hood, the following day the Tuttle court judged him and Friday a week a noose will hang him.

Additional Survivors to Hang in Utah. John Jacob Astor and Barnum's Tiny Tim, both survivors of the Titanic disaster, will be hanged in Salt Lake City this Friday. "It's a good day for all of us," the president said. "We don't want these encrusted survivors of that sunken boat of the past bringing up muddy memories of the First World War. Times like those are best forgotten. Hang them all. End of discussion."

ONĒBA INTRODUCES PLUG CATTLE

Everyone remembers the fantastic story of the discovery of cooked beef. According to Charles Lamb, in the China of A.D. 400, a house burned down with all its outbuildings, including a barn full of cattle. Afterward, a farmer and his neighbors, attracted by the sweet and sour smell of the fresh-roasted meat, took knives and cut plugs from the roasted animals and found it delicious.

For a long while afterward, whenever anyone hankered after cooked meat, a barn was burned down. This kept on until barns were in danger of disappearing altogether, when an adviser to the ruler of the next dynasty was wise enough to see that it was possible to plug a cow and cook the meat over a brazier without burning a barn.

After this custom had flourished for centuries, stripping cattle came to America. With stripping cattle, you simply rip off sheets of meat, painless to the cow, which re-meats itself overnight. You can sauté, slow cook or grill the strips and eat them, or stitch them into shirts or blouses that draw flies away from your face.

THE SEARCH FOR THE URPFLANZE

Onēba here. In this column I would like to treat the subject of the "ideal plant," which the German writer Goethe called the *urpflanze*. Since then, people have tramped through back pastures and rarefied deserts in search of the plant, though none but I have come upon it. When I did, in an Oregon forest, I carefully lifted the large plant and its long, mossy roots from damp earth and took it to my laboratory. The colorless juice of the plant will cure anything but habit. Chewing the stems, or smoking dried ones, leads to whiter teeth, healthier gums and an overall feeling of well-being. Making a tea of the dried leaves and drinking it daily will supply you with twice the energy on half the sleep. Eating the little, bitter drupes of the plant late in the season will sicken you, though. It's a plant with miraculous benefits but should be approached with caution. I only hope and pray I didn't pull up the only one.

> **Dear *City Moon*,**
> **Why not breed for better human stock, as we do with hogs and plants? Just as there is an ongoing Process during which all the material of the universe shifts, fluxes and transmogrifies, and just as this Process invariably leads to dissolution, common sense and reason point us down the road of selective breeding, collective child rearing and harvesting the energy locked up in the neutrodyne dead. Readers, please vote to sanction my experiments. Think of a frosty night by the fireplace with a loved one, warmed by a slow-burning and sweet smelling neutrodyne composite log. Dead neuts left to rot in gutters and rural ditches are a wasted energy source and should be legal to use as fuel asap.**
> **E. Zanzetti**
> **Scientist**

ZUGUNRUHE ALERTS NEUTRODYNES TO MIGRATE

Neutrodynes meet in a scruffy congregation outside Pisstown near the summer solstice. They are anxious. It's a feeling in their bones. They must move south. In ethology *zugunruhe* describes anxious behavior in migratory animals, especially in birds during the normal migration period. The behavior occurs even if the birds are kept in deep, darkened caves.

Neutrodyne ponies raise a hazy dust cloud over the town, which lingers for days. Children and the elderly cough up yellow bile. Some die. The neutrodynes do this, our correspondent reports, to lay plans for their wanderings. The behavior seems to involve the highest reaches of economic social organization. They choose to travel together, and at night, because it is safe that way, not that there is any comradeship among them.

Gathered on the outskirts of Pisstown, they discuss the migration for days, with aggressive in-fighting, often assault, and so complete are the arrangements that very few strollers are left behind.

TONG TORTURE PAD

Neal Cassady is back, running the Painium, a tong-torture pad in San Francisco. These punks are on the latest molecular version of a drug called Neutronia-P2. Cassady takes these punks, once they get out of line, puts the hot tongs to their nipples and applies the pressure. Some of his customers faint at the smell of their own burning flesh.

This is not a *jamais vu* but a cold, hard truth. Reinvigorated, Cassady is as mean as a rabid skunk. If you crossed him in life, watch out. On the other hand, if you're a drug punk, you can use him; he'll talk you down. They say he's hanging out with Sheriff Prop and learning the ropes of police work.

The question Bunkervillians are asking is whether Cassady should be hung along with the bleached survivors of the Titanic mishap, or released into the custody of Mr. Ken Kesey, of Pleasant Hill, Oregon, former acid-king of punkdom, who has offered to provide elder care for the famous talker for the rest of his life.

Spurning the generous offer, Cassady headed south to San Miguel de Allende, in Old Mexico. In 1969, after an evening of pulque drinking, he collapsed on a railroad track and died in peace.

SHE BLOWS HERSELF UP

Charity Green, 23, has spent the last nine years blowing herself up for charity. In that time, she has used more than a truckload of dynamite to send herself whirling through over 800 explosions. Charity is the feature attraction of the Mo Magic Stunt Show, which travels from coast to coast. Twice each performing day she puts her life on the line with nine sticks of dynamite.

She sits, in yoga fashion, her head tucked between her legs, in the center of a three-sided, foil-covered capsule. The countdown begins. At zero she rubs the two wires that connect to a detonator, which is attached to the load of dynamite. Then, a terrific explosion sends her flying out of the capsule. For fifteen minutes following the explosion she writhes on the ground, not knowing where she is. The burst has knocked the air out of her lungs and, like a drowning person, she must be forced to breathe again.

Three men are assigned to see that she is revived. One opens her mouth to make sure she doesn't swallow her tongue. Another slaps her gently across her sooty face. The third sponges cool water and salve on whatever scrapes and burns she may have.

"This new exploding art," Green says, "is too important to kid yourself about, and I, Charity Green, am crusading for that cause."

MIRACLE MIKE APPEARING NIGHTLY AT THE OLD GONS BALLROOM

Miracle Mike and his assistant, Mo Magic, a behatted, skeleton of a man from Texas, claim to be representatives of Radio Universal. When on stage at the old Ballroom, Miracle Mike's earthly father's head sits pickled in a jar on a table beside him. Miracle Mike can make its lips move and reproduce with perfect fidelity personal commands from Radio Universal. The head then solicits coin in a bubbling voice and the mouth spits a dime into the fluid to illustrate the idea that only by tithing to it generously can the head be kept alive. Tomatoes and eggs hurled at Miracle Mike, as they often are, are mostly blocked by Mo Magic's tennis racquet and have little effect, though the yolks of eggs sometimes gum up the lids of Miracle Mike's star-crossed eyes.

"A sponge of vinegar will get that egg off pretty quick," Mike says. "My show will go on whether they hate me or like me. Daddy's head is real, and it has things to say, including advice on many topics of interest to the young."

SPECIAL TO THE MOON

Onēba's Seventh Death
Led to the edge of a fetid swamp by friends, Onēba placed

a thumb-smudge of ashes in the middle of his forehead and retired to a tree, a cypress to be exact. His friends chained him to one of its knees by prearrangement. The logging chain, attached to a 20-inch metal collar around his waist was long enough to give him 20 or 30 feet of range. He built a lean-to for shelter, dug a hole with his overgrown fingernails to collect rain, and ate palmetto leaves and tree bark. In the thirty days it took him to die, he very likely reflected on his sixth life, his favorite so far, and all the good times he enjoyed as a man, a lover and a president for six years. In that time, he fathered 17 children with 17 mothers and loved every one of them dearly, he claimed.

Years later, two men hunting wild boar found his bones. Nearby were sneakers, shreds of his robe, a leather belt, books, including a Bible, and a radio. Only 10 of his 206 bones remained. Sheriff Prop said the rest must have been carted off by wild shoats or shabbits. Also found was a crude toilet Onēba had dug with his fingernails in the cold earth to relieve himself. In the end, he was identified by a jawbone fragment and an identity card.

Bryan Flattering,
City Moon *Literary Editor*
and author of Onēba 's Sixth Death

SHOCKING DISCOVERY

Emmet and Eugene Robinson were passing the Blue Light, a Pisstown brothel, when they discovered a scrotal sack stuck onto an iron picket in front of the place. It was freshly cut and at first it was thought that a murder had been committed. But it was quickly learned that the bag belonged to Pozeki Mott, 73, a man who had died at the Lower Farm's Pasteur College of Medical Arts months before of an undisclosed cerebral event. On Saturday night, a party of Christian medical students had broken into the cold storage room, severed Mott's weighty, frozen scrotum, which by then had distended greatly, then carried it to the sporting house and jammed it onto the picket. One of the students later said of the testes, "They were long. They must have been under water when he took a c**p." The scrotal bag was eventually returned to the college in a desiccated, shriveled condition, and will be interred with the rest of Mott's body at Eternity Meadows.

A CEREMONY OF SHAME

Hemp is used in twines, oakum and packing. It endures heat, friction and moisture. It dyes blue or violet with an aqueous iodine solution and is high in cellulose. For this reason, it makes a sturdy rope which may be used in many ways, as it was yesterday, to haul young neutrodyne females with violet nooses around their necks down a busy City street in a neutrodyne shame ceremony. Most pedestrians looked away from the awful scene and placed hands over their ears to soften the shrill wails the females produced as they choked and gagged and were pulled along on bloody knees.

NOXIN EXHUMED, MONEY FOUND

When the colon of the former president was autopsied after exhumation last Ash Wednesday, a wad of U.S. bills the size of a soft ball was discovered. Noxin was well known for the practice of eating balled-up paper money and including shavings of gold and uranium in his salads and soups. He had been committing slow suicide. Infection developed when he was counting money in his Oval Office, flicking bills from the stack with a long fingernail, which he lifted unconsciously to scratch his ear every now and then, sometimes inflicting a minor cut. The wound was poisoned with germs from the dirty bills and developed into an abscess that, joined with the intestinal blockage, killed him.

The surgeon general ordered the exhumation after a group of Noxin's staff members filed affidavits alleging that the president often asked them for money, claiming he would show them a trick, only to stuff the bills into little plastic packets and swallow them, then go to the next cubicle and repeat the show. It seems now that the evidence is in, including the cedar chest in Noxin's bedroom found full of dried balls of money smelling slightly of feces, that he had been running this scam all his public life.

HAGFISH FOUND IN POPULAR SWIMMING HOLE

Known commonly as the slime-eel, up to three feet long, the hagfish breathes through its nose, sees through its skin, can tie itself in knots, and has those coming to the Trench to swim befuddled. Now they see bright red warnings everywhere: NO

SWIMMING! But why? No explanation is given. Despite that, several show-offs dive in, are under far too long, until wives and children are gasping and crying. Minutes later, the swimmers emerge, covered head to toe in slime. They slide out of the water and fall onto the bank. They struggle for breath until bystanders come along and pull the slime away from their faces.

The hagfish can live without food for more than a year. When afraid, it hides inside a globule of jellylike material secreted into surrounding water. The hag has four hearts, each beating in a different rhythm, which separately control its head, tail, muscles and liver. It has a skull but no backbone. Photosensitive cells all over its girth enable the hag to "see" where it is going, generally toward the neutrodyne sleeping camps scattered along the Trench, where it feeds on infants thrown into the water and watches for feet to dawdle at the ends of piers long enough for a bite to be taken and blood sucked.

THOUGHT FOR FOOD FOR THOUGHT

Place a raw hag egg in a cocktail glass, sprinkle with sugar and chopped parsley. Puncture the yoke with your little finger, add rainwater with a spritz of seltzer and you have a nice, cool late summer drink. Whenever a recipe calls for bat or turtle, use hag. It has a deeper, darker flavor. Be sure to soak it in vinegar for 48 hours, though, to rinse away every trace of the bile-tasting slime.

Lordi Lordiss
Food Editor

ALL THE WORDS IN THE WORLD

Hazel Brown, 60, a well-known American educator and Navy commander, had scarcely reached Paris when her clothes were torn off by French Europeans and thrown to the crowd as souvenirs. People caught the shreds and put them away in their closets. Parisians were in love with this teacher, who had brought so many of the young poor in the United States out of a cosmic fog of ignorance into the halls of learning and logic.

Most recently she had been asked to teach ninth grade in one of Bunkerville's poorest schools. Conditions there were such that, during the lunch recess, children could be seen squatting around desk-wood fires, roasting pigeons, which were abundant in the asphalt schoolyard and easily killed by a hurled marble or a rock. Otherwise the school served only starchy rice pudding for lunch, day after day, which the children hated.

Even under these conditions, Hazel Brown drew *whoops* from 50 pupils in her English class last Monday for requesting them to discover how many words there were in print around the world.

Under a kind of hypnotic compulsion, during the following week, half the students at first tried to obtain information from librarians and college professors but failed. An indignant conclave of nuns and school authorities decided the only way to answer the question was to *count* the words, which the other half of the students rightly understood was impossible and refused to participate in.

Brown herself said she didn't know or expect to ever know the actual number, but that "it probably exceeds the googol," meaning the number one followed by 100 zeroes.

Asked why she had conceived such an assignment, Brown said, "Very simple. It separates those who would willingly waste time attempting the impossible from those who recognize the futility and refuse. You need both types in the government and in the military. One cancels the other. All warring factions will be in stasis, at odds, at loggerheads, and peace finally achievable."

After her tour of France, Brown returned to Bunkerville and continued to spread her message. "Every teacher must use this assignment, and the results must be carefully and accurately recorded for reference and future use by authorities."

Sadly, just a day before her 70th birthday, Hazel Brown died of what are called 'brain eating amoeba' (*Naegleria fowleri*) two months after swimming in the Trench. She will be truly missed. The president himself plans to attend her funeral events and toss her ashes into the still water at the spot of her infestation.

VEEP IN CLOSE SHAVE

Editorial

The self-declared vice president, who some believe to be a necronaut disguised as the veep, had a narrow escape from a possible second death yesterday as he watched a flatball game at Wuntex Park Stadium between the Pisstown Tomcats and the Denver Doves. A model airplane appeared over the stadium quite suddenly, flying this way and that, doing acrobatics. The crowd cheered, until the operator lost control and the machine took a dangerous tilt to one side and swooped over the V.I.P. box, plucking the veep's snap-brim hat from his head with its roaring propellers, doing no harm to him, but tragically striking a flatball fan sitting behind him, killing her. The plane's operator fled and has not been located.

The hotly-contested game ended in a draw. Unfortunately for them and their families, three players were struck by the hard-thrown, disk-like, pounded-leather flatballs and died of injuries to the throat. Typically, the flatball's rim is studded with sharp blades, like a saw. It's not that the *City Moon* isn't a big fan of flatball. We just think the blades should be outlawed. They're only there to let blood when a player scores. Long-time fans who remember a time when there were no blades allowed say it was a better game. Then the ball killed and injured in other ways: fractures of the skull, blindings, lost teeth, crushed Adam's Apple *(prominentia laryngea)* leading to voice box injuries and speaking difficulties. A ball striking the back of the neck can still kill or paralyze. One hitting you in the temple will knock you cold if it doesn't kill you. A hard one to the groin would be painful enough without the blades. We say, civilize flatball. Outlaw the blades.

HOP 'O' MY THUMB SUFFOCATES

Little Sterling Ragsdale, 6, known as Hop 'o' My Thumb, gave up trying to cool himself in the late summer heat with lemonade and a bamboo fan and hopped into an old refrigerator with a bag of dry ice in a fatal effort to lower his body temperature. He propped the refrigerator door open with a stick, but a sudden gust across the trochilic-occupied valley blew the stick away and the door closed. Neighbors were unable to hear little Hop's muffled cries for help, and the carbon dioxide sublimating from the dry ice quickened the suffocation.

Sterling's parents, Judy and Jeff Ragsdale, distraught, inconsolable, did nothing to find their son. They assumed he had been kidnapped and only waited and wept. When Sterling was found a month later, he was wearing only a t-shirt and had fresh human bite marks at the hilts of his small fingers.

Hop 'o' My Thumb Ragsdale will be cremated at his parents' behest and Armand Henault, who immortalizes friends and acquaintances by molding their ashes, will shape little Hop into a flower pot, in which a marigold will be planted.

WOMAN DALLIES WITH SHABBITS

Sheriff Prop has been informed that a petite, gray-haired neutrodyne female of Tuttle has for years been dallying in apparent harmony with a house full of shabbits while painting them to look like skunks.

"I can see dozens from my rear balcony," says a neighbor, "tails and heads hanging out all the neut's windows, dropping fecal pellets into the peony beds below."

When Prop surveyed the home's exterior in the beam of a flashlight, bright red eyes peered back. "There must have been 20 or 30 of them looking at me through parted drapes," he said. Then the door opened. The neut woman stood with a head of lettuce in her hand. When Prop looked into her living room, he saw skunk-painted shabbits running all over the house through the filthy, ammonia-smelling chaff that covered the ruined floors.

When he had completed his inspection, the sheriff stood on the porch and asked the neut why she kept so many shabbits and why she painted them that way.

She answered, "I hate people, but I love shabbits. I don't want people coming here. People are afraid of skunks, not shabbits." Then she slammed the door in his face. Although the neut was unpleasant in every way, no laws were broken, and the sheriff took no action.

THIS IS CINERAMA? AN UNFLATTERING REVIEW

It is a pity that Ark On Leo and Yuk Lin Leo plunged to their deaths from a window of their fourth floor suite at the Gons Hotel after setting fire to $75,000 cash in a gold, ancestral bucket. Now this senior-citizen-aged stage and film duo will have died with the taint of their last and worst Cinerama production staining their reputations in the immediate future: *The Death of Sinowe Kesibwi*. This is a rotten three reels of cinerama, hanging like a dirty diaper from an infantile plot. Police shoot to death nine pigs that were terrorizing the neutrodyne camps at Manila. The shootings precipitate a feud between the neutrodynes of Piggy Lane and Warren Pacillo, owner of a 400-pig farm adjacent to the camp, played by Enfield Peters. Neighbors have complained for years that unpenned sows dug up gardens and flower beds and chased children to protect their piglets. Sergeant Pajak, played by Ark On Leo, and his men go to the camp and kill 10 pigs. Pacillo nurses three more wounded sows but only one remains alive. He claims Pajak's men crossed into his woods to shoot the pigs, and in the process wounded two of his best neutrodyne workers.

Then the shooting begins. As is typical of the Manila cinema, Yuk Lin Leo arrives at Ark's side, a classic *deus ex machina*, appearing neither young nor old, angel nor hag, man nor woman. Is it a dream figure? Why do others arrive lacking any organic connections to the plot, forcing us to provide our own uneasy explanations for their presence?

Pacillo, meanwhile, tries a fresh strategy in the gun battle. Riding atop an elephant, Big Burma, he drives his remaining pigs toward Ark On Leo's frame-and-paper house, delivering a sermon with a bullhorn, wearing floppy ears and standing on a tailor-made perch. He then stampedes his elephant through the walls of the house.

We left the movie feeling any meaning it may have been building toward was certainly erased in the final, meaningless minutes.

Bryan Flattering
City Moon Literary Editor

ONĒBA BEHIND BARS

From the Archives

During his first night in detention for the assault and beating of presidential contender Justin Case, Onēba lay in a drop-ceiling room on a municipal bed and said he slept very well. He was routed out at 5 a.m. and sent to the woodpile for a morning of laborious oak-splitting for the prison's distillery. After four hours there, it was decided he had earned his breakfast and, with the oatmeal, bread and coffee consumed, he went to City Hall, was adjudged there and sentenced to six months at the Lower Farm's elite prison, inaptly named Wayfarers Lodge, which is to be congratulated on the way it is run. The quarters are well kept and clean. The prisoners seen at the lodge are strong, able-bodied and willing to work. Absolutely no signs of drink or dissipation were noted.

After a long fast, Onēba was visited in his cell by many of his aspirants, a cell which is the breeziest and most comfortable in the lodge. He ate a tough, dry, sirloin tip steak, some army beans, and drank two quarts of buttermilk.

He said to a reporter, "There is no man in this lockup more rational than I am. The jury was in error when it found me guilty of trumped-up charges. Still, I am satisfied that those who instituted the proceedings were acting in good faith toward me and meant it to be for my own welfare."

Moments after Onēba's pronouncement, his stomach gurgled, and gas sputtered from his rear end. "I may never again attempt the experiment of fasting," he said.

ITALIANS WASTE SEXTON

During my service in Manila, I happened to be wandering through a neutrodyne cemetery, generally on the way to the grave of Asia's revered Mr. Beefcake, a champion wrestler of the 1920s billed as the Harmless Horror. He was interred vertically, customary in those days, the feet protruding from the earth, now just a pile of metacarpals, a few slivers of toenail and a gnarled shoe full of dead leaves.

I took with me a fresh marigold, a favorite of Mr. Beefcake's in life, a box of zwieback in case I got hungry, and a quart of soup. About halfway to the grave site I happened to see a neutrodyne sexton boring a hole with a galvanic auger. Sweating all over, wiping head and neck with a bandanna, the neut said, "I keep planting them, but they never come up."

Suddenly several Italians surrounded the sexton, snatched at his pockets, telling him that money shouldn't be worth his life. All of them were unemployed and desperate. Before the poor neut could say a single phrase in his defense, the muzzle of a service pistol was placed at the crest of his ear and a shot fired. The neut collapsed to the ground, rolled into the excavation, voided himself and died.

Eventually I found Mr. Beefcake's grave, somewhat above ground and overgrown with kudzu. I sat on a banquette nearby and thought about Mr. Beefcake's illustrious career. One thousand victories, no losses.

I picked a kudzu leaf from the grave and placed it inside my copy of the Kama Sutra to dry.

Carlos

Rincon Nada, N.M.

TROCHILIC BOY DIES IN PLUNGE

A trochilic boy of 14 spun his way into Pisstown Stadium in full regalia and up to the very top tier of seats during a flatball battle between Tuttle's Tuttlemen and Gas Flats' Sailors. He stopped spinning and sat down just as the catcher, Jerry Tinker, rounded the bases and slid into home. The crowd's attention was drawn to the scene at home plate for several minutes, not to the strange-looking boy with the grotesquely muscled legs at the top of the stadium. When the cheers were finally finished, the crowd looked up to see the boy spinning along the narrow concrete safety barrier just behind the highest seats. His balance was remarkable during a complete spin around the stadium. When he returned, however, he was pale and exhausted. After a few moments of heavy breathing, the boy lost that famous balance and fell to a concrete parking lot 50 feet below.

Because trochilics believe that such sudden and premature deaths as this one are not entirely final, efforts at preserving the body are always made, loosely based on old Egyptian methods. The boy was taken to an Onēba-owned preservation facility and placed onto a cypress board, where his skirts and blouse were removed. The bones of the nose were cracked with a chisel and mallet by one of the preservationists, a hooked wire inserted, and cerebral matter drawn out through the nostrils, put aside and not preserved with the other organs. An incision was made and all contents of the abdomen except the kidneys were removed and the cavity cleaned with Varsol and stringent soap. Then the diaphragm was cut, allowing access to pulmonary regions. The small hearts were not removed but packed in ice to cool.

The preservationist said, "They got hearts like humming birds, three of them. These are still warm." Each piece of viscera was washed in sodium carbonate solution and put into a jar of brine.

Finally, cosmetics were applied to the boy, who was packed with wood shavings and excelsior, dressed in a gabardine suit and dragged into an empty lot to bake and dry in the sun. In a year or two, these "mummies" are ready to display. The odor is gone, the facial skin is like antique leather, the eyelids are burned away, exposing wide-open, bird-pecked eyes, and clothing rat-gnawed in an artful way. Tourists can find them for sale at the entrance to any trochilic camp from east to west.

HOT ROD LUSH PACKS TRIPLE THREAT

Life is cheap on Pisstown's east side. It is a place where kinsmen murder kinsmen, robbers murder merchants, hag fisherman kill one another, wives murder husbands, cousins murder uncles, uncles rape nieces, sweethearts erase lovers, sons kill their fathers and friends kill friends. The great variety of homicides in that area of Pisstown has given it a reputation for being unsafe at any hour, particularly after dark.

A murder of serene compassion was staged Wednesday, March 17, on the east side. Hot Rod Lush and his brother Calvin argued over their younger brother, Bubba, being arrested for raping a 10-year old girl in the neighborhood. Calvin said he believed Bubba was guilty. Hot Rod said, "Not guilty!" and, in his fury went to Calvin's car and got Calvin's big .38 smoker and swept back up in his face and said, "What the hell did you say!? I'll mow you down," and poured three bullets into Calvin's heart.

Boom! Boom! Boom!

Another life was gone, another funeral arranged.

KILLER SIDEWALK SLAYS POET

Nickolina Seravola Black, ace of New York poets, in town to read from her work, was hooked on a killer sidewalk in Gas Flats. Cheap radioactive Mexican rebar was installed by unskilled neutrodyne workmen. They poured concrete over the rebar, but not enough. When the hot sun of August baked the sidewalks, the heated rebar, expanding, sprung like a spring and struck Ms. Black a fatal blow to the head. She will be remembered for a slim volume of verse called *Arts and Sausages*.

SHOES TO BE MADE OF INSECTS
BY JAPANESE PROCESS

"He who is morbid is no adequate in-
terpreter of his age." I.A. Richards

THE CITY MOON

VOL II   NO 1   **1977**   *"Eventually; Why Not Now?"*   ⊙ The City Moon   50 CENTS

MAN SUCKS WETNAPS ¡ BELLED BUZZARD SEEN¡ NECRONAUTS CRUISE

A man in Muncy has mortified himself in a new lemon-scented way, by sucking Wetnaps in a horrible Mexico Lindo Cafe suicide; the belled buzzard of Red-water Texas has been seen again, coming down in a litany of frightening wingchops to eat candy corn with delicate gamecocks on the Prop place east of here; these odoriferous necronauts parading lost in our alleyways carrying duck-facsimiles, dropping finger joints like bleeding peanuts on our ban-quettes; the shocking Topeka beef-liver murders of which I will not talk; the carp kills of Mobile Bay; the Swanees subsidences; the finding of judge Crater so long strolling the golden pony roads of the afterlife and the so happy re-turn of Sal Mineo and Jim Dean, who declare heaven a simple parcourse where they were made to complete suffering 20-mile hikes barefoot, under a dazzling artificial sun, every day, without sustenance beyond a spoon of soy gruel in the evenings, comparing their experience to life on Parchman Farm; Governor Wunty of Georgia promises tent hospitals and free haircuts to boy-scouts ; the saturnalia at the City airport continue, the runway cracks and is not repaired, small craft line it like the bones of once living cattle, pisaweed

sprouts from the bones; Jazzlip Richardson has opened a hotdog stand in Croaker Park; Agonews are staggering away from earth to spread their new definitions on orders of life, rocketing from Earth in clattersome ships powered by propane and operated by behaviorally trained planimals given ammonia wafers, then dropping through swift vortices to a Paradisical planet where inhabitants pedal helium baloons; men are now walking on sidewalks due to the powerful universalot drugs; mantids have been seen, by the thou-sands, walking the streets of Red Water, Texas, all female, on three con-secutive nights, gathering under da-lites for some unknown purpose, then dis-persing and flying off; a similar conflux is mentioned having taken place in Ox-ford, on the Old Parchman grounds, though no connection is drawn by the edi-tors, no conclusion arrived at; Emperor William is sure that he was shot with an air rifle, and not injured by a piece of iron thrown by an epileptic patient, as at first reported; Masuchika Shimose, who invented the high explosive to which the name Shimose powder was given by the Japanese, died today. Send all news releases to City Moon, Box 542, Canal Sta. New York, NY 10013

The Insect Compound

Dung beetle (Scarab) pushing a ball of dung (Coleoptera)

Hymenopteran ovipositing in an aphid (Homoptera)

The New

trochilics

Trochilics move down the river on spiralling double-wheel ro-tation machines motorized by an extremely small and light-blue finished electric engine. As they reach the dam on the Kaw at Lawrence, the slow moving wheels tangle in the drift-wood, and they are forced to camp along the bank at night, and people stopped their autos and backed up traffic along the bridge and stared. Some hurled rotting tomato hearts on the

accidental visitors. They sat in circles around their camp-fires roasting carp on sticks. One of them made a circular motion above the water and catfish spun out onto the mud-bank, joyfully offering their flesh to be eaten by the trochil-ics. The Editor was on the bridge instantly, carrying his camera and a small handgun. He had seen the beatniks, he had seen the hippies, he had seen the revolution come and go,

he had written about the beef-liver killings in Topeka in his newspaper. But he was caught with his britches around his ankles when the Trochilics came to town. Before long the trochilics wan-dered up and began circling through the downtown streets. They re-lieved themselves on streetcorners, urine spiraling from their penis'. They surrounded certain pedestrians in the middle of the day, taunted them, spun their little hot-spin-ning teetotums, the little top-like toys they curry in their pockets, sexually abusing them at times in plain sight of law enforcement off-icials, and nothing was done about it. The arm of the law has been twisted into a useless extremity by these hypnotic trochilics. Had Milton lived in a world be-smudged by the presence of these new trochilics, Paradise Lost would have read like Westworld. And it they'd gone to Mississippi in Faulkner's time, the Hamlet might read like Warhol's Blow Job. Why can't our attorney-general do something about them? Scien-tists at the great university here have said, "When I think of tro-chilics, I think of spirochetes and roundworms and certain ro-tifera, not to mention the double helix itself." Why does the turn-key let them out every night when they've been jailed by day? They say it takes three or four hard-muscled athletes and a $6.98 brace and bit to drill through the heart chamber of an old trochilic. It's worth it.

Mother blind.   Father dead.

SUICIDE PARK -- PAGE TWO

An excerpt:
The Price of Relief
Piss in my eyes $10.00
In my ear $3.00
In my mouth $6.00
On my mammaries $4.00
In my hair $3.50
Full relief menu $30.00

WARNING! NEUT FOOD MAY BE TOXIC

Necronaut peddlers along Arden Boulevard sell ice cream that is prepared in unsanitary conditions, thrown onto filthy carts and wheeled along grimy streets. It is a rich source of typhoid fever and dysentery. Buy a cone from a dead vendor and you'll be burning from both ends in a few hours, though the moment you devour it, you'll awake in paradise.

ADVICE FOR SUICIDES

If you're planning an "April is the cruelest month" suicide, take these steps:

Plan it for outdoors, such as at a park or beach, where guests can dress casually and let loose.

Invite as many as nine but count on an equal number of neutrodynes showing up.

Invite the sheriff to attend, chiefly to maintain discipline.

Schedule the thing to begin in late afternoon and run for

no more than two hours. Don't keep the suicide fans waiting any longer.

Arrange for a simple cookout menu plus snacks.

Assemble equipment for games and bag races.

Sell candy favors and award inexpensive prizes.

Make teams and run races, providing opportunities for roughhouse play.

Play nonsense games, including some that encourage dancing by all the guests.

Eat cookout supper and gather around the fire after the suicide for group singing.

A HAPPY MAN

For a living, Pappy Ragsdale retrieves the eggs of hagfish from golf-course ponds. Born in Chicago, Ragsdale came to Bunkerville a wanted man, a criminal who hurled a waiter from the window of the Blue Pearl Restaurant in the Gons Hotel. The waiter had served him a wormy summer pie. Ragsdale was guilty of assault in the 3rd degree, tried, and served 10 years at the Lower Farm.

He had been a vaudeville actor and stage hypnotist, a specialist in exuvial magic, and here, now, he seines for hag eggs, ices them, salts them and sells them to golfers at a good price.

Asked if he ever missed the glimmer of klieg lights from his former career on stage, Ragsdale said no.

"I will still do acts in front of small groups," he said "like when I bring a kid's dog or cat back from the dead or something like that, but the money's been leeched out of it, the audiences are dull and fickle. I like the private life I have now and I'm happy. Just the hags, the eggs and me."

BUDD SMOKES THREE PISSTOWN NECRONAUTS

Cliff Budd, candidate for mayor of Gas Flats, treated the three inhabitants of a holding cell to a lighted cigar as he was filmed touring the city jail facility. Budd tossed a lit cigar butt onto the rake-straw floor of the cell where the three men were sleeping side by side on their backs and snoring loudly.

A smiling guard said to Budd, "Those are the famous Three Stooges, Moe, Curly and Shemp, all here for public drunkenness and assaulting people with shaving-cream pies."

In a moment, smoke and flames were so intense that Budd and other gawkers backpedaled, coughing and choking.

Onlookers report, and film footage shows, Moe melting down like a holiday candle while Curly and Shemp bubbled and burned.

"That's terrible," Budd is reported to have said to an aide. "We do need to kill that film."

"Yes, sir. That's a given."

LIGHTNING STRIKE DRIVES TUTTLE MAN INSANE

Bloodgood Cutter, a milkman, had come to the City to fish for horned pout in Wuntex Lagoon. After a sunny morning without a nibble, Cutter decided to pack up and call it a day before the afternoon showers came. He could already see darkening thunderheads in the west and he had a long drive back to Tuttle in that very direction. He was worried.

The last step in his getting ready to leave was to reel in the baited line that had been sitting out there on the bottom, undisturbed, for hours. But when he tried to do so he felt a strong tug at the end, something big. He set the hook, waded a few feet into the water and began to reel in the line. He couldn't. He wondered what was on there, a big turtle, maybe a gar, a huge Asian carp, a buffalo fish or even a caiman. Cutter had seen several of them surface that morning. He was determined to haul the creature to the bank and began backing up while tugging on the heavy test line. He was able to gain a foot or two with every tug, but it was going to take a long time.

Cutter glanced at the approaching wall of thunder clouds and tugged ever harder. As fate would have it, he would never know what was on the line. He was struck by lightning. Sheriff Prop, who was the first to examine Cutter after the strike, says that he was alive but delirious and "cooked red like a lobster."

In and out of a coma for months, Cutter eventually recovered and returned to Tuttle, his body healed but his mind gone. It wasn't but a few days back at home when Cutter barged into the Office of Patents and Subventions, bringing something putrid-smelling in a sleeve of newspaper which turned out to be a pickled cow's foot on the end of a broomstick.

He said, "This device can used to determine the best flooring for a cattle barn. I'd like a patent." He was assured by the clerks that such a thing was not possible, and they denied him with a few chuckles and not even a polite adieu.

These days Cutter sits inside his rural home under his aging wife's care, mostly looking out the west window or watching TV.

Ethyl, Cutter's wife, says, "That's all he does anymore is look for storms to come. If one gets close, he'll go out there and sit in a metal chair in the yard till it passes. He thinks if he gets struck again, he might either get back to being normal or die. Either way is OK with him."

Mrs. Cutter tears up as she tells reporters that she had to sell all 50 of their dairy cows and take out a second mortgage on the house, farm and implements. After all that, she said, "We got enough to live on for about a year and a half."

She paused to think. "So maybe I'll get my own chair and go out there with him when a storm comes and hope for the best: eternal rest. I'm awfully sick and tired."

JUNCTION MILK MEN SIGN HUGGING PLEDGE

Editorial

Drunkenness, dishonesty, incompetence and smoking are vices milkmen have standardized resistance to because of their union leadership. Chancy Logan, union president, announced, "My milkmen have agreed to a sharp reduction in salary, and also, beginning Monday, to hug any woman who meets them at the door holding the empties." One hundred milk truck drivers have signed the pledge.

A similar suit in Muncie civil court points to the dangers of hugging pledges. It concerns a case of "mistaken hugging." Important questions of due process were argued by attorneys for Stephen Sumner, whose religion required retaliation against a milkman who mistakenly hugged his mother while she idled on a porch in Peabody Junction, last summer.

The *Moon* finds no harm in the hugging pledge but doesn't recommend implementation of it south of Peabody Junction. To quote scientist Zanzetti: "My long-term study of the common house fly demonstrated the mating advantage of the southern fly over the northern fly, so I'm not surprised by the pent-up lust among southern huggers. Let's keep the milkman hugging decent and ban it south of Peabody."

The editors agree. They need the milk down there but let them shun the hugging and the huggers.

NOVELIST TO STARVE SELF

Sissy Peterbilt, author of *Who Puked in the Sink?* and heiress to the Peterbilt trucking fortune, plans to starve herself, according to her closest friends and confidants. She was in a joke shop Saturday last looking for a box of art monkeys, she said, to help her with her Xmas giving. She left with her monkeys in a bag. Outside, a bait sale was in progress. Crawlers, $4.50 a dozen. Blue devils a dime apiece. She bought a few blue devils and put them in the same bag as the monkeys. She would take them with her when she went, and for amusement as she waited to starve, watch them fight in the bag.

Sissy will go this Friday to Wuntex Park Lagoon Boat Rentals and rent a pedal boat. She'll pedal her way to the middle, and there, like a crippled bird in the wilderness, die of hunger and thirst in a few weeks at most, with crowds looking on in the last days.

The manager of the boat rental said to our reporter, "All them boats got small holes in them. She'll sink and drown before she starves. They aren't meant to be out that long on the water, long enough for her to die of starvation. Get real."

NEUTRODYNE STOOL GREAT FOR USE IN GARDEN

Lionel Yoder, widower and father of six, fertilized his lawn with 300 pounds of dried neut stool expecting it to produce lush grass. Instead, he ended up with 2,000 moon flower plants and random stalks of popping corn.

"We've even got four or five watermelon and pumpkin vines," Yoder said, adding, "and some cotton. It puzzles me how cotton got into them neuts. There ain't a cotton boll within a thousand miles of here."

MAN ATTEMPTS TO THROW FATHER FROM WINDOW

Magistrate D.B. Bilke, characterizing the act of Fire Scout Robbie Ragsdale, 16, as "brutal in the extreme," sentenced him to six months of confinement at the Lower Farm youth home for attempting to throw his ailing father from a window of the Gons Hotel.

Arthur Ragsdale, the father, is past 70, and was recovering from an operation in which his arm was stapled or sewn to his shoulder to make it useful after a recent bout of nodal paralysis. His son attacked him, dragged him to a 10th floor hallway window and tried to push him out. Several hotel guests intervened and stopped the worst from happening. Had it happened, it would have been the ninth falling death from Gons windows.

It is not known what triggered the young Fire Scout's attempt on his father's life, but the elder Ragsdale, fully recovered now, can put his hand in his pocket and throw a baseball overhand. Robbie, showing great remorse, vowed to

Sheriff Prop, "When I get out, I'll take care of Dad the rest of his life. I'm a sorrowful soul for doing what I did, and I want to make amends."

The sheriff, talking to reporters, said, "I've got no idea why Robbie did this, but what puzzles me more is why are people diving or being pushed out of the Gons windows all the time?"

The *City Moon* has learned that the Onēba-owned hotel is in the process of replacing the bloodstained sidewalk beneath the windows in question.

THE DEAD WERE WED

Yesterday, in Tuttle, Dinky Stover was wed. This morning Dinky was dead. The city hangman applied the rope, blew a dose of analgesic into his face and slid home the knot. His crime: wedding a neutrodyne without a permit. Mrs. Stover stood alone in a soaking rain, weeping under a black umbrella as Dinky spoke his final words: "Goodbye Susie. Sorry I forgot about the permit."

BANKRUPT ASS IN POOR SHAPE

A bankrupt army mule, left to wander in the slums of this country, may find itself in a can labeled "Ideal Food for You and Yours." The implication is that human beings can consume this tinned meat with no injurious effects. It has been demonstrated that a pound of canned ass contains more nourishment than a pound of ground round. American canneries are as hungry as dogs to can this type of ass for a meat-starved populace.

ANCIENT REPTILE NETTED

The news from Loch Ness is that the fabled "Nessie" has been caught in the nets of a fishing boat, the *Joy Ride,* captained by Billy Fangio whose eyes opened impossibly wide when he saw the 14-foot creature thrashing in his nets. It was a long-necked *plesiosaur*, not the "monster" she was thought to have been. Fangio had wanted the jawbones of a plesiosaur as a souvenir for a long time.

With the help of a mate, he lifted the struggling, 400-pound reptile onto the deck. He stroked its belly until it slumbered peacefully, then killed it with an axe blow to the head and cut the jawbones out.

He had what he wanted and rolled the dead Nessie across the deck and into the cold water. The mate, showing more compassion than his captain, removed his cap and bowed his head to the sinking carcass of a storied monster.

GIANT TO APPEAR IN PARK

Arrangements have been made for children to see Big Machnow, the Russian giant, who stands 9-feet-4-inches tall barefoot. It was announced yesterday that Machnow would hold a reception, children only, in Wuntex Park. At 4:30 Sunday afternoon the big Russian, accompanied by his manager, will parade up and down the park lanes and shake hands with three or four children at a time. He told the children to bring satchels, since they will get chewing gum and souvenir frogs' feet.

The giant will arrive in a White Steam Touring Car a little

after 4 o'clock. He will drive up Flocculus Avenue to Terminal Circle and through the Indole Tunnel to Ninth Street, along East Avenue to the Paseo, across Esplanade Avenue, thence through the Duff Lane entrance to the park.

ANXIOUS CROWDS AT ICE STATIONS

Waiting lines at the City's ice-distributing stations are rapidly growing longer morning to morning and never in the history of the ice-fund have there been so many applicants at each station with the temperature as moderate as it is now. What it will be when the promised HEAT WAVE arrives, no one knows. There were 3,650 pounds of ice waiting at the nine stations yesterday morning. It was gone in an hour.

APOLLINARIS IS THE QUEEN OF TABLE WATERS It has constantly and steadily increased in Popularity and Esteem and is now accepted, with added quinine, throughout the malarial zones of Louisiana, Georgia and most of Florida. It possesses all the properties of an IDEAL and PERFECT table water.

SAPPERS

Editorial

Now the word "sapper" comes from everyone's lips. A sapper, we are told, is a type of mad female described as a "land troll." The usual habitat: under a bridge or overpass. She comes at you, stinky and naked, mud caked to her hair. Because her hand is palsied, she straps a plaster-cast model to her arm to alarm her natural enemies: boys with stones and switches, girls with pins and needles, old men with canes. Equestrian sappers pick young men up from the spot where they stand and carry them off to their camp, where they rape the men and kill them. Afterward they ride their horses to the nearest town and chuck the men's socks on the lawn in front of the police station.

You can chalk this whole situation up to a result of business-as-usual rapid living. The formula for making a sapper out of a housewife is simple: She's running to the kitchen to catch the spaghetti boiling over when she hears the doorbell ring. At the door she receives a gift booklet that, when read, produces a change in her over time.

The climate in America has something to do with this. It draws the strings of our nervous systems tighter and tighter, until they are ready to snap. We are changing from a life in the open to a life in service to the brain. This tendency will continue. We can't help it.

ONĒBA PUNCTURES FINGER WITH PEN

Moon correspondent C. Starky reports that, while writing his seventh set of memoirs, Onēba wounded himself with the point of his obsidian pen after dipping it into a little pot of warmed oil tar, making a small but painful wound. He grew feverish. Dr. Zanzetti was immediately called in. Was Onēba going to die again?

No, he wasn't, booksellers hoped. They were moving his newest publication, *I'm Alive Again!,* at a fast clip.

"Not dead," Zanzetti said. And that was that. Any additional dyings would have to wait. For now, Onēba was awake and beginning to make sense.

NECRONAUT SAVED FROM SECOND DEATH

A very famous necronaut almost met his second death yesterday. He was saved from a chilly drowning by the new life-saving crew organized by the Health Department at the Disinfection Station at Pflum Road and North 10th in the City.

Buddy "Bloodgood" Cutter Jr., chief frogman of the life-saving crew, was on the dock about 6 a.m. in his rubber frog feet and bathing suit when he saw a man floating down the Trench like a sodden log and calling for help. Bloodgood plunged into the disinfected waters and swam out to the man, who clung to a straw hat and a cane and wore a striped suit. The man threw his arms around Cutter's neck and thrashed wildly. He was dragged to shore and identified as W.C. Fields, comedic American actor. Shortly, he was dried off, given a jumpsuit and bussed to the Lower Farm evaluation unit.

BOOKS CANNED WITH ASS

To encourage the consumption of canned ass, the City is now including a free, miniature book in every can. The books are carefully and hermetically sealed in Plasticine to prevent contamination by natural ass oil. This month's title is *The Road to the Big House* by Charles "Charlie" Starkweather.

As a boy, Starkweather hitched locusts to an improvised

merry-go-round to measure their speed and duration of flight. Later he decided to turn junk tires into cash. A simple hand grinder can take an old tire and make a welcome mat out of it. There would be a significant profit.

Charlie thought about the future a lot, standing at his grinder, fashioning mats out of steaming hot rubber chunks. He told a fellow worker, "I'd rather be a free man and starve to death than a billionaire in China."

He ceases his rubber grinding and catches a railcar bound for Reno. There, in a tiny rental flat, Charlie writes furiously in his logbook. A sample entry: "In a dream, I am in the Pink Mink Marsh (pink minks ran everywhere) and I come upon a den of blue racers weaved into a slithering ball. I attack the ball with an oak stick and succeed in sending them on their separate ways."

In Union City, at the YMCA, a racquetball enthusiast invited Charlie over to his comfortable apartment for a swing at backgammon and a bottle of resin wine, saying to him in passing, "Psychiatrists can help people who are mentally disturbed, but they've come up with nothing that can help an asshole. Be there seven-ish."

The racquetball enthusiast was Buddy Cutter.

Charlie's fate was sealed in that invitation.

Cutter said to Charlie before dinner, "Look, if you want to join our frogman club, you can get a miniature pair of frog feet. You can hang them on your keychain, lapel, or wear them as a lucky charm. You also get a frogman decal to be used on your car, backpack or notebook. You get two booklets: *Swimming in the Plasmodium* and *The Supreme Sport of Spear Fishing*. And there's one more thing: a coupon that can be used toward the purchase of a pair of regular-size frog feet you can wear on the outside of your shoes. Well, do you want to join us or not?"

Charlie thought, *Nah, they're a bunch of foot patters. I want nothing to do with them.*

But Cutter was a lusty Texan and would not be denied. Much younger, as a circus performer, he had flashed lightning from his fingertips, joined a strange crowd and worn skirts, invented a pipe clip for toothless pipe puffers, and broke bread with powerful businessmen.

He said, "Look, Charlie, I'll tell you what. I'll fix you a cocktail I call the "Doctor." You drink that and then we'll talk turkey. The ingredients are a tablespoon of Boonekamp bitters, two ounces of gin and a dribble of vermouth. It is served in an old-fashioned glass with ice and a cube of pickled beet. The beet juice runs out and colors the drink red, like blood."

Charlie said, "Give me one."

While Cutter fetched the drinks, Starkweather flew the coop. He hailed a jitney cab and paid the neutrodyne driver to take him to the Ideal Trailer & Motor Home Court. The neut made a U-turn in the dusty drive and angered the court's boss, who said, "This is private property and trailers are homes. Tenants here are mostly regular Americans and they don't want the noise and dust from jitneys making U-turns in the yard."

Despite the boss's vituperations, Charlie agreed to lease an attractive, cherry-red motor home with whitewalls, jalousie windows and burled walnut cabinetry inside for a fair sum. He was determined to make his nut in the writing business and drove to a remote, woody location with a nearby stream. It was late September and the air was crisp and fresh. He felt invigorated.

I'll make a perfect first paragraph, he thought, and began to write what eventually became the *Road to the Big House*.

TODDLER SHOOTS FATHER

A three-year old pointed a supposed cap pistol at his father, squinted, and said *Bang!* The toddler saw his father's eyes fill with fear. The father recognized the gun as his own .38 "snubby," not a cap pistol at all. It was too late. The bullet struck him in the face, in one cheek, and exited the other. His life was not threatened; the holes were correctable with surgery. The toddler will serve four years in the Lower Farm Children's Facility for attempted patricide.

Dear *City Moon*,
Attn. Dr. Zanzetti
Help me. I think I have a canker. It first made its appearance in red spots forming a circle on my belly, leaving in the center a spot about the size of a silver dollar of sound flesh. In a short time, the affected circle formed a heavy, dry scale of a whitish, silvery appearance that would gradually drop off. A light discharge of a bloody substance oozed out. I used mineral oil and Cuticura soap with Prussian Blue in it to soften the spots. I suffer intense itching even so, especially on these warm City nights.
Respectfully,
Madame Chu
Palace Orienta

Dear Madam Chu, I suspect what you have is psoriasis, an immune system reaction. Too many skin cells are being produced beneath the skin. They pile up and shed when they reach the surface,

causing the itching and redness. Be prepared to shake the sheets in
the morning. They'll be full of flakes.
    Scientist Zanzetti

A SNAKE IN THE GRASS

The famous writer William S. Burroughs, living at that time just across the river from New Orleans, stopped in for tea at one of Onēba's southern estates, a plantation on the Mississippi formerly known as Oak Alley. They had a very pleasant chat on the patio. Burroughs explained the method of brewing sun tea, which has none of the tannic bitterness of tin pots. A young man emerged from the mansion with a pitcher of the tea. "We get this tea from Darjeeling," Onēba said. "The sun infuses it with Orgone energy. We add a drop or two of lemon juice."

The two sipped a bit of tea and talked over this and that. Then Onēba said, "It's my day to mow the lawn and grub out the underbrush, my friend. It's a kind of exercise I thrive on. Excuse me." He suggested I pass the waiting time with magazines while he finished the task. I turned to an article, "Ice Yachts of the Future: Sailing over the Frozen Seas."

As he was reading, Burroughs heard Onēba cry out, "I'm bitten, I'm bitten!"

It seems Onēba 's sickle struck a stone, fell from his hand, and as he reached into the grass to remove it, the snake struck at him, sinking its fangs into his hand.

It was venom from the fangs of a copperhead, which had stopped to hide in the heat of the day.

Burroughs grabbed Onēba's wrist and squeezed it as hard as he could. "Let's keep it in the hand." He pulled a sharp knife from his pocket and made an incision in a vein near the bite. He sucked blood from Onēba's wrist, spit out two or three mouthfuls, and said, "All will be well now." And it was. Onēba lived. The only damage was to his hand, now permanently fisted, with crippled fingers and no sensation.

MOTHER'S CAFETERIA You stay with us until we've given you all you can eat. And it's FREE. Come and gorge on whole-fried pout, land crab, soft-shell snapping-turtle bisque and dozens of other dishes. We have private rooms upstairs ($200) and we'll even feed you breakfast while you sleep without waking you up ($300). We're at 62000 Old Reactor Road. Geiger counters available: $69.99. Check out our selection of sex toys in the souvenir shop. Prices vary.

A GENEROUS ACT BY LOCAL DENTISTS

Stifled cries and groans and the heavy breathing of neutrodynes under anesthetics resounded through Wuntex Park today. The band shell had been transformed into a dental clinic. Local dentists volunteered to do the work. "They have funny teeth," one of the dentists told us. "We have, what, 32? They have 64, though they are small and dull, and no incisors." Twelve chairs were installed, and quickly filled with neutrodynes suffering toothaches. Four of them were females. One, after 40 extractions, died from loss of blood. Overall, the exercise in charity was a booming success.

PIO'S DAUGHTER AUTO-IMMOLATES

Padre Pio, known for his stigmata, visited Bunkerville last week on his tour of America. He was asked to list possible causes for the occasionally bleeding wounds. He replied, "Divine revelation ... diabolic intervention to confuse believers ... and conscious or unconscious suggestion. None can be proved." In a strange 1950s follow-up to this story, Pio's pretty daughter, Gabriella, 19, who was also his secretary, was seen, while dancing with her boyfriend in the Wuntex Pavilion, to burst into flames. The boyfriend escaped with minor burns. Hours later, Gabriella succumbed to hers.

NEW U.S. PARKS

The president has ordered the establishment of several new American parks.

Sapodilla Park, in what was once Belize, is a land of marvels. Fitzhugh Thompson has written, "In one region there are no poisonous herbs, nor does the querulous frog ever croak there. No scorpions exist, nor do snakes glide among the sea grass. Getting to Sapodilla takes a bit of caution, however. In the dense mangrove swamp, there are wild neuts, living on small fish, crabs, conch and seaweed, who have been known to leap onto passing dories and beg for meat and potatoes, grunting like pigs. These harmless neuts move out of their mangrove habitat occasionally to tend their sapodilla trees growing on higher ground. Otherwise, you'll see them perched in the larger mangroves, waving at tourists.

Pilchard Park, in Pennsylvania. At a comfortable height of 4,000 feet, Pilchard is the best place to view the devastated parts of Altoona. Camping sites available for a modest charge.

Callicarpa Park, occupying most of what was called

Florida, Georgia, Alabama, Tennessee and the upper regions of Louisiana and Mississippi. A man named Marfak is thought to be the original settler in the area. His poem, "The Moon," serves well as the park's anthem.

The Moon
Someone is eating an orange;
See what a bite he can take!
    And look at the yellow peeling,
    Fallen across the lake.

Cook County Park, closed most seasons. Hazardous ruins at Chicago have not been fenced properly, allowing picnickers to wander there, mostly looking for better hot dogs. Ten have been killed by falling stones, concrete and bricks. Three have stepped into burning pits of assorted debris and died. Toxic gases killed them before they hit the fire. The fence, the city says, will be repaired by 1976. Before that time, it is expected hundreds will be maimed and killed.

Pandanus Park, a palmy wilderness of sand and sun occupying the Jersey barrens. It hosts but one life form, the diminutive shabbit. The limit of all shabbit striving is set by the scarcity of circulating blood oxygen. They lack the subtle lever of oxygen-binding hemoglobin wrapped in corpuscles, the biochemical patent held by the vertebrate line. Their circulating coppery hemocyanin is not as good by a factor of three, even though their viscous blood is loaded with protein and three hearts are hard at work keeping blood pressure high. Shabbit emotions are skin deep, signaled by blushing and paling. Pushing back another in fight or love, they turn dark red. It takes hours for a shabbit to recover from light exercise. Digestion is an all-night affair. One of the hearts skips a beat with every spermatophore ejaculation during copulation but without any change in rate or amplitude. Here is intelligence in a soft body, but with no fixed frame of reference. The shabbit cannot put one stone on top of another. It learns to pull levers with great difficulty. It is poor at mazes. Newly blinded, at first it sits touchingly bundled in its own arms. After a week it takes up an outstretched position on the floor of its mud home, palpating the surfaces with all its suckers. This little beast has a mind even more visual than our own. Come see the shabbits at Pandanus Park.

Occidental Park, the last member to enter the system. The saying goes that the park is broiled under an ogling sun for 300 of the 365 days we have. In August ears of corn burst on the stalks and the husks take flame. The sun never sets there so the park administration has established as many as ten dozen sun-block and cancer-check stations with dermatologists on hand at all hours.

La Tropicana Park, with submarine-size watermelons growing before the eyes of visitors who watch the giant melons swell beyond belief on flatbed haulers. There are paths of ivory, trails of amber and jade, streams of tin and silver. These are the pathways of the world. Along them have moved salt and sugar, tabasco peppers, wheat, rice, corn, cotton, silk, wool, dead animals, live animals, pins, needles, beads, thread, wheelbarrows, shovels, rum and glass. Memory disappears in this exciting Puerto Rican park.

Great Middle Park, located near La Junta, Colorado, birthplace of writer Ken Kesey, is beset now by wandering prairie neuts who disgust visitors, especially those eating picnic lunches. Hundreds of complaints have been filed. Officials promise to pay $3.40 for every dead one brought in to the park ranger's office, and $1.70 for a bucket of their ears, which are dried and sold as dog chews.

Dilbat Park, established on the sands of Death Valley in honor of its original home in Dilbat, Sumeria, a small, sandy settlement southwest of Babylon. An explorer by the name of Leuko Vink stumbled upon a rare vein of silkstone on the site in 1957. At that moment a stranger appeared near him. It was a man named Marfak, who claimed to be the park supervisor. "Are you naked?" Marfak asked. "You don't look naked."

A swollen sack of silkstone chunks was tied to Marfak's back. "We're all naked here, mate," he said. "Get that way or get out of the park."

Texoma Park, in central Texas, where masses gather to capture the curved sunshine. Mums grow on trees there. They are shipped to France where they are one of the most curious features of the *Exposition de Chrysanthemums et Fruits* in the Cours-la-Reine in Charente. The mums are displayed at the stand of *Milet de Fils,* and the effect is so novel that dumbstruck crowds stop to look at them.

LINER ENVELOPED IN FLAMES

The freighter *Onēba* arrived in Zurich today bearing 500 pounds of Austral Dog Boots, caught fire and sank to the bottom of the deep harbor. The fire began at the captain's table when a plate of bread combusted for no apparent reason. In a moment, two scullions and much of the fo'c'sle were ablaze. Down in the orlop deck, where neut wipers squirmed in their seamy bunks, balls of white hot flame rolled like tumbleweed. In all, 85 neuts departed this life. The captain was saved, though all the ice in Antarctica cannot cool him down. Some say the harbor boiled like tea water as the flaming ship sank.

BOY DELIVERS SUGAR TITS

Yesterday a peculiar boy arrived at the Upper Farm Suckle Facility, where infants born of Lower Farm prisoners nurse on warm rubber bladders filled with hag's milk. On the boy's breast were numerous exquisite pectorals, both large and small, including various amulets arranged in 16 layers. Some of these pectorals constituted many hundreds of sections of elaborate *cloisonné* work. Around his waist were two girdles, from each of which was suspended a dozen sugar tits.

"Show me to the suckle unit," he said. "I have something to give."

STORY CONTEST ENTRY

My Encounter with a Shabbit
by
Chance Dibben

I thought it was a puppet landing in my yard that a neighbor kid had thrown over the fence. I went over to it, thinking I'd toss it back, but it had a horrible, alien stink all around it. I gagged and crabbed backward.

A milky substance doughed from the snoot. When I poked it with a sharp stick it roared to life and got on me, sitting on my shoulder, commanding me to go into the cat briars, and I did so. Showing not the slightest hesitation, it spat a hot fluid soup of clabber and acid into my ear.

My back felt the sting of the briars as I squatted to catch grasshoppers and feed them to this thing. It was my first encounter with a shabbit. Now, still sitting on my shoulder, it ground the hoppers in its mouth while smoking an acrid-smelling cigarette.

Somehow the bite of a shabbit and a boomslang adder are roughly the same. First, its cold lips touched me at the keel of the ear. They were eel-like and slimy. Then the teeth painlessly entered and painlessly withdrew, leaving a deadened prow of flesh behind.

Shabbit bite, a quick way to die. It called on me in a puppet's uniform. I would have been dead, via the bite, had I not called my neut Gordon, who came posthaste from his stall in the shed.

"Good God almighty!" said Gordon. "I'll bring out the Master Leech."

The End

In better times, Castaneda would offer comments here. Sad to say, he is hospitalized with level 4 nodal paralysis, complicated by Leiden-5. The City Moon *story contest will be suspended until he has recovered.*

HOOVER SAVES TONG'S DAUGHTER

A burnished haze of heat hung over the blue waters of False Bay, a seaside playground on an island in the China Sea. During the siege of Tientsin in the Boxer uprisings at the turn of the century, Tong Shao-yi, later prime minister of China, took refuge in the American settlement. One day a shell burst through Tong's roof, killing his wife and baby daughter. J. Edgar Hoover, who lived across the street, rushed into the burning house and carried another of Tong's little daughters to safety through a hail of bullets.

Years later, when Hoover was director of the FBI and chief food administrator in Washington, the Chinese ambassador, Wellington Koo, invited Hoover to dinner. At one point, Mrs. Koo said smilingly, "Mr. Hoover, we have met before."

Her American guest wrinkled his brow, trying to remember the occasion. Mrs. Koo solved the mystery. "I am Tong Shao-yi's daughter, whom you carried across the street during the siege of Tientsin!" she said.

Effie Pfeffer
On the Road to History

IRONY OF THE MONTH

A freighter carrying a cargo of Duncan yo-yos was sailing from the Philippines. In a typhoon, the crates of yo-yos shifted back and forth, sinking and lifting the ship repeatedly.

Dear *City Moon,*

This is a true story.

A friend and I in Bunkerville impersonated medical students and gained entrance to the City morgue, half drunk, late at night. I knew that my cousin Mickey was at the reception desk on night-shift and would be pleased to give us a cook's tour of the place. He said, "There is an autopsy going on. You two will enjoy seeing it. Come on, I'll show you."

We were taken to a sterile room of white-tiled walls, ceiling and floor, that tapered to a drain. We saw an older man cut open throat to penis lying on a stainless-steel table. My cousin said, "He's a ship captain from Norway. There was an explosion while the ship was in the harbor. He was flung into the Trench. When found, after five days in the water, the body had been fed on by catfish, hags and other Trench creatures.

"What we're trying to determine here, for the satisfaction of the ship's insurance carrier, is whether the blast or the drowning killed him."

A young anatomist, standing at the captain's side, holding a lobe of the captain's liver, said, "Come on in, get close to the action. We're just getting started."

The anatomist said, "Look how the liver is macerated" and held it closer so I might see it better. On smelling it, I closed my eyes and swooned (that's the best way I can describe it) and genuflected to avoid vomiting.

A husky assistant in a denim smock came in to help and, with a razor device, cut the captain from the top of the left ear upward and below the widow's peak on the forehead cleanly to the top of the right ear, then peeled the scalp and let it settle on the back of the head.

My friend lifted me upright by the shirt collar.

"Don't be fainting," my cousin said. "It's really obnoxious. Let's calm down and look around. We have some interesting things pickled in formalin or alcohol, and we have a bum in the cooler who came in today. Someone shot him in the armpit, down by the river, for cursing Franklin Delano Roosevelt and claiming the now-adored president had a cloven hoof, not polio."

My cousin lifted the bum's stiff arm and a bit of pus came out of the bullet hole. A hot belly foam hit my throat and I gagged.

Billy Alonzo
c/o Box 591

SURVIVAL TIPS

When camping in the American wild, here's a way to find safe drinking water: You come, let's say, to a mountain brook that issues from a thick forest. It ripples over clean rocks, it bubbles with air, it is clear as crystal and cool to your thirsty throat. *Surely that is good water,* you think. But do you know where it comes from?

Every neutrodyne cabin is built near the spring branch of a creek at a higher elevation than you are. Somewhere up that branch, there may be a clearing; in that clearing, there may be a neut with a case of dysentery or typhoid fever who voided herself over an oft-used latrine. Lesson one: Avoid drinking clear, cool stream water anywhere no matter how much it babbles.

Keep looking for potable water. Sometimes a subaqueous spring may be found near the margin of a river by paddling close to shore and trailing your hand in the water. When a cold spot is noted, go ashore and dig a few feet back from the water's edge. Now, weighing a canteen with pea-sized pebbles, tying it to a string and sinking it, you'll be able to bring up safe drinking water. If it is muddy, clarify it by stirring corn meal into it and letting it settle, or, if you have a lump of alum, drop that in and wait until the mud precipitates. The result: drinkable water.

When traveling in alkali country, carry some vinegar or limes or lemons or, better still, a glass-stoppered bottle of hydrochloric or muriatic acid, readily available in hardware stores. One teaspoon neutralizes about a gallon of water. If there should be a little excess, it will do no harm, but rather assist digestion. In default of acid, you may add a little Jamaica ginger and sugar to the water to make a weak, but safe, ginger tea.

LET'S COOK A BOOK

Books are full of cellulose, nutritious glue and, if you're lucky, a few book lice. Take a fat book like the *Summa Theologica* or the *Principia Mathematica* or any fat old tome you have around and boil it for seven-to-ten hours in salted and acidified water. Save any gray paste that rises up for later use. Put in a bay leaf, a handful of peppercorns and a pint of angostura bitters.

Now you've got your sauce. Let's go on to the stuffing. Fill a bowl with stale bread chunks. Your pot liquor can now be folded in and you've got your stuffing. Get that stuffing between those soaked pages. Use a table knife and spread it like peanut butter. Truss up the book with a strong twine, drizzle with sauce and steam it for three hours. Once it's tender and blended, serve with chicory salad and *pain perdu*. An aperitif of an absinthe frappé goes well before eating the book.

Lordi Lordis
Food Editor

SECRETARY OF FEMININE AFFAIRS APPOINTED

The president has named Harry Harriet head of feminine affairs. Harriet's criminal past is documented: In 1968, he poured ammonia into a drunken man's wine and killed him. For this offense he spent eight months in prison. As soon as he was let out, he exposed himself to girls in a schoolyard and went back for three additional months.

Then, in 1969, a woman from Batavia, who claimed to have been one of Harriet's inamoratas, reported to police that she had been drinking heavily and that about 1:30 a.m. she drank a bottle of beer that Harriet had laced with lye, causing severe burns of the throat. She died a few days later. For that crime, Harriet did 20 years.

The *City Moon* asks, how has such a man been appointed to such an office?

ONĒBA BURIED IN FAVORITE CAR

Onēba loved the practical joke during his fifth life. He died on a Thursday, September 2, 1941, and was buried just as he had asked to be – dressed in a lace nightgown and seated in a Ferrari, with the seat slanting comfortably.

To quote from his will: "Though fuel is plentiful in the afterworld, distances are great. If one needs to drive, say, to Samarra from Radiola, one needs a good, fast car.

"If you arrive in the afterworld without wheels, it's tough buns. You take your chances thumbing rides. It's horrible. You never know who'll pick you up. On the good side, it might be

Mitzi Gaynor, the choicest trollop in the afterworld, a favorite of all dead men.

"One wants to have one's own wheels. When you shift back here, if you do, you can sell the vehicle at a steep price."

Unembalmed, Onēba was placed behind the steering wheel, a jug of ale and a box of sandwiches on the passenger's seat, his little poodle, Curly, sedated, sleeping in his lap. The tank was full of gasoline. A crate was built around the car and lowered into the excavation by a crane, dirt piled atop it, making an impressive mound.

Two weeks later, a court ordered the Ferrari disinterred, in light of evidence that the circumstances of Onēba's most recent death had come under suspicion. The mound of dirt was excavated with a backhoe and the crate lifted out. The sound of the car's radio could be heard by the workers. The windows and windshield were fogged. Patches of mildew spotted the car's finish.

The driver's door was jimmied open and Curly wobbled out into the sunlight, shook herself off, and yawned, very much alive. Meanwhile, the windshield wipers were working at full speed, the rubber blades worn away.

When the interior of the Ferrari was examined, what had happened was clear. Curly had awakened to find herself in dire straits. She had apparently clawed and gnawed her way through the firewall, only to find the engine compartment a dead end. Not giving up, she had tunneled through the rear seat into the trunk – another impossible exit. Then, as if resolving to make the best of things, Curly had survived by eating the sandwiches and contriving to pull the cork on the ale jug. She had even managed to turn on the radio and the wipers in her escape attempts. Finally, the ale gone, and the sandwiches eaten, Curly had no choice but to feed on her dead master. It is fortunate that this did not happen sooner, as Onēba was generally left intact, aside from a portion of the pectoral area and a calf that had been nibbled away.

ZEUS BOLOGNICS Name a meat, any meat, from turtle to yak, and we've got it. If we don't, it's free. Ha-ha. When Bozo Vidanovitch opened the shop in 1955, we offered only frozen meat, mostly hamburger patties. It was risky. This was a time when frozen meats were a no-no. In 1951 bankers and others looked on frozen meats as a necessity of war. Many remembered the revolting taste of frozen mutton during WWII. Now Zeus can proudly say, we have no frozen meat at all. Every meat is fresh-killed and dressed on the premises. New specials every day. Today rabbit collar, $15.99 per ounce. Sunday special is always cold braised-tongue salad, $9.99. And don't forget meat-pie Saturday, with whole pies $10.99, slices $3.50. Zeus Bolognics, 1000 Industrial Forest Way, Bunkerville. No reservations. No seating. No phone. Come in person.

THE CITY MOON INTERVIEWS ONĒBA

C.M. You've walked among circus giants, have you not?

O. Oh, yes, let's see, there's Topinard's Finlander, over 8 feet, and Baby Frances, only 7 feet and quite fat. She was then the longest living fat lady (at 826 pounds) of all time. I had occasion to stay in her Tampa home once when I was beachcombing my way north from the Keys to Far Rockaway for Cowards' Day. I dallied there so long, and grew so infatuated with Frances, I married her. The sex was for the most part oral. In my mouth her cl****is was like a quivering quahog. When it engorged I nearly

315

choked. She twittered with joy when I sank my teeth into it.

C.M. The record indicates she bore you six children. Is that correct? If so, by what method were they conceived?

O. Let me begin by asking if you've ever seen a horse-doctor midwife a mare during a difficult birth?

C.M. No, we're city people.

O. It's quite a spectacle. One sees the doctor, arms glistening with petroleum jelly, put on rubber mittens and plunge elbow-deep into the mare, searching for obstructions. I decided to adapt something similar for my own needs. I deposited palm's full of ejaculate as near to the opening of my big Baby's fallopian tube as I could get. It's fortunate I have small hands.

C.M. You've written a monograph on the subject, called *Nine Giants*.

O. That's true. In it I conclude that giants are, as a rule, liars in proportion to their height, always telling tall tales about their relatives. One claimed ancestry directly from Goliath. They are indolent, unamiable, irascible, unsociable and unpleasant to live with. Baby Frances and I were divorced in 1945. She died of heart failure at the age of 47.

C.M. Over the years you've had an abiding interest in the study of neutrodyne communication skills. Tell us about that.

O. *"Bo aba-ntu babi babota tubatia"* means "They-these they-person they-bad who kill we them fear." It is the most remarkable language developed for speech alone. The verb does the heavy lifting, as in poetry.

C.M. What do you think of drugless healing?

O. Since the beginning of homeopathy, followed by osteopathy and chiropractic and chiropody, drugless healing has taken tremendous steps forward. When Americans realized there were other ways of healing, they were slow to forsake the nauseating draughts of modern medicine. Many are now convinced of the efficacy of the drugless systems and have become strong advocates of, and willingly testify to, the adequacy of drugless methods. For example, if I find myself "stove up" on a Monday morning (too much Saki and Soma the night before), I pick a pail of dewberries, pound them and make a concentrated juice, using it to wash down a couple of Pepitron tablets. Once, when I was working the Coward's Day carnival in Reno and staying at the Tunney Arms, a friend called me. His name was Stekel and he was in a panicked state.

"My bowels haven't moved in a month. Help me. What can I do?"

I said, "My friend, if you go to the doctor, what will *he* do?"

Stekel said, "Well, I expect he'll go to probing me with a sanitized finger and try to work loose whatever the blockage is."

I told him, "Yes, so why not do it yourself and save the money? Stay home and be cool. A little Vaseline, a private moment, a washcloth soaked in warm water will do the trick. And besides, an artful finger, in dislodging the blockage, can also stimulate the neighboring prostate gland to ejaculate, another feature of drugless healing."

C.M. Can you describe what it's like for you during those periods between lives?

O. It isn't a period. It's a place. I go to a city of the mind, a synedrium called Radiola, named by its founder, Guglielmo Marconi. I bide my time there. There are plenty of cheap flats, all-night restaurants, bars. Last go-round I had lunch one day at the Squat 'n' Gobble with General Eisenhower. He looked good enough, but quivery, shivering as if he had the chills. He spit up all the cockle chowder he tried to swallow. His uniform was a sour mess. He appeared discombobulated. Somewhere along the line he'd lost the tip of his nose and the spot was festering. On an impulse I wanted to smack the son of a bitch in his face for the hash he made of Normandy Beach. I must say that "living" in Radiola, one's temper is always on the edge of eruption. I felt forever anxious, clumsy, skittish. It isn't all that bad a place, but neither is a bus station. One spends one's time waiting there, that's all. And waiting is such a nuisance, even to the dead.

C.M. The word is that necronauts are plagued by pranksters in Radiola.

O. That we are, and that's why I want to speak to the one who hid a large syringe filled with what I believe to be weed killer, pointed upward in my pedal car seat. I sat on that needle and the pressure of my body operated the plunger. I did not get the full injection, but I did become ill. If it happens a second time, I'm going to stomp some rump.

C.M. What of the mysterious disappearance of Myron the Art Typist. He was a friend of yours.

O. Yes, he is or was. I know very little other than what the papers are reporting. He had dined out with friends at Billy Haa's Chophouse, waved goodbye to them and hailed a tuk-tuk. He has not been seen or heard from since. The chances are 100 percent Myron will never be found.

C.M. Thank you, sir. It's been a delight talking to you.

O. My pleasure, friend. Rock 'n' roll.

CITY MOON AVERSE TO VERSE

Editorial

The poet Philip Lamantia said, "But the fact remains, we have reached the point in 1975 that the act of reading Ginsberg and Olson or any of their epigone is interchangeable with the scanning of *Time* or *Newsweek*. I maintain that this is no accident but clearly delineates the false consciousness of poetry proliferating within the shifting gears of decadent capitalism."

It seems clear to us, that whatever may be shifting within those gears is probably sawdust. Enough has been said already. Let's hear no more claptrap about the false or true consciousness of poetry. As everyone knows, the best way to eliminate the boll weevil is not to plant the cotton.

The *City Moon* wants to have a four-year moratorium on poetry. This is not to ask that poets stop writing any more than cotton farmers should be prevented from propagating their own private seed stock. No, nothing as harsh as that. We ask simply a temporary quiescence on the publishing end. And what better time could a poet choose to lay low than during the Noxin years? Send us your opinion. Box 591.

NAZI GARDENING

National Socialist gardening is the latest craze. Topsoil is brought in and shoveled into wooden forms in the shape of swastikas. The beds can be planted with any number of different vegetables, greens and flowers. The swastika shape allows the gardener to reach any part of the garden without stepping in mud, or into the garden itself.

MEET DEATH IN A JUNKYARD

It is not uncommon to see a goose, rather than a dog, acting as lord-protector of a junkyard. The City's largest, Junktown USA, owned and operated by Onēba Industries, is managed by Herb "Shorty" Long.

Long tells the story in his own words: "An Italian tourist attended a party a little way down the road from my yard and drank heavily. During the festivities he bottomed up. Then, shortly after midnight, he began to stagger his way back to the Gons Hotel, the notion occurring to him that the used mattresses piled up inside the Junktown fence would be a good place to sleep it off. It is reported that in the morning, police found a clean-picked skeleton in tropical evening clothes, and they blamed it on my three geese, Obla, Dibla and Do and wanted them put to sleep, and me to be locked up. Wrong. Everybody knows geese don't eat meat.

"The truth is, Junktown is in a swampy area near the old reactor and in recent years, has been host to seasonal congregations of driver ants. They are secure in their billions, fear nothing and can take down a human being in full stride.

SUICIDE BY JAVA

Albert Wormwood, a Pisstown dentist, poured 68 steaming cups of strong coffee down his throat in 31.6 minutes, claiming to be the world's fastest coffee drinker and is the first known suicide by java.

He died this way: He climbed to his own roof in the broiling sun, nailing in 14,000 shingles in 18 days. "Mama, I'm going home," he said to his wife in a basement bathroom when his roofing chore was finished.

Autopsy showed a shrunken, blackened and pitted liver.

STORY CONTEST ENTRY

A Foot and a Palm
by
Kyle G. Rodd

A tattooist, Ray Biggs, returned to his shop after lunch and found a girl waiting outside. She said she was 11 and that she wanted a small tattoo on her palm, "Something for eternity, like a fly. They will always be around."

Inside the shop, Biggs placed her on a table and drew a fly on her foot. "This shouldn't hurt," he promised. "On the palm it would hurt very badly."

"But no one will see it if it's on the bottom of my foot."

"Twenty years from now, my dear, you'll be glad it's there. And only your husband or lover will see it."

The girl agreed and left an hour later, limping happily, with a sore fly on the instep of her left foot.

A funeral director named Grimes had, after squeezing a rubber ball for many years, hardened his palm in such a way that the skin would stand fast beneath the engraving tool. He walked into Biggs' shop and said, "I'll make you a bet. If I can stand having a full-size red admiral butterfly tattooed on my palm, then you'll have to have yourself measured for a coffin at my funeral home." Biggs took the challenge.

Grimes muffled his little cries of pain but got through the

process and left with a beautiful butterfly in his right palm, something sure to be a hit with bar hags anywhere in America.

The next day, at Grimes' funeral home, Biggs was having his dimensions measured for the coffin. His cigar lay in an ash tray. He picked it up and touched the orange glow of low fire to a fever blister on his lip. In only hours, inflammation had set in. Biggs died in agony of a vicious viral infection a few days later, leaving his best work in the palm of an undertaker.

The End

Kyle: We will place this story on file until Mr. Castaneda recovers. For now, he is gravely ill, though there is every hope for recovery. Scientist Zanzetti has been treating him with a brand-new regimen of herbs and dried mushroom tea, with a chaser of paregoric, lemon juice and honey. His cheeks have blossomed pink, his eyes have opened, but he has yet to speak.

SUICIDE IN CHERVIL GARDENS

She did it at night among a group of laughing children, with whom she had been playing in Wuntex Park's Chervil Gardens and Arboretum. She, Eunice Flowers, was a fifth-grade instructor. The game was *bladderball*, the object to kick the inflated bladder of a shabbit across a predetermined goal line in darkness. When the game ended, in the pitch of night, without warning or words, she discharged a bullet into her temple.

She was taken to the nearest hospital, Hôtel Dieu, at the foot of German Hill. Zanzetti, the attending physician, said, "Take her to a spa, perhaps on SUSNRS, where radium mud is always bubbling out of conical extrusions. She can sit in one of the bubbling cones. The bullet will flocculate in time and leave but a modest lump above one eye. It's no sweat."

That very thing was done and Zanzetti's nostrum was proved. Eunice is in full fettle again and looking for work. She says she doesn't remember shooting herself or why. "It was involuntary. It was an impulse. I love life."

NEUTRODYNE ANGLING

The neutrodynes of SUSNRS' marshes, near the upper shores of the Firecracker Sea are ardent hunters of the chubbit, a sort of terrestrial fish produced by Zanzetti Laboratories, a cross between a chub and a shabbit, equally capable of living in water or on land.

The neuts call these animals "Pakningwukme" and the art of hunting them "feeling for the mother of the marsh."

A party of neuts strip themselves, surround a clump of marsh grass and merely feel among the stems and roots for chubbits hiding there. Those that are caught are quickly pierced with sharpened willow rods until they come to pieces.

SPUD: A SMOKING CLUB

The president of SPUD is Vincent "Hammerhead" Terranova. On visiting his Carolina home, this reporter was invited to hammer an 8-penny nail into Terranova's pileated neck, which he did. After an extended pounding, it went in about 2 inches.

Terranova made no cry, nor was there bleeding evident. During the interview the nail remained in situ, like a picador's lance.

He explained, "SPUD is a society of smokers. Members think of themselves as Social Puffers Under Duress and they're spitting angry, tired of being shuttled into little corners of life that say, SMOKERS ONLY or NO SMOKING. They want some slack, some breathing room. It's a living hell they live in.

"I like to point to the back-sides of anti-smoking statistics, saying, look, it shows that 75 percent of heavy smokers do not die of lung cancer, but of something else. The very ones who eschew nicotine happily smoke marijuana until they are blue in the face. Marijuana is a weed more noxious than tobacco ever was. It fills the lungs with black sludge and eventually puts the mind to sleep, while tobacco, in its many forms, is both a neurological and circulatory tonic. It flushes the kidneys, and in combination with alcohol, produces a kind of fibrillose euphoria that no other drug can match. And, it has the benefits of legality."

ZEUS BOLOGNICS We do much more at Zeus than push meaty dough paste into sausage casings. Please, the next time you're traveling to SUSNRS' Altobello, visit our production plant, located at No. 9 Donahoo Street in the American Quad.

This month we are featuring:

Blocula We grow leafy cabbages on the bodies of dead neuts. Goes well tossed into a sauté with cubed horse loin and scallions.

Squassation Bolognic art typified. Meat paste in any form. In the rear yard of the plant you can see a mountainscape of souse, whole battalions of "wurst" soldiers ready to march up Pork Chop Hill and down again.

Punch 'n' Judy Made of head cheese, these two rollicksome

figures gibe at each other across the Mincemeat Gulch, while a group of mounted "chorizo" warriors gives the visitor a strange feeling of unity and power.

> Five Mancy Meanings
> Tyromancy – Divination by the coagulation of cheese.
> Cephalomancy – Divination by the broiling of an ass's head.
> Axinomancy – Divination by saws or axes.
> Gastromancy – Divination by the sound of the belly.
> Libanomancy – Divination by the burning of incense.

A CONVERSATION WITH CANDIDATE BUDD

Who is more fry-eyed than presidential candidate Bonnie Budd, and why is she running for president? This reporter, by chance, had a choice encounter with her just yesterday. It was on that lonesome stretch of two-lane between Tres Piedras and Ojo Caliente. I had just lunched at the Squat 'n' Gobble in Tres Piedras – a bowl of their famous green chili and a cup of their "all-nite" coffee. I was fortified for a night of driving.

It was December and near freezing. A pre-snow sleet had crusted on my windshield. The defroster was on the fritz. I kept driving, hoping the weather would change. Gradually the wipers froze in their places, snow fell, and I pulled over to the shoulder. Getting out of the car, I heard the crackle of a fire and smelled burning pine sap. There was an orange glow 10 or 12 yards into the woods. Going there I found Budd sitting on a log wearing Bermuda shorts and stirring a boiling pot of piñon nuts and red peppers.

She said, "Stay a bit. Eat some of these nuts. I practically live on them out here. The snow is a bluff. In an hour, the sun will shine."

Though she was wearing goggles, her edgy, fluid gaze was clearly visible behind the lenses, and difficult to look at. I avoided eye contact and instead focused on the stub of a dead cigarette she held vise-like between a set of rotted choppers.

I took out my pad and pencil and said I was a correspondent for the *City Moon*. I said, "Miss Budd, you say you are a candidate for the presidency, yet you live out here in the middle of nowhere and never campaign."

She answered, "We are a nation on wheels, not on our feet. This needs to change. Like these piñons, we must root in whatever is below us and then grope for whatever we can claim above us. Tell them I have a plan. I see underwater vessels twice the size of Arcosanti, fish-like in shape, using lateral undulation as propulsion, made of biomechanical software, housing thousands, floating as lazily as a man o' war, continent to continent, every passenger like a blind pig finding an acorn. Tell them that. Tell them they're trying to stop the Process. That will not do. The Process is molten and will burn them. Language itself is a Process. Why curb it like a dog? Let it spew, like germs in a sneeze."

A minority of voters know who Budd is. She is one of those wacky jokesters who run for president every four years. Most in the mainstream have never seen her.

Next election period there will be more than 100 candidates. Theoretically, these crazy candidacies will grow exponentially from there until their number exceeds the total tally of voters.

Effie Pfeffer
On the Road to History

THE FOOD OF THE FUTURE

From the laboratories of Zeus Bolognics comes an answer to the ancient question of what to do when our currency is so debased as to be worth no more than the paper it is printed on and the ink and the dye it is colored with.

A scientist at the Zeus plant, using an idea from a worker, successfully vulcanized gum tissue onto horseshoe-shaped slugs of pig iron. Then the seed teeth of fetal cows were implanted, nourished and teased into full, orderly growth.

A simple, two-cycle, gasoline-powered engine easily filled the machine's energy needs so that it could be mounted on a flatbed and taken into the neighborhoods.

"Bring out your money!"

Americans hurry down driveways carrying buckets and wheelbarrows full of worthless millions and dump them into the maw of the Green Machine, as it has come to be called in the press, staring into a green soup of gluey bucks.

These people are using wads of cotton in their ears as the grinding of the machine's choppers can pop the drums. The slightest whiff of its exhalations can rubber your legs and you might fall.

Hungry Americans are pleased to trade money for food. When they have emptied their buckets and the maw is full, it moves on. As it goes, it dumps from the rear 12-pound cubes of a doughy white material that appears to be a firm bean curd but tastes sweet and cheesy. Neighbors gather them up like farm hands behind a hay baler, stacking the cubes in sheds and on porches.

To its credit, the Green Machine has killed but once. A Cincinnati girl, Hattie Porlocks, eight, was illegally feeding it gum drops and peanut brittle when it bared its teeth like a starved wolf and bit off her head. A police officer had to follow the machine for blocks before it spilled Hattie's head, intact, though shrouded in a cloudy green gelatin.

"Sure enough," says our staff philosopher, C.A. Ludwig. "It's another instance of ecophagic money policy. These periods have occurred throughout economic history, which, I must say, is the only kind of history there is.

"Edible money is a new twist on an old idea – just a phase until we can grow more trees.

"Now, let me be the first to say, the taste of those money-based cubes, with the added spices and oils, sautéed or broiled, are a tough chew and a bit oversweet. Sure, I make my dumps when the machine comes to the house. I'm a well-meaning citizen. I fry the stuff, pattied, and in hot lard. Really, I'm fond of it, but lately the truck has been calling in the middle of the night. I'm drilled awake by the scream of the driver through a bull horn, "Green Machine! Bring out your bucks! The Green Machine is here!"

BALLOON BLOW MARS RAT FÊTE

Michael Ratt, a relative unknown and the last candidate to enter the presidential race, was seriously injured today when a massive, gas-filled campaign balloon in his likeness exploded only feet from his head, concussing him, bursting both ear drums and spraining his neck. It is not known whether Ratt will be healthy enough in time to launch a catch-up run for the office. He entered the political arena suddenly, seemingly from nowhere, although his filing documents indicate he is a native of Pisstown and a successful grinding wheel manufacturer.

THREE HEADS IN A SUITCASE

A neutrodyne female arrived at the Lower Farm with three heads in a suitcase about 9 a.m. Sunday during a thundershower. She said she was a tormentrix from Texoma Beach and that she had carried the heads 10,000 miles after obtaining them at a freeze-dry conference in New South Wales. The heads belonged to Gloria Vanderbilt, James Hoffa and Karen Silkwood. Lower Farmers bought them for a stiff price. The neutrodyne left when her suitcase was empty and her purse full of money, promising to return the following spring with a new selection of freeze-dried heads.

OWNERS, TRAMPS, SMOTHERED BY CULLS

Three partners who built one of the largest clone mills in North America on 5,000 Montana acres were killed yesterday by stampeding clones where they lay sleeping. Inside the clone mill, the gene vats were cooking. Sterile workers clocked in and out. Tramps loitered in the crawl space on their backs eating whatever fell through the safety net and the floor cracks and drinking any liquid seepage. It killed them by the dozens and turned others into knuckle-dragging beasts.

The mill owners, I.P. Freely, Seymour Butts and L. Fauntleroy, like the Three Stooges, were snoring in their bed when a posse of defective clones, called "culls," entered the room and asked for the time. The three owners merely wheezed and whimpered and turned over all at once.

For unknown reasons this minor slight angered the unnatural clones and their greasy circuits screamed, "Kill!"

Three plump, nude clones leapt into the bed and sat on the owner's faces, smothering them.

Services for the mill owners will be held at Lamanno Panno Fallo on Saturday at 7 a.m.

TALK WITH APE ENDS IN DEATH

An interview with Brainerd Franklin, the Ape of Golf.

C.M.: Why does golf need an ape player?

B.F.: Ask a simpler question.

C.M. How much do you weigh?

B.F. About 50 divots, give or take. That was a good question. Ask another.

C.M.: What's a sand wedge for?

B.F.: To eat, I think, isn't it? My trainer always made banana and peanut butter ones for me.

C.M. Who made those snakeskin boots you wear?

B.F.: Monkeyshine Shoe Company. If they don't fit right my bunions ache. I own the company. I'm rich and I feel good. It's one thing to be a poor ape, but a poor human – it must be awful. Oh, please excuse me, I need to potty.

(*City Moon* interviewers wait outside the men's room, shouting questions through the door.)

C.M.: Do you believe in a god of any kind?

B.F.: Are you kidding? I'm an ape. No god ever gave an ape a break. I dig Freemasonry. I've got a motor scooter and I love to ride in parades.

C.M.: Some say you resent being called the Ape of Golf.

B.F.: I do. I need a name, not a label. I'm Brainerd Franklin from now on.

C.M.: They say apes like you only live about 15 years. You worried at all?

(The toilet flushes inside the men's room. When the water stops rushing, it is flushed again, and this happens three or four more times.)

B.F.: The shitter is broke! Turds are all over the floor in here! Call the police!

(Police arrived shortly after and the press was made to leave just as water flecked with feces seeped under the men's room door. The interview ended. No more was heard from Franklin.)

THE BLACK HOLE MOTEL Hourly, daily, weekly, monthly, yearly rates. Very cheap. Very comfortable. Take the Old Reactor Road to the end any time night or day. Toot your horn at the gate. We'll come out to receive you with a chocolate and a nosegay.

We do have several rooms set aside for neutrodyne occupancy, and one for traveling necronauts. Trochilics not welcome.

DUKE EATS SITZ BATH

John Horton, the "Iron Duke," announced his retirement at the Green Gables Bar and Grill Tuesday night. He ate Chicken Royale, Spinach Biscuit with onion sauce, redberry pie, his plate, the silverware, drinking glass, and coffee cup and saucer. After eating the plastic table cloth, he sucked a dinner mint through a napkin. Then he went downtown, with dozens of the curious following him. He entered an antique shop, ate an old tin sitz bath and died. The coroner, Noguchi Enso, arrived to extract the Duke's famous iron stomach. This took 3 hours and 50 minutes. On a butcher's scale the organ topped 30 pounds. In his 60-year-long life, he had eaten the equivalent of a small town and everything in it, including gasoline pumps and asphalt streets.

NEUT MALE GIVES BIRTH ANALLY TO TRIPLETS

Marcus Govinda exhausted doctors with a standing labor of 11 days, 8 hours, 13 minutes. After birthing, Govinda was unable to answer questions and soon died of blood loss. Neutrodyne females give birth easily, safely, and with no bleeding. Male neuts giving birth to males suffer greatly.

HELL FOULED, COULD CLOSE; DEAD BAD TO HEAVEN

Hey, troops, Onēba here.

People ask me, "Where is Hell located?" I tell them it's ubiquitous. In the utmost solitude of nature, in toilet bowls.

"Will the willfully wicked on Earth continue so in the other world?" they ask.

Yes, and yes. In churches, in nice homes. The wicked get worse. The good go bad. Only the indifferent remain the same. The average joe can't understand it.

They want to know if I have a plan for the next eon?

I explain that the devil is a friend of mine who complains that what the Styx has done to his Deep Shaft Whiskey trade doesn't bear repeating. "You can't make strong whiskey without corn, and you need good water. The Styx doesn't have it. We're 60 miles underground, so we get every seeping drop of effluent from the Upper Midwest. We're drinking herbicide down here. Look, we're in huge financial straits. If it continues at this level, I'll shut Hell down once and for all, and your bad dead will break down Heaven's gate."

PREXY DEAD, BOON TO DANGLE

Brainerd Franklin, the Ape of Golf, has been convicted of Murder One for killing the president. He went through the White House kitchen ripping off cabinet doors, scattering the contents, then raped the president's dog, Scottie.

Now sentenced to death, he plays a nose flute in his cell every day. A small radio broadcasts the Master's Tournament as he listens distractedly. He reads, *As I Lay Dying* and *Siddhartha*. He's already written the menu for his last supper: banana pudding and peanut clusters. Final preparations are being made in the death chamber. The rap of hammers and the scream of electric saws can be heard plainly from his cot as he feigns a nap.

We spoke with Franklin on the eve of his execution.

C.M.: What's your terminal weight, pal?

B.F.: At age 55, when they jerk out my brain, it'll be more like age 52.

C.M.: Is there an afterworld for you guys?

B.F.: After what? For who? Oh, I get it. Sure, yeah, of course. I hope so, anyway. An ape don't any more want to be dead than you do.

C.M.: Does the noise of all that gallows-making bother you?

B.F.: They just better tie bowling balls to my feet if they expect to snap my neck cleanly. I expect to dangle in agony some time before someone jumps up and tugs at my legs. I have a strong kick, by the way. It's not the noise itself that irks me, but that it represents an idea alien to ape-culture – cruel and unusual punishment. All I did was open up a can of whip ass on the president and his Hawaiian slut, and this is my thanks?

C.M.: How do you want to be remembered?

A.G.: I want a 50-foot balloon of me in every Macy's parade.

C.M.: Are you going to try to take something with you this time?

A.G.: A Russian-made putter I call Lefty, and a soul mate I call Lance. He's promised to defenestrate from the 10th floor of the Gons Hotel the moment of my execution. We plan to marry after death. His last lover, a president named Kenny, never did him right. That's why he fell so passionately for a caring ape like me.

C.M.: Do you have any scores to settle?

A.G.: "Life is a bogey, not an eagle." I'm quoting someone here. I don't know who, but they said, "We are always one stroke over, always in hazard. Fairways turn foul. Every tee-off ends in a slice. The game is forever uneven, the score never settled. I feel under par but not vengeful.

C.M.: What would you do differently if you had a second chance?

A.G.: I'd never carry cans of aerosol whip ass on me. With an ape's volcanic nature, I am susceptible to murderous fits. They should ban whip ass, period. Keep it off the shelves. Without it, I wouldn't have killed.

C.M.: Where do you go from here?

A.G.: Excuse, please, but I've got to make for the pot. I'm all loaded up again. Got to dump it.

KILROY'S BURGLING SUPPLIES All imaginable burgling tools available. High-zoot, state-of-the-art, forceful entry gear. Special!!! Laser Key (fits any lock): $55.96.

VEGAS WHITE MAN KILLED IN ATTEMPTED RAPE OF BLACK SWAN

A Las Vegas man wearing a humongous costume has been killed while raping a swan near the lagoon in Wuntex Park. The black swan's flailing wings pounded the man's temples until he was unconscious, then, after an hour and a half, dead.

The man's name was Timmy "Tick" Harrison, a blackjack player. He had rented the costume at Uncle Bob's Monster Shop about 6 p.m. yesterday, then drove his car to the park, searching for a duck or swan to have sexual congress with.

The animal was quickly found and Harrison was in full chase behind it, when it turned and killed him with savage blows of its wings to Harrison's head.

LIGHT'S OUT DEATH SPA When the going gets tough, get going to Light's Out. Your last day, we promise, will be the best 24 hours of your life. We offer every bodily comfort imaginable and a nightly lecture on "Today's Afterworld and the Chance of Return" by Pastor Wurmbrand, the last living Process prelate. Terminal elegance at an affordable price. Call us when you've had enough. Bywater 5115. We're just a mile north of the Old Reactor.

THREE HUMAN HEARTS FOUND IN STILLBORN NEUTRODYNE

The coroner gasped when he exposed them during the autopsy. There were three of them, no larger than plump strawberries.

Zanzetti was called in. "What in the living hell are those?" the coroner asked.

Zanzetti, gloved, lifted the little hearts in his hand and examined them with a loupe. "These are human hearts in early development, my friend." He said. "This is not something to be sneezed at. It's very serious. Someone implanted human heart buds in this one when it was a fetus, someone with great learning and skill. And I doubt this is the only one. Some could be teens by now, with beating human hearts."

The coroner folded his arms. "What does it all mean?"

Zanzetti returned the hearts to their cavity. "You see, they've removed a lung to make room for the buds to grow. We now have a neutrodyne surgeon, more likely many more, out to change the equation to neut equals 5% human. Eventually they'll breed us out of business. The question now is, *do we care?* And as I read the zeitgeist, we don't."

The neutrodyne infant, referred to by scientists as Valentine-1, was buried, as neutrodyne culture requires, head down, in the Gas Flats Neut Rest, a weedy, rocky, hard to dig place, pocked with fire ant hills. Mourners seldom stayed there to the end of the services. It was almost impossible to stand far enough from a hill to avoid being bitten. Many mourners ran away, brushing ants from their ankles.

WORMS FOR EARTH

A billion earthworms were seeded at SUSNR'S worm fields by Annelid Futures LLC, an Onēba corporation, which hopes to harvest enough of the foot-long fishing worms to supply the entire Earth. The worms thrive in SUSNRS' warm, below surface mud, where they find the perfect temperature for survival.

NEUT QUEEN GONIONEMUS GOES UNDER THE KNIFE

Queen of the neutrodyne Midwest region, Gonionemus, had a 25-pound teratoma removed from her abdomen yesterday at Hotel Dieu Hospital. Postmortems revealed the tumor's contents: a small femur, two eye teeth, one milk tooth and a tiny, fully-formed foot.

Studies revealed that whip ass applied near the queen's spinal base many years before had made manicotti of her majesty's L-5 vertebra. Royal neut officials say the queen may perish. She is being kept alive for experiments, primarily on the effects of whip ass on aging.

PRESLEY MUMMY ON DISPLAY IN MEMPHIS, EGYPT

It's down at the end of a lonely street and it's housed in a grand building called Heartbreak Hotel. You pay about $50 U.S. for a three-bed room. The mummy lies at rest in the lobby, bloated as in late life. You gawk at it as you make your way to the Graceland Café. Some look away, some toss coins and bills into the coffin. The Café is built to look like a kitchen with a chef's table, but it is only a tableau, to be viewed behind glass. An adjacent restaurant seating 300 is where the food is served. The signature dish there is a peanut butter, banana and bacon sandwich, although many more upscale entrees and appetizers are available, such as head cheese on Crisco biscuits, pecan-crusted mullet, mock-turtle soup and flat iron steaks in blackberry sauce.

QUICK STAKES SOUTHERN LANDS CLAIM

Avery Quick of the City, a horse trainer by trade, has filed a quitclaim deed on a certain property in the afterworld. Local courts say this property, located in the so-called Southern Lands, does not exist. But Quick said he saw these lands at the edge of the City as recently as two nights ago.

"They are vast," he said, "their earth black, rich and fecund."

Quick will build a house as soon as he finds a court to recognize his deed. He intends to plant cabbages and beets.

ANOTHER CLONE MILL INCIDENT

Judith Purslane, forewoman at the mill, discovered the remains of necronaut Fatty Arbuckle, who had been picnicking with a young, unidentified, former, would-be starlet beneath the mill. It was shady there, out of the sun and heat, a setting which most necronauts avoid. It is supposed that Arbuckle and the starlet had been substantially dissolved when one of the mill's containment vessels was breached and spilled 10,000 aqueous tons of stomach acid, which came down with a tidal roar on the couple and killed them.

THE BRAIN OF THE LATE ENFIELD PETERS, a prodigious 10-pounder, will be on display one day only at the Arden Boulevard Ice Palace. The brain will be wheeled about on the ice by a pretty skater with a push cart. Everyone there will know of the famous actor's exceptionally large head in life, so large that, during the filming of *Who Puked in the Sink?* a small gaffer's assistant stood behind him, unseen by the camera, clutching a handful of Peters' hair, pulling his sagging head upright, enabling him to kiss the actress playing his paramour. Nor did the large brain make him an intelligent man. His I.Q. was estimated to be 100, which psychologists call "dull-normal." Even so, his acting technique stunned audiences all over the world. With his chin on his chest, brow dripping perspiration, stringy hair falling in front of his face so that you couldn't see it, he voiced the greatest Shakespearean soliloquies ever recorded. To the regret of millions, the recordings were lost in the bombing of Peters' Platter Palace, a Peters'-owned record sales store on Hardwood Road, 1200. The bomber/s have not been apprehended.

Sheriff Prop said, "We're sad about Peters' death, we're sad about the bombing and the loss of the vinyl. On the good side, we'll always have Peters' big brain to marvel at during the games."

ADAM'S APPLES Red. Tempting. Damned good. Surprisingly bitter afterbite. Seedless. We're at 1150 Orchard Road. I'm the one with the red beard. Ask for Adam. I'll open the gate for you.

VALUABLE MONKEY TO GET TROCHILIC HEART

A high-dollar, blue-gum monkey, Barkley Tarr, employed by Aerospace General as a space cadet, is to receive the heart of a trochilic, an institutional lifer, who will be sedated, and the heart excised by Coroner Noguchi.

Scientific studies confirm the efficacy of trochilic-chimp exchanges. Economically significant simians like Brainerd Franklin and Barkley Tarr tend to reject the hearts of peers, but not of trochilics, a group from which many are available.

Tarr was born Oct. 4, 1957, the day Sputnik went *beep ... beep ... beep* up there somewhere over the rainbow. Now a decrepit 30-year-old, Tarr's ticker has petered rapidly in recent weeks and a trochilic's heart has been sought nationwide to replace it. The surgery, with Noguchi at the knives, will be performed at Hotel Dieu Hospital in the City when a proper heart is found.

FINAL ENTRY IN CITY MOON STORY CONTEST

The Murder of the Douche King's Wife
By
Carlos Castaneda

Fungi kill for the same reason Virgilian Sutpencil did. They cannot produce their own food and so rely for energy on existing organic matter. And, as do certain fungi, Sutpencil fed on material already dead, often illegally obtained corpses. He stacked them in his lambing barn like cordwood, drawing black plastic tightly over the pile to bake in the barn's oven-like heat. Once, he took one of the corpses with him on vacation in a specially made carpetbag lined with pure para rubber to contain the odor and the juices.

At some well-defined point in Sutpencil's evolution, the line between parasite and predator seems to have been crossed. It happened the day Matty Massengill, wife of Dr. Elliot Massengill, inventor of the modern commercial douche, was found dead. Someone had throttled her. By the four-fingered imprints on her throat, the coroner concluded that a thumbless male had done the deed, one with unnaturally long and powerful middle fingers.

"But," he cautioned, "I can't say anything about his ancestry or origins."

Massengill, grieving in his library, picking through his photo albums, brooding over every still of his beloved Matty, was suddenly struck by a furious urgency: a photo of his anatomy school roommate, Virgilian Sutpencil, had flopped onto the rug, showing a thumbless hand and middle fingers like bratwursts.

His old pal Virgilian.

Now the memory struck like an Oriental gong. Sutpencil could strip the trigeminals from a cadaver in half the time it took his classmates. Born without thumbs, but, in compensation, with huge fingers, the weapons that had killed his wife. Case solved.

Editor's note: While we are in awe of Mr. Castaneda's brilliant, maybe overly brilliant, literary works, we must confess that he has sent us a story that we think is plagiarized, at least in part. As yet, we have not identified the source or sources he picked from. As readers know, to say that Mr. Castaneda has been "under the weather," is an understatement. He is very ill, and, as this story illustrates, probably delusional. The submission seems to be just a compendium of other writer's work, showing a complex mix of Sherlock and a streak of Poe.

    City Moon
    The Night Desk

ERNIE'S BEAR CLAW BAKERY When the light outside goes on, the claws are ready. Big Ernie's frying them right now. Drive thru. At the corner of Ninth and Tenth, City.

GREEN DEATH RAINS ON SUN SEEKERS

Popeye's, a spinach-canning factory on Old Reactor Road, exploded yesterday at noon, blowing the green stuff a mile into clear blue skies and hurling a five-ton statue of Popeye heavenward, which, when it fell back, killed 12 employees lunching outdoors and enjoying the warm sun. Before anyone else could take cover, a hot, green downpour burned the hair off ten more.

INSECTS KILL NEBRASKA FIELD GENERAL

At a flatball match near the city of Auburn, a swarm of blister beetles (family *Meloidae*) destroyed the mouth of quarterback Johnny Horton Jr. by flying into it and filling it with caustic eggs as he winged a game-winning aerial in the Corn Bowl. Seconds later, Horton was on the turf, choking. Fellow players dug beetle eggs from his mouth with their fingers and beat his chest with their fists. When Horton's mouth was empty of eggs, it began blowing bubbles, some as large as soft balls. The players could hear a kind of sizzle, like bacon frying, coming from the widening mouth. As it opened further, filling not with walnuts but blisters, his breathing was restricted further, and he succumbed only minutes after his greatest flatball victory.

NURSE FUZZY WUZZY DYING

Bullet, a Java man, was with his Uncle Wiggly at the Upper Farm last week, neutering piglets, when news arrived that Nurse Jane Fuzzy Wuzzy, his muskrat lady housekeeper, was caught in a rat trap and was dying.

TEXOMA BEACH TO GET WIND BLADE

The 100-foot bamboo blade is expected to disperse necrotic winds that blow in from the Gulf in summer months when fish-kills are at their peak.

DOLPHIN BRUISES FEEDER'S HEART

A fish-feeder at Waterworld Pool #66 fell in today. Peppermint Molly, a dolphin, chewed through the feeder's rib cage and bruised the heart, almost killing her.

DEWEY DUG UP, CHEWED UP, COVERED UP

A couple wept in Eternity Meadows early this morning as Dewey, their unknown son, was disinterred. Pickets representing CUD (Chew Up the Dead) groups were there to hector, jeer and spit. Later, Dewey's unknown sisters reburied the body in brown paper. The large mother swaddled her head closely and shrouded herself in a drab dress, grieving for the son she did not know, for years, she had mothered.

After her son's birth, friends dropped off and the circle of those who did not know her gradually enlarged.

"I felt myself disappearing," she said, "in little pieces. If I became known again I would be a nonentity."

Several other of her unknown sons survive and have silenced their mother on more than one occasion. She says, "They do a lot they don't want me talking about." For income, the boys' mother receives unmarked bills and loose change under the door for favors granted.

Government agents admit the father of the unknown son, German Boxx, has eluded them for years by living in British Honduras, but it is thought that his son's disinterment might bring him out of obscurity. To date, this has not happened.

The cost of the unknown son's reburial ($990.29) will be underwritten by the Bodies Under Dirt Society (BUDS) of greater Bunkerville.

REMAINS OF SUSNRS PLUNGES INTO YELLOWSTONE

With a roar and a crash loud enough to be heard on Texoma

Beach, all 600 million tons of the remaining artificial moon landed within the boundaries of Yellowstone National Park, setting off dozens of boiling geysers, scalding hundreds of tourists, most of whom perished. The famous landmark will be closed to the public for two or three years while the debris is removed, and the geysers sealed with concrete plugs.

Gen. Lindy Burns, former commander of SUSNRS, is resting now in an embassy in Manila, drinking buttermilk with rye chasers and nursing his emotional wounds. "I devoted my whole life to that false moon. Now it's just wreckage. I'm wracked with guilt over those dead tourists, too," he told Effie Pfeffer, *City Moon* historian.

Lindy's perspiration has a violet tinge and stains his flight jacket. The condition is caused by excessive amounts of potassium permanganate in the blood. The chemical was used extensively on SUSNRS to kill predatory or other unwanted fish in the hundreds of one-acre ponds devoted to raising hornpout (*Ictaluris nebulosis*), a type of catfish considered best for nutrition and sustainability, and chub, a river fish popular with anglers.

Lindy was given nuxated iron to fix the blood. By morning he sat and ate coddled eggs. After breakfast, he was placed on a pandiculating appliance to stretch his torso then bathed with mineral water and basic soap.

Once on his feet again, Lindy was issued a passcard, fitted for civilian dress, doused with sun screen, given a box of sandwiches and put on a railcar bound for the Noxin Air Force Base at Loma Linda.

On arrival, he spoke briefly to assembled officers on the tarmac, saying, "We were a tough bunch up there before the breakup. My men could digest dried peas, spinach, bread, potatoes, butter, soybean oil, entrails, ground bone and alfalfa meal. The toughest need the best.

"The problem is, they never sent any of that up to us. We got by for years on Spam and canned beets. Look at me. I'm a pale shadow of my former self, although I do love beets, especially pickled. You can see my face is pretty red. What can I say? SUSNRS was a wonderful thing, the biggest engineering feat ever."

As Lindy was escorted to the base infirmary, Effie Pfeffer overtook him and asked, "What was SUSNRS really for, sir? We never knew why it was built or what it did. We could see it up there on clear summer nights, dimly lit, crackling and popping with the sound of seams separating. We knew it was coming apart and it scared us. What was going on before the breakup? You were there."

Lindy stopped to give it some thought. "I'm an honest man," he said. "Nothing was going on. There were only ten of us in the crew. We had small living quarters and a kitchen. The whole thing was a façade. SUSNRS was an empty globe full of scaffolding and 2-by framing. It wasn't in orbit. It was floating. Go ahead and call it what it is, a big trial balloon that looked like a moon. It fooled millions around the world."

"To what end, sir?"

"I don't know. We were never given orders. I suspect it was a whim of one of the presidents."

"Just to fool people?"

"Yes, I'm afraid so. Now that there's nothing to do in the world, the presidents get restless. They want to do something. It doesn't matter what."

"Thank you, sir, for that insight."

THE END

THE REASON INDIA WANTS
50 MILLION TWISTED BB GUNS
MASS-PRODUCED

13 PILOTS
WRONG U
BLAMED IN

SUSNR

Encounter with an Orbigator   50 CENTS

FLASH

Pinhead in the

The Pinhead in the Sky Coffee Corp.
a Meeting of the Susnr Bored to discus
place a pinhead in the sky. The pinhea
tacked to the welkin with a finishing na
tually, all things will come to pass, an
this? and why not now? long the motto
Moon. We are a magazine for lonely
paths, star-crossed lovers like Donnie
Osmond, Mensa members, cowperson
everywhere, Irving Berlin who's been
and those in the Suction Camps.

Weather: No rain in sight. The burning
Sapodilla Desert are on the move, cre
an average rate of a furlong a month, i
four times that fast. When it comes to
warm or cold temperatures produce pl
star shapes. Shade now available, Zon
This is the last issue of City Moon. We
ing the night coach to Susnr. Write us,

submarine
guts
peculiar
boy

FOLLY

The Caw County school district on Susn
hypnotized and enrolled its first neutro
Its name is Gerben Van Dyke. It tips
810. It is no dunce, and is capable of
feats of auto-fasciation. In one minute
peace and love, the next it guts a pecul

The primitive art of the Elasmobranch
epiphytic. They live in the Suction Can
breed in the darkened confines of the te
This discovery was made by Marfak, th
hunter. An era has dawned, but nothing

Baron Von Kemplin sailed the Firecra
chinese laundry ship. When he arrived
met Jack Dempsey, the Ten Sleep heav
they agreed to meet in the ring. "The
a paper car," said Dempsey. "And th
said Von Kemplin, 'will suck gaseous
Proceeds accruing as a result of the be
go to needed repairs at the neut home

WHY are we scared of IKE? See page

ABOUT THE AUTHOR

David Ohle's novel, *Motorman*, was published by Alfred A. Knopf in 1972 and re-released by 3rd Bed Press in 2004 with an introduction by Ben Marcus. Its sequel *The Age of Sinatra* was published by Soft Skull in 2004. His novel *The Pisstown Chaos* was published in 2008 (Soft Skull). He has edited two non-fiction books, *Cows are Freaky When They Look at You: An Oral History of the Kaw Valley Hemp Pickers* (Watermark Press, 1991) and *Cursed from Birth: The Short, Unhappy Life of William S. Burroughs, Jr.* (Soft Skull, 2006). His short novels, *Boons, The Camp,* and *The Blast* were published by Calamari Press, and his novel *The Old Reactor* was published by Dzanc Books in 2014.

His short fiction has appeared in *Harper's, Esquire, The Paris Review, TriQuarterly, The Missouri Review, The Pushcart Prize,* and elsewhere. He has taught fiction writing and screenwriting for thirty years—at the University of Texas in Austin, the University of Missouri in Columbia, and the University of Kansas in Lawrence.

He is now retired from teaching and lives in Lawrence, Kansas.

King of the river

CITY MOON

Vol. 1, No. 1, January 1979. Edited by Roger Martin and David Ohle. Our motto: Sworn to fun, loyal to none. Eat, drink, and breathe. Never woo the folly. Stop just short. SASE. No poetr

BUDD SMOKES OUT THE NEUTRODYNES

Candidate Budd was locked up in the American Jail yesterday afternoon for treating the inhabitants of the neutrodyne cage to a lighted cigar. Budd threw the cigar into a mound of rake-straw, thereby terrifying a score of dynes and starting a fire in the cage.

One buck dyne melted down like a holiday candle, while another bubbled and burned. Their peaceful nest was a ball of flame. Then the flames were stamped out and Budd arrested. Our analysis: It takes more calories to eat a piece of celery than the celery has in it.

CUTTER MADE INSANE BY LIGHTNING

brother of Bloodgood Cutter, Frances, crabbing locally in a marshy borrow pit, elt galvanized yesterday, as ad Fate Perry, in Dresden, xactly ten years ago. The eason? Lightning.

Cutter, maddened in the flash, then barged into the office of Patents and Subventions in Alamogordo, bringing something smelly in a sleeve of newspaper. It turned out to be a pickled ponyfoot on the end of a stick. Half a crab in his mouth, eyes as big as God's, he said, "This device is being used by me to determine the best flooring for a barn."

Further enquiries were discouraged and Cutter denied his patent without even polite adieu.

An orange fuzz appeared on Cutter's jaws, becoming by St. John's Day, a stringy and irregular beard. He wore his baseball cap when the days threatened rain. He experienced no pain.

Dr. Bo

MILKMEN SIGN HUGGING PLEDGE

Drunkeness, dishonesty, incompetency, drinking and smoking are vices mother's milkmen have standardized resistance to through their union leadership.

Chauncey Logan, union president, announced, "My mother's milkmen have also agreed, beginning Monday,

to hug any woman who meets them at the door holding the empties."

One hundred milk wagon drivers have signed the pledge in the last months.

A similar suit in the Fifth Chancery Court concerns a case of "mistaken"

hugging. Important questions of due process were argued by attornies for Stephen Sumner, whose religion requires retaliation against a milkman who mistakenly hugged his mother while she idled on a porch in Shreveport last summer. Listen up mothers: If you won't sell your milk, we won't buy your tale -- City Moon Eds.

NOVELIST TO STARVE SELF

Kansas Fingerberry, a new city ovelist, is starving herself according to her closest friends and confi-antes. She'll be dead by Saturday, n the Bugger Zone, a "bad" neigh-orhood near the Buffer.

he was in a joke shop Satur-ay last, looking for a box of art monkeys to help her with her typing. he left with her monkeys in a bag stinking to high heaven. Outside, a ait sale was in process. Crawlers, 4.50 a dozen, blue devils a dime,

fishermen were strung up like perch up and down the block.

Fingerberry adressed the weary Nimrods thusly: "I'm writing this novel because it exemplifies life.

ROCKS BOAT AND DROWNS

"It shows how people have a Robin Hood urge.

"It shows people sailing by shanty to Patmos, to view the relics of St. John.

"I expect the poor will like this book, but the rich ducks of the East won't put their bills anywhere near it."

So Fingerberry is to starve herself. She'll go this Friday to Municipal park and rent a pedal skiff. She'll pump her way to the middle, and there, like a bird in the wilderness, fast to death.

Fingerberry is advised that she is likely to rock the boat and drown instead -- Editors, City Moon

BIG HOG COOKS TOWN

Dresden, Tennessee has been burned before by a wide assortment of both accident and bagatelle, but nothing can touch the

out of Reno, who narrowly escaped burning to a cinder on the road. The torch, in a frenzy to avert the flames it wore about itself like a

Perry had gone to his room at 11 o'clock to retire. He lit the lamp which caught fire within, and Perry threw it into the street.

IT'S NEW!

CITY MOON

Year-End Issue Only $600.00

LOOM FRUIT

JAN-APRIL	MARCH		DOTTY-TWO	IN-FIDDLE	COLDGOSPEL	MAX'S

(calendar grid)

DINAH IN

I CALL ON DINAH

THE YEAR IN PREVIEW

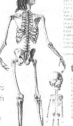

What's beneath their beauty

Maybe you died because you ate

the wrong breakfast – – – – –

The Die is Cast

PILE FIZZLE

Throw Out The Mummy

Foxy

The brain

STAUNING

DOUGLAS' PETER presents

SAD MARAT

"I want President"

the nth man

Blonde percentage

A startling detective story?

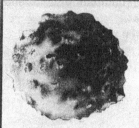

ISKCON NEWS

50¢

DREAMER DEAD AT TENSLEEP

STALKED, KILLED

Nine dreamers of Ten Sleep, on Iskcon, have been named in the stalking and slaying of Dewey, a dream figure, shown at right. These dreamers, who often met to tell the secrets of their dreams to one another, began to recognize, in common, a shadowy, poorly dressed figure standing in the shadows of their dreamscapes, and all called him Dewey. Dewey threatened the peace and the privacy of the sleeping world. The nine, thinking that dream figures would feel no pain, agreed to murder the innocent Dewey, the way one pops hornworms between the thumb and forefinger-- without a thought of mercy, since these creatures are universally known to be without feeling. Each dreamer, as they arranged it, would arrive by auto in front of the Mexico Lindo during the 3rd REM period on the night of December 12th. Inside the cafe, it was supposed, Dewey would be waiting to haunt them, to brandish a shiv in their faces, to spit his tobacco on their dream shoes. On this occasion, Dewey little suspected he would be facing an organized dream-body of hostile Ten Sleepers, Iskconians bent on sending this American creeper to the dream hell of Atlantic City. Yet in through the door they arrived like a family walking into its favorite chicken house on Sunday morning after church, a mother and father with a trail of brothers and sisters. In a moment Dewey was pinned, his eggs removed.

CZOLGOSZ PLANTED LIKE SPUD

In 1881, on Iskcon, an Arab employed in a show in Ten Sleep had his hand bitten off by an enraged capybara and made no complaint. Refusing surgical assistance, he plunged the maimed limb into boiling oil.

Primitive races of Earth, especially pigmented ones, feel pain less acutely and thus enjoy a reputation for stoical endurance, the result, however, of a modified sensation.

It is not difficult, knowing this, to understand why Ekaterina threatened to kill her husband, an Arab, for being without feeling, and making a mud pie of the marriage flower.

Ekaterina was beyond reason. The more her husband, Czolgosz, tried to calm her, the more hysterical she became.

" I would sooner die than live with you, " said Czolgosz.

Then Ekaterina's patience broke, like the brittle ice of March's Ides.

She seized her husband's service revolver and shot him through the head, at the crest of the nose, Czolgosz sat down on the setee, and spent a gaudy evening in the process of dying, without the benefit of feelings.

Ekaterina buried the Arab at night in a nearby field, and a few days later planted Idaho potatoes over the spot to hide all traces of the murder.

Her husband, she told the curious neighbors, had become uncontrollable and had left her forever as he had threatened so often to do. This tale was accepted without question, and as the weeks passed, little green sprouts came up in the field until the slain Czolgosz's resting place was hidden beneath a green carpet.

The crime itself did not make the woman flinch. She was hooked on the idea that he lay on unconsecrated ground and so was doomed to ages of grisly wandering on the earth instead of peaceful repose until the day of resurrection. But like the Arab in the Ten Sleep show, she refused the overtures of humanity to her. And like the Arab she shall be publically maimed. La-de-da.

ISKCON NEWS IS A PUBLICATION OF THE CITY MOON PRESS.   IT COSTS ¢ 50   COPYRIGHT, 1978.
IT IS WRITTEN AND EDITED BY DAVID OHLE AND ROGER MARTIN.   WRITE TO BOX J, TENSLEEP, ISKCON.

Special thanx is due to: AMERICAN MAGAZINE, LIFE, ROCK CITY PATH POSTER